A Nuclear Step Too Far

A rocket tipped with a dirty bomb hits Israel. *Mossad* immediately jumps into action to discover who is responsible and seeks to prevent any further attacks.

BOOK NINE OF THE GEOPOLITICAL TECHNO-THRILLER SERIES

ANDREW B. LOUIS

For information regarding permission, please write to:
info@barringerpublishing.com
Barringer Publishing, Naples, Florida
www.barringerpublishing.com

Cover, graphics, and layout by Linda S. Duider
Cape Coral, Florida

ISBN: 978-1-954396-85-2
Library of Congress Cataloging-in-Publication Data
A Nuclear Step Too Far / Andrew B. Louis

Printed in U.S.A.

DEDICATION

*To all secret service agents who risk
their lives to protect their fellow citizens
against terrorists around the world.*

OTHER BOOKS BY THE AUTHOR

Other novels by Andrew B. Louis include:

 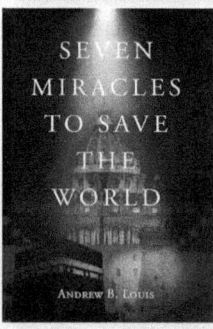 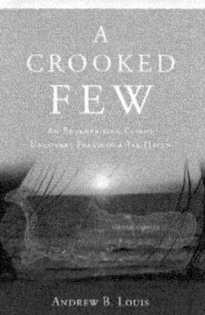 

Operation Kovesh, The Shadow Experts, Below the Surface, The Crypto Trap, Escaping the Bear, Glitter and Smoke, Trouble in the China Sea, Destruction Along the Nile, The Improbable Collector, Seven Miracles to Save the World, A Crooked Few and *Tough Choices* available at Amazon.com.

www.AndrewBLouis.com

ACKNOWLEDGMENTS

Though all the writing and errors are solely my own doing, a number of people contributed to the creation of the text. I would like to thank the numerous friends and family members who were kind enough to comment on various drafts and led me to make material changes for the better, particularly Jeff who provided the first in-depth edit.

SYNOPSIS

Israel is placed in an always feared but never experienced situation: one of the rockets which hit Tiberias, and was presumably fired by Palestinian terrorists, had a "nuclear tip": debris which was recovered confirmed that the rocket was what is routinely called "a nuclear dispersion device." Though considerably less dangerous than a full-fledged nuclear bomb, it marked an unacceptable escalation in the nature of the hostilities between Isarel and its enemy neighbors. *Mossad* and *Shin Bet*, Israel's two main security agencies, are both drafted to elucidate the challenge, together with Countess Renate's Shadow Experts. After having concluded that the nuclear tip of the rocket was probably made of radioactive elements sourced from nuclear waste, the Israeli secret services follow a couple of different threads to identify the guilty party and punish them.

The first thread involved working back from the apparent geographical location from which the dirty rocket had been fired. That led *Mossad* to Iraq and to the discovery of an unknown ISIS camp just across the Iraqi Syrian border. The agency had to find a way to destroy the lethal elements of the camp's activities and, if possible, to inflict further damage on Iran, the suspected backer of this new terrorist unit. The second thread was to trace the origin of the nuclear waste which seemed to be available in Iraq and led *Mossad* to Paris first and then to the southeast of France where suspect activities were being carried out. Could this area be for nuclear waste what Marseilles used to be to the narcotic trade half a century ago?

In the end, though the reader will be able to note a number of successes in the anti-terrorist activities of secret services in Europe and Israel, one might ask whether the defensive attacks engineered by *Mossad* will be sufficient to stop the nuclear traffic? Or was it the escalation in the rocket launching activities of terrorists toward Israel the one step too far which would inflame the region?

Disclaimer: All the parties to this story are fictitious and if there was some resemblance to individuals or institutions, it would be purely coincidental.

PROLOGUE

TIBERIAS, ISRAEL

The sound of sirens woke up everyone in the usually quiet town of Tiberias, on the western shore of the Sea of Galilea.

■ ■ ■ ■ ■

The second lowest freshwater lake in the world, after the Dead Sea, the Sea of Galilea is lying about 700 feet below sea level. In the first century and before, the Sea of Galilea was a valuable resource for Galileans, the inhabitants of Galilea, as it offered plenty of fishing opportunities. The city of Tiberias lies about ten miles southwest of Capernaum, the city from which St Peter, the apostle and future first Pope of the Catholic Church originated, according to Christian Gospels. It dates back to that time period, having been built about twenty years after the birth of Christ by Herod Agrippa, the last Jewish king of Galilea, who is said to have spent much time there.

Though fishing remains an important activity in Tiberias today, cultivating the land has over time tended to take over as the main generator of employment and incomes. Horticulture dominates, with a particular emphasis on fruits such as citrus, avocados, bananas, cherries, figs, strawberries, and many others. The area benefits from wonderfull fertile soil and a southern exposure which provides all the sun these plants need. Beyond agriculture, as the town developed and its inhabitants became more affluent, at least by regional standards, a variety of services grew to meet the incipient demand. They included those designed to cater to tourists and in particular the numerous Jewish and Christian pilgrims visiting the Tomb of Maimonides, the Abulafia Synagogue or St Peter's Church that is a rare crusader-period church almost hidden between a restaurant and a bar along Tiberias' beach promenade.

Sitting almost directly opposite to the Golan Heights on the East side of the Sea of Galilee, the inhabitants of Tiberias have had to get used to and prepare for the numerous Palestinian attacks which prevailed virtually as soon as the state of Israel was created. Though Jews were the first inhabitants of the region, their various migrations led the Palestinians to become the majority of inhabitants in the region which had been administered by the British since the fall of the Ottoman empire. Thus, Palestinians were the people whom the United Nations displaced, when, on November 29, 1947, it adopted Resolution 181, calling for the establishment of a Jewish State in Eretz-Israel and providing for the future of the original British Palestinian mandate which was slated to end in May 1948. That was when the territory was divided into separate Jewish and Arab states. All parties at the time, possibly in a bid to atone for the Holocaust, seemed aware that it would force the resettlement of people who lived in the area granted to the Jewish state.

Since the creation of Israel as a state, Tiberias's inhabitants, as has been the case throughout Israel, have become used to a semi-permanent state of warlike conditions. Though these would surely make many westerners in Europe or the U.S. cringe, they have come accept this as the normal way of life. Residents have been thoroughly trained as to how to react in the case of any suspected incoming missile attack. They know that they have to move as quickly as possible to shelters either hidden below their homes or more often located nearby, throughout the city.

■ ■ ■ ■ ■

On that day, from the relative safety of shelters where the sirens had directed them, people initially heard the shrieks associated with the ignition of the missile engines as the Iron Dome fired them. Soon, the rumbling of those missiles breaking the sound barrier would be followed by explosions as the Israeli rockets were intercepting and blowing up incoming enemy fire. On that particular day, the Iron Dome had been quite successful: it had prevented any of the rockets that had been fired at the city from hitting the town itself. Everyone agreed that the missiles had originated from places either in the Golan Heights or possibly even further east.

■ ■ ■ ■ ■

The Iron Dome is Israel's all-weather, air defense system, which was designed, with the help of the U.S., to protect the country against incoming rockets or artillery shells. It comprises both radars to pick up early signs of airborne objects launched toward Israel and missiles which are fired to intercept any incoming projectile that might be hurled at the country, most likely by terrorists based in Lebanon, Syria or Gaza. Though the Iron Dome is focused on short-range missile attacks, two other systems provided further safety. One, David's Sling, took care of short- to medium-range rockets, while ballistic missile defense was entrusted to the various Arrows systems developed by Israel Aerospace Industries, a state-owned company, in cooperation with Boeing. This had been made necessary as the risk of missiles launched from further away, from Iran or Yemen, for instance, had become quite real.

More importantly, Israel started to realize how asymmetrical the costs of attack and defense might be. The projectiles that were launched toward Israel could be relatively cheap to manufacture for as long as there was only a limited need for extreme accuracy and thus guidance mechanisms. On the other hand, defense was always expensive as it was required to pick up the incoming fire, track it, fire at it, and hit it. Accuracy was key. Israel had recently implemented a couple of key artificial intelligence enhancements to the systems' radar which were designed to distinguish between threatening and non-threatening incoming rockets. For instance, rockets that were judged likely to fly into areas that might be cultivated—as most of the territory was in the region—but where loss of life and serious physical damage were deemed unlikely were designated as non-threatening. They were allowed to run their course. This allowed the Jewish State to save its expensive missiles and avoid having to fire them at rockets unlikely to cause much harm.

■ ■ ■ ■ ■

That night's attack might have been lost in the noise of frequent terrorist activities in the area if it had not been for at least one of the few rockets which the Iron Dome had allowed through as it was deemed not to threaten any inhabited area. All rockets that represented a real threat to the town and its inhabitants had been destroyed in flight, and debris fell mostly into the Sea of Galilea, where they would eventually rust and serve as shelters for the fish, including the famous local delicacy, the Galilean tilapia, locally called "St. Peter's fish." Accidentally, that fish has nothing to do with the often-prized John Dory, a fish that lives alone or in small groups on the sandy bottom of the continental shelf from Australia to Africa and from Japan to Europe, and which is called St Peter's fish in several languages.

The real surprise which caused a routine challenge to explode into what could become a major confrontation rested in the debris of a so-called non-threatening rocket which had landed about 2.5 miles to the southwest of Tiberias. What the analysis of the debris revealed was distressing to say the least. Had a new phase in the war between Israel and its neighbors just started? Was it the second leg of the war which had already started between Israel and Hamas?

■ ■ ■ ■ ■

Josh Steimetz, better known locally in Mosul, Iraq, as Abu Musa, knew that one day, soon, questions were pretty sure to be coming his way[1] and these questions would come from his Kurdish friend, Ibrahim.

Without going into too many details here, Josh had, a few years earlier, played a vital role in a very successful *Mossad* operation in and around Iraq. A *Mossad* agent deeply imbedded in Iraq, Josh had penetrated a narcotic trafficking network where opium was sold in exchange for cut and polished diamonds. The Mosul-Erbil region of Iraq sat in the middle of routes to bring Afghan opium to the West. Among the many opium sellers, one particular group was connected to Kurd nationalists: they used their profits to finance their century-long resistance to what they viewed as the foreign occupation of Kurdistan. To them, Kurdistan was a geographic territory comprising the Upper Mesopotamia and the area around the mountain chain that separates Iran and Iraq today, the Zagros. That geo-cultural territory had not been maintained as a separate nation ever since Kurdish-inhabited areas were split between the Safavid and Ottoman empires, in the 16th and 17th centuries. In fact, at present, Kurds as a people found themselves spread into Turkey, Iraq, Iran, and Syria. Irrespective of which country they actually inhabited, a keen sense of tribal identity based on Kurdish culture and language, not to mention the remnants of a diffuse national identity persisted among them. Though more moderate than the surrounding ethnic groups on political and religious matters, the Kurds still strived for political

---

[1] By the same author, see *Glitter and Smoke*, Barringer Publishing, 2023.

autonomy, if not outright independence. Many unabashedly conceded that their goal was the re-creation of Kurdistan as a country.

On the other side of the opium trade, were Palestinian terrorists who used the opium which they then sold in the global narcotic marketplace to purchase arms and finance Palestinian terrorist operations. Historically, most Palestinian terrorists participating in the narcotic trade had been connected to the four better-known groups at war with Israel: Hezbollah, Hamas, the Popular Front for the Liberation of Palestine, and Islamic Jihad.

Mossad's operation in Iraq had uncovered a new entrant in the opium market: ISIS, or rather a rebirth of ISIS. Rather than simply seeking to defeat Israel and have Palestinians return to the territory they had had to give up when Israel was carved out by the United Nations, ISIS was dedicated to more grandiose goals: the "ISIS" acronym stood for "Islamic State of Iraq and Syria" and they wanted to recreate a califate in that part of the Middle East. The acronym described very well the geography of the califate which ISIS wanted to recreate: a combination of Iraq and Syria, where Islam would be strictly followed. After its defeat on the field—though it most certainly saw it as but a temporary setback—ISIS had regrouped in the north of Iraq and the northeast of Syria. Both contiguous areas bordered Turkey and overlapped territory with a strong Kurdish population. As a part of its intended rebirth, ISIS had muscled into the opium trade which served principally as a funding source for Kurd nationalists and Palestinians further down the chain.

Jewish from his mother's side, with a father of Lebanese Christian Maronite descent, Josh cast an impressive figure. Many people would observe that he had a lot of the traits of the famous "men of the desert" which translates as "*Bedouin*" in Arabic. Respectful of the keen sense of Jewish identity which flows from mothers in the Jewish tradition, Josh had not adopted the Muslim faith of the bulk of the local population. He had also been careful not to show any indication of his ancestry, or of his parents' religious convictions, neither of which would be deemed acceptable where he lived. His beard had been allowed to grow as is traditional within the Shiite Muslim community and framed a rectangular face with sharp, dark eyes. He had a wide forehead and, despite his beard, showed perfect white teeth when he smiled. A shade more than 6'2" tall and tipping the scales on the high side of two hundred pounds, he surely stood out in a crowd, being quite a bit taller than many of the local Iraqis, be they of Kurdish or Arab descent, as he also did when he was in Israel.

■ ■ ■ ■ ■

Quite recently, Josh had received an invitation from Ibrahim; he wanted them to get together for one of what they both like to call their "chats."

■ ■ ■ ■ ■

Ibrahim was quite a bit shorter than Josh. Yet, though ostensibly older than Josh by at least twenty years, his demeanor would certainly not lead anyone to consider him an old man. Beside a strong sense of purpose, he exuded class and charm as several members of the Kurdish ethnic group often do. His white hair and white beard could not dissimulate his perfectly aligned white teeth framed by darker lips. His bearing seemed aristocratic, with well-coordinated and elegant moves, without ever looking contrived or artificial. Whether walking or sitting, his back seemed always quite straight, except when he leaned toward you seemingly to share something with you that was not to be repeated.

■ ■ ■ ■ ■

Josh had met Ibrahim a few times since the successful completion of their informal partnership a few years earlier, though he had been careful never to bring up their adventure together. He never acknowledged his *Mossad* connections and kept the story which Ibrahim had originally accepted that he was somewhat of a bounty hunter. That Ibrahim really did not know what bounty Josh was after hardly ever came up; and when it did, Josh would simply reply:

"I'm an opportunist . . ."

Ibrahim preferred to use these short meetings, often over a cup of coffee or tea, to exchange information with Josh. Both men respected the other and realized that though their sources had to be quite different, they could learn by comparing what they were told. On that day, Ibrahim's phone call had been meant to suggest something new had come up:

"Abu Musa! It's been a while since we last chatted."

"Indeed, my friend, indeed."

"Would you have an hour or so for me?"

"For you, always. When and where?"

"Should we meet at the Al Shatee Café? We've been there before."

"We have indeed. Sounds like a brilliant idea. When?"

"Let me see. How about tomorrow. I'll be driving up the Erbil to Mosul Highway, you know, Highway 80. Al Shatee is just off the main road, virtually on the beach of the Tigris River. I could be there no later than 11:45 a.m. Would that work for you?"

"Sure, we could then also have a snack. By the river . . ."

"Great. The first of us to arrive should order *mezze* for two. See you then."

■ ■ ■ ■ ■

Josh did not need any explanation when Ibrahim used the term *mezze*. He knew he referred to a selection of small dishes served as appetizers, similar in many ways to Spanish *tapas*, Italian *antipasti*, or Chinese *dim sum*.

∎∎■∎∎

The stretch of Mosul where Al Shatee was located was simultaneously quite picturesque and touristy but also partially in dire need of a facelift. It had been the center of much fighting when American troops worked to dislodge ISIS from the area. Originally, one could think of the area as a wonderful garden district, where tourists could congregate and take in the sights. Located on the bank of the Tigris River as it makes a 90 degree turn to the west, the Al Shatee Café offered wonderful views of the beach and of the Al-Jazeera Recreational Park located on an island in the middle of the river. It was also quite close to the former Presidential Palace Complex and what was arguably the best hotel in town until it was abandoned, the Ninevah Oberoi International. The streets, which used to be well-tended and lined with various tree essences, were now considerably less elegant.

CHAPTER.01

MOSUL, IRAQ; TEL AVIV, ISRAEL

Josh had arrived first at Al Shatee Café. He had chosen a table on the front terrace, allowing a full view of the Tigris River and the Island Park just beyond. He ordered both food and drink and sat back in the plush chair to contemplate the scenery. Seeing Ibrahim approaching from the corner of his eye, he stood up to greet him. After having exchanged a few pleasantries, Jost suddenly noticed that Ibrahim's body language was changing. He was leaning toward him as if he wanted to share a secret:

"My friend, I've heard a rumor which I think could be quite important."

Josh was genuinely surprised and simply said:

"Really?"

Before replying, Ibrahim sat in his chair and sipped from the cup of hot tea that was on the table in front of him. He lifted his eyes again, though rather than looking directly at Josh, it seemed he was admiring the running water of the Tigris River and the greenery in the middle of its flow. Eventually, he said:

"Yes. But before I go there, I need to tell you that your success in dealing with the rogue fellow on my team and ISIS haven't made my job any easier. We've had to find new buyers . . ."

He paused and immediately added:

"Yet, I've got to concede that I'm happy that ISIS was eliminated from the buying population . . ."

Josh elected not to reply, as something was telling him that Ibrahim had more to say. He was correct as Ibrahim added:

"However, I'm not so sure they've been totally eliminated. Something tells me that the cell which had tried to infiltrate the opium trade has by now disappeared, but I'm not sure they haven't reappeared elsewhere. Anyway, back to the opium trade, our main challenge has been the fact that the Taliban have managed to cut back opium cultivation in Afghanistan by more than 90%."

Josh was truly not interested in the opium trade at that point. He had earlier conceded as ordered by his superiors that the trade was a necessary evil if it was meant to help the Kurds maintain themselves in existence. On the other hand, the idea that ISIS might be reappearing in some new shape was surely smack in the middle of his mandate. He asked:

"What makes you say ISIS may not have been eliminated?"

"Well, this is exactly the point of this conversation. One of my people picked up a rumor the other day. One of his contacts asked if he had any interest in radioactive materials . . ."

Josh, allowing his real self to appear, however briefly, could not resist raising his voice as he exclaimed:

"What?"

"You heard me right, my friend. I had exactly the same reaction when I was told."

Ibrahim paused, drank a few sips of his hot tea and continued:

"At this point, we don't know whether the radioactive materials were on offer or in demand, but someone has some interest. Think of it and it isn't a huge step to jump to the conclusion that some people engage in the trade of radioactive materials. Could ISIS have abandoned opium and turned to radioactive material?"

"Radioactive materials?"

"Absolutely."

"What kind?"

"That, frankly, I don't know. My guy only replied to his contact or acquaintance, I don't know which, that he needed to talk to his leader about it. I wish he'd asked for more detail, but unfortunately, he didn't."

"Do you have a sense of what is involved and where it comes from?"

"Not really, I'm afraid. Now, I've heard of scavengers who looked for abandoned radioactive material in the old Soviet Union. I'm told there are plenty of sources, but frankly saying what I just said, I've told you more than I know. It's also possible that some people have gotten their hands on nuclear waste. There are plenty of reactors within a couple thousand miles from here."

Josh looked perturbed:

"Hold it. Let me kind of think aloud . . ."

Ibrahim nodded his concurrence, smiling to encourage Abu Musa to keep going. Josh first mentioned that he could not imagine any sufficiently enriched uranium or, worse yet, plutonium that was available on such a loose basis. That led him to conclude that whatever was on sale or in demand did not appear related to the creation of a true nuclear fission device. Ibrahim nodded his agreement, though he immediately added:

"You're already way ahead of me, Abu Musa. For a bounty hunter you seem to know a lot . . ."

Josh smiled, but he ignored Ibrahim's bounty hunter comment and continued his reasoning:

"So, if it's not to create a nuclear device what would be the point?"

"Don't know. What about a dirty bomb?"

Ibrahim's response startled Josh. He hesitated a second and then exclaimed:

"Wait a minute my friend. That's it . . . No! That has to be it. That's exactly it. A dirty bomb. Nobody would buy radioactive materials on the black market for any legitimate use, like medical equipment needs or nuclear research."

Ibrahim came right back:

"Don't want to take you away from your reasoning. Yet, your comment is right on with respect to medical equipment, but I'm not so sure when it comes to nuclear research."

Josh conceded the point, but came right back, arguing that their reasoning so far seemed to be telling them that someone was thinking of making a dirty bomb. Ibrahim nodded again and agreed. Josh did not give him the time to take the point further. He mused on whether terrorists in the region would be likely buyers. Ibrahim sternly noted:

"I can assure you that no sanctioned Kurdish resistance group would **ever** entertain such an idea. We don't operate that way. So, I hope the terrorists you are considering have to be of the Islamic variety."

Josh noted the special emphasis Ibrahim had paced on the word "ever." He conceded the point but kept on digging:

"Sure. But isn't it true that Islamic terrorists would likely be buyers? ISIS might be one of them. But who's the seller?"

He paused and took his point further:

"Many, if not most, of the terrorists in this part of the world have some relationship with Iran. We know that Iran mines its own uranium, near the Fordow plant, northeast of Qom. So I can't imagine they would be in the market for radioactive materials. Also, if they do support the terrorists, why wouldn't they simply supply them the material they need. After all, they have a couple of reactors already operational . . ."

Ibrahim interrupted Josh:

"Abu Musa, my friend. Neither of us knows much on this topic, though I must admit that you surprise me with how much you know. Let's agree to do a bit more digging. I'll be happy to help, but only if I can stay in the shadows."

"Deal."

■ ■ ■ ■ ■

David Heller, the head of the *Disruption* group within *Mossad*, was sitting at his desk and quietly sipping his second morning cup of coffee when the phone rang. His group, probably the most secretive within an already very secretive organization, was generally in charge of activities which many would consider illegal. However, these activities still needed to be conducted in the interest of the state of Israel, which possibly in the today's world seemed uniquely faced with terrorism rather than declared warfare. These controversial activities were thus considered within the spirit if not the letter of Israel's Constitution: assassination of foreign leaders, sabotage of certain installations of which Israel did not approve, internet warfare and the like. His group did not appear on any organization chart—that anyone could procure. He picked up his phone and as was his habit simply said:

"David here . . ."

"Sorry to bother you, but I need to speak to you quickly. Are you free now?"

David had recognized the voice of his key lieutenant, Mark Levi. Mark was very special to David because of the clever work he had done for him in earlier missions. David invited Mark to come straight into his office. Less than a minute later, David was holding his office door open for Mark and pointed him to the cream leather sofa with the matching side chair. Mark walked around the glass-top coffee table and sat down. David asked:

"Coffee?"

"Sure, please. No milk, no sugar. Just an ice cube to cool it down a bit."

David turned to his assistant, Uschi:

"Could you please get us a cold coffee for Mark and a hot one with milk for me?

"Of course. No problem, sir.

Without even allowing any time for a transition, David then asked Mark:

"What's the urgency?"

Mark made a face which David read as meaning that it was indeed a serious matter. Yet rather than replying directly to the question, he asked in turn:

"Remember Josh Steimetz?"

"Sure do. Mosul, Iraq. Anything happened to him?"

"Yes and no. But given the spirit of your question let me assure you he is alive and well. Quite alive and very well I should add."

"Excellent. So, what's going on?"

Mark took a sip of his now almost ice-cold coffee and summarized for David's benefit the phone conversation he just had with Josh. Knowing David's preferences, Mark gave him the punch line first:

"Josh has just picked up a rumor that there may be some trading in radioactive material in Iraq, in the region around Mosul."

David figuratively jumped up in his chair:

"Hold it. Radioactive material?"

"Yes. But one of the problems we have is that we don't know much more than that, and Josh's contact didn't know either, or at least wouldn't say anything more. So, given that there's an entire range of materials which could be radioactive, we need to find out more."

David was about to continue on his current line of questioning when he paused as if he had had an important thought. He asked Mark how Josh's contact had heard of the rumor. Mark replied that it was in fact somewhat more than a rumor and yet something less than a hard fact, explaining:

"Josh's contact said that someone approached one of his contact's informers and asked if he would have any interest in radioactive material."

David looked surprised. He immediately asked:

"Selling or buying?"

Mark smiled and deadpanned:

"That's one of the points. We don't know."

"What do you make of that?"

"At this stage, very little . . ."

Mark paused as was his custom. He liked to make sure his thoughts were all in the correct order. And in the current instance, he hadn't had much time to think about the matter. His gut reaction when he heard the news from Josh was that the tip was important, and he said he felt he needed to share it with David as soon as he could. David nodded his agreement, but yet asked:

"Any initial thoughts? Half-baked as they might be?"

"It's hard for me not to have one major thought front and center. As you know, we, *Mossad*, have always had one major worry. Could this be the first sign?"

"Hold your horses. You don't mean the risk that nuclear weapons would somehow be brought into the regional conflict which has Israel opposed against its Arab neighbors virtually since the establishment of Israel."

"Afraid so!"

■ ■ ■ ■ ■

David and Mark knew that nuclear fears had quickly expanded and led Israel, though this was never confirmed officially, to develop its own nuclear weapon capabilities. They were aware that the danger had not seemed to moderate with the announcement that India in

1974 and Pakistan in 1998 became the next nuclear powers. Yet, in the more recent past, the risks had appeared to rise even further that Arab countries would seek nuclear capabilities as Iran looked like it was a few short steps away from acquiring technology needed to make nuclear bombs. Would they use these capabilities to defend against anyone attacking Iran or to try and obliterate Israel?

■ ■ ■ ■ ■

Mark concluded:

"Bottom line, I think we should investigate. At one level, I can't think that the Palestinians would seek or even be allowed to develop a nuclear weapon. Iran is near to having one and I can't imagine it being prepared to fund a redundant Palestinian research and development effort . . . And if not Iran, who would fund them?"

David nodded his agreement and then paused for what felt like quite some time, until he looked straight at Mark and said:

"Can see that? But what if we're talking dirty bombs?"

■ ■ ■ ■ ■

Wikipedia defines a dirty bomb as follows:

"*A dirty bomb or radiological dispersal device is a radiological weapon that combines radioactive material with conventional explosives . . . It is not to be confused with a nuclear explosion, such as a fission bomb, which produces blast effects far in excess of what is achievable by the use of conventional explosives. Unlike the cloud of radiation from a typical fission bomb, a dirty bomb's radiation can be dispersed only within a few hundred meters or a few miles of the explosion.*"

■ ■ ■ ■ ■

David's question, which he may well have meant to be rhetorical, did not unsettle Mark. In fact, he smiled just as he was about to get to that point. Mark had already concluded that the use of a "real" nuclear bomb by some fringe group was unlikely, as he explained:

"First, I can't believe that given the relative unreliability of terrorist organizations any power would "give" a nuclear bomb to a fringe group . . ."

David interrupted:

"Can't debate that, though we know that Pakistan has helped Iran develop its own nuclear technology. Pakistan, for the first time, admitted in 2003 that it may have been the source of both knowledge and equipment for Iran's nuclear program. If I remember correctly, Pakistan became suspect when it disclosed that it had arrested an individual and was questioning the man who drove the nuclear project in Pakistan, a certain Abdul Qadeer Khan about his ties to Iran, if my memory is correct."

"Be that as it may, the danger of a terrorist group which had just been gifted a bomb to turn around and use the bomb in a blackmail against their supporter would seem too big."

"I see that too. But how about sharing with terrorists the technology needed to make dirty bombs and the whole situation is turned on its head. Do you agree?"

Mark smiled and replied that this was exactly what he had concluded himself, adding:

"Can't disagree. I would come to the same conclusion that it's the most likely case. However, it surely isn't a slam dunk."

David raised his eyebrows and asked with a half-smile on his face:

"You're going to explain that to me, right?"

"Absolutely. Anything nuclear is bound to bring the ongoing partially undeclared war in this region to an entirely different level. The various nuclear powers know that they are all carefully monitored by their adversaries. Who else besides Iran would give nuclear material to Hezbollah, Hamas, or the Muslim Brotherhood? Wouldn't Iran need to worry of any consequences to its own country? I know that you can always argue that any country that is first to use a nuclear bomb is attracting attention and should know that retaliation would be immediate and terrible. The end of the world . . ."

David had another thought up his proverbial sleeve:

"I can see that and can't disagree with you. Now how would you react if I suggested that the nuclear material might not have been given per se but somehow stolen?"

Mark replied that he had also considered that angle:

"The key would be from whom. You don't mean from Iran do you?"

"Not specifically, but why not?"

"Anyway, at this point, we haven't heard of any large-scale theft anywhere, but I'd like to set up a task force and have them investigate the issue in more depth."

He paused for a second and then asked:

"One of the things we need to look at is the motivation behind one of the two or three main Palestinian terrorist organization launching a dirty bomb toward Israel. We know that the main purpose behind these kinds of explosives has to be to deny civilians as well as soldiers the use of some territory. However, the contamination with radioactive material around the area touched by conventional explosion does not distinguish between friend or foe."

Mark kept going, making the point that, to his knowledge, dirty bombs had never been used in a real situation, only tested. He added that the real damage they inflicted was the costs associated with the decontamination of victims and of the affected areas which he added could extend from a few hundred square yards to a few square miles around the point of impact. David interrupted with a smile:

"Excellent point my friend. A dirty bomb wouldn't make it any easier for Palestinians to regain territory against Israel. By the way, we need to find out how long such contamination might last . . ."

Mark replied that he did not know but would find out. Immediately, though, he added:

"To me, even if whatever decontamination is needed requires both considerable time and expense, I can't imagine inflicting this damage can be the main motivation."

He was going to continue when David interrupted and said with a very serious tone of voice:

"Agreed. I don't think we need to debate this any longer. To me, they would principally be used to create mass panic as a weapon of terror. I think that we both need to take this up to Simon and do that as quickly as we can."

CHAPTER.02

TEL AVIV, ISRAEL; AND SOMEWHERE IN THE AUSTRIAN ALPS

General Simon Rabinowitz, the overall head of *Mossad* had been traveling within Israel and would not return until about 5:00 p.m. He therefore could not meet David and Mark until then, later in the day than had originally been requested. Yet, he asked his assistant when she contacted him to make sure they were the first two people he met upon his return.

Advised that Simon would be back a shade earlier than antici-pated, David and Mark arrived at 4:45 p.m. Simon ushered them into his comfortable office, with a wide smile. Though a casual observer might not understand why Simon would be smiling as he was about to discuss a very important matter, one need not go much further than the fact that he had a particular relationship with David Heller. David had been his second-in-command until Simon had succeeded the legendary General Ariel Landau, the former the Head of *Mossad,* when he retired. Simon also knew Mark quite well; he had risen steadily through the ranks though probably faster than most would have expected. He was now at the point where he was widely considered to be David's most senior lieutenant.

A jovial younger man in his late thirties, Mark had been involved in a number of missions, several of which proved to be critical to the safety of Israel. His rapid promotions were the direct result of his unusual abilities to see a situation, appreciate it, imagine the various possible outcomes, pick the best, and execute it. It was not that he had never made a mistake. More than once he had found himself coming up short in his analyses; yet, he had been unusually quick at learning from his experiences. David Heller would readily say that one of Mark's strongest qualities was his ability to recognize a mistake and correct it. Rather than digging in and burying himself deeper and deeper when in error, Mark had made the famous quip his personal motto: "if in a hole, stop digging immediately."

Simon pointed his guests to the sofa in the corner of his office. He had by then quickly returned to his usual purposeful demeanor; he was about to get a briefing which he had been told could be very important—duty called. He would give his two colleagues his undivided attention and undertook to make sure they received as much of his wisdom and guidance as he could muster. When he had briefly spoken to him on the phone while Simon was in Jerusalem, David had given him the main reason for the meeting and done it with simple, powerful words, no unnecessary detail. Simon's immediate reaction, including a willingness to return to Tel Aviv by helicopter rather than by car and call a meeting at 4:45 p.m. had demonstrated that he viewed the matter as crucial to the safety of Israel. He asked:

"Mark, can you give me a summary of the two or three main points we need to discuss? As you know, David has already given me the elevator pitch and I just want to make sure I don't miss any important color."

Mark proceeded with a simple preliminary conclusion:

"To me, Simon, the major issue can be broken down into three questions. First, what is it about the rumor which Josh has picked up; in particular, is there any echo of it anywhere within our system?

Second, assuming the rumor is correct, what can we find out about it? Third, who are the main parties involved?"

He paused for a second and surprised his audience adding:

"As for myself, I don't take it for granted that it is either one of the three main Palestinian terrorist groups or that it is directed toward us, at least initially."

Simon let out:

"Wow. You've thought about it in some depth haven't you? Had you shared your last point with David yet?"

Looking at his boss in an embarrassed and almost contrite manner, Mark conceded that he had not had the time to do it yet, as both David and he had been quite busy during the day. He immediately made amends and added:

"Sorry, David. I probably should have found the time . . ."

"Don't you even think of worrying about it, Mark. At your level and mine in this organization, we don't worry about politics. We worry about getting the job done."

Simon was smiling, ostensibly delighted and probably also somewhat proud that the team he had selected was working as well as it was. Turning to David he asked:

"Will you need additional resources?"

David spent no more than a few seconds thinking and blurted out:

"I think it'd be great if I could talk to Countess Renate and see if she has any resource she can share with us . . ."

"Countess Renate? I think I can understand. But before we get there, do you need anything from within our own organization?"

"Well, truthfully Simon, I feel I need to know a lot more with respect to radioactive materials before I even know what question to ask."

"Have you considered talking to Marvin?"

■ ■ ■ ■ ■

Marvin Goldstein was a veteran of the service responsible for all technological development for *Mossad*. He had an encyclopedic knowledge of the capabilities of each of the branches of the Israeli Defense Forces. He also knew exactly what was being planned for the future and even what research directions were emphasized and those which were not. At fifty-five, Marvin had worked with nearly all the key players in the service. He knew his stuff better than anyone and had a mind that thrived on challenges. He loved innovation, even if this was going to stretch his capabilities nearly to the breaking point. He was a man of vision; his vision was focused on technology. His only well-known shortcoming was that he loved technology so much that, often, he would extend his explanations into levels of detail that many considered unnecessary. Many felt that he often veered away from common Hebrew, or English, to speak in technobabble. Yet, most people still gave him a pass on those, as he was so good at everything else.

■ ■ ■ ■ ■

Countess Renate was the founder and head of The Shadow Experts[2]. This network was as secret as its leader. It consisted of specialists across a wide variety of disciplines who cooperated with and were directed by Countess Renate to defend "good causes." They ranged from micro-biologists to advanced material engineers, to art experts, to cyber engineers, to electronics gurus, and to many other specialties, each as esoteric as the others. All associates knew they were members of the network, but most did not know who the other members were, other than those people with whom they had worked on one or another assignment. They all knew Renate; most, if not

---

[2] See *The Shadow Experts*, by the same author, Carringer Publishing, 2021.

all, had seen her in person or on some video conference call. Yet, no one could claim that he or she had met with her regularly. These specialists were all "part-time associates" who punctually came into a team to solve a problem and returned to the shadows when they were no longer needed. Besides the honor of being a member of the network, they were all generously rewarded when they participated in a project.

Renate had no board of directors. Her only employees were a handful of individuals who worked for her at the castle, her residence in the Austrian alps. The castle had a completely hidden lair which allowed Renate to remain linked to everyone without giving away where she was. She even had a corporate jet which had been modified to include vertical take-off and landing capability and could thus be hidden underground. She could leave or return to the castle without anyone seeing how she had flown in or out, as the castle grounds did not include any visible runway. The handful of employees were the only ones who knew of her twin identities—her real name was Princess Alexandra, a wealthy orphan and distant heir to the Habsburg imperial crown. Her husband, Prince Karl, of Danish royal blood, also had a twin identity as he morphed into Captain Frederik, her pilot and all-around aide when she became Countess Renate.

■ ■ ■ ■ ■

David agreed that Simon's suggestion was high on his list of things to do next, though he argued that an initial overall conversation with Countess Renate might still be useful even in the absence of a complete understanding of all technological issues. He added:

"In fact, I know that Mark is scheduled to meet with Marvin tomorrow in the early afternoon."

Simon nodded and suggested that they could try to get her on the video conference phone then, adding:

"I never know where she is, but, if she is at home, the one-hour time difference shouldn't be a problem. If she's anywhere else, I know she always tries to accommodate us."

Mark blurted out:

"By the way, do we know where she lives?"

"No, my dear Mark; we don't. And trust me, it's not because we haven't tried. She takes her personal security quite seriously. In fact, I thought I saw a shadow come over her face the day she had to concede that she lived on the European Continent. At the time she had casually mentioned that Tel Aviv was an hour earlier than her place; I had mentioned something to the effect that the detail told me she lived on the European Continent. That's when she replied that I might know more than most, but that thankfully the European Continent was still quite vast."

■ ■ ■ ■ ■

David and Mark had left Simon's office as he had other pressing matters to attend to and he and Mark connected to the conference line. David immediately recognized the always joyful and partially throaty sound of Countess Renate's voice. He did not have to say many words before Countess Renate interrupted him:

"David; it's so nice to hear from you. Anything interesting?"

Countess Renate could see the wide smile on David's face as they were using a video conference call service. He replied:

"Nothing more than the usual, Countess."

Nobody on the call could miss the partially dissimulated laugh of both Countess Renate and Mark. David continued:

"But let me ask you a question if I may . . ."

"Fire away."

"Do you have a way of giving us access to a nuclear energy expert?"

"That should not be a problem, on the surface, but you're going to have to tell me more. Nuclear energy covers a very wide waterfront, my friend. I should also add that I'm flattered: you guys should not be short of first-class nuclear engineers."

"Touché. You're right. But we're looking for the best of the best and for someone who does not involve a risk of leaks. In fact, I am more interested in the topic of nuclear armaments. Dirty bombs to be specific, though there are ramifications in a number of different directions."

"Dirty bombs, Hey! Sure. Can you tell me more or would you like to reserve the details to the time when I can have Dr. Marcel Delagrange on the phone?

"Marcel Delagrange?"

"He's the most knowledgeable man I know in that field. He is a graduate of the absolute best math and physics school in France: *Ecole Normale Supérieure*; in fact, he was first in the competitive exam you have to pass to get into it! I'll spare you excessive detail about that, but the school is a part of what the French call the four aces: the four schools sitting at the top of four key disciplines, engineering, business, government administration as well as education and research. However, add to that highly desirable diploma, post-doctoral work at MIT in Massachusetts and a stint at the CERN—*Conseil Européen pour la Recherche Nucléaire,* the European Organization for Nuclear Research just outside Geneva—and then a full career as a consultant to the French nuclear power industry, and you'll get a sense of his qualifications. Do I need to add that he still finds time in his spare time to teach at Ecole Normale Supérieure in Paris? Don't know anyone who has a better résumé in this field, though I must add that I would be surprised if he had ever been involved in building a nuclear weapon."

She paused for a second and jokingly added:

"Though I'm pretty sure he would shine there as well . . ."

Mark jokingly made a sign of submission and added:

"Impressive indeed. Impressive. Can we assume he is an associate of yours?"

"My dear Mark. You know that normally I wouldn't be able to tell you . . ."

She paused for effect, and almost immediately continued:

"But, for once, I'll surprise you. Yes, he is and yes, I can tell you about it. In fact, he was one of my first associates on this side of the Atlantic Ocean, with Dr. Armand Duchemin[3], the fellow from the Institut Pasteur whom you all know."

Mark could only utter:

"Wow!"

Then remembering Countess Renate's initial question, he changed his train of thought and replied:

"In as few words as I can, let me simply say that we have heard a rumor from a usually reliable source that there is talk of traffic of radioactive material in Iraq. It immediately made us think of dirty bombs."

"Wow. I see. That's serious indeed. Can I assume that you wouldn't call me if your source was not as solid as they come?"

"Correct, but you need to know one thing. As we speak, we know very little other than the fact that the rumor I mentioned exists. Yet, we feel we would love to be guided in our analysis, and we suspect that you might in fact have ways of getting certain datapoints faster than we."

Countess Renate simply replied:

"Thanks for the confidence. Let me organize a three-way video conference call with the usual provisos in terms of who everybody

---

3 From the same author, see *Shadow Experts* (2021) and *Trouble in the China Sea* (2024) both through Barringer Publishing.

on the line is and the need for absolute secrecy. I'll get back to you as soon as I have anything to report."

She paused and before leaving the call added with a smile:

"Give my best to Simon please."

CHAPTER.03

TEL AVIV, JERUSALEM AND TIBERIAS, ISRAEL

Though he surely did not have more than a few pieces of whichever puzzle he might be contemplating, Simon had, in the meantime, decided to inform both Jesse Benaroya, the Prime Minister, and Jeremy Bensoussan, the head of *Shin Bet*. Truth be told, this was the way the Israeli system functioned: total transparency across the very top of the security apparatus. Anything which might appear secondary or even unimportant could rise to a crucial level of relevance when brought together with other, on the surface, equally small elements. *Shin Bet* is Israel's domestic security service. Thus, though less well-known outside of the country than *Mossad*, it fulfils a critical role, as illustrated by its motto: "Defends and shall not be seen." The distinction between *Mossad* and *Shin Bet* seems to be broadly the same as that which prevails, in the U.S., between the FBI and the CIA, though the usual cynic would surely argue that transparency and an absence of interagency competitiveness are more visible in Israel. After all, that should not be surprising as security, for Israel, is a matter of survival.

To simplify the process, the three men had decided to meet in the Prime Minister's office, so that only one briefing would be needed.

That required Simon and Jeremy to travel from Tel Aviv to Jerusalem. They thus decided to share a helicopter ride. Simon boarded the official government helicopter just outside his office and picked up Jeremy on the way to Jerusalem. The headquarters of *Shin Bet*, or *Shabak* as the security agency is also called in Israel, are located on the outskirts of Tel Aviv University, about four miles due south from *Mossad*'s headquarters. Coincidentally, *Shabak*'s senior officers work a couple hundred yards away from *Palmach* Museum, which is dedicated to the *Palmach*, the strike-force of the underground *Haganah* defense organization.

Though always welcoming to his guests, Jesse Benaroya's face was somber as he showed Simon and Jeremy to the light green, suede leather sofa in the corner of his office. Coffees were awaiting everyone on the table in front of the sofa. Jesse had chosen to sit in the matching armchair which was at a 90-degree angle to the sofa. Simon was to his left and Jeremy to Simon's left. Jesse opened the meeting with an expression of his serious worries:

"Gentlemen, I don't need to tell you how serious this is. Simon, many thanks to your organization for procuring our starting point, but I feel that both you and Jeremy will need to cooperate quite closely on this one. But I know I don't have to say it; you two always do."

Simon smiled and replied:

"For sure. As you know, Jesse, Jeremy and I travelled together from Tel Aviv to see you. Though the noise of a helicopter engine can be deafening, we managed to exchange a few thoughts. I'd say we have had a chance to discuss our first reactions. I think I'm not putting words in Jeremy's mouth when I say that we both agree this is very serious and deserves a dedicated, joint effort within the country's security services."

Jeremy concurred:

"Couldn't agree more. In fact, we agreed, subject to your OK, that we're going to bring Noah Raman, the head of *Aman*, into the loop. We'll have all bases covered."

Jeremy did not need to remind anyone that *Aman*, Israeli Military Intelligence, is the third agency in the trio of organizations dedicated to the security of the country.

Jesse nodded his agreement, though he qualified it:

"I didn't call Noah into this meeting because I wanted to have your full input on what you felt must be done. But I'm totally prepared to follow your recommendation if you believe he should be included."

Simon supported Jeremy's comment and added:

"At this point, I think our recommendation, if you agree, Jesse, has two main dimensions. First, we should keep the whole thing firmly concealed; the press should not know about any of it. Whoever participates in that nuclear waste traffic can't know what we know. Second, I think that the senior managements of all law enforcement organizations in the country should be made aware of a non-specific rumor, couching it as absolutely top secret, need to know only. They should only be told that it concerns nuclear material theft."

Seeing Jesse nod his concurrence, Jeremy replied that maintaining secrecy would mean that instructions should take two different forms. Some form of communication, possibly coming from the Prime Minister's Office, or the War Cabinet should inform the most senior personnel of the need to monitor all news relating to nuclear issues very carefully. He was glad to see both Jesse and Simon concur with his first suggestion. Jeremy continued:

"Lower down the totem pole, all relevant personnel should be made aware of a need for any suspicion of any form of radiation leak or dirty bombing to be immediately sent up through reporting lines. There is no need to discuss any background, such as the rumor, but we want anything that can help us reach Tel Aviv or Jerusalem within minutes, hours at most."

"Totally agree, Jeremy. Let me entrust this to the two of you. Please make sure that I am kept aware of any development."

■ ■ ■ ■ ■

Meanwhile, in Tiberias, Eli Schonberg and his son, Jacob, emerged from the shelter on Shatzer Street. It was quite close to their modest home and was part of a network which seemed to have been designed so that no shelter was further away than one mile from any other. They were delighted to see that there was no trace of bomb damage; the projectiles had to have fallen elsewhere. Eli and Jacob, like many people in Tiberias, were both farmers and businessmen. They had a shop which catered to the tourist trade and at the same time they followed the family tradition: they were avocado growers. In fact, while in the shelter, they had learned on the radio that a bomb had hit an area which they suspected was not terribly far from their three main avocado tree fields. These were located about two and a half miles to the southwest of town. Eli and Jacob felt that now that sirens had stopped sounding, they needed to go and assess the damage, hoping it was minimal.

Though father and son, the two men did not really look much like each other. Eli could not hide the weight of the years on his shoulders and that also showed on his face which was wrinkled, particularly around the eyes. His hair had long lost its brown tint to become more white than grey and his posture had stooped a bit; he retained the vigor which people who work the land often maintain thanks to their daily physical activities. Jacob, on the other hand, was at least six inches taller than his father, and, in fact, quite a bit more as he stood straighter where as his father already had somewhat of a vaulted posture. His face, though bearded as his father, was dominated by two piercing brown eyes that darted from right to left as he surveyed his surroundings. He exuded the energy of youth, though, somehow, one could not miss the fact that he looked quite mature and ready to take charge.

Father and son calmly walked back to their home and climbed in their grey pickup truck, with the tools and equipment they usually needed to tend the trees and the soil between the many rows. They drove 600 feet to the roundabout and turned right on Levi Eskohl Street. A third of a mile further on, they entered another roundabout and took the first exit, the only one in fact, which took them virtually due south. A couple of roundabouts later and about two miles on, as they were about to enter Hazor'im, a small village, they veered sharply left onto a dirt path that ran along a number of cultivated fields. The fields were quite similar to everything else in the local landscape: fruit trees galore. It was easy to imagine the landscape a few months earlier when all these trees would have been in full bloom, showing a symphony of bright colors. The leaves of the trees in the early summer varied from the light green color of mango leaves to the almost greyish turquoise blue of olive trees, and from relatively large to quite small. Another significant difference which could only be noted in the fall and winter was whether the trees shed their leaves or were evergreen. In the end, the simplest observable difference from one plot to the next at any time of the year probably was the height of the various trees. For instance, while an almond tree might reach 40 feet, avocado trees could grow to be 60 feet high.

Less than a half a mile down the road, they were surprised to see something that looked like the edges of a small crater. Though they could not see the impact point precisely, they quickly estimated that the crater was probably not more than 10 yards in diameter and at most two feet in depth. The two men decided that forward progress by truck was going to be difficult as the edge of the crater obstructed the dirt path. They thus left the truck and kept going on foot. It took them no more than a few seconds to draw the obvious conclusion: an enemy rocket had escaped the Iron Dome and had fallen near the path, in the process damaging fields on both sides of the path. Eli noted:

"Sure hope that our fields were not too damaged but am convinced we couldn't have escaped unscathed."

Jacob was equally cautious:

"Darn right! I'm prepared for some sad news. The fire has surely burnt quite a number of trees."

He paused for a split second and added:

"And the fire surely has touched one of our fields."

Their three fields were on the right-hand side of the dirt path. They did not need to get all the way to the crater to estimate that a good 20% of the first field that ran along the path had been burned by the impact. Eli and Jacob could see pieces of metal, a few of them seemingly still smoldering, all around them among the small rocks that littered the sides of the trail. Both were strong men, who had built up the farm on their own, after various wars had damaged their historical land; they were well aware of the dangers and risks. They were therefore somewhat angry, but certainly neither distressed nor ever depressed. They had done it before and could do it again. And they would surely get some help from the government to deal with the loss and rebuild what had been burned.

All of a sudden, Jacob saw his father clutch his chest.

"What's wrong, Papa?"

"I don't know. It feels like my heart is fibrillating . . . You know. Not beating regularly."

"But you have a pacemaker, don't you?"

"I do, but it feels almost as if it isn't working properly. It feels like before they put it in."

Jacob immediately took control:

"OK Papa. This is serious. More serious than any avocado tree plantation. Let's go back to the truck. Walk calmly, we don't want to stress your heart. I'm driving you to the hospital."

Eli did not seem to enjoy the experience of being told where to go by his own son. Yet he reluctantly followed Jacob's strongly worded advice; he had to concede, at least in his mind, that Jacob was right. Once in the truck, Jacob decided to drive to the urgent care center on Ha-Yarden Street, in the center of town. He knew it had the best heart care in Tiberias and felt that his father deserved the best. He avoided all the side streets and though it was at least a couple of miles longer he was convinced that Highway 77 would be faster. It was a major artery to travel around and into town. As he was driving, with his cell phone in hands-free mode, he called his mother to tell her what he was doing and asked her to call the hospital. She gave the hospital his cell phone number and the staff there immediately reached out to him, calling to give him directions and find out more about the patient. He described the symptoms broadly and they agreed that he was doing the right thing driving his father straight to the hospital. They told him a crew would be ready at the emergency entrance.

■ ■ ■ ■ ■

Marvin's office was just as one would have expected it: messy like the office one would imagine belonged to the proverbial absent-minded professor or scientist. The wide bay window offered a beautiful view of the Mediterranean and of the Herzliya marina. Inside the office, he had drawings, blueprints, mock-ups, and detailed models of several of his current works-in-progress. The coffee table in front of his visitors' sofa was littered with technical magazines and papers or articles that he had not yet read or still wanted to read again before deciding what to do with them. There were even a few folders on the floor in the general area of his desk; only Marvin knew what was in them . . .

"Mark what a pleasure! What can I do for you?"

Mark started with a brief summary of the rumor he had picked up through Josh Steinmetz. As usual, he chose to keep non-essential information off the table, not because he did not trust Marvin but simply because training within *Mossad* emphasized that even internal communications should be limited to need-to-know information, as much as possible and reasonable. He then asked:

"Is there anything that you need me to add to that?"

Marvin smiled as he leaned back in his desk chair. He then asked:

"Are you aware of the tests we have carried out on nuclear explosives?"

"I know about the work on the creation of a nuclear device, but you can't possibly be talking of that, are you?"

"No! You're absolutely correct. I'm referring to a series of tests we ran during a four- or five-year period of time; can't remember exactly. We wanted to measure the effects of nuclear explosives if they were ever used against us. We focused solely on small nuclear devices. Dirty bombs would be at the low end of that scale, but a few tests dealt with real fission explosions. Haaretz, the longest running newspaper currently in print in Israel, reported in 2015 or so that high-level radiation was measured only at the center of the explosions. We found that the fallout, the radiation carried by the wind, was low. In short, we concluded that the main issue was psychological, not real damage, unless obviously you were dealing with a massive blast."

Mark replied that this seemed quite encouraging. Marvin immediately urged caution, arguing that the key to the experiment had been the power of the explosions. He added:

"I wouldn't rely on any of this to evaluate a threat coming from people like Iran . . ."

He paused for effect and finished his sentence:

"As and when they develop a full-fledged nuclear bomb. At that time, I'd bet they'll be higher than the top end of the range of devices we tested. Add to that the belief I have that they wouldn't care much about collateral damage to Palestinians living in the vicinity of their target and you must conclude that this remains an area of top intelligence priority, as I'm sure you know."

"How can we protect ourselves against that?"

Marvin allowed himself a heavy sigh as he said:

"I'm not sure I know where to start, my friend."

Mark refrained from any reaction to encourage Marvin to keep going; he did not need to trigger the massive flow of explanations, many of which would not be directly relevant. Marvin still started by mentioning the obvious steps of basic caution such as preventing illicit radioactive materials in shipping:

"Here I mean via, cars, boats or airplanes."

He added:

"There are plenty of tools or measuring devices, more or less sophisticated, that can be used at official checkpoints. However, what if the device or the raw material is brought into the country across unguarded stretches of coastline or some other barren border area? We've got plenty of those, you know . . ."

Marvin paused and then added:

"A prototype dirty-bomb detection device with nanosecond neutron analysis demonstrated that it could detect uranium from behind a 2-inch thick was . . ."

"I thought uranium was not the best material for a dirty bomb . . ."

Marvin was impressed by Mark's knowledge. Yet, he thought he needed to take a detour in the current conversation to explain to him how a dirty bomb operated. He said that the simplest way to think of a dirty bomb was to imagine a conventional explosive charge surrounded by radioactive material. He added:

"Though the radioactive material does not have to be powdered, the smaller the particles are the easier it would be to disperse them in the explosion."

He then returned to the earlier point as to the potential use of uranium. He explained:

"The more radioactive the material is, the less of it you need or the more impact you will have assuming the same volume. So, it's true that certain isotopes or chemical compounds are more suited to a dirty bomb. Do you know that, in a nuclear fission reaction, uranium loses some of its energy and it is replaced by rising radioactivity?"

Seeing Mark vaguely nod, Marvin continued:

"As the process of fission takes place, the atoms of uranium are consumed and split into smaller atoms which are intensely radioactive. Anyway, remember two key things. First, most terrorists are after a psychological impact, not a maximum kill rate on the spot. Second, what detection we can carry out with uranium, we can do even better with caesium-137 or strontium-90, to name only two alternatives."

Marvin paused for a short few seconds and concluded:

"Bottom line: we have some defenses, but the risk is certainly not contained as far as I know. In fact, let me ask you a rhetorical question: why do we have to assume that a dirty bomb would be brought into the country? How about placing it at the tip of a rocket or dropping it somewhere from a drone?"

CHAPTER.04

Back in Tiberias, everyone was just as surprised as Eli and Jacob, minutes after they had arrived at the hospital. Eli's condition had improved perceptibly during the short trip from the fields to the hospital. Furthermore, he said he felt almost normal as he walked through the door of the hospital, refusing the gurney which had been brought out to wheel him in. Despite his pleas that he and his son should return to the avocado plantation, a wheelchair appeared, and he was asked to sit in it as he was still ushered into a room where he was thoroughly examined, and the functioning of his pacemaker checked. Most everything did indeed seem normal. The only conclusion anyone could offer at that time was that some external factor had caused the pacemaker to misfunction. The emergency physician on duty suddenly observed:

"Wait a minute. Coincidentally, yesterday, I read a piece which said that certain forms of radiation can cause chemical changes in the structure of the pacemaker."

Jacob immediately saw where the physician was heading and asked:

"If there was radiation, why did it not affect my phone or other electronic equipment we had, starting with any solid-state component in the engine of the truck?"

"Reasonable question, sir. Quite reasonable in fact. To tell you the truth, I'm not sure I know the answer. The only thing I can do is formulate the assumption that the dose of radiation might have needed to be stronger to interfere with their functioning, though it was high enough to disturb the pacemaker."

Suddenly, Eli exclaimed:

"Could the bomb that caused the crater in our field have emitted radiation? We saw a number of small metallic bits, a few of them still smoldering. Could it be?"

Jacob was surprised and could only reply:

"Could it be what, Papa?"

"Could the rocket that hit our field have been a dirty bomb?"

▮ ▮ ▮ ▮ ▮

Countess Renate was the first to speak on the videoconference call she had organized with David, Mark, and Dr. Marcel Delagrange:

"David and Mark, let me introduce my friend, Dr. Marcel Delagrange, to you. Marcel, I have already shared your background with David and Mark, and they were quite impressed; but who wouldn't be?"

Marcel replied in a voice which surprised both David and Mark as it was particularly deep as he spoke deliberately:

"It's a pleasure to meet you gentlemen. May I suggest that in keeping with the good old American tradition we use first names to communicate. So much simpler than the French or German habits of using full names and titles . . ."

He paused and briefly laughed:

"Come to think of it, unless I'm mistaken, there are no Americans on this call. So, let's just call it an international tradition and be done with it."

David and Mark could only nod their agreement.

Marcel continued:

"Rather than asking you to repeat everything which Countess Renate told me she learned from you, I thought I should prepare a short presentation on dirty bombs. How they're made and what the key issues are. Any problem?

David and Mark nodded their agreement. Marcel went on:

"Good. So, here it is."

Marcel paused again and noted:

"As I was preparing this, I've tried not to get into too many details for you. Yet, there are a few technical issues which I must put on the table. Please bear with me, as I suspect that it will allow us to get more quickly to the key questions and to identify the areas where the Countess and I might be able to help."

With that said, Marcel mentioned that the starting point of any such conversation has to deal with what is it that anyone, terrorist organization or any other entity, should have in order to construct and detonate a dirty bomb. He reminded the group that a dirty bomb is made with classical, non-nuclear explosives and some radioactive material placed around the explosives. With a smile, he added:

"If you ask, that's why they're often called Radioactive Dispersion Devices, or RDD for short. As you know, in the military around the world, people love to use acronyms rather than full words."

He laughed heartily and jokingly said that he probably did not have to spend any time discussing conventional explosives, adding:

"You gentlemen have a lot more experience with them than I do. Or at least you have surely used them more than I would have."

He continued with the comment that the challenge, therefore, was in the acquisition of radioactive material. He paused and suddenly said with a seriousness which surprised Mark and David:

"I hate to admit to it, but there are literally millions of radioactive sources used worldwide. The most obvious would be found in the nuclear industry. But there are many, many others. Think of hospitals needing x-ray equipment; think of universities and research establishments which conduct experiments requiring some form of radioactivity. Think of pharmaceutical companies. Now for the decisive factor, think of any company which makes radioactivity detection equipment. I could go on, but I'm sure you get the point. Many people and corporations need and use radioactive sources."

Seeing that no member of his audience seemed lost, he continued:

"The key is that each of these establishments produces waste which consists of a mixture of radioactive material, and other stuff, be they liquids, gases, or solids. They start with some radioactive source and when they're through working with it they find themselves with waste which is in certain cases even more radioactive. Now, you can be sure that waste, which is considered quite dangerous, is closely supervised and supposedly well-guarded. But you'd be surprised how much can fall through the cracks."

Mark could not resist asking:

"Are you always such a pessimist, Marcel?"

"I'm not and don't think I ever was. Remember, my background is in scientific disciplines. The data and the data alone should guide your conclusions. Frankly, I've never thought of myself as a pessimist. In truth, I see myself as a realist. I'd rather know the dangers to which I am exposed even if they might worry me than live blissfully ignorant and die of ignorance."

Seeing that Mark did not want to add anything, Marcel continued his presentation, arguing that of the many potential sources he had just listed, only nine reactor-produced isotopes are considered suitable for dirty bombs. With a smile, he added:

"I'm sure you don't need me to enumerate these possible sources."

Countess Renate, David and Mark smiled and waved their hands in a fake sign of submission. Marcel turned to a discussion of what he called the key question:

"Now, where could one find these radioactive materials? That's where the news isn't good. I've read several pieces arguing that the U.S. Nuclear Regulatory Commission has estimated that one source, i.e. one possible supply of radioactive material is lost, abandoned or even stolen each and every day of the year . . ."

Mark could not resist repeating Marcel's last sentence with special emphasis on the last five words:

". . . every day of the year?"

"Unfortunately yes, Mark. And things don't get much better when you look outside of the U.S. In the European Union, for instance, losses or suspect disappearances work out to nearly 10 per month, one every third day! In short, around the world, you should assume that there are thousands of these sources, with new ones added to the list weekly."

David could only note:

"That's even worse than I thought . . ."

"And I'm sure you have excellent data . . . Now let me help you with a quick point. Remember when the Soviet Union was broken up. Remember the question of who should have custody of nuclear weapons, since quite a few of them were in fact in Ukraine. I'm not going to be drawn into a discussion of how well or badly that particular issue was resolved, but I just want you to imagine the number of sources, spread throughout the former Soviet Union, for whatever reason though usually the main one was communication and thus producing energy in desertic area. Before the dislocation there were people who were responsible for them. Afterwards? No one!"

Marcel paused to drink from a glass of water on his desk and then quickly added:

"Now for the better news. Probably less than 1 in 5 of these sources reported to have been lost could pose significant challenges. Where would we find them?"

Marcel paused again to verify that his audience was following his point. Satisfied that they were still with him, he continued:

"Unfortunately, as I just implied with my Soviet Union example, most analysts believe that thousands of them are in Russia where various organizations lost count of them when the Soviet Union collapsed. A large but unknown number of these sources probably belongs to the high security risk category."

Marcel could not resist telling the story of a couple of woodcutters who fell very sick because of a radioactive source on which they stumbled. They were from Georgia, in the former Soviet Union. One day, they happened on a radioisotope thermoelectric generator. These devices convert heat generated by the natural decay of enriched plutonium into electrical power. Marcel went off his story briefly to remind David and Mark that these kinds of generators powered dozens of space missions and could produce heat and electricity under the harsh conditions of deep space for decades without maintenance. He paused and said:

"Sorry for these arcane details, but you needed them to understand the rest of the story."

Mark and David signaled that everything was OK. Marcel returned to his earlier story. In Georgia as anywhere else in the former Soviet Union, generators just like the one these fellows found were used to emit beacons in lighthouses in remote areas of Russia. He went on with a half-smile on his face, as his position as a scientist would have surely taught him not to touch the generator:

"The two men dragged the generator back to their camp as they badly wanted something there to provide heat. Within hours they suffered from acute radiation sickness and needed to be taken to the nearest hospital."

Regaining quite a serious demeanor, Marcel added:

"The story does not say whether they survived or not, but I wouldn't rate their chances of doing so at more than 50/50. Just to help you put that accident in the proper perspective, let me add that the International Atomic Energy Agency later estimated that the generator in question probably contained the equivalent of the radioactivity released immediately after the Chernobyl accident. Note that the total radiation released by Chernobyl over time was much, much larger."

David had to ask:

"So, Marcel how big of a risk are these loose sources, really?"

"I'd love to give you a reassuring reply, but in fact the truth is that the danger is real—very real. First, I'm told that there has been an increase in the illicit trafficking of radioactive sources, though it may have gone deeper underground in the more recent past. The better news, if you will, is that there are logistical issues which makes life harder for terrorists trafficking in nuclear waste."

Marcel paused and continued after having taken another sip from his water glass:

"First, you want to make sure that the source can be transported from A to B with enough shielding to protect whoever is carrying it from radiation. Not everyone is as naïve as our Georgian woodcutters. So we need protection, though that protection can't become unwieldy—I mean too heavy and restricting your freedom of movement. Remember, lead is an excellent shield against radiation, but it's also the heaviest common industrial metal, aside from mercury, platinum, gold and a couple of others, among really special metals. Second, your source must still have enough radioactivity to be effective when the bomb explodes. Finally, and this may be a bit too technical, the source should be sufficiently dispersible to contaminate the area that the bomb targets."

Mark had to ask:

"Has there been any instance of actual terrorist use of dirty bombs?"

"Truth is the answer is no, at least to my knowledge. But they have come close, in fact too close for comfort in my book. For instance, in 1995, Chechen separatists buried a caesium-137 source wrapped in explosives at the Izmaylovsky Park in Moscow. The plot unraveled. A similar approach was used in 1998, though the attempt was again uncovered before it could explode. In 2002, some fellow was arrested in the U.S. on the grounds that he was planning a dirty bombing. Another instance occurred in 2006, this time in the U.K. Again, no explosion, but what if? There have been many others, but their common feature is that each and every one was discovered before any damage could be done. But it's hard not to see a trend and therefore a risk. Something is bound to slip through the cracks at some point . . ."

David thanked Marcel for the lengthy but incredibly instructive explanation. Marcel made a sign with his right hand that no thanks were necessary. He suddenly added:

"One last thing I should mention. I wouldn't discount terrorists using some very minor radiation release, say a 'not-so-dirty bomb' if I can call it that. They might then publicize the action to capitalize on the general population's fears of radiation. I once saw this somewhere, could even be in Wikipedia, and I want to leave it with you: make sure you distinguish between weapons of **mass destruction** and weapons of **mass disruption**."

David noted the emphasis which Marcel had put on the distinction between the two phrases and could not resist applauding Marcel's last comment, concluding:

"Marcel, I read your comment to mean that the goal of such an activity would be to gain publicity and destabilize society, possibly even through the normal political process."

Mark interrupted:

"I see what you mean. Create fears if not panic in the voting public. The terrorists would then hope that a more supportive party comes into power."

Marcel nodded and said:

"That's one option. The other is that the party that comes into power to fight the terrorists, probably the other extreme of the political or ideological spectrum, creates such a mess that this eventually allows the terrorists to seize power."

"Might you be referring to the move to the extreme right in certain European countries?"

"Bingo. But don't focus solely on the extreme right when the extreme left offers you similar example, albeit in different regions. Even simply stealing radioactive materials may trigger a panic reaction from the general public. Similarly, a small-scale release of radioactive materials or a threat of such a release may be considered sufficient for a terror attack."

"Any suggestion for us?"

Marcel hesitated as he had to concede that he was entering a zone which was beyond his real area of expertise. Yet he said:

"Were I a terrorist in that frame of mind, I'd think that hospitals have to be quite vulnerable to an attack aimed at stealing radioactive material. We've all heard of hospitals and even certain pharmacies being targeted by drug traffickers . . ."

Mark jumped to the conclusion:

"Why not target them to steal radioactive material? Would it be as simple as that?"

Marcel smiled and repeated his earlier point:

"That's not my area of expertise. So, I can't be sure about any details. But the broad outline does not strike me as crazy or simply not feasible. However, remember, there are thousands of these sources around the world. So, there might be a simpler or easier solution."

CHAPTER.05

TEL AVIV, AND TIBERIAS, ISRAEL

While it was decided to keep Eli in the hospital so that the pacemaker could be monitored for a full 24 hours at least, the resident invited Jacob to join him in his office. From there, they called the municipal authorities to inform them of the incident.

Chaim Messer, the Head of Police in Tiberias, was one of the people who had received the warning from Tel Aviv following the meeting that had taken place in Jesse Benaroya's office with Simon and Jeremy. He had instructed all members of his staff to find him if anything relating to radiation was to come up and get him on the case immediately. The phone call from the resident at the urgent care center definitely fit that bill, and Chaim was on the phone with him in seconds. A couple of minutes later, he ordered two police officers to go to the hospital to get depositions from Eli, Jacob, and the medical staff. Simultaneously, he and two of his direct subordinates plus a couple of police officers jumped in two police cars and drove to the Schonberg family field to investigate the nature of the explosion. Within less than thirty minutes, the conclusion was inescapable. The Geiger counters which the police brought to the field had unmistakenly detected radioactivity.

Chaim first ordered his two men to create a map of the radioactivity around the crater. They put on the protective clothing they had brought in the trunk of their car. They started from the middle of the crater and moved in the opposite direction one from the other, observing and reading out on their walkie talkies the level of radioactivity every ten yards or so, stopping when the level fell to below a 200 millirems per hour threshold. It quickly became apparent that the charge had contaminated an area which was just short of 200 yards in diameter.

As the men were walking, they also indicated to Chaim the location of any piece of metal they could identify in terms of its distance from the center of the crater. They picked anything they saw and placed it in a radiation-proof bag that was attached to their belts. Once they felt they were done with what they called the salvage and recovery work, they still had one final avenue to explore. They started again from the center of the crater and collected about a small shovel full of dirt every ten yards or so and placed it in an individual plastic bag which bore the coordinates of the spot from which the dirt came. Afterwards, they noted with some humor that they could have combined the two steps into a single operation: recovering metal debris and picking up dirt samples. Chaim agreed but added with a smile that the observation came too late that time but would be a useful improvement to add to their standard procedures if something similar happened again.

After his men had carefully collected all the various pieces of scrap in the crater and around it, Chaim called Tel Aviv and was put through to Jeremy Bensoussan at *Shin Bet*. By then, his men in Tiberias had tested all the fragments they had found within the crater and around it. Chaim was able to report that they had all tested positive for radiation, with various degrees of intensity as could be determined with the equipment at their disposal. Jeremy asked him to keep everything under his own direct control, with great care given to protect everyone from the effects of radiation. He added:

"By the way, I'll need you to send all the various samples to Tel Aviv as we will now need to determine whether we can identify the kind of radioactive material which was used."

He paused and added:

"Chaim, this is a state matter. Please make sure that you do what needs to be done in a way such that no one in the town is aware of anything untoward."

Chaim asked:

"How about the two farmers and the medical personnel at the urgent care center?"

"Give me the phone numbers of anyone that might have heard the reference to radiation, and I will have someone call them immediately. They'll receive a very superficial briefing and will be told that, officially, nothing special happened other than the fact that a rocket was not shot down by the Iron Dome and hit an avocado field. Nobody should doubt the story as everyone knows that we do not aim to shoot down rockets or missiles which are not likely to hit populated areas."

"Will you want us to monitor their contacts and conversations?"

"Routine matter my friend."

Jeremy moved to his next question:

"By the way, did any other rocket get through the Iron Dome?"

"So far no news of it, but my men are still canvassing the whole area."

"Thank you. Don't be surprised if you see someone start doing some search and recovery work in the Sea of Galilea. Simon Rabinowitz and I want to see whether any other rocket might have had some nuclear coating or anything that emitted radiation."

Mark Levi, who had been put in charge of the mission by both Simon and Jeremy, had elected not to start his underwater inspection of the Sea of Galilea at the Fisherman's Anchorage in Tiberias. Rather, he chose the Marine Center of Ginosar, 5 miles north of Tiberias in the direction of Capernaum. While the marine facilities that were available in Tiberias would have been more convenient, Mark felt that Ginosar offered a more discreet alternative. Indeed, the chances that anyone in Ginosar would have heard of the accident in the Schoenfeld's field had to be much lower. Though a news blackout had been imposed on the Tiberias bombing, Mark also worried that leaks might still have occurred somewhere between the hospital and the dock. The operation started in the middle of the night, precisely to avoid anyone being aware of it. Yet, a few fishermen plying their trade off Ginosar, could not help but notice something unusual was taking place.

Mark had organized for a two-man mini-submarine to be brought by truck to Ginosar from the marine base in Haifa where it was normally kept when not in use. Though this might have surprised someone not used to the Israeli road network, the truck started driving due south despite the fact that Ginosar was due east of the Navy Base in Haifa. The apparent detour allowed the driver to use highways and thus to offset the longer distance with a higher average speed, not to mention peace of mind during the 1-hour drive very early in the morning. Once a mile from Ginosar, he kept going straight on Highway 803, bypassing the town and looking for Highway 90 which he would take until he reached Ginosar at which point he would look for the Marine Center. All expectations were that at that time of the night, it would be totally deserted. Depending upon how long it would take for the minisubmarine to complete its search and recovery mission, the decision would be made as to where to take it out of the water, though everyone was aware that it would take a few days before that decision was required.

■ ■ ■ ■ ■

Marvin and Mark had thoroughly discussed the process which could be used to retrieve any debris they would find. Mark was indeed concerned that he did not want his crew members to be exposed to frequent and significant changes in pressure. A critical issue which all scuba divers know very well is that pressure increases as one goes deeper and deeper into a body of water. Typically, recreational divers cannot exceed 130 feet, though professional divers with special equipment may be able to reach 300 feet. While the issue of the time it would take a professional driver to reach a 300-foot depth is valid, the men agreed that it was a moot point in the circumstances: the diver would not need to adjust to the change in pressure if the pressure within the submarine was gradually adjusted so that it corresponded to the water pressure outside. Further, with the maximum depth of the Sea of Galilea not exceeding 141 feet, the men would be well within the parameters of a routine dive. There would not be any need to provide for atmospheric diving: small one-person articulated submersible with sophisticated pressure joints to allow some movement on the diver's limbs while maintaining internal pressure equal to one atmosphere. These allow divers to go all the way down to 2,300 feet, a massive overkill in the circumstances.

In short, the conversation reassured Mark that the work would be relatively routine and only require well-tested equipment. This did not mean that the effort would be easy as the scope of the search would likely be larger than usual.

■ ■ ■ ■ ■

On the shore of the Sea of Galilea, the minisubmarine's trailer which was sitting inside the truck was rolled off onto the beach. In fact, more precisely, it was rolled off at the top of the boat ramp that Mark knew was there. With the trailer slowly guided down the ramp and into the water, the mini submarine was soon floating off the trailer. The depth of the sea both around Ginosar and pretty much all the way across the sea's entire length and width averaged about 85 feet, except when immediately near the coastline. The plan was to dive to a depth of 80 feet and follow a classical virtual grid pattern offshore Tiberias. The two men who were going to work with it climbed aboard through the upper hatch and settled in their driving positions. The submarine did not linger on the surface. The men quickly dove so that they could start the reconnaissance mission without attracting undue attention from people coincidentally passing by, however improbable. Yet, everyone knew that the effort would last longer than a couple of days: it was a foregone conclusion that it was bound to attract some attention. On the other hand, local inhabitants had grown used to searches in the Sea of Galilea; with any luck their curiosity would not be so acute that any sort of crowd would assemble.

The submarine's two large underwater projectors and cameras allowed the two divers staffing the operation to see the bottom of the large lake quite well. The automated guidance system allowed them to set specific beacons and thus stay on track, while a radar made sure that the ship was never at risk of colliding with some underwater object or worse yet to become grounded. The men were ready to pick up anything which looked like it had not been in the water longer than a couple of days, all the while using the onboard radioactivity monitors to note and report whenever a measurable reading was observed.

Once they found something they deemed interesting, one of the two submarine crew members would exit the craft through its air lock and pick up the piece of debris. Mark and Marvin had attached a container to the rear end of the minisubmarine, using a rigid anchor system so that it remained at the same depth as the submarine itself and at a constant distance behind the craft. The diver would deposit the debris in the container and return to the submarine the same way he exited. Marvin had recommended that each time a man re-entered the submarine he should spray himself with a radioactive decontaminant while in the air lock to avoid bringing any radiation inside the cockpit.

Given the importance of the issue, Mark had decided to search the whole Sea of Galilea or a full 64 square miles. He knew, and David had agreed with him, that this represented an ambitious goal, which would surely extend the duration of the operation beyond a day or two. As a rule, well-trained teams take about 3.5 hours to search a square mile. Here, Mark had assumed that he could use a less concentrated grid pattern as the minisubmarine was equipped with radiation detecting devices and warning lights driven by artificial intelligence. They helped the men make sense of the multitude of debris which would be found at the bottom of the Sea of Galilea. Thus, the submarine could move at a faster clip than normal and could afford to allow some more distance between two parallel grid lines. Yet, Mark realized that the whole operation would have to last at least four to five days. This would require refueling the submarine and rotating the crew, although the plan was that this could be done at the same time.

As a rule, the team had agreed that they would always initiate such a "rapid return to port" when the searching pattern had the submarine roughly abeam Ginosar. When a change of crew was due or some additional fuel required, the submarine would carefully note its coordinates, sail back toward Ginosar, switch crews, fill up the tank, and resume operations. Simultaneously, the container attached to the tail of the submarine would be emptied into a radiation-proof receptacle which would immediately be airlifted by helicopter to Tel Aviv so that analyses could be started. Though Mark and Marvin had initially hoped for the operations to be conducted surreptitiously, it quickly became evident that people would eventually figure out that something was going on. They eventually agreed that the party line would suggest that they were looking for fragments of the rockets which were aimed at the Tiberias region, with no mention whatsoever of the radioactive dimension of the problem.

The minisubmarine first sailed in a north-easterly direction aiming for Capernaum, the main town near the north end of the Sea of Galilea. Once there, it turned around and sailed toward Tiberias. It went back and forth in parallel tracks until the large bay which was found between the two towns had merged into the whole lake. From that point onwards, the submarine shifted the search pattern to a slightly different grid which was aligned almost perfectly north-south. The first few passages were not particularly eventful, as they were too close to the shore. The Iron Dome would surely try to intercept incoming missiles at some further distance from places where people might live. Yet Mark elected not to ignore that area: it would really be stupid to miss something, particularly where the search was at its easiest.

The first interesting piece of debris was located about two nautical miles due east of Ginosar. The instruments on the minisubmarine indicated that it was laying by 105 feet of water and that there appeared not to be any trace of radioactivity. One of the two crew members, Sheldon Shamir who had already slipped into his diving gear, except for his oxygen bottle, regulator, flippers, and diving mask, got up from his front seat and walked toward the air lock. He knew that many scuba instructors would have chided him for leaving aside a number of the crucial pieces of equipment that one is always supposed to have in any dive, but that did not trouble him too much. He reckoned he was never going to be more than twenty to forty feet away from the submarine. As he was about to enter into the air lock, he waved to his crewman, Adam Leibnitz, who was then in charge of piloting the submarine. Adam gave him a thumbs up, indicating that everything was ready for his exit. He opened the reinforced steel door and walked into the air lock and within a few seconds was outside

105 feet below the surface of the Sea of Galilea. The size of the piece they had located was at the high end of their expectations, but the buoyancy created by the water allowed Sheldon to maneuver it with little difficulty into the container at the back of the submarine.

He was walking back toward the outside entry into the air lock when Adam motioned to him that his instruments had picked up another piece of debris in the vicinity. They had agreed to a few hand signs prior to starting the mission; this would allow them to communicate as there was no use for a radio underwater. Sheldon gave a thumbs up and stayed outside of the craft. Adam very gently moved the submarine forward about twenty feet, while Sheldon was swimming alongside and to the left of the craft, where he and Adam could maintain eye contact. Sheldon had no difficulty locating the second piece of debris which was quite a bit smaller than the first. He picked it up and dumped it into the container. This time, Sheldon re-entered the air lock, sprayed himself generously with the decontaminant that had been provided, removed the breathing apparatus and the flippers and left them inside the air lock. He walked into the cockpit and took his seat to the right of Adam. Smiling he said:

"Piece of cake, my friend."

"Great. You know, though, one thing I thought about while you were outside: what do we do if a piece turns out to be too big?"

"Well, as Mark told us, Marvin calculated the likely range of sizes we were likely to find given the type of encounter the incoming rocket would have with our missiles."

He paused for a second and added:

"Good question though. Let's send a sonar message to base and see what they say."

CHAPTER.06

TEL AVIV, ISRAEL

A week later, back in Tel Aviv, Mark had called a meeting to discuss the results of his team's exploration of the bottom of the Sea of Galilea. He had invited Simon and Jeremy as the two most senior individuals tasked with ensuring Israel's safety as well as David Heller, his boss, and Marvin his technical *compere*. Two junior members of his team were also present: Sheldon and Adam as they were the people who had conducted the operation. Mark wanted them in the room both in the event that someone might need details which they would be better apt at providing and to be able to give credit where credit was due. His opening statement demonstrated how much more work was needed:

"I'm not sure where to start, gentlemen, as I see our results as both good news and bad news."

He paused briefly to let his punchline sink and continued:

"On the one hand, it's clearly good news that we didn't find any radioactive debris in the Sea of Galilea . . ."

Simon interrupted:

"I see that you use the word 'find,' Mark. Are you suggesting that there still may be radioactive debris which somehow you might have missed? Might we need to go back?"

"Excellent question, sir. The short answer is that it's always possible that we missed something. We're all human."

Mark paused and then developed his logic, arguing that they had used the time-tested 'belt- and-suspenders approach. He proceeded to list the various elements of their effort, starting with the visual search which was carried out from within the minisubmarine. He expanded the point making it clear that the mission was to identify anything which the pilots thought had been in the water for not more than a few days and might be of interest. He added:

"Once anything was identified as warranting their attention, one of the crewmembers would step out of the submarine, pick up the object and place it into the container."

Simon insisted:

"That's good. So, there is minimal uncertainty. We can safely assume that there would seem to have been only one rocket with a dirty bomb. Correct?"

"I would say so, but I would add that the people near Tiberias are looking for any other debris on land which might signal there was more than one dirty rocket."

Simon interrupted again:

"Isn't it safe to assume that any rocket that would have escaped the Iron Dome would have exploded as it hit the ground? Doesn't that leave enough visible traces to argue that we should by now have picked up any such spot?"

Mark took a quick sip from his water glass and replied:

"Absolutely, sir. I'm only being cautious because you don't know what you don't know. However, let me add something important which would add weight to your conclusion. We also had a second layer of search, which I might call evaluation. Marvin's team had placed a couple of Geiger-2 Counters, one on either side of the submarine's hull, with a monitor for each placed in the cabin. They should have picked up any sign of radioactivity in the water. That would have immediately led the team to stop the submarine and go look for what had triggered the alarm. Bottom line: no sign of radioactivity."

"Excellent. Thanks Mark. Now, you talked of bad news . . ."

"Yes, Simon, to me at least, and I have already discussed this with David, it is troubling that there should be only one suspect rocket . . ."

Simon thought the statement needed correction as he said:

"Sorry to interrupt, Mark, but to me on that front we are past the point of mere suspicion. We know there was a dirty bomb . . ."

"Sorry, General. I misspoke. My problem is that we saw a volley of missiles, most of which were intercepted by the Iron Dome. We picked up the debris of those that were allowed by the Iron Dome to hit the ground to the north of Tiberias: again, no trace of radioactivity, other than the one which hit the orchards of the Schonberg family."

Jeremy interrupted:

"Mark, am I correct assuming that your worry is that there seemed to have been only one missile which had some radioactive explosives?"

"Absolutely, sir. That makes no sense unless . . ."

Simon looked like he was going to interrupt, but he apologized and motioned Mark to continue his thought:

"Unless either it is meant as a threat . . ."

Jeremy volunteered:

"That would be one heck of a double-edged sword. What if we decided to treat the threat as a major menace and mounted a counteroffensive?"

Mark replied:

"Perfectly valid hypothesis, sir. We would then be retaliating against the Palestinians of Hezbollah who we assume are behind the other missiles, since they came from the northwest of Israel. This would likely have led us to think quite seriously about our response. But we could have been mistaken. The more I think of it, the more I think we should accept that there's another possibility . . ."

Mark could see Simon move closer to the front edge of his chair, a sign that Mark's comment suggested something which he had not anticipated. Mark smiled as he noticed and kept going:

"What if it was fired by somebody else?"

"Somebody else?"

"Yes Simon. Someone other than Hezbollah which as I just said we assume were responsible for the other rockets. I can't tell you who at this time, but the list isn't as long as we might think."

Mark could see that Simon was taking his point quite seriously when he asked:

"Hold it, before you go there, what would be the point?"

Mark stayed silent for a few seconds as he was wont to and then argued that anyone who would be responsible could well simply be called a "spoiler."

". . . a spoiler, Mark?"

"Yes, Jeremy. The idea would be that someone might be trying to point a finger at some Palestinian group, in order to weaken that group."

Mark paused again for a few seconds and developed his hypothetical scenario:

"What if it was meant to trigger a response from the Israeli Defense Forces? Exactly what Simon suggested we might do. One would assume that we would attack the most obvious target, Hezbollah, which we know has at least one cell in Syria in addition to their bases in Lebanon. That would potentially achieve at least two goals from the point of view of that hypothetical third party. First, it should get rid of or weaken a competitor. Remember how Hamas got rid of Fatah in the Gaza area, not as far-fetched as it initially looks . . . Second, it might get us in serious international trouble."

"International trouble?"

"Yes, Simon. Depending upon how we reacted, disinformation from Palestinian, or other sources could claim that we made first use of something nuclear."

"You're assuming that our response would involve nuclear weapons, right?"

"Right, Simon. My worry would be much less serious if our response was only through traditional weapons. Yet, it remains a worry because we might be accused of a response that was too heavy unless we disclosed their use of a dirty bomb. And even in that case, which I dislike because we don't want to give ideas to other terrorists, how could we prove we knew Hezbollah was the responsible party."

Simon smiled and replied:

"I see. Now, you were going to tell is more about who that other faction might be . . ."

Mark took another sip of water and said:

"Indeed, who could that other faction be? How about some other terrorist group, say Islamic Jihad; we know they have cells in Iraq. Could even be more ominous. What if it was some Iranian unit which meant to do damage and missed?"

"Why would they do that?"

"You know they are trying to get to us. What if they wanted to hurt us and yet felt better taking cover behind Hezbollah?"

Simon nodded and with a wry smile added:

"That would be really devious . . ."

He paused and concluded:

"But not necessarily out of character. Could even be ISIS, right?"

■ ■ ■ ■ ■

Mark's next order of business was to pay another visit to Marvin Goldstein. As usual, Marvin was all smiles when Mark arrived at the door of his office. When setting up the meeting, Mark had given him a heads-up on the main topic he wanted to discuss. Very much in character, Marvin relished the opportunity to deal with the intellectual challenge.

"So, Mark, what can I do for you? You told me it related to radioactive material which your teams collected, but that's overly broad, right?"

"Can't disagree with that. However, before we start, let me ask you a generic question."

"Fire away."

"Is it possible to determine what radioactive material was used in the making of a dirty bomb from debris recovered on site?"

"Excellent question Mark. A simple yes might suffice, but let me expand a little . . ."

Marvin noted that Mark's facial expression changed, used as he was to Marvin's forays into technobabble. Marvin insisted that the point was quite relevant:

"Let me say that, in fact, it is easier to tell the original material with a dirty bomb than it would be for a true nuclear device."

Marvin paused and took the change on Mark's face from exasperation to a quizzical look as his permission to dig further:

"In a fully-fledged nuclear explosion, you know, with a fission bomb, you get both ground impact and the radioactive fallout. That includes weapon debris for sure and traces of relevant material in the radiated soil, but it also comprises fission products. They are the products which the fission reaction generates. They are the problem as there can be hundreds of them. In fact, there are always more of them that the sole source of the nuclear explosion."

"So, in the present case, would you be able to determine what the radioactive material was from the debris that were picked up on the site?"

"Absolutely no problem, my friend."

Marvin paused and then could not resist asking a question:

"Why is that important to you, by the way?"

It was then Mark's turn to take what amounted to a teaching role before Marvin. He explained that his research taught him that there really were two kinds of radioactive materials which would typically be used in a dirty bomb. Marvin's arched eyebrows told Mark that he had all his attention. He continued:

"One of Countess Renate's associates told David and me that the two isotopes most likely to be used in a dirty bomb were caesium-137 or strontium-90. Now I should honestly note that he cited a whole list of other possibilities, but he did say that the two I just mentioned might both be best suited and most frequently used. I should also candidly tell you that I am repeating what I've heard as all that is way beyond what my Bachelor of Sciences degree taught me."

"Quite correct. Where does that get you Mark?"

"Well, it so happens that they are the two fission-products accounting for most of the heat and penetrating radiation in high-level nuclear waste."

Marvin jumped on the idea, exclaiming:

"I understand. Brilliant. Let me guess . . ."

Mark reluctantly agreed to let Marvin steal center stage:

"You are asking yourself what radioactive material the terrorists used, because you hope to be able to deduce from their nature how the terrorists got ahold of them . . ."

Mark nodded as Marvin continued:

"So, if we find the two you mentioned, or at least one of them, in the debris that were collected in Tiberias, then the odds would suggest they come from nuclear waste. So, they would have to have come from places where nuclear reactors are operated."

"Exactly, Marvin. Now, let me put some meat on those bones. Marcel Delagrange, of The Shadow Experts, told us that one of our options might be to go after the millions of radioactive sources used worldwide in industry, for medical purposes, and in academic applications for research. He said that the U.S. Nuclear Regulatory Commission estimated that one potential source of radioactive material is stolen, abandoned, or lost on average each and every day of the year."

Mark paused and noted that Marvin, for once, appeared genuinely surprised. He continued:

"Plus, it's not only a U.S. issue. Within the European Union, losses around about one quarter of what they are in the U.S. So, in short, we'd be looking for the proverbial needle in a haystack."

Marvin came right back:

"Makes total sense. Plus, I'm sure that the problem of lost radioactive sources isn't limited to the developed world, right?"

"Absolutely."

Mark went on to explain that Marcel made a couple of important points on this issue. First, he highlighted the importance of what he called "orphan sources." They were particularly numerous throughout Russia after the collapse of the Soviet Union, adding:

"The Soviets used thermoelectric generators to produce beacons in remote areas of Russia. That was the only way they could know where the various important installations were. These beacons typically didn't need maintenance and lasted for quite a long time. But they were ideal for Russia, as it wanted to remain in touch with people in remote locations; remember, there are eleven time zones in Russia. And guess what these typically used for their power? Strontium-90!"

"One of your two candidates!"

"Absolutely. The other is caesium-137. It's a radioactive isotope of caesium and one of the more common fission products generated by the fission of uranium-235. And remember, the first nuclear reactors used uranium-235 because it's an unstable substance, which could thus more easily trigger and maintain a chain reaction. Anyway, I don't know why I'm going on discussing this. I don't need to explain that to you, Marvin. You've probably forgotten more on the topic than what I ever learned."

Marvin smiled but humbly appeared surprised by Mark's comment. Mark went on to suggest that terrorists would not have too much trouble trying to get caesium from the nuclear waste created by many of the world's nuclear reactors, while scavengers might source strontium-90 from remote sites in Russia. He concluded:

"Though I know you can punch a whole bunch of holes this early in the process, I'm working on the initial assumption that if the dirty bomb that fell near Tiberias used caesium-137, we need to look for nuclear waste traffic. If it is strontium-90, we've got to look at rogue scavengers from Russia."

"Smart. Smart, but, as you say, your intuition needs to be confirmed. Now, let me ask you another question: have you written off the risk that the radioactive material is provided to the terrorists by one of the global terrorist state sponsors, you know, Iran, Russia and even China?"

"We sure haven't, though I am currently leaning against it."

"Why?"

"Simple. The terrorists in question can have one of two motives for creating a dirty bomb and launching it toward Israel. They might want to attack Israel, but I am guessing that they would know that we would retaliate quite possibly not with a dirty bomb but with the real thing. Why would a state terrorist sponsor take that risk at this point?"

"I see, but it is surely possible. Say, Iran could argue it was not involved. How could we prove otherwise? The terrorists would hope that international pressure would prevent us from retaliating."

"True, but we have sources within Iran and the risk for that country would still be huge, we don't have to launch a ballistic missile tipped with a nuclear device. There are many other ways that we can help engineer or facilitate a nuclear accident in Iran . . ."

Mark paused and went back to his earlier logic:

"Now, the terrorists might have a different motive: create fear and hope that Israel's retaliation would lead to the destruction of the terrorist group that would initially be suspected. We're back to my earlier point: that might be a way, devious as it would be, for them to trigger a confrontation to eliminate competition. In the case of Tiberias, if the dirty bomb didn't come from Hezbollah, which we would currently view as the most likely enemy in that geographical zone, we might still retaliate against Hezbollah. By the way, I went over that logic with Simon, and he didn't shoot it down, at least not right away."

Marvin whistled and concluded:

"You've got yourself a serious mess. Best of luck my friend . . ."

"We'll always need luck, but let's start with your analysis of the debris we collected at the site. I will also include debris we gathered at the bottom of the Sea of Galilea, offshore Tiberias. We assume they were part of the rockets destroyed by the Dome. We already know they didn't appear radioactive, but it would be interesting to know if they involved any sort of common material . . . For instance, what if the rocket debris we picked up in the lake were made with mostly the same material as the one which exploded in the Schonberg field? Wouldn't it be easy to assume that all rockets, both 'clean' if I may say it that way or 'dirty' came from the same group?"

"Or were supplied by the same external provider . . ."

Mark paused for a moment and asked:

"Marvin, would we find the same kind of radioactive materials in what I might call commercial or research reactors?"

"I'd have to check myself on that, Mark, but I can't see why not. Why are you asking?"

Mark smiled and simply explained that this hypothesis, if valid, would also open a number of other sourcing avenues, adding with a disturbed look:

"Don't need to tell you how many laboratories or hospitals there are in the world where one could steal some of the needed material . . ."

CHAPTER.07

TEL AVIV, ISRAEL; AND ISTANBUL, TURKEY

Mark's next message went to Josh Steinmetz in Mosul, Iraq. He did not waste much time with context and details, and simply said:

"Important development. Could we meet in Istanbul at your earliest convenience?"

Mark knew that it would not be difficult for Josh to find a flight to Istanbul from Erbil, where the major regional airport was, about fifty miles south-east of Mosul. Mosul had an airport at one point in time, but the hostilities in 2017 had led to severe damage which had not yet been fixed: the airport was still not fully functional and certainly not able to handle commercial traffic. He also knew that Josh could not find a flight to Tel Aviv from Iraq as regional tensions had led many Middle eastern airlines to suspend or simply not initiate flights to Israel. On the other hand, though Josh could have flown to a country closer to Israel than Turkey, Mark would have had difficulties getting there without taking the option of a disguised corporate jet. This might not have worked if a flight plan had been requested: it might have had to disclose that the origin of the flight was Tel Aviv. There were certainly ways around that, but Mark wanted to go for the simplest possible solution.

Istanbul offered the best compromise and had in fact, over time, become the waypoint of choice for many *Mossad* and official Israeli officials. Istanbul offered a couple of solutions as it happens to have two international airports: the "old" Sabiha Gokcen Airport (SAW) on the Asian side of the city, i.e., east of the Bosphorus, and a newer airport, New Istanbul Airport (IST) on the European side. The new airport was conceived to be the world's biggest airport and it is expected over time to see all the traffic that used to land at or take off from Sabiha Gokcen move to the new facilities, as Sabiha Gokcen is still the world's busiest single runway and single terminal airport.

With all flights from Iraq going to New Istanbul Airport and Mark having chosen to use a corporate jet, they would naturally meet at IST. Mark had chosen to arrive before Josh so that it would give him the time to deal with a few details. For instance, his first step once on the ground had been to rent a car, as he knew they were not going to stay and have sensitive conversations anywhere near the terminal. He had in fact ordered the car ahead of time and the Kia Optima he had selected was ready for him as he arrived at the private jet terminal. He confirmed that the two rooms he had reserved at Mare Negro Villa were indeed available. Mare Negro Villa is a Zen hotel which, though a bit more expensive than many, happened to offer secluded amenities, a few hundred yards from the Kumkoi beach. Once he had picked up Josh, Mark would simply drive almost due East on Highway 0-7. About 25 miles later on, they would arrive at the beautiful villa-hotel, where they would have ample time to confer in a relaxed atmosphere and spend the night before returning to their respective home countries the next day.

As soon as they got into the car, Josh could not help asking the obvious question:

"Your message didn't say much. What's going on?"

Mark surprised Josh with an indirect reply:

"Do you remember a short while ago the rumor which you heard from your friend Ibrahim?"

"Sure do. The trading in radioactive material . . . What about it?"

"Well, and this is absolutely top-secret, we have reasons to believe that Tiberias has been hit by at least one dirty bomb-tipped missile . . ."

After a short whistle, Josh simply said:

"You're kidding?"

Josh paused and did not allow Mark the time to reply. He had immediately realized that his question and particularly the use of the word "kidding," though automatic, was completely off base. He added:

"Wait a second. Sorry. 'Kidding' is definitely not the right word. Nothing funny about that here. How much do we know? Or, maybe the better question, how much are you allowed to tell me?"

Mark smiled and replied that he would be happy to share everything he knew, adding:

"Because, believe it or not, I would like you to be on the team that helps address and hopefully solve the issue."

Without giving Josh a chance to say much of anything, Mark went on to reply to Josh's earlier question: what was known? He said that the only known facts were that at least one missile that had been "allowed" through the Iron Dome carried an explosive charge that involved a measurable dose of radioactivity. He also said that there was no question about whether the device that exploded was a bona fide nuclear bomb, however small: it wasn't. He emphasized that it could not be a fission device, both because the damage was too small and radioactivity too low. He added:

"I won't bore you with the gory details, but there is a minimum size for a nuclear device and that size is determined by the critical mass of radioactive material needed to trigger a self-sustaining explosion."

Josh smiled at the explanation and indicated by his body language that he did not need any additional information. Mark concluded that the current thinking until anything more surfaced was that the rocket or missile that hit was somehow tipped with a dirty bomb. The missile crashed on the ground near Tiberias in an area which was not populated, though it involved substantial agricultural activity, principally related to the culture of fruits and vegetables. Mark added that he still did not know what material had been used to generate the radioactivity, but should soon have the answer, though he also noted that they now had what he called:

"A pretty decent map of remaining radioactivity a few hours after the explosion. The overall zone was in fact rather small. We found that there was no threatening radioactivity more than five hundred yards from the center of the crater. That's about 20% to 25% as much as the strongest dirty bombs that were ever evaluated."

He also mentioned that they had not found any radioactive source in the Sea of Galilea, as they searched for debris from missiles which had been intercepted. Before he could finish, Josh asked:

"Sorry to interrupt, but I have what may be an obvious question: did the various rockets conventional and 'dirty' related come from the same place?"

"Excellent question my friend. As you know, the Iron Dome will let certain missiles go through if they are deemed unlikely to hit areas where they could cause casualties. The dirty bomb slipped through precisely for that reason: it didn't seem likely to hit any populated place. Now all the rockets and missiles came from the same general direction, namely the Golan Heights. However, your guess is as good as mine as to whether they were launched from the same spot or even by the same people."

Mark paused and concluded:

"You could easily imagine that one set came from the Golan Heights and another from some place further than the Golan Heights though still in the same general direction. So, frankly, at this stage there are more things we don't know than things we know, but I want to get a head start if I can."

By that time, they had arrived at the hotel and thus interrupted their conversation to check in, drop their luggage in their respective rooms, and freshen up. They agreed to meet thirty minutes later in the lobby. Mark added:

"Make sure you wear comfortable, light shoes as I'd prefer for us to discuss this away from the people around the pool and the gardens.

■ ■ ■ ■ ■

Josh was the first to come down from his room, as he had to admit that he was impatient to hear more. His first question to Mark as soon as Mark had signaled it was OK to "talk business" as he said was:

"What do you want from me?"

Mark did not reply directly to the question. In fact, he initially conceded that he was not really sure of just about anything. Seeing that Josh was not following him, Mark added:

"Frankly at this point I'm just looking down the list of things that I know or have heard of which might somehow be related to or have a bearing on the issue."

"So?"

Mark explained to Josh that the one element which possibly linked him to the matter at hand was the conversation they had had a few weeks earlier. He argued that the rumor that there might be some traffic in radioactive materials in Iraq could well be germane to the current situation. More specifically, he made the point that a key question with respect to the suspected dirty bomb had to be where those who launched the missile got at least the nuclear material if not the whole missile assembly. Josh smiled though he noted that something seemed odd in what Mark was describing:

"Correct me if I'm wrong, but a missile hitting Tiberias had to be launched from the Golan Heights or thereabouts as you said earlier. That's Hezbollah territory. Right?"

He paused and noting that Mark was smiling, he added:

"I thought that Hezbollah had a direct line to Iran. By this, I mean that they got all their weaponry and cash from Iran. Why would they need to go through some other, more circuitous route?"

Mark smiled and replied that the question was valid, though he cautiously added:

"At least on the surface."

Josh raised his eyebrows as Mark went on to discuss two variations on the same theme. He first conceded that Hezbollah should not need to get missiles tipped with dirty bombs from anyone else given what everyone knew of Iran's nuclear capabilities. But he then surprised Josh with a simple rhetorical question:

"What if Iran was not willing to give them any nuclear material? After all, Iran must know that anything that looks or smells like a nuclear expansion of the conflict would have dramatic consequences, not least of which on its own territory. Obviously, there would be negative consequences for Hezbollah itself, but Iran would also be a sitting duck."

Josh agreed that Mark's rationale was reasonable. He said he understood why Hezbollah would want to score a significant victory on their own over Israel. Yet, he also understood why Iran might not want to satisfy their dirty bomb needs because, as Mark had said, of the consequences on Iran itself. So, he concluded,

"If Hezbollah wanted to hit Israel with a dirty bomb they would have to act on their own."

Mark replied:

"Totally agree, my friend. In fact, you're taking me to my other two alternatives. Imagine this: what if Hezbollah was trying to loosen its links to Iran, or simply needed to take a next step on the nuclear front to deal with intra-Palestinian rivalries?"

Josh stopped walking for an instant, turned toward Mark and only asked:

"Why?"

"Because some other Palestinian group was trying to upstage them. Hamas has been very much in the news recently, don't you think?"

Josh nodded, so Mark continued:

"Go back to the early days when Hamas had gained power in the Gaza Strip but had to share it with Fatah. Remember, in June 2007, after Fatah had lost the 2006 legislative elections in what they called Palestine. Hamas initiated a military conflict to get rid of Fatah and it took them five days to eliminate them."

He paused for effect and simply concluded:

"These guys are not altar boys. They are after power, and I can easily imagine someone being upset by the fact that Hezbollah is so well established in Lebanon and surrounding countries. Why not try to dislodge them?"

Josh smiled and played the idea further aloud:

"I don't know anything and am thus only speculating. But one thing troubles me. We have at least three different Palestinian factions, Hezbollah, Hamas and, Islamic Jihad. At one point, why wouldn't there be some form of internal warfare with one of these three wanting to become the driving Palestinian authority? They'd be most likely not to achieve this through elections or negotiations; so how much easier does it seems to be to try a military operation, however disguised?"

Mark laconically replied:

"Totally agree. The next question is obvious: what comes afterwards? Well, why not play a game which would in effect implicate one or the other factions?"

Josh was now thoroughly enjoying himself with the hypothetical dialog:

"I see, you mean Hezbollah appearing to be shooting at Israel when it would actually be the work of Islamic Jihad . . . on its own or on behalf of Hamas, or even someone else."

Mark was smiling broadly as he replied to Josh's latest hypothesis:

"Absolutely. And you can add any variation of which you can think. Given the geography of the region, your choice of belligerents might actually be right on, though I wouldn't exclude ISIS. Remember, they were trying to expand their Syrian beachhead into Iraq when we last had to deal with them around Mosul. You were on the front lines then, weren't you?"

Josh accepted Mark's invitation to complete the scenario. Thinking aloud, he argued that Islamic Jihad or anyone else might have thus procured radioactive material to make it look as if Hezbollah is escalating the conflict. Mark nodded adding that in such a case Islamic Jihad or ISIS would not be asking Iran for the material. He concluded:

"I see, they would probably want Iran to think that Hezbollah was going rogue . . ."

Josh could only nod his agreement. He argued that in both hypotheses, a key assumption had to be that Hezbollah was not willing to let Iran know what it was up to. Mark concluded:

"Agreed, though in one case we assume that Hezbollah might have asked Iran for some nuclear help, and they, Iran, refused. Yet, from that point forward, the two alternatives are in fact quite similar. The only real difference, from Tiberias's point of view, is simply who fired the dirty bomb missile. In the first case, it could be Hezbollah. In the second, it is someone else. Now, both alternatives could work whether there were or were not cracks between Iran and Hezbollah."

CHAPTER.08

TEL AVIV, ISRAEL; ISTANBUL, TURKEY; AND
SOMEWHERE IN THE AUSTRIAN ALPS

Mark and Josh had by then returned to the lobby of the hotel. They both agreed to take some time off on their own to relax and think about the conversation they just had. They would continue their talk at dinnertime. The two men were happy to note that they were almost alone in the dining room when they sat down for a before-dinner cocktail. Josh remarked:

"This may be because we are dining at such an early hour . . ."

"Couldn't agree with you more, but both of us need to get up early tomorrow morning to get back home."

"Goes without saying. Tell me, Mark, I'd like to get back to your idea of missiles having been shot at Tiberias by separate groups . . . Are you suggesting that someone, presumably Hezbollah would have fired several traditional missiles from the Golan Heights, while a single one, tipped with a dirty bomb, would have been fired at the same time from a different location?"

Mark was happy to see that Josh's mind was still totally focused on the issue he wanted to address. His first comment was that the issue of a single or two firing locations was not crucial, though he added:

"There could in fact be two different sources for the missiles, though it might require either cooperation or just coordination between two terrorist groups."

Josh immediately picked up on the idea, arguing:

"Could be. But a real Machiavellian thought would be that some common head of the two groups is working to weaken Hezbollah in favor of someone else . . ."

"ISIS?"

"You said it, my friend."

Mark paused and, as an afterthought, added:

"By the way, that wouldn't necessarily mean that Iran is dropping Hezbollah. It might simply be a case of Iran realizing that with Hezbollah an entrenched political entity in Lebanon, . . ."

Josh interrupted:

"Just a second Mark. This does not compute. Let me be humbler, at least it does not compute for me. If ISIS, let's use them as a place holder until we know better; if ISIS fired some missile helped by Iran at the same time as Hezbollah did, wouldn't you expect that Israel would retaliate against Hezbollah?"

"Sure. But what if Israel elected not to react too strongly because of the potential civilian casualties? After all, we know that the dirty missile didn't cause casualties. So, Iran would have vicariously scored something against Israel and created a serious fear of other radioactive activities. And yet, we couldn't respond without proof. That's where we are at this time . . ."

"I see your point, Mark. Now back to my earlier question how can I help?"

Mark kept silent for a good thirty seconds and simply said:

"We can talk details and strategy later, but my first concern is elsewhere. I am asking myself whether your friend, Ibrahim, could give you enough information or access to allow you to penetrate the network of which he has heard."

■ ■ ■ ■ ■

Mark was quietly sitting at his desk in Tel Aviv when his internal phone rang. He picked it up, noticing on the screen of the phone that the caller was none other than Marvin Goldstein.

"Marvin, what a pleasure. Any news?"

Marvin seemed to hesitate, which Mark thought seemed odd; after all, he was the one who had initiated the call. Eventually Marvin blurted out:

"Well, Mark, nothing totally definitive, but I felt I ought to call you as soon as I heard."

Marvin paused and then added:

"We can categorically state that caesium-137 was involved in the dirty bomb."

"Caesium-137? Does that mean that you've ruled strontium-90 out?"

"Unfortunately, not. In fact, we found traces of it, but we need more work to have a final determination. Let me explain, though I don't want to go too deep into the process of nuclear waste management, but, ever since the 1970s, both isotopes . . ."

"Isotopes?"

"Yes, sorry. Atoms with the same number of protons but different numbers of neutrons are called isotopes. They share almost the same chemical properties but differ in mass and therefore in physical properties."

Marvin paused and seeing that Mark was back on board continued:

"Caesium-137 and strontium-90, have typically been packed together, in the form of caesium chloride and strontium fluoride . . ."

"Not sure I need that level of detail, Marvin . . ."

"Sorry again. I'm letting myself be carried away. Anyway, the bottom line is that these two chemicals are products of the nuclear fission process. They also are the main radioactive agents in nuclear waste."

Marvin noted that Mark was listening attentively and continued his exposé. He explained that in the process of safeguarding nuclear waste, which can be dangerous for several decades if not longer, the two radioactive isotopes are packed together into capsules. These are then placed into storage units which are very cautiously safeguarded. Casually, he then added:

"So, it wouldn't be terribly hard to assume that we should find both elements if nuclear waste is the source of the radioactive material used by the terrorists. The only issue is that their relative concentrations might differ, so we might not identify them both at the same time."

"Relative concentrations? How does that get you to the conclusion that you might not find out about them at the same time?"

"Ah! Again, I want to keep details to a minimum. As I said earlier, we found traces of strontium-90. Let me simply say that the way they are put together in the capsules means that the concentration in one relative to the other can vary from a bit less than two times as much caesium as strontium to as high as eight times more caesium than strontium. In short, first you would typically expect to find more caesium. In fact, at times, caesium dominates to the point of overwhelming strontium. Am I making sense?"

"Thank you very much, Marvin. You definitely are. How much longer before you have a full answer?"

"A week at most, probably a bit less."

Marvin paused again and added:

"I want to make sure I answer your question adequately Mark. I'm afraid that I may be misleading you."

"Really?"

"Hopefully not. But here is a summary of the findings. I'll leave out all the details, technical or not. The samples we received contained radioactive material. The dominant source of radioactivity was caesium-137. But we have seen traces of strontium-90. I want to see the results of the analysis of more samples to be more definitive about how dominant caesium is. Is that clearer?"

"Definitely my friend. One last question for you. Earlier you said that we should not be surprised to find what you called these two isotopes, if we were talking of nuclear waste. Correct?"

"Absolutely."

"Well, then is it not true that given that you have found these two isotopes, the source of radioactive material most likely is nuclear waste?"

"Most likely indeed, however as we discussed it a while back it does not exclude other forms of nuclear waste such as what hospitals and research laboratories generate."

■ ■ ■ ■ ■

Mark had asked Countess Renate also to organize a conference call, with or without video, with Marcel Delagrange. He felt that whatever additional information he had was sufficient to go into more detail with Marcel. He thought that . . . *he might even start snooping around as well.*

Countess Renate opened the meeting with a smile:

"Gentlemen, it's nice to have you all around this videoconference. Glad to see that you were able to join us, David."

"Too important to miss, Countess."

"Understood. So, Mark, what's new?"

Mark went on to relate the information which Marvin had provided to him, drawing one preliminary conclusion, as he put it:

"My guess from what Marvin said is that the source for the radioactive material found in the dirty bomb in Tiberias seems to be nuclear waste."

Marcel interrupted:

"You mean waste produced by nuclear fission, as in a nuclear power plant?"

Mark hesitantly replied:

"I guess so."

"What makes you say that, Mark?"

"Marcel, I must be careful and remind you that you have probably forgotten more on the topic than I ever learned. But the presence of caesium-137, and possibly though that is still not proven of strontium-90, would suggest that to me. Wouldn't it be true that you might find other isotopes if the origin was different?"

Marcel retorted admiratively with a wide smile:

"I have to tell you that you amaze me. Please, don't take this the wrong way. Yet, when we last talked it seemed to me as if you knew very little about the topic. Now, you articulate not only a feasible scenario, but in my view maybe the most likely. Congratulations."

David interrupted Marcel and asked what next steps the findings suggested. Marcel replied:

"To me, it points to a need to quickly work with the national nuclear energy authorities in the various countries which use the correct type of reactor and ask about their waste management processes."

He paused for a second, as if deep in thought and suddenly added:

"We may need to access sources which might tell us whether there has been any theft of nuclear waste anywhere."

"Theft?"

"Yes, David."

Marcel went on to explain his statement arguing that several people have argued that waste storage is the weak link in the chain, though he immediately added that the popular view is somewhat erroneous. He reminded the group that 97% of the waste produced by the nuclear power industry is classified as low- or intermediate-level waste, adding:

"It has been widely disposed of in near-surface repositories."

With Gallic pride he took this further:

"In fact, the implied 3% levels of high-level waste are exaggerated. In France, for instance, nuclear fuel is routinely reprocessed so that only 0.2% of all radioactive waste is classified as high-level."

Marcel returned to the safety of nuclear waste focusing briefly on its transportation from a power plant to a storage site. He argued that the key to safety is the way nuclear materials are packaged, as those are designed to shield anyone from radiation even under the most extreme accident circumstances. Taking the point further, he mentioned that most high-level waste is held as stable ceramic solids or in vitrified form, adding:

"In short, with the radioactive isotopes secured within the glass or the ceramic, it would be exceedingly difficult for terrorists to disperse that material. To me, the threat from so-called 'dirty bombs' isn't high."

David had to interrupt:

"Understood, Marcel, but we have definitive indications both that a bomb that dispersed radioactive material hit not far from Tiberias and that debris contained caesium-137 and traces of strontium-90."

Marcel smiled and replied:

"Don't get me wrong, David. I was arguing the theoretical point. We know that dirty bombs have been made. So the key question I am asking myself is whether the terrorists stole some waste material from somewhere and converted it into the one or two components you mentioned or if the radioactive material which you all identified might not have been provided to them by someone who knew what they were doing."

He paused and added:

"Beside the safeguards I just mentioned, it's clear that it's no slam dunk to get your hands on nuclear waste, if only because it is quite radioactive. You need a lot of protection both procuring it and then distributing it if I can use that word. However, the unused, new fuel rods are typically kept under close guard, mostly because they're but a step away from being enriched to material needed to construct a nuclear device. So, upstream of the fission process, it would be hard to break into the chain. Not saying it's impossible you know, but it would be difficult. Downstream in relative terms is less of a challenge."

He drank from a water glass with his right hand and concluded:

"I agree that we can't rule out any form of nuclear waste theft and that this is something we should investigate. I would only add that I would also be looking into avenues where the waste was not stolen but provided as such."

David looked pensive for a few seconds though he signaled to Mark that he wanted to keep the floor. He then asked:

"Right at the outset, we had assumed that the terrorists would be acting without agreement from Iran and possibly without even having informed the authorities there. The alternative described by Marcel would completely change that, wouldn't it?"

Marcel replied that he really had no basis on which to push the dialog in that direction, though he would happily draw up a list of all countries which operated at least one nuclear power reactor, adding:

"Anyone with a nuclear power reactor generates nuclear waste. The last time I looked, 32 countries operated at least one nuclear power plant. And that total does not include countries which have nuclear reactors for purposes of research, rather than electric generation. When those are counted the total number of countries rises to 50."

Marcel paused for a few seconds and suggested that many of the countries with nuclear power generation would be on the list of potential enemies of Israel or supporters of Palestinian interests. He concluded:

"I am not sure how one would proceed, but it would be interesting to look around and see whether these newer entrants into the industry have as solid nuclear waste disposal practices as others. Further, as I know we discussed it a while back, you have all the 'loose sources' found in the old Soviet Union, a few of which would be able to provide caesium or strontium."

Mark paraphrased Marcel's conclusion:

"In short, Marcel, you're telling us that we should use a very broad net."

"Absolutely."

"I'm also hearing you saying that we should not waste too much time looking for waste theft in countries like France or the U.S."

"I agree, although everything is possible."

Marcel paused again and surprised the group:

"One generic place I might look very carefully would be in countries where a very strong political opposition to nuclear power has developed . . ."

"You mean . . ."

"No special place per se but think of places like Germany. They're the most anti-nuclear country of the European Union. Terrorists might find a readier audience there but note that this is pure speculation on my part."

"Is there anything you can do to help?"

"Let me contact a few of my friends in the key centers. But, what may I mention?"

David simply replied that the fact that one dirty bomb had exploded in Israel could not be made public. He suggested:

"Can you operate in a hypothetical mode?"

"Sure can."

CHAPTER.09

MOSUL, IRAQ

Back in Mosul, Josh, aka Abu Musa, sent word to his friend, Ibrahim, that he would appreciate meeting him for coffee, in his words, "at the habitual place," if still convenient. Though Ibrahim was travelling in the country and thus unavailable the following couple of days, he let Abu Musa know that he would welcome a meeting. In fact, he suggested that they could meet on Sunday or Monday, the following week.

At the agreed time early on Monday morning, they got together at Al Shatee Café. It was too early for either of them to be looking for anything savory to eat. Thus, they ordered what many people consider the ultimate Iraqi breakfast indulgence, Kahi. It comprises layers of filo pastry, with butter basted between each layer, the whole thing being then soaked in sugar syrup and topped with clotted cream called *geymer*. They also asked for a couple cups of tea, with lemon for Josh and honey for his guest. Rather than sitting at one of the usual tables inside, they chose a corner terrace location where they sat in plush armchairs, both facing the Tigris and its beach, with a coffee table between them. Ibrahim started the conversation with a question:

"So, my friend, what can I do for you? I guess you're the one who called this meeting . . . If I can call our pleasant get-togethers formal 'meetings' . . ."

Abu Musa conceded with a wide smile that he had indeed felt a need to chat with Ibrahim. He started with a general observation indicating that the comment which Ibrahim had made almost in passing the last time they met had intrigued him. With Ibrahim not taking the bait and jumping into the conversation, waiting to hear more, Abu Musa expanded his point further, as he explained:

"The idea that there could be some nuclear traffic around here had me quite perturbed."

Ibrahim smiled. He had guessed that Josh had that topic in mind but had elected to remain uncommitted for as long as he could. Beside the fact that such behavior was quite typical of the local 'cat and mouse' culture, he had reasoned that it was the one that gave him the largest number of options. He replied:

"Why? Don't tell me that you're involved in that too? Just like I discovered you were in the opium-for-diamond traffic after we met a few years back . . ."

Abu Musa smiled in response and with somewhat of a contrite air said:

"Well, I must come clean on at least one thing. I am not involved in that traffic; you can trust me on that . . ."

"Don't tell me I couldn't trust you not on other issues? That would sadden me my friend."

Ibrahim exploded into loud laughter, providing a cue for Abu Musa to appreciate that his friend's latest comment was in jest. Still, Josh replied:

"Seriously, I can assure you that you can trust me. But you need to know that I am a bit of a spy."

Ibrahim looked genuinely startled. He paused for a second or two and could only ask:

"For whom? I seem to remember that there was speculation that *Mossad*[4] was in the loop the last time we were involved together professionally if I can put it that way. You work for *Mossad*?"

"Well, the problem is that my answer won't help you, initially at least. You see, I honestly have to respond that I do, and I don't."

He paused and saw that Ibrahim was paying quite a bit of attention, though his facial expression had remained almost neutral, with his usual quiet smile; yet Josh thought he could catch his friend showing some surprise when Ibrahim heard Josh say that he might work for *Mossad*. Josh knew he had to expand on his reply, as it was clear that his ambivalent answer had not satisfied Ibrahim. He started with a small correction to the original statement, arguing that his use of the word "spy" was not appropriate. Ibrahim looked at him even more attentively. Josh finished his thoughts saying that, more specifically, he saw himself as a roving informer, adding:

"In short, I am always on the lookout for information which I am then ready to share with anyone who is willing to pay me a fair fee. That's why I initially called it spying, because the information that has any value must be new and has to have previously been hidden. I can't simply read from the front page of the daily newspaper."

He paused again and seeing that Ibrahim was on board, he concluded:

"So, I have indeed done some work with *Mossad*. In fact, your memory serves you well. *Mossad* was involved when you and I last crossed paths professionally, but I do not work exclusively for them. More than that; I was not personally involved in the opium-for-diamond trade. I had just stumbled onto it. Remember how I just happened to be near the spot where a plane that crashed that supposedly carried payment for opium traffickers? It turns out that

---

4 By the same author, see *Glitter and Smoke*, Barringer Publishing, 2023.

Mossad had been interested in the information, and not only bought it, but had asked me for a few additional services . . ."

Ibrahim returned to his trademark smiling face. With a wave of his right hand, he casually dismissed the information Abu Musa had just given him. Yet, he offered:

"My dear friend, it's not for me to give you advice, but you're living on the edge. Be very careful whom you choose as your business partner. Double agents have a bad habit of turning up dead."

"Thanks, Ibrahim; very fair and excellent advice. But don't mistake me for a real spy of the type that makes up what people usually mean by the term double agents."

Abu Musa paused for a second to sip from his lemon tea and explained that, as he had suggested a short while ago, his use of the word "spy" was not appropriate. Looking at his friend squarely in the eyes, he added:

"From what I just told you, you must have gathered that I am just a mere informer. The people with whom I deal do not tell me anything sensitive about their activities. In fact, I would never sell information from one 'client' to another. They just like the idea that I can bring stuff to them which they can't get through their usual channels. I should add that, occasionally, they might contact me with a question, though this was not what started my interest in the opium-for-diamond trade nor is it the case on our current conversation."

Ibrahim did not immediately react, as if he was looking for the right way to reply. Finally, he said:

"That's a bit better, I'll concede; but it's still pretty risky. Many organizations do not like to allow people who know something about their activities to live peaceful lives ever after."

He smiled at his humorous comment and then returned directly to the topic at hand, being quite sure that he did not have the job of keeping Abu Musa safe. In fact, truth be told, Ibrahim was himself concerned by the potential intrusion of some trade in nuclear waste in the Kurdish area of Iraq. At a minimum, working with Abu Musa on the issue might allow him to keep himself in the loop and thus be able to manage the activities of the Kurdish resistance in such a way that it did not fall into any trap that could give someone a reason to try and wipe them out, as several groups had attempted to do in the past. With a straight face though he offered:

"Anyway, what can I tell you other than that a rumor has been circulating? I surely haven't run into anyone offering me any piece of such business. I don't even know which side of the trade they might have been on—the buying or the selling."

Ibrahim paused again noticing that Abu Musa seemed decidedly quite interested, and quietly added:

"I heard what I did from someone within my own organization who had been approached to gauge our interest, I guess."

Though he was a bit disappointed by Ibrahim's reply, Abu Musa still kept the conversation going, thinking *I can't tell him anything more about me. That lie is big enough already, though I hope I can keep him as a friend. I doubt that he would ever find out about my official Mossad role. After all, the rest is a fable!* He asked:

"Could I meet that person?"

Seeing the quizzical look on Ibrahim's face, he clarified the question:

"You know, the man who was approached . . ."

Ibrahim matter-of-factly interrupted him and replied that he could ask the man if he would be willing to meet Abu Musa. He explained that he could not control the man's decision to agree to meet him or not. After all, the man might have felt he had to report whatever he found out to Ibrahim but might not be comfortable sharing the same information with a stranger, even if introduced by Ibrahim. Yet, Ibrahim immediately told Abu Musa that first there should be an "agreement" between them. Abu Musa reacted to the word "agreement" as he was unsure what Ibrahim might have in mind. He asked:

"What kind of agreement are you talking about?"

"Well, something that covered us both as well as him, my friend. I need to know what you are looking for, why it may be important and what your position would be if there is stuff behind the rumor."

Abu Musa smiled. He was relieved, but not surprised, that Ibrahim had not effectively asked for any piece of the action. He told Ibrahim that he would be happy to go through all these details. He in fact volunteered right away that he surely did not want to get involved in the nuclear waste material trade, adding:

"What I did in the diamond for opium trade was highly unusual for me. I am not interested in taking sides."

He concluded by saying that he would be more interested in finding out enough about it to share the information. Not surprisingly, Ibrahim asked who might be interested in that information. Abu Musa replied that he could think of many organizations, starting with the CIA in the United States, *Mossad* in Israel, MI6 in the U.K or the DSGE for France.

"I see that you are only considering countries which already have nuclear capabilities . . ."

"All but one have them and have made it known officially. Israel is assumed to have them but has never said whether they did or didn't . . ."

"Come on! Don't tell me you have any doubts.

"Fair, I don't. More than that, I'm quite sure they have nuclear capabilities. But that's my guess, my informed guess, not a fact."

"OK, I'll buy that. You also didn't mention countries like India, Pakistan, China, Russia or even Iran . . ."

"I didn't mention them for two reasons, Ibrahim. First, when I sell information, I choose those with whom I deal carefully. I am just not willing to deal with anyone who asks for information and offers to pay for it. I am not interested in fomenting trouble. I hope that I might contribute to cooling hot spots, not to throw oil onto any fire."

He paused and was delighted to see Ibrahim smiling more broadly. He continued:

"Secondly, while I am reasonably convinced that the countries I mentioned first wouldn't have an interest in making trouble in this part of the world, I can't be sure about those on the second list you suggested. After all, it's common knowledge that Iran's nuclear capabilities were built with the help of a Pakistani nuclear scientist, Abdul Qadeer Khan . . ."

■ ■ ■ ■ ■

A.Q. Khan is known as the father of Pakistan's atomic weapons program. He was a nuclear physicist and metallurgical engineer. Though no unimpeachable proof has ever been found, people believe that he ran a secret, underground network which provided nuclear help to Iran, North Korea and even Libya. He took advantage of all the connections which he openly developed in the West to buy what is referred to as dual-use materials and even technology; they were called dual-use because they could be used for civilian as well as military purposes. With respect to Iran, people have a strong conviction that he provided the country with uranium enrichment technology, which the regime used, through the Amad Plan, to get perilously close to being able to build a nuclear bomb. He was tried in absentia in 1983 and sentenced to four years in prison for stealing Dutch uranium enrichment secrets.

■ ■ ■ ■ ■

Ibrahim nodded at Abu Musa's explanation and even offered an encouraging smile. Yet he surprised Abu Musa with the next question:

"On a different track, what makes you think that these people might be interested?"

"You mean, the agencies on my first list?"

"Absolutely."

Abu Musa replied that, except for Israel, they were on record for being against nuclear proliferation. He added that Israel has not said anything, but it made sense that they would likely not want any of the local players, as he called the various terrorist groups in the Middle East, to acquire these capabilities, even if they involved little more than constructing dirty bombs. Ibrahim smiled and simply said:

"You do make some sense."

He paused for a few seconds and concluded:

"Tell you what. Let me talk to my man and see the lay of the land. Once I am satisfied, I'll contact you. It is obvious that everything we have discussed stays between us and that I would never go behind your back."

"That's exactly what I would expect of you, my friend. You can be assured that I would follow exactly the same route. I would be happy to collaborate with you on this if you are interested. After all, a few of these terrorist groups that might be intend on building dirty bombs do operate in your backyard, and possibly even against you and your people."

Ibrahim indicated his agreement with a smile and made it clear that the meeting had run its course, as both cups of tea and their small plates were empty and there was no offer to ask for more.

CHAPTER.10

TIBERIAS AND TEL AVIV, ISRAEL; PARIS, FRANCE; AND MOSUL, IRAQ

An unexpected phone call from Marcel Delagrange interrupted Mark as he was drinking his first cup of coffee at the office. Marcel wanted to have a short conversation with him, in order to bring him up to date on what he saw as an important development.

"Mark, sorry to bother you this early."

"Wait, I don't quite understand. Unless I'm very mistaken, if it's early for me, Marcel, it is even earlier for you given the one-hour time difference. Right? What's up?"

Marcel conceded that he had gotten up quite early because something had been going around in his head that prevented him from sleeping. He proceeded to tell Mark that he had talked to a small number of sources in Continental Europe, as well as the U.K. What surprised him was that virtually everyone was aware of small leaks of radioactive material in their respective countries. Mark asked:

"What do you mean by leaks?"

"Nobody is aware of significant amounts of radioactive material that might have gone missing."

"That's good; I guess . . ."

"Sure is. But they all said that they were also aware that here or there some small amount of material had gone missing. They confirmed what the scientific community knows but has been told not to disseminate to the public: you don't need more than a few pounds of radioactive material to create a dirty bomb which would contaminate an area a few hundred yards in diameter centered on the bomb's point of impact on the ground."

Mark told Marcel that he needed a crash course on the nuclear process. Marcel replied with a smile that they would need more than the rest of the day to get hardly more than a basic overview. Mark conceded that he had misspoken and that what he needed was a way to get a better perspective on nuclear waste. Marcel said that he totally understood the point and offered what a called "a few simple pointers."

He started with a general principle, as he called it, saying that the weight of nuclear waste produced by a nuclear reactor is about equal to the weight of the radioactive matter that had been introduced in the reactor. He added:

"So, to give you some perspective, a one-gigawatt nuclear power plant will typically use just under 28 tons of uranium fuel. Thus, you will need to dispose of just under 28 tons of radioactive spent fuel, of which 90% is low-level and 3% high-level waste."

Marcel paused and asked Mark if he followed. Hearing his positive answer he kept going, explaining that nuclear power reactors depend on fuel assemblies, which comprise a few hundred fuel rods. He went on:

"Typically, a rod will need replacing every two years or so. Now, this is complicated. Let me try to keep it as simple as I can. Though the numbers vary from one reactor to the next, depending upon the type of reactor, there can be up to 200 fuel assemblies in a core and up to 250 rods in a fuel assembly!"

He paused and asked:

"Still with me?"

"Yes, but the numbers are baffling: 50,000 rods in one reactor! How can I simply visualize how often waste is removed from the reactor?"

"Now, that's an excellent question. As a rule, you will need to shut the reactor down, which does not mean it has stopped completely, but means that it isn't producing electricity. The whole fuel rod exchange can take up to 30 days. So, for any given reactor, it usually happens every two years or so. Typically, a rod serves three cycles of two years. The newest rods are at the periphery of the core and the older ones in its center."

"How much do they weigh?"

"The correct answer is: it varies. But as a rule, you have about 6 pounds of uranium in a fuel rod . . . A uranium pellet weighs about 20 grams and there are upward of 250 pellets per rod."

All of a sudden, Mark appeared to wake up and said:

"Wait a minute. It seems to me we are barking up the wrong tree. Given what you've just told me, Marcel, how could anyone steal a spent fuel rod?"

"Excellent observation my friend. Something makes it even harder than you think. As they are removed from the reactor, spent fuel rods are plunged and submerged for five years into a water reservoir at least twenty feet deep and with constantly re-circulated cold water so that they can cool. That reservoir is still usually within the reactor complex. It's only after they've cooled down for that length of time that they are removed and placed in casks for long-term storage."

Mark whistled and offered a simple conclusion:

"OK that does it. As I said earlier, though I will never rule out anything, I don't think it's reasonable to worry too much about spent fuel rods being stolen. There must be some other weak spot somewhere . . ."

Marcel noted that one could more easily steal uranium pellets prior to them being assembled into rods. He explained to Mark that the process involved transporting the enriched uranium to a fuel manufacturing plant where it is converted into dioxide powder and then pressed into a hard ceramic material, the pellets; these are then stacked and sealed in long metal tubes . . . Mark noted:

"Don't know about you, but I do see an opportunity to steal pellets, but what good would that do? They are not more than slightly radioactive before the rods have gone through nuclear fission, right?"

"Absolutely."

"Good. So it's clear that this is probably not the point I am interested in. What's the weak link? Or rather maybe where's the weak link?"

Marcel replied that he was surely well beyond his main area of knowledge. Yet, he had always assumed that the point that presented the greatest opportunity for 'leakage' might be in the transportation of waste material from one location to another, whether that other location was the final storage place or some intermediate step. Mark slapped his forehead with his right hand and said:

"Why didn't we think of that any earlier?"

■ ■ ■ ■ ■

Josh, aka Abu Musa, was delighted when he picked up his phone as he realized that his friend, Ibrahim, was calling him. Ibrahim dispensed with all light conversation. His greeting was short, as he quickly moved into the meat of the subject:

"Abu Musa, my friend, I may not be a bearer of good news . . ."

Josh's heart initially sank. Yet, he elected not to let it show and with a joyful tone of voice replied:

"What do you mean?"

Ibrahim explained with some degree of embarrassment that the man who had started the rumor recanted some of what he had initially said. In the light of the lack of reaction from Josh, he expanded on the point, first apologizing for having used the word "recant." More precisely, he told Josh:

"It turns out that what my man, Rezna is his name, told me is somewhat different from what I had initially understood."

"In what way?"

"Let me first say that I am not blaming him. For reasons I will discuss another time, let us say that something in the back of my mind made me more than ready to believe that some form of nuclear waste traffic could well develop here."

He paused. As Josh seemed to want to hear more on that point, Ibrahim simply said:

"Again, Abu Musa, my friend, I'll get to that some other time."

He then proceeded to argue that the way Rezna had expressed his understanding when he, Ibrahim, talked to him the first time could be interpreted as suggesting that there was real traffic going on. He added:

"Well, this time, my questions were more precise and his replies correspondingly more detailed as well. Now, it seems that a friend of his had asked him about the nuclear waste trade in a generic manner. So, the request he had received was not nearly as blatant or clear as what I had been led to believe. He now says that the question he was asked was simple. The interlocutor indicated he had recently started to see a new trade appear. He then just asked whether there was any interest in that trade, within the group of people which he knew Rezna was a part of."

Josh asked:

"That trade, does it still relate to nuclear waste?"

Josh was quite a bit relieved when Ibrahim told him that it was still indeed what was suggested. Ibrahim however immediately added:

"The one thing which is clear as mud is whether the gentleman was looking for buyers or sellers . . ."

"Ah! What does that tell you?"

Ibrahim replied that he was totally confused. On the one hand, the fact that one was still talking of trading in nuclear waste meant that something new was developing. Further whatever it was surely required careful monitoring. On the other, he was confused as to how Iraqis could play a role in a process where they were not a substantial player in the nuclear world. Josh interrupted:

"Just a second, there might be an interesting tidbit in there. Does the 'Tuwaitha site,' just south of Baghdad mean anything to you?"

Josh did not let Ibrahim answer his rhetorical question and continued:

"Didn't former president Saddam Hussein build a research center there?"

Ibrahim's eyes widened and he smiled more broadly as he said:

"Hey! You're correct Abu Musa; I know that Iraq bought a couple of research reactors from France . . . In the mid-70s I believe. One of them was quite famous as it was a large one, they called it Osiraq; the other, the second was smaller, much smaller in fact. Can't recall its name."

Josh had to ask:

"What happened to them?"

"They were both located at Tuwaitha as you said. Technically, they were part of a research effort. Unfortunately for Iraq, Saddam Hussein, only a Vice President then, bragged that this was a first step toward nuclear armament and that Iraq would thus be the first Arab state to do so."

"Not a terribly smart thing to say, right?"

"Absolutely. Israel reacted quite quickly. It organized Operation Opera which bombed the core of the reactor in 1981 before it had even come online."

Ibrahim paused and then concluded:

"Anyway, weapons inspectors of the UN Special Commission and the International Atomic Energy Agency conducted quite a number of inspections. They found numerous pieces of evidence that the Iraqi regime had failed to disclose, activities which should have been reported. Even more, they discovered indications Saddam had planned to resume his nuclear undertakings as soon as he could. Experts both from the U.N. and from the U.S. said the status quo was unacceptable. They called for re-establishing an inspection regime in Iraq that was 'effective, rigorous and credible,' fearing that the risk that Iraq might reconstitute its programs would become serious anew."

"Not a real surprise, right?"

Ibrahim easily granted the point and argued:

"True. In fact, it was totally in character, particularly after the Israeli bombing in 1981 led Saddam to a change of strategy. He wanted to build the full sequence of activities needed so that he could have a nuclear capability. Codenamed Project 601, he directed Iraqi scientists to recover safeguarded highly enriched uranium from French- and Russian-supplied research reactors in August 1990. Further, he decided to take control of the whole nuclear fuel chain, with the only exception being that he would still buy yellowcake, the processed uranium ore. He had started to build a nuclear enrichment plant which would eventually yield the pellets which would be made into fuel rods in a fuel manufacturing plant which he had also begun to build."

Josh could only ask:

"So, what did the U.N. do?"

"Well, with the help of the Americans, they effectively tried to destroy most of what they found."

"So, there is no remaining nuclear activity in Iraq?"

Ibrahim's voice on the phone suggested to Josh that his friend had to be wearing his usual trademark smile as he said:

"Well, not quite. Officially, the only nuclear activities conducted within Iraq involved medicine and agriculture. But who knows what's happening away from the sun?"

"Is there more to the story?"

"Nothing official my friend. Yet, many of us believe that some nuclear waste was surreptitiously 'removed' before the U.N. finished their work."

Ibrahim paused again and continued his explanation after having taken a sip of the cup of tea which he almost always had next to him, particularly when he was at home, in his beloved sitting room. What he said was a real surprise to Josh:

"That's what I was talking about when we started this conversation. I had forgotten about the sequence of events which led to people believing that Saddam's weapons of mass destruction program had been completely stopped. Yet, for some reason, it recently came back to my mind. You know, it's one of these things which often makes little sense: you know something; you forget it and one day, unexpectedly, you remember it . . ."

He explained that one day he had what he called a frightening thought: *what if the nuclear waste which we supposed had been taken away before the U.N. and others could clean up the place had suddenly been brought back into the open*? Ibrahim continued:

"You see, my friend, I never knew where the waste had been hidden and by whom. I was too young then to be in a position where I would have been in the decision-making loop. Yet, I always asked myself who could have taken that waste. Would it be members of the Kurd Resistance or former Iraqi government officials?"

Josh interrupted:

"So, you are sure that there has been some nuclear waste hidden in Iraq . . ."

"Abu Musa, one is never sure about anything unless one is a witness, and even then, who knows? Time has a way of distorting memories . . ."

"Turning philosophical on me? I see, yet back to your question; who could have taken that waste?"

Ibrahim did not reply directly to Josh's comment. Rather, he continued his prior train of thought:

"Again, the short answer must be, who knows? Yet, I couldn't believe that anyone associated with the Kurdish Resistance could have been involved; that's simply not the way we conduct ourselves. Further, the risks simply would seem to be too big. So, for lack of a better solution, I concluded that it had to be former members of the Baath Party, still loyal to Saddam."

Ibrahim paused and smiling at Josh through the telephone added:

"But now I'm a bit older and hopefully wiser. So, I still can't believe that the Kurdish Resistance would plan to use it. But I have gone further than stopping at Baath politicians loyal to Saddam. For instance, someone from whatever political persuasion, including some sub-group within the Kurdish resistance might have gotten ahold of the loot and treat it as something they could later use as a bargaining chip."

"With whom?"

"Probably some Western power. I still can't believe the Kurds would be prepared to trade it to someone who might use it. Anyway, even if you exclude us, there are so many mini groups within the Iraqis, possibly extending into neighboring Syria, ranging from religious extremists to those who would like to return to Saddam's days . . . I never took that any further. Now, with the question of the whereabouts of this waste, however much or little there was, kind of floating around, I wouldn't be surprised if this is the kind of trading Rezna heard about."

Josh interrupted:

"Let me guess: trading some of Saddam's old waste which would still be radioactive and also looking into ways to get more nuclear waste to satisfy their needs if they wanted to build dirty bombs, whenever they had run out of Saddam's waste . . ."

"Couldn't have said it better myself. However, you realize that these are two totally different problems, right?"

CHAPTER.11

TEL AVIV, ISRAEL; MOSUL, IRAQ

Josh immediately called Mark in Tel Aviv. The phone conversation he had just had with Ibrahim both provided information which he deemed new and raised important questions as to how he should proceed. He knew he had the option of using the secret flashlight-like communication device which all *Mossad* agents had. The agent sending a message would compose that message on a computer, a tablet, or a phone, most often through the voice recognition feature. The system would then encode and transform that message into high intensity light pulses. These pulses would then be aggregated into a single signal or at most a few flashes which would be sent, via a high-intensity light beam and in mere milliseconds, to a satellite. The message would then be sent to its intended recipient while the process would follow similar steps in reverse.

Yet, he chose to use a satellite phone which was encrypted and thus almost tamper-proof. His main worry with the other tool is that it made it more difficult to have a fast back-and-forth dialog. The small delay it introduced was definitely worth it if the agent was in enemy territory and probably under some surveillance, but it did not seem necessary in the current circumstances. Mark picked up immediately and was very surprised when Josh shared what he had found out from Ibrahim. Josh did not go into the myriad of details he might have reported, he simply mentioned what he believed were the two main new elements:

"In short, Mark, the conversation with Ibrahim was a bit of a game changer. He first told me that what his man had initially described as a rumor that there was some form of nuclear waste trade was more in fact an indication that someone was looking for participation in that trade . . ."

Mark came right back:

"Let me make sure I get this right. The key point you're making is that we're not sure that the earlier implication that there was trade in nuclear waste in Iraq was correct when we first heard about it. But now you conclude that the rumor simply pointed to the fact that someone wanted to participate in that trade if they could figure out with whom, where and how."

"Correct."

"And by the way, we still don't know whether the individual was a buyer or a seller; right?"

Josh replied:

"Correct again, though my intuition suggests the fellow would more likely be a buyer than a seller."

"What makes you say this?"

"Let me get to the second point and you'll see. Ibrahim told me that there was a solid belief within Iraq that some nuclear waste that had been created in Iraq under Saddam Hussein had been preserved."

"The U.N. inspectors didn't get everything. Is that what you're saying?"

"Yes, though I must remind you that the idea of that residual nuclear waste was just an early conjecture on the part of Ibrahim. He initially said he had no direct knowledge. But frankly as the phone conversation went on, I became convinced that he most likely knew of it and was probably even aware of more than what he said."

"Really?"

"Can't prove it, but this is what my instinct tells me. The only thing I'm willing to believe is that he doesn't know where that waste has been or where it still is. That's what makes me think the individual who spoke to Ibrahim's contact was more likely a buyer."

Mark replied with a broad smile:

"Hey, whether Iraq had any weapons of mass destruction was one of the major issues that bedeviled a President of the U.S."

He paused and added:

"Now, seriously and more to our point. From your earlier experience with Ibrahim, do you believe that last statement?"

"You mean that I suspect that Ibrahim does not know where the waste has been or now is?"

"Yes."

Josh hesitated. On the one hand, he clearly remembered that Ibrahim took quite some time in an earlier adventure to reveal that he was a leader of the Kurdish Resistance and that he was a direct participant in the opium trade which transited through Iraq, as a means of funding the Resistance. On the other hand, Josh had always felt that Ibrahim was above board. That in fact, even in the opium trade his willing participation was conditioned on the need for him to help fund the Resistance. He concluded:

"I've always seen Ibrahim as a gentleman, but a gentleman dedicated to the Kurdish cause and whatever came with it. I can't imagine him taking part in activities which could lead to mass murder."

Mark nodded though Josh could not see it and simply replied:

"I understand your view and can't prove it wrong. Yet we both know how bad the drug trade is and how many victims opium addiction has created, don't we?"

"You're right, Mark. I have no answer to that. Where my view has evolved as I said earlier is Ibrahim knows more than he is telling us. Yet this does not change my conviction that he isn't involved in the nuclear waste trade and that he would like it neutralized. Push me hard and I'll even bet that he's hoping I might help him get rid of it . . ."

Mark did not pursue the train of thought further, rather, changing tack, he said:

"Let's go beyond Ibrahim's role. Listening to the two points you've related; I can't escape the idea that you may have uncovered an explanation for the provenance of the nuclear waste used in Tiberias . . ."

Josh was smiling broadly as he said to Mark:

"It's funny. I hadn't yet made that link, but now that you've made it, it looks almost obvious. Where does that take you?"

Mark explained that he had the luxury of being a bit further away from the action. That gave him perspective, adding:

"Remember. You go to a museum to see impressionist paintings. Often, you won't see anything if you stand too close to the canvass. A few of these paintings are literally just a myriad of dots. However, take a step or two backward and all of a sudden, an image appears. It's the same thing here."

Josh was still not convinced and just replied:

"I need more . . ."

"Well, let me help you."

Mark went on to explain the whole sequence of events which Josh's information had suggested to him. He started with the observation that he had just found out that some old but still radioactive nuclear waste may have remained in Iraq. He added:

"From there we can eliminate one of our key questions when we looked at the dirty bomb attack on Tiberias. The terrorists didn't need any third party to supply them with the radioactive material; they simply needed to know that there was some of that stuff somewhere in Iraq, to find it, buy it and create the dirty bomb . . ."

Mark added a couple of important points to help Josh get to the same juncture he had reached himself. He reminded Josh that the mission which he and Josh had discussed near Istanbul Airport was based on the first incarnation of the rumor which Ibrahim had reported. To make the point clearer he added:

"We started this before we had all the details about the dirty bomb coming from the East had hit Tiberias . . ."

He paused for a second and continued his train of thought:

"One of our main questions was who might be involved. Now, coincidentally, we find out that the origin of the nuclear material might be much easier to trace. This will force me and you to add a dimension to your mission."

Josh's ears perked up when Mark talked of expanding the mission. Though he thought he was beginning to follow Mark's point, he asked another question:

"Are you saying that now that we believe that some old waste may have surfaced, we are ready to jump to the conclusion that whatever that waste was it had to be material that was used to attack Tiberias?"

Mark initially sighed and simply said:

"Whoa Horsey. Not too fast. I'm not suggesting that this is the only explanation. Far from it. However, what I'm saying that it could be **an** explanation. Said differently, the nuclear waste **does not have to** have been sourced from outside Iraq or Syria, but it still could."

Josh surely understood the emphasis which Mark had placed on a couple of points in his last comment. He answered:

"That's what I thought. But talking about my mission, what's next?"

"At this point, I don't think we can do anything more. After all, we don't know who had taken the waste before the U.N. inspectors arrived. We don't know who used it. In fact, we don't know whether we are talking of one and only one party, or whether there is some conspiracy going on. If there's a conspiracy, how did the parties connect, how did one know where to ask?"

Josh interrupted:

"You give me a thought, Mark."

"I'm all ears."

"OK. Now, please appreciate I am thinking aloud . . ."

"That's when we're often at our best. Go right ahead."

"Let's go back to Rezna, Ibrahim's man. In fact, let's go back to the question he was asked, whatever it was that started the rumor . . ."

Josh went on to construct a scenario which assumed that the party that was asking the question might well be the group that wanted to use that nuclear waste in a dirty bomb intended for Israel. Mark's words of encouragement next took him to a preliminary conclusion:

"What if that party was aware or had heard of the existence of the waste, but didn't know who had it and where it was stored?"

Mark interrupted:

"I love it. Let's concede that this is only one of several possible scenarios, which quite frankly I haven't even begun to create in full. The guy asking the question was going through a list of contacts, which may or may not have been assembled in a random manner. So, the reply that he heard from Rezna only told him that Rezna and the Kurd faction he was suspected to belong to didn't know, but that left several other names on the list . . ."

"If I may interrupt, Mark, there is a variant in this logic. Rezna was not aware of the connection between his group and the nuclear waste. But that should not mean that the Kurdish Resistance didn't know about it or even didn't have control . . ."

"Absolutely. Now, unless your friend, Ibrahim, is bold face lying to you, we may be able to assume that they are not in that loop. Correct?"

"True. But does that mean that some outsider, say me, couldn't try to get into the action?"

"I see where you're going, Josh. However, remember that whoever it is, they must have found some of that waste if they are indeed the ones who shot the dirty bomb toward Tiberias."

Josh replied:

"Can't disagree. However, who knows whether the custody of the old nuclear waste remained with one solitary group? So back to something you said earlier, they may have had some of that waste but not all of it. After all, wouldn't it have been more prudent to separate the waste into several packages and disperse them around Iraq?"

"I see what you mean."

Mark went on to reshape Josh's mission to include at least three different threads. First, in Mark's mind, nobody as yet knew who had fired the dirty bomb rocket; that then meant that there was work to be done on that front. He added:

"I don't think this is part of your role as of yet. I'm going to have someone else on that. I don't want to put you in a position where you might end up being squeezed between two enemies. Way too dangerous."

Josh thanked Mark though he added that he and whoever was behind the firing of the dirty bomb rocket might well end up crossing paths. Mark replied that this was surely possible, though he argued that he had to think it through in much more depth to decide whether knowing each other would help the men or hurt them. Continuing his discussion of the three threads, Mark turned to the second and did not surprise Josh when he said that it had to do with uncovering whatever could be found with respect to the old Iraqi nuclear waste. Josh asked:

"Am I getting this straight? Is it reasonable for me to involve Ibrahim? Whatever I do, first I've got to create the story."

"Makes sense . . ."

Josh concluded:

"And then, after having discussed it with you, I'll get him into the fray, or not . . ."

"Agreed. The third and quite important thread relates to whether this was an isolated event or something more . . ."

Josh had to ask:

"What do you mean by 'this'? "

"Excellent question, my friend. So far, we've provisionally established, at least as some working assumption, that the tip of the nasty rocket that hit Tiberias used old Iraqi nuclear waste. We're also assuming that the party which Ibrahim's friend, Rezna, met was looking for that waste."

He paused to check his logic and concluded:

"Now, the key question, beyond verifying our key assumptions, is for us to find out what it is the terrorists who fired the dirty rocket are up to. Remember, we had a lengthy conversation on Kumkoi beach during which we discussed what the goal of whoever fired the rocket might be. That question is still on the table. But a new dimension is now obvious:

Without paying attention to the fact that he was interrupting his boss, Josh blurted out:

"I see. Are they going to look for more radioactive stuff? And if yes, from where and for what?"

"Right on. I don't need to tell you that you're going to need help if there is a global dimension. The one thing that I'm going to focus on in the short term is this: let's assume that these guys are not trying to build a nuclear device but rather working to create a dirty bomb capability. Whether they'll use it just against us or more broadly to achieve their goal is still unknown. Whatever this is, I've got to tell you that history will one day write that this was one nuclear step too far!"

CHAPTER.12

TEL AVIV, ISRAEL

As soon as he hung up with Josh, Mark asked his assistant to set up a meeting with David, Simon, and Jeremy Bensoussan, the Head of *Shin Bet,* as soon as possible. While he did not feel he had learned anything which would force him to redirect the operations initiated when he learned of what he called "the Ibrahim rumor", he was still convinced that there were enough new elements that a "meeting at the top" would not only not hurt but was in fact the right thing to do. The meeting was set for a day, hence, which allowed Mark to have a pre-meeting with David. After all, he was a "good soldier" and respected his hierarchy. David ought to have a complete briefing as well as the opportunity to comment and help Mark better prepare the following day's discussion.

David listened to Mark's recapitulation of the story and of the developments so far. Mark was delighted to see the smile on his face; it was telling him that he had not made any egregious mistake or missed something big. His impression was more than confirmed when David offered his most sincere congratulations:

"As you know, Mark, I've always felt that I'd rather be lucky than smart. So, don't let this get to your head. Yet I have to tell you that the operation has made more progress so far than I would have dreamed."

David paused and uncharacteristically rose from his chair to shake Mark's hand as he was sitting on the sofa in his office. Mark smiled and thanked David, gave credit to Josh. He reminded David that most of what had come out was a direct result of Josh's special relationship with Ibrahim. David conceded the point, but reminding Mark of his decision to go meet Josh at Kumboi Beach in Turkey and of the numerous conversations he had had with Josh since, he simply said:

"Good bosses help their people give their best . . ."

As if he had flipped a switch, David's face returned to a serious expression as he wanted to discuss with Mark what the next steps in the current mission were, prefacing his remarks with the usual:

"Assuming that Simon backs us up."

Mark was not surprised by the change of expression on David's face: he was now used to his almost unique ability to change facial expressions as he moved from one topic to the next. He was also gratified that David had used the term "us" rather than "you" when it came to Simon's backing. He briefly toyed with the idea of a joke to the effect that he could not recall a situation when Simon had not backed David up but decided that the matter was serious enough that levity was neither called for nor even appropriate.

David remained silent for what seemed like at least a minute, as Mark, correctly as it turned out, thought David was getting his ideas in order. Mark was still surprised when, rather than giving Mark his conclusions as he expected, David asked him how he would suggest attacking the issue. Mark reminded himself that he had learned quite a while ago that David's attitude was exactly what a good boss should do: allow the subordinate to come up with as many ideas or suggestions as possible. The boss's role indeed is never to impress his subordinate with his skills and knowledge. They're assumed to be there; he's the boss. Without the required skills, the individual would not have gotten the job. Rather than seeking to impress, a good boss is supposed to model those skills on the job. Allowing the subordinate to conduct his own analysis in a low-pressure environment was exactly the way the subordinate could learn and develop, provided, as David knew and modeled very well, that the boss did not jump on the subordinate if he made an error.

Mark had had some time to think things through, both since and after his conversation with Josh and as he was preparing his presentation to the larger group. His first point struck a note when he said:

"I think we need to break the problem into at least two fundamental dimensions, with possibly two more facets."

Encouraged by David's body language, he started with a listing of what he called the fundamental dimensions. In his mind, the first crucial issue had to do with the attack on Tiberias and the dirty bomb. That also included at least two elements: who was behind the attack and, especially, the question of whether all the rockets were fired by the same group, or the dirty rocket was launched by some other party? On that front, he said that whether there was one or two aggressors would have a strong bearing on what the point of the dirty bomb was. In passing, he noted that he would be surprised if there was only one aggressor, as the use of the dirty bomb looked almost suicidal if it came from Hezbollah. Finally, he added that he should confirm where the dirty bomb had been made, by whom and with what radioactive material. David nodded and simply said:

"So far, so good, my friend. Now you talked of two fundamental dimensions . . ."

"Absolutely, sir. Let me turn to the second now. There the question has to do with whether the nuclear dimension is an exception aimed at reaching some specific goal which we have yet to uncover or whether it represents a bare expansion of the range of armament used in the regional conflict."

Again, after having taken a sip from his sparkling water, he noted that the two dimensions as he just characterized them were neither unrelated nor even independent. Seeing that David looked particularly interested, he offered an explanation of his thoughts.

"Assume that this is only a one-off, . . ."

"Just a minute, what is 'this?"

"Sorry. I'm referring to the dirty bomb."

Seeing that David was back on track, he continued:

"If the use of a dirty bomb is a one off, it's a fair question to ask which came first, the chicken or the egg?"

David was making a face, which told Mark that he needed more clarity. Mark explained that one could think of two scenarios. Whoever was behind the dirty bomb might either have planned to use such a weapon or decided to use it because it had come across the radioactive material which would make the dirty bomb feasible. Mark summarized his point:

"Was the dirty bomb a planned development or an opportunistic use of the right resources?"

David interrupted:

"You know what? This is a great question. Given what you reported earlier, would you be thinking that finding the old Iraqi nuclear waste was what caused the hypothetical decision to create and then use or even maybe just test a dirty bomb?"

"Exactly, but it isn't as simple as this. The scenario I'm mulling over involves whoever shot the dirty rocket. At first blush, it seems to be missing internal cohesion. Why suddenly use a nuclear-tipped weapon. Let me explain."

Mark went back to a recent situation which he needed to deal with. He recalled the operation mounted to deal with the machination of the Muslim Brotherhood in Egypt[5]. He argued that they found out that the Muslim Brotherhood, in that instance at least, was not monolithic. Mark recalled that there were at least two parties within the Brotherhood: one was principally focused on religion and Egyptian politics to the extent they interacted with religion, and the other driven by revolutionary motivations, possibly imported from Afghanistan with help from Iran. David nodded though he asked:

"I'm lost. You're going to explain the parallel here, right?"

"Sorry. Absolutely. Assuming that the dirty bomb was fired by a group different from Hezbollah and not taking any side as to why that group would do that, one could imagine two scenarios. In the first, the group wants to send a bomb, more powerful than usual, or aimed at an unusual target but isn't thinking of taking a step beyond conventional warfare. Now, there could be another faction, let's call it a splinter group, which would like to do more but does not have the means to do it."

Mark paused and simply concluded:

"Now, assume that this splinter group coincidentally comes across some nuclear waste material. That could be the trigger that got them to go for a dirty bomb."

David smiled. His protégé had made an excellent point. Yet he needed to bring him back to the main issue: his second fundamental consideration:

"Can we get back to your second fundamental dimension?"

"Sure. I was asking whether the nuclear dimension was coincidental or intentional."

David interrupted:

"If it's coincidental, we can assume that the hypothesis that a nuclear waste traffic in or through Iraq isn't a very important issue."

He paused and seemed to think for a minute and added:

---

[5] By the same author, see: *Destruction Along the Nile*, Barringer Publishing, 2024.

"However, now that they've let the cat out of the bag, their position vis-à-vis nuclear weapons may be changing."

Mark finished David's earlier sentence:

"Yes, but identifying who, why, and from where would be even more of a priority if the use of a dirty bomb was not coincidental but intentional . . ."

■ ■ ■ ■ ■

The next morning, Jeremy, the Head of *Shin Bet*, David, and Mark met in Simon's office. In truth, only Jeremy Bensoussan was discovering anything new. David had indeed briefed Simon on the main points which Mark would cover. Simon started the conversation with apologies to Jeremy, bemoaning the fact that he hadn't the time to give him a preview, as David had only managed to reach him, at home late in the evening. He still made the commitment that Mark was going to go over all the relevant information, irrespective of whether it would be repetitive for other attendants or not.

Simon surprised David and Mark with his subsequent comment:

"Jeremy and I have been aware of one element which will be a bit of a surprise to you, David, and Mark. To tell you the truth, I only found out about it when I received my last briefing before I took over the leadership of *Mossad* from Ariel."

David and Mark exchanged glances and noticed that Jeremy was smiling. Simon proceeded to tell them that *Mossad* had been aware that some nuclear waste material had been taken away by people loyal to Saddam before the U.N. inspectors had a chance to recover it. He added:

"This has been considered a national secret which only the heads of *Mossad* and *Shin Beth* know. I know that Ariel told me that this was not to be shared with anyone in the political sphere, except on a need-to-know basis. I assume that you received the same instructions, Jeremy . . ."

Jeremy nodded and replied:

"Absolutely. In fact, a cell within my agency is still tasked with finding where the waste had been stored, yet they do not know what it is that they are looking for, other than the fact that a rumor was going around to the effect that Iraq had some nuclear material, though nobody knew what it was or even how it was acquired."

Mark interjected:

"This secret which you just shared, Simon . . . It fits directly with something which Josh's Iraqi contact told him in so many words."

"Really?"

"Yes, he talked of residual nuclear waste generated during Saddam's years which would have been hidden . . ."

David took this further:

"Thanks Mark. In fact, you had gone beyond that point. Did you not tell me of a plausible scenario where the waste that tipped the Tiberias dirty rocket had come from Iraq?"

"I did. But, first, Simon, is there more to that secret?"

Simon replied:

"The knowledge that nuclear waste was around was obviously something that figured in my thinking, but I surely didn't make a direct and conclusive link. In fact, even today, given the additional information which you gathered Mark, I am still not ready to draw a categorical conclusion. It's still just one more plausible hypothesis."

Mark made the point that he agreed that it was too early to draw a formal conclusion, though he added that the first rumor mentioned by Ibrahim and its subsequent correction made a link more probable than not. Simon agreed with Mark's conclusion and invited him to discuss what he judged to be the two most principal issues.

"Thanks Simon. Well, simply put, David and I agree that the first issue is directly related to what happened in Tiberias. It is a fact that someone launched a dirty bomb toward us, though what we don't know is who is behind that and why it was done. The second issue is equally important. It relates to the fact that whoever launched that rocket took a huge step: it introduced a nuclear dimension to the local terrorist warfare that has been going on for a half-century if not more. We don't know but need to know whether the use of nuclear material was coincidental or a deliberate fundamental expansion of the conflict."

"I like your summary, Mark. David, anything you need to add?"

"No, Mark and I are on the same page."

"Jeremy, any question?"

"Well, Simon, as you would expect, I don't have one but a multitude of questions, Yet, at this point, which I define as information sharing, I'm OK."

Simon smiled and turning to Mark asked him:

"Are you ready to make any recommendation in terms of what comes next, or do you need more time."

"David and I discussed this, Simon, and we believe that we have two distinct missions coming out of what we have learned. It may well be that the two will converge at some point, but we are not ready to consider them one and the same."

He paused to take a sip of water from the glass to his right and concluded:

"We believe that we should continue to learn as much as we can about the circumstances surrounding the Tiberias events. We believe that this is a mission which Josh Steinmetz should lead, though we may need to provide him with some help."

Mark was gratified to see David nodding in support. He continued:

"The second mission deals with the introduction of a nuclear dimension into the local conflict. This would involve identifying whether whoever used the nuclear waste they placed into the dirty rocket did this because an opportunity arose or because they have a broader plan. In that case, who is behind the plan, is it the usual state sponsor, read Iran, or is it something quite different?"

Simon asked:

"Can you say a bit more on this last point?"

"Sure, but please appreciate that I am totally in the realm of speculation. For instance, could it be that some other state is interested in inflaming passions and yet do it in a way that can't be attributed to them? Think Russia or China. They surely generate plenty of nuclear waste on a routine basis: would they surreptitiously supply some of that waste to a terrorist organization in the Middle East and if yes for what purpose? I'm sure there are other variations on which I haven't yet stumbled, but I suspect this gives you a sense of where our minds are . . ."

Simon seemed to conclude:

"Thanks, Mark. Anything else from anyone?"

Mark suddenly raised his hand, as a schoolboy. He had had another thought. Simon invited him to share it:

"I know this is really half-baked. But imagine this. Let's assume that Iran is definitely trying to get more and more control over the region. Let's also assume that Iran was behind the savage Hamas attack, you know, the one they called 'Operation Al-Aqsa Flood'—or the Deluge—on twenty-one communities in the south of Israel. One could conclude that Iran would like to unite all Palestinian terrorists into one single entity, possibly led by Hamas. Then who stands in the way of that goal?"

Mark paused and Simon immediately jumped into the fray:

"I get it Mark. I get it. Hezbollah becomes a problem. So, Iran orchestrates a dirty bomb attack at the time Hezbollah is shooting missiles at Tiberias. They hope we're going to reply as if the dirty bomb came from Hezbollah. In short, they could be trying to get us to do their dirty work for them. Weaken Hezbollah to make way for Hamas over which they might believe they have better control . . . Brilliant! Great work you all. Anything else?"

Seeing that nobody offered any additional contribution, Simon added:

"Jeremy, can we spend a few more minutes together?"

CHAPTER.13

Josh knew exactly what he had to do.

As soon as he heard from Mark that his part of the mission was ready to start, Josh looked for flights to Istanbul and back where he would meet Mark. Of the three flights available on Turkish Airlines, he chose to avoid the two which either travelled in the early morning or arrived just after midnight. That meant that he knew he would land just before 1:00 p.m., leaving him and Mark not more than an afternoon to meet on the first day. He would have to return on the 6:10 p.m. flight the next day. Mark did not have to worry about airline schedules as he would fly one of the agency's corporate jets. Mark decided to return to the same Zen hotel, Mare Negro Villa, near Kumkoi beach. With Josh needing only carry-on luggage, they met in the car which Mark had already rented and drove straight to Kumboi Beach. They decided to have a late lunch immediately after they checked in but before they had taken the time to drop their limited luggage in their respective rooms.

Josh let Mark give him as detailed a briefing as he was able to and refrained from asking any questions until Mark indicated that he was through. Josh was not surprised by what he heard, which was exactly what Mark had planned, as he chose not to share with Josh the national military secret which he had learned from Simon. His main rationale was that there was no need to confirm that the information which Josh had heard from Ibrahim was a reality that was already known to *Mossad*. He also elected not to share the hypothesis about Iran standing behind the dirty bomb, as it remained but a hypothesis, and he did not want in any way to influence Josh's views of the various alternatives he would have to consider. This made a lot of sense as Josh would be responsible for tracking what he could find on nuclear waste trading in Iraq. They spent the next several hours going over a number of scenarios, most of which Mark had already constructed and a couple which Josh had developed during their conversation.

In the end, the two men agreed that Josh's first order of business should be to collaborate with his friend Ibrahim. He would need for Ibrahim to introduce his man Rezna. Josh and Mark debated long and hard whether the best approach would be for Josh to be the one to contact Rezna or whether he would need someone else to help him. The logic for having Josh in control was obvious: it would be the simplest by far. On the other hand, there was a real risk that Ibrahim would detect some contradiction between Josh's activities and the description he had given earlier of him being nothing but an informer. Eventually, the decision was made that the risk was worth taking. Mark had to maneuver carefully with respect to the military secret. Though he surely accepted that the 'Saddam' or 'residual' waste as he had come to call it might be the source of the nuclear material in the dirty bomb, he wanted to ensure that Josh would still investigate all other potential sources as well. Josh mentioned a couple of ideas that he could use to finesse his expanded role which he believed Ibrahim would accept and even believe.

They discussed a number of possible reactions which Rezna could have and it became obvious that the number of variations on the theme was too large to plan for each one in any real detail. Yet, they planned for at least six different scenarios all of which assumed first that Rezna would agree to meet Josh, aka Abu Musa, and second that the individual whom he would introduce would also be willing to help at least some of the way. Josh initially argued that the two assumptions which they were making were already somewhat of a stretch. Seeing Mark's quizzical look he expanded on the point:

"First of all, I think it's fair to assume that Ibrahim will agree to introduce me to Rezna. He's virtually already said so. But that's only half of the problem . . ."

Mark interrupted:

"Sure. But more to the point, will Rezna agree to tell you anything?"

"Even before you get there, Mark, the question remains: will he agree to meet me? Remember, my official activity: I'm an informer. How likely will someone with shady connections agree to meet someone like me?"

"I can see that. However, with Ibrahim's help, do you think the odds are better than 50/50?"

"I do, but not by much. In fact, I would give myself 2 chances out of 3. I must be prepared to accept a first meeting with him with Ibrahim present."

"Would that work?"

"Initially sure. But at some point, Ibrahim has to recede in the background."

"By the way, do you have a carrot for Ibrahim?"

Josh laughed as he replied:

"I'm not sure that's the right word. We have two strings which we can play. The first is Ibrahim's love for his country and its people. I'm sure that he wouldn't like the idea of Iraq becoming a playground for nuclear traffic."

"Makes sense. The second?"

"Whoever is likely to get involved in the nuclear waste traffic only has one currency with which they can deal: opium. The supply out of Afghanistan has dropped considerably and though prices have moved up correspondingly, I'm sure that Ibrahim does not want competition there. Maybe, there's something which we could offer to help him make sure that no one comes hunting on his territory!"

Mark nodded his general agreement on this front. Still, he asked:

"What about our second assumption?"

"That's the one where I think we've got to start with expectations that are less than 50/50. After all, why would Rezna's contact agree to talk to me?"

Josh paused and told Mark that he saw two possible scenarios with respect to that individual:

"Assuming that he suspected that some nuclear waste had been removed before the inspectors could get to it, either he was asking Rezna to see if he knew anything, or he had bigger plans."

Mark cut in:

"You're going to explain that, right?"

"Sure. Again, my scenario has no value if the rumor about that residual nuclear waste is baloney."

Josh did not notice a wry smile which appeared briefly on Mark's face. Mark was indeed thinking that he had not confirmed the existence of the residual waste. Thus, to Josh and any other person not in the know it remained no more than a hypothesis. Josh had just demonstrated the worth of Mark's strategic decision: Josh would surely not create a risk that the information would become anything more than a possibility. Josh kept going:

"Assuming that some of that waste exists, you want to find out if he, Rezna's contact, was only trying to find whoever knew where that waste was. In any case, you'd have to assume that he or somebody he knows well and is allied to has found it."

"Only if you assume that his group is behind the dirty rocket fired on Tiberias . . ."

Josh agreed only up to a point:

"I can see that. However, why wouldn't you assume that the group to which the man belongs is the provider for whoever fired the rocket?"

Mark conceded that the chain of events which Josh was painting was as feasible as any other. So, he asked:

"OK, grant you that. Where does that leave you?"

"Well, if the residual waste was all he was looking for, he's done."

"I see. So, you would assume that he would only be interested in further talks if he is prepared to look for more waste, either for his own organization to use or at least for it to sell to potential buyers . . ."

Josh replied:

"Absolutely. I think it's clear that I may have to morph from someone trying to figure whether there is nuclear waste for sale to a different person who might be looking for nuclear waste buyers . . ."

"I like it!"

■ ■ ■ ■ ■

Mark asked David for some time on his calendar to work on the planning of the other mission flowing from the use of a dirty bomb against Israel. He had already spent quite a bit of time thinking of the various steps he wanted to take but felt that he needed to bring David onboard as there would be at least a couple of issues which he could not resolve himself. They dealt with resource allocations and the limits which ought to be set so that the effort did not end up in a free-for-all.

David was smiling as he welcomed Mark into his office. The duo had already spent enough time together, with David the boss and Mark the subordinate that they had a well-oiled routine when it came to meeting in David's office. Mark had already asked Uschi,

David's assistant who replaced Joan who had retired, for a large glass of sparkling water. David, while greeting Mark at the door, had also requested a beverage, though, in his case, he preferred a glass of iced coffee. Mark walked into the office and went straight for the sofa which he found to his left, while David naturally chose the armchair which stood to the right of the sofa, at the end of the rectangular glass-top coffee table.

David surprised Mark as he said:

"One thing you need to know, Mark. Simon called to tell me that he and Jeremy had agreed that they should pursue the various leads *Mossad* and *Shin Bet* have independently."

David could not fail to notice that Mark's face expressed astonishment. He decided to forgo asking Mark for his thoughts and immediately volunteered:

"Simon and Jeremy know that this may lead to some overlap, and thus to the potential for some waste of resources. Yet, they felt that both agencies have their own people and their own protocols. They believe that it would be best for them to adhere to them."

Mark could not resist asking:

"What about cases when we might be working at cross purposes or in competition with each other?"

"Excellent question, my friend. The way they're going to deal with this is simple: there will be a weekly coordination meeting."

He paused for effect and smiling announced:

"And you will be the main project coordinator . . ."

Mark stood flabbergasted as if he initially could not believe his ears. Intuitively, when he had heard David start to talk of the coordination of the agencies' efforts, he had assumed that David would play the leading role. David repeated the original message, adding:

"Obviously, I will be available to help you if needed. Any question?"

Mark replied that he was honored with the responsibilities but was simultaneously worried that he might be stretched too thin. In response to David's request for additional details, he explained:

"In truth, given the broad outline I wanted to discuss with you with respect to the second leg of the mission, I had come to the conclusion that I might have to play a very active role in it."

"How active?"

Mark conceded:

"Well, frankly, I thought I might have to take day-to-day responsibilities, including liaison with people overseas as I suspect it's going to be a requirement . . ."

"Solid assumption I should add. But why you?"

"Oh, believe me, it's not because I don't think that none of my guys could do it. Rather I'm worried that whoever it is will have to consult with senior individuals in the agencies or government departments which will need to get involved."

David interrupted:

"And you worry that someone more junior than you might not get it done?"

Mark replied with a weak and embarrassed "yes." Any worry which Mark might have had at that point dissipated in a second as David smiled and said:

"Mark, this is exactly what Simon, and I expected. But you need to appreciate a couple of things. First, anybody reporting to you isn't nearly as junior as you think. Second, you are more valuable to us as a coordinator and planner than as a field agent."

He paused briefly, drunk from his iced coffee and continued:

"There is little doubt in my mind that you will have to be present, in the field, at some point in time. However, I know you, and Simon does too. Unless you have broader responsibilities, you are going to go deep into the weeds. I need you to know about the weeds, but you're too valuable to us to spend your time there. So, trust me, appoint one of your best deputies to take the lead and simply make sure that you are around to help him or her whenever needed."

Mark could do little more than simply agree, adding with a wry smile that he would need to think of what it meant in terms of his current tentative plan. David asked him then to give him the broad outline of the plan. Mark was happy to comply:

"The key mission as I see it is to find any potential external link to some sort of nuclear waste trafficking. At this point, subject to confirming it with both Marvin and Marcel, I tend to think that we are talking of theft of nuclear waste during transport from the reactor cooling site to wherever it is placed in long-term storage."

"Remind me why?"

"Unless we speak of those so-called 'orphan sources' which remain in places where there was some nuclear activity and no longer is, I believe that the move of the spent fuel rods from the reactor to the five-year underwater storage is too complex and too supervised for anything to happen. More to the point, the radioactivity of the rods as they are extracted from the core of the reactor is at its highest. You need machinery to conduct the work. Humans would die if they came in direct contact. And machinery would be unlikely to go unnoticed."

"Makes sense. However, help me understand what you mean by 'orphan sources.' Isn't that exactly what we may have found being used in the stuff that came from Iraq?"

"Absolutely, though it's Josh's job to confirm that such is the case. So, the question remains: where are the other orphan sources? Principally in the old Soviet empire if I believe Marcel. While everything is possible, we also heard that many of these are 'lost' in the middle of nowhere."

"Mark, I'm not here to tell you what to do, but my own guess is that I wouldn't ignore these sources. In fact, it's a lot easier for me to get my mind around the idea of a Russian gang, without any relationship with their central government, to go 'harvest' these various sources of nuclear waste than to imagine how someone would manage to steal spent fuel rods."

CHAPTER.14

MOSUL AND ERBIL, IRAQ; TEL AVIV, ISRAEL

Ibrahim was not surprised when he saw that the phone call he was receiving was from Josh. He had in fact been expecting it. It had been a while since they last talked, and it was not in the character of the Abu Musa to drop something that could be so important.

"Ibrahim, my friend, any chance we can meet. I've done some research on the topic of our prior conversations, and I'd like to take them to the next step if you agree."

"Always ready to have tea with you, preferably in the mid-morning. By the way, any chance we could meet in Erbil?

"Sure. How about the small plaza right after the main gate into the citadel . . ."

■ ■ ■ ■ ■

Erbil, also called Hawler, which was known in ancient history as Arbela, was the capital and most populated city in the Kurdistan region of Iraq. Though smack in the middle of the Kurdish territory, Erbil was quite a diverse city from both ethnic and religious viewpoints. In fact, certain people within the city tended to feel that trouble or strife had always been brought to the town by "foreigners."

And, by "foreigners," they meant people who did not live there and had not lived there for at least a generation, though they could well be Iraqis. Importantly, "foreigner" was never used to describe differences of religion or ethnic group. The historical heart of the city was a citadel which is estimated to be close to 7,000 years old; it has stood on a mound about 100 feet higher than the surrounding plains for millennia. It has been claimed that urban life in Erbil can be dated back to at least 6,000 BC. The citadel was at the center of the walled old town. The metropolis had expanded from there in some concentric circle fashion. Thus, there were five ring roads loosely following the contours of the walls of the citadel.

The main gate through which one entered the citadel was "guarded" by an immense statue of a Kurd reading. The message thus imparted was one of wisdom and solemnity rather than of military might. The houses of the citadel behind the statue were built into the stony ground of the mound and looked down on the streets and the tarmacked roads that drew concentric circles around the citadel.

■ ■ ■ ■ ■

For once, the two men did not meet in a coffee house. Ibrahim knew that Abu Musa was aware of a house which he, Ibrahim, had used at some point, not to reside in, but as a sort of meeting place. In fact, it was in that house that Abu Musa had saved Ibrahim's life when a member of his opium trading network tried to blow himself and Ibrahim up.[6] Josh recognized the living room where he had first met someone who eventually was revealed to be Ibrahim; at the time of their first encounter, his friend, Ibrahim, had introduced to him a man that could help Abu Musa and spoke from behind a curtain and with a disguised voice. It was only after the fact that Josh realized that Ibrahim and the hidden man were the same.

---

[6] By the same author, see *Glitter and Smoke*, Barringer Publishing, 2023.

A couple of cups of tea, together with a few pieces of *kahi* with *geymer* appeared and were placed on the low table in front of the two armchairs in which they were seating. Kahi is the ultimate Iraqi breakfast indulgence, reminiscent of Baklava, which is probably better known around the world, as it is found in almost every country around the eastern Mediterranean basin rather than principally in Iraq.

Once the young man who had brought the coffee and pastries left the room, Ibrahim wasted no time and simply asked:

"So, tell me what I can do for you, my friend?"

Josh was ready with a simple reply. He told Ibrahim that he would like to give him his conclusion first and then offer any explanation which his friend might need. He paused and looking straight at Ibrahim added:

"I would like to meet your man, Rezna. Can you arrange it for me please?"

Ibrahim smiled broadly replying:

"I can't tell you I am surprised. That wouldn't be true. We've been dancing around that question for a while. Yet, I still don't understand why you want to speak with him and how it can help you."

Ibrahim's reply was one of the three possible scenarios which Josh had rehearsed with Mark when they were last at Kumkoi Beach. Their main concern was for Josh to maintain his cover as a broad informer with a preference for "good causes" and yet have rational explanations for what he was asking.

Returning Ibrahim's smile, Josh matter-of-factly explained that the rumor which Ibrahim first communicated and then amended was very interesting, adding:

"I can even tell you that I know that more than one party would be interested in anything I can dig up. I haven't made a firm commitment to anyone, but I believe I have a buyer if I can find out more about the nuclear waste trade."

Looking both surprised and almost disappointed, Ibrahim interrupted:

"Don't tell me you would facilitate something like that Abu Musa. That's not something which a friend of mine would do. There's got to be more to it than what you're saying. What's up?"

Again, Mark and Josh had anticipated that direction in the conversation and Josh replied with a great deal of candor:

"Ibrahim, I didn't say that my contact would conduct such trade. I just said that he would be interested in it. In fact, I can go a bit further: I'm sure that he wouldn't consider conducting such trade . . ."

He purposefully left the end of the phrase hanging. Mark and Josh had agreed that not being crystal clear at the outset gave them a few more options later on. Yet, they had concluded that he could take the statement a bit further if he had to. In such a case, he was ready to say that at least one of the two parties he had contacted would do more than not conduct the trade: they would try to combat and stop it. Ibrahim seemed more at ease, but his body language conveyed the message that there was something he still did not understand. He had to ask another question:

"OK, that's better. But where's the catch?"

Josh decided to outline his mission in broad terms. There was no need for Ibrahim to know that *Mossad* was behind it. In fact, he was ready, if it came to that, to point to several regional security agencies which would fall into the same basket as *Mossad*. He first told Ibrahim that the first key element of what he deemed his mission was to find out who was involved and whether they were buyers or sellers. Ibrahim interrupted:

"Wait a second, Abu Musa. You're talking of a mission, and you tell me you haven't made a firm commitment. Something does not add up here, am I wrong?"

"No, you're my friend. I misspoke. I used the word mission to describe what I set myself out to do. Let's be honest. I couldn't approach anyone with a simple rumor and hope that they would immediately open their checkbook to buy the information or to hire me, or both."

He paused to eat a piece of his *Kahi* and went straight ahead:

"With the information I had, thanks to you let's not forget, I drew up what I might call a scenario. I focused on the nuclear waste trade and concluded that no one is going to go after windmills. Don Quixote does not live either now or around here. So, I decided that I had nothing to sell if I didn't know who was involved. At the same time, being involved isn't enough. How would you approach someone if you didn't know whether they were interested in buying or selling?"

Josh was relieved to see that Ibrahim's demeanor seemed to become more relaxed. He added to the story that he had just offered that there were a couple of other elements which he would like to know if he could, arguing:

"Besides knowing who is involved and which side of the trade they're on, I'd also like to know a couple more things. If they're buyers, I'd like to know to whom it is that they're selling whatever they're buying. If they're not selling, they'd have to be buying, right? Then, I'd like to know what they want to do with it."

He paused and offered an aside:

"Can't believe it could realistically happen, but someone might argue that they need that waste to conduct experiments . . . That doesn't mean that they're about to build a nuclear device. By the way, I know enough to know that you can't build a nuclear bomb with nuclear waste unless you first have the capability to reprocess it. And that, my friend, isn't something that you do in your garage . . ."

Ibrahim smiled, allowing Josh to conclude:

"By the same token, if they're sellers, I'd like to know where the waste they want to sell comes from. Maybe, it's as simple as the waste being part of what was salvaged from the Saddam Hussein era. However, what if it comes from someplace else? Then what? You see, nothing but plain information. All within a general storyline. This isn't to say that the story will hold. I'm ready for my hypotheses to be proven wrong, but until then . . ."

Ibrahim appeared satisfied, but he still surprised Josh as he said:

"I can see that. However, let me tell you this, Abu Musa: if you were a member of a secret service, from Israel or from anywhere else in the Middle East, you wouldn't be acting differently."

Josh was not surprised by Ibrahim's comeback. In fact, it was the first assumption that he and Mark had made. So, without batting an eyelid, he simply replied:

"I can't contradict you. But let me offer an additional twist: what if such secret services didn't have the resources to do it themselves? And here I'm not talking about money. You need contacts, knowledge of the culture and many other minor elements which I can bring to the party with respect to Iraq and that several secret agencies couldn't offer. Then, wouldn't they be willing to use a discreet free-lancer?"

Ibrahim had to concede:

"Touché. Help me understand what would actually happen if you got to speak with Rezna."

Josh had also rehearsed that part of the conversation with Mark. He was ready with an answer:

"Simple. I would only have one major question and a series of secondary queries. My key question would be whether he would be willing to introduce me to whomever mentioned the possibility of nuclear waste trade."

"Isn't that a bit risky for Rezna?"

"Don't think so. I am assuming that he would first ask his contact whether he would be willing to speak to me. I can imagine a conversation very much like the one we're having here."

Seeing Ibrahim sit back in his chair and smile, Josh continued:

"My secondary queries would involve learning more about Rezna, the man, and what he could tell me about how he got to meet his contact. I suspect that these questions are probably more personal, and I wouldn't be surprised if he initially refused to answer. My hope is that he would change his mind as he realized that I was just trying to understand what might be an important development."

■ ■ ■ ■ ■

As he was driving back to Mosul, Josh kept thinking of what the conversation with Ibrahim had taught him. He quickly zeroed in on two main questions: would Ibrahim help him or not? Would Rezna talk to him or not? Josh realized that his position was incredibly weak. He and Mark had alluded to it when last in Kumkoi Beach, and Mark's suggestion that Josh would need reinforcements became absolutely inescapable.

When he arrived in Mosul, he called Mark and told him that he would need foot soldiers and that he would probably need between three and five of them. Before Mark could ask how he got to that conclusion, Josh explained that he had realized that he was going to need people to tail at least a couple of the parties he would like to meet. He added:

"In an ideal world, Ibrahim introduces Rezna who greets me like a long-lost friend, tells me where he lives and invites me to his place to meet his contact. I don't need to tell you that the odds of this happening are perilously close to zero. Ditto with his contact. So, I suspect that I will need to have people keep a watch on these characters, if only to make sure that I'm not walking into a trap, but also to find out more about them without me having to ask them."

Mark told him that he was surely not surprised and still asked:

"Are you sure you only need foot soldiers? Shouldn't one or two of these people be fully trained agents who can do more than simply trail someone?"

Josh immediately saw the wisdom in Mark's recommendations, though he said that at the outset at least they should probably aim lower rather than higher:

"Why don't we have one solid agent and a couple of foot soldiers first. After all, there won't be a need for more if I can't get to talk to Rezna . . ."

CHAPTER.15

PARIS, FRANCE

Mark travelled to Paris to meet Dr. Marcel Delagrange. He expected Countess Renate to be present as well as Nathan Stone, the senior *Mossad* representative in France. Nathan would be introduced with his official title of Vice Consul for Military Affairs. That Countess Renate might strongly suspect what Nathan's real job was did not overly concern Mark. Yet, he had made it a point to invite Countess Renate to keep her suspicions to herself. This did not prove to be an issue, as she had demonstrated numerous times in the past when she and *Mossad* had worked together. She introduced individuals without conceding whether they were members of The Shadow Experts or not.

Marcel had organized a conference room at the Bristol, a very nice yet discreet hotel on Rue de Rivoli, a main Paris artery which goes from Rue de Sévigné in the Marais, east of the Hotel de Ville to Place de la Concorde and which runs along the north side of the Louvre and its gardens, the Tuileries. The avenue is well known for its arcades which are found all the way from the Palais Royal to the Place de la Concorde. They provide a covered sidewalk lined with all sorts of shops, from fine clothing or other luxury goods all the way down to touristy knick-knacks. Changes to traffic patterns implemented over the prior several years completely altered the look of one of the greatest avenues in the world. While it used to allow one-way automobile traffic from east to west, the street has been reserved mostly for buses and bicycles from May 2020 onwards. The only positive thing which many old residents might say is that it has lowered the noise level, though a cynic here or there would point to the few additional horn-blowing instances as traffic jams formed near cross streets.

Marcel started with an apology for the much too large size of the room that his assistant had been able to book. He told the group that he originally was hoping that he could find a simple, smaller, and more intimate "salon" or sitting room but was told that he would have had to book a suite and, more to the point, book it for the whole 24 hours. His next choice was between two rooms, the Salon Marigny and the Salon Rambouillet. He concluded:

"Though the Salon Marigny was quite a bit cozier for a group like ours, I didn't like the fact that there was no window. So, I picked this one and asked them to remove extensions to shorten the conference table and place four chairs and a coffee table at the west end of the room."

The Salon Rambouillet is on what the hotel calls the lower lobby, which really means the ground floor. It opens onto the interior garden located between the two buildings, one facing Rue de Rivoli and the other Rue St Honoré, a commercial street parallel to Rue de Rivoli and running from Rue Royale to the Palais Royal and beyond.

Marcel also noted that the light from the garden seemed even more brilliant as the walls were painted in a pearly white color. The furniture, including a wonderful, gilded mirror on the east wall, was in a Louis XV style, and the coral-hued cabriolet chairs contributed to creating a warm and refined space.

After everyone had arrived and sat down in the improvised sitting area, Marcel turned to Mark and invited him to tell the group what his main concerns were. Mark started with sincere thanks to Marcel and Countess Renate and proceeded to give a formal introduction to Nathan Stone, Israel's Vice Consul for Military Affairs in France. Turning to the issue at hand, he explained that he had caught wind of a rumor suggesting that some traffic in nuclear waste might be taking place in the Middle East, most likely somewhere between Iraq and Syria. He was pleased to see Countess Renate smile, indicating that she was totally in the loop. He made the point that Israel had incontrovertible reasons to believe that some nuclear waste had made its way to the region though he asked the small group to forgive him for not going into details. Marcel briefly interrupted:

"Can you confirm that you identified the radioactive material?"

"Yes. Though it was principally caesium 137, there was also some strontium 90."

"Do you have proportions for us?"

"Not yet. Remember, we didn't have a large number of pieces of debris to analyze."

Mark returned to his flow with the idea that there were really two dimensions to his investigation. One part, which would not be a burden for the group assembled in the room, sought to identify whether the sourcing of the radioactive material was regional. Marcel interrupted again:

"Are you thinking of Iran primarily?"

"Yes, sir. In fact, quite frankly, the operative word here is 'primarily.' There are enough nuclear reactors within the Middle East if you extend the region all the way to Pakistan and even India, that pinpointing the source, if it is local, won't be a walk in the park. I should add that we heard someone who might be knowledgeable, emphasis on 'might' by the way, argue that some indigenous waste from the Saddam Hussein area might have resurfaced."

"That would be terrible . . ."

"Couldn't agree with you more, Marcel, but there are so many ifs and buts to this hypothesis that I have temporarily decided to keep it on a back burner. I'll reactivate promptly if anything further suggests it is reasonable."

Mark was smiling and interiorly bemoaning the need for the pious lie he just foisted on the group. Yet, at that point there was not enough proof to breach the national secret which Israel had maintained for many years. Marcel nodded with a smile. Mark concluded his brief exposé:

"I am hoping that with your help Marcel, we might be able to identify whether there might be people in this region who might supply nuclear material to the Middle East."

"A whole series of 'might' I should note."

"Excellent observation, Marcel. That is the unfortunate truth: we don't know as much as we would like to. I also expect that Nathan will be able to provide contacts both within France and throughout Europe."

Marcel was about to intervene, but Mark asked to be allowed to finish his point:

"In fact, our analysis, but you are the expert Marcel so you may disagree, suggests that the likelihood of radioactive material being taken directly from power reactors when spent rods are replaced with new ones is next to zero. The operations are much too supervised, not to mention the fact that they create a major contamination risk and require equipment which anyone would have a tough time smuggling into a power plant, unless you assumed some form of complicity in the personnel at the higher echelons of a nuclear plant. However, we have thought of two potential avenues."

He paused to drink from his glass of sparkling water and concluded:

"We believe that the greatest vulnerabilities are when waste is being transported. For instance, we found out the spent fuel rods are eventually transported to a permanent storage site after they have been removed from the core and been placed into cold water for five years so that they can cool down. Is there a window of opportunity for terrorists there? Another vulnerability which we haven't yet seriously investigated relates to waste produced in small research or operational industry reactors."

Marcel was smiling and said:

"Excellent analysis. Just like you, I can't believe that anyone could steal spent rods when they're taken out of the core. I am not convinced that it would be much easier to grab one or two after they've cooled in water, but I would concede that, to my knowledge and thus still to be verified, that part of the process involves fewer controls. However, I'd have no trouble believing that vials from laboratory reactors might well be the easiest, or rather the least difficult to steal. The only problem is that quantities might be much smaller."

Marcel paused and his demeanor changed as he said:

"The one thing we can't forget my friends is that caesium, for instance, must be separated from the small pellets of spent uranium found in the rods. Again, using the same analogy you did, Mark, it's not a walk in the park. The technology isn't simple, but it is well understood. So, you must all appreciate that this, caesium-137, with or without some strontium 90, must be recovered from a water-based solution into which the pellets have been soaked: they become caesium hydroxide. It requires a decent laboratory, with significant protection for all operators, though the process is relatively quick."

Mark then asked:

"Can you imagine some terrorist organization creating that capacity?"

"Sure. Again, the process is complex but well understood. I should also add that it is costly, principally because of the robust radiation protection that must be put in place. By the way, that is why I am told that the U.S. does not recycle any of their spent fuel. It's easier and cheaper to get new yellowcake uranium and enrich it."

Mark concluded:

"So, it is worth our while to investigate this avenue, but we should not assume that these activities would be carried out by many independent entities."

"Absolutely. If this has been on the radar of terrorist organizations, we have to assume that we don't have too many of them to find, and, I assume, for you or others to eliminate."

Nathan changed the topic and asked:

"Mark, do you have a sense of what can realistically be done without raising all sorts of alarm bells?"

"Not in the detail. But I am hoping that once Marcel has confirmed what is or isn't feasible, we might be able to get together with local secret services and find out whether there is anything that could be of interest."

Nathan asked:

"Any idea?"

Mark replied:

"I think we would need to find some outfit who is stealing spent fuel rods. My intuition tells me that we won't find them on our own. The key question, in my view, is this: are there any rumors which may have been picked up by authorities and not yet acted upon as they were too vague, for instance?"

Countess Renate could not resist interrupting:

"Realistically, Mark, how likely is that?"

"Well, the truth is I don't know. But the massive and largely uncontrolled immigration into Western Europe has led to some unrest in Muslim populations, whether it be in France, in Germany, in the U.K. or in the U.S. among others. It's not terribly hard to assume that 'some agitator' might have seen that as an entry into certain industries."

"Like what?"

"Good question, Countess. Let me stay with our current assumption which could well prove dead wrong. How about having a small cadre of people who are already employed within the waste transportation industry? Imagine that these are not visibly active in the Muslim advocacy movement though they are receptive to its ideas; they could well be young people who have still gone through studies reasonable enough to get the sort of job that would be expected to place them in the right positions."

Mark paused and looked around at his three colleagues and concluded:

"Radicalize them all the while making sure they remain neutral on the outside and you might be able to design a plan allowing you to steal the occasional rod. I could go on with this scenario, but I am sure you all get the point."

Mark paused and after a short while almost as an afterthought added:

"And, by the way, I haven't thought it through sufficiently to go down into the operational details."

Marcel applauded Mark's exposé:

"I can't tell you your scenario is right, but from what I know, it's plausible. In fact, the only two other components you would need are not terribly complex. You would want for that rod, which you have to assume would be incredibly tightly packaged, to be taken to wherever the reprocessing laboratory is. There, the caesium-137 would be extracted, returned to a dry pellet form, and it could readily be delivered to terrorists."

Marcel paused and decided to modify his latest statement somewhat:

"In fact, it could be even simpler. I would start with the same premise: a spent fuel rod is stolen. Rather than taking it to a reprocessing laboratory, I could imagine a simpler sequence. Remember there are around 250 uranium pellets in each single rod. Well, how about collecting the pellets, placing them into some well-protected case and then carrying the case to a reprocessing laboratory."

Mark's face displayed a quizzical look as he asked:

"Not sure I understand why that would be simpler."

"I see the issue. A reprocessing laboratory isn't a place which you improvise. As I said earlier, the process is well understood, somewhat rapid, but still complex. So, you might want to conduct these activities in a place that is more discreet and possibly closer to the location where the waste might be used . . ."

Mark thanked Marcel and offered a couple of concluding thoughts. First, he cautioned his friends that they should not be "wedded" to the scenario that had just been suggested, adding:

"That's one of the dangers we all know about. You become so invested in the image you have of what you're looking for that you may end up missing a minor variation which is there, staring you straight in the eye."

His second thought was a bit more subtle. He noted that however plausible the scenario he had concocted was, it remained orders of magnitude more complicated than imagining that Iran is supplying the radioactive material to terrorists in the Middle East. He concluded:

"We do want to carry out that operation with all the appropriate caution and deliberateness, but we can't forget that there are easier ways for Middle Eastern terrorists to buy radioactive materials before they turn to stealing spent fuel rods."

Marcel interrupted:

"I don't want to steal your thunder, Mark, but there is another source which we have discussed at least once in the past . . ."

Mark suddenly looked more intensely at Marcel who continued:

"Remember, we once talked of all the orphan sources as we called them which were one way, or another abandoned within the Soviet Union when it disintegrated."

"I haven't forgotten, Marcel. But thanks for bringing them up. I've been thinking that one through in my spare time."

He paused and laughed at his own joke and continued:

"Without boring anyone with details that could change in a few days, we need to develop two different pieces of intelligence. First, we should find out whether there exists a list of these places somewhere in Russia. The library of the old KGB would seem like a place to start. The real question is how to proceed? Second, does the solution require someone retrieving the waste or is there a way to destroy it in a remote-controlled manner."

Mark was totally surprised when Countess Renate spoke up and simply said:

"This may be something for us to discuss when you have the time, Mark."

CHAPTER.16

MOSUL AND ERBIL, IRAQ

Meanwhile, three unrelated individuals arrived at Erbil Airport, at various times the same day and from three distinct locations. Nobody needed to know they were all *Mossad* agents on their way to help Josh. Mike Robert, somewhat of a veteran in *Mossad* arrived via Beirut, Lebanon. He had been driven across Israel's northern border and was travelling on a Lebanese passport. In fact, Mike Robert, or more correctly Michel Robert, emigrated from France to Israel over twenty years earlier; that was when he changed his name to Mike in a bid to erase the French connotation. He did not have much to say against the country of his birth other than the fact that antisemitism was already too much for his family, and this despite the fact that they were reformed Jews and not Hasidim. The almost two hours flight on Lebanon's flag carrier, Middle East Airlines, easily recognizable owing to the Lebanese Cedar painted on the red and white tail of the aircraft, had been uneventful. Mike had retained the beard he had grown to carry out a mission in Iran, as he was often called to perform in that part of the Middle East because he was totally fluent in Farsi, though he also spoke Arabic with no accent.

Joseph Asher was quite a bit younger than Mike Robert, by at least ten to fifteen years. He had joined *Mossad* after his normal course of engineering studies, followed by the required stint in the army. Though he was young, he was quite perspicacious and was known for being able to disappear in crowds. Most people indeed would find very few adjectives to describe any aspect of his physique other than "normal" or "average." Joseph had somewhat strong semitic facial traits, which were the norm in that part of the world. This included a beard which seemed to be growing so fast that he would need to shave two if not three times a day to fit the classical "freshly shaven" description. He had recently been stationed in Turkey and lived in either Istanbul or Ankara depending upon where his services were most in demand. He was travelling on the Turkish national carrier and used the Turkish passport which *Mossad* had made for him while on assignment.

Frank Mauser shared more with Joseph than with Mike. He was also quite young for a *Mossad* agent, having only recently joined the agency after commando work in the army. His claim to fame, if one could say it that way, was that he was a redoubtable athlete with a specialty in the triathlon. Thus, one might not expect him to look like an impressive, bulky bodyguard. Rather, he was best described as muscular but lanky, his discreet and hidden strength being all about tenacity, flexibility, and the ability to sustain long efforts with different muscle groups alternatively taking the lead. He had been posted in Damascus six months earlier and provided with a Syrian passport for the occasion. Nobody was thus surprised to learn that he had flown Syrian air.

The three men had followed the instructions which Mark had given. First, they had each rented a car in Erbil and were surprised to discover that alongside Iraqi outfits, several international car rental companies were available. The focus being placed on discretion, they had all chosen Iraqi car rental agencies and had selected vehicles that would not stand out in the local environment. The SUVs which they chose would allow them to follow any vehicle of interest, although Mike reported to Josh on the phone that he was surprised to see a few automobiles that almost belonged to the exotic car range. Josh simply replied:

"People also use cars, even rented cars, to impress around here . . . Similar to Tel Aviv, Dubai or Cannes."

Josh had indicated that it would be best if they did not stay in the same hotel, for obvious reasons. Unfortunately, with only two hotels close enough to each other and in a suitable area of the city, Mike booked himself into the Modern Plaza International, while Joseph and Frank had to choose the Royal City Hotel. They each walked to the address Josh had given them: a shophouse he rented in a strip mall, five blocks north of University Highway, near the eastern border of Al Shurta, a major neighborhood in the center of Mosul. Josh had indeed suggested that they should avoid driving to the shop, unless they knew they would need a car just afterwards. Parking spots were at a premium, though they would find out over the time they were to stay in Mosul that it was not as hard to find a place to park as in Tel Aviv, Istanbul or Damascus.

Though the shophouse was small and comprised only two rooms, one in front and the other in the back, Josh had elected to keep the lease he had taken for another mission. After all, he viewed it as a cheap and conveniently "local" place where he could meet people he did not want to see in a public place and to whom he did not want to give his real address. Josh had slightly changed the layout of the back room, initially not more than a large storage space. He had transformed it into a sitting room, with four armchairs, a tribal rug on the floor and a couple of coffee tables, one between each pair of chairs on the right and on the left. The so-called lavatory had been improved and offered both hot and cold water in the shower that was there. Finally, he had also added a small fridge and a microwave oven, which would allow anyone that needed it to heat up something to eat. Though there were no formal sleeping facilities, Josh had stored four inflatable mattresses, just in case they were needed.

Josh had given specific instructions to the three agents. Principally, he had advised them to avoid arriving at the same time, or even close to one another. Since they all had smartphones connected to the internet via SpaceX's Starlink satellite, they could be in constant contact with one another, using ear buds; they had selected *Mossad* standard issue buds, which were black rather than the usual white, as the black of the buds was more discreet than white against their black facial hair. Even a careful observer could not have noticed that they did not have one, but two phones and that each was connected to only one of the earbuds. This allowed them to remain accessible at all times. Josh had also advised them to alternate between the front and the back door as an entry point into the shophouse. Joseph and Frank were to use the back door that opened onto an alley; this was the way all the shophouses would use to bring in new goods into the shops. Mike on the other hand would be using the front door.

■ ■ ■ ■ ■

Once all together in the shophouse, the four men discussed the mission. Their most important topic was to coordinate their actions as Josh told them he would meet Ibrahim and Rezna a short while later at Al Shatee for *mezze* for three. Josh concluded his short exposé: "Well guys, we don't have much time. Let's get going."

■ ■ ■ ■ ■

Mike had been designated as the one agent who would be first to arrive at the restaurant. He backed his car into one of the many spots available, choosing one which would allow him the best view of all the cars in the parking lot. He stayed in his car for the first few minutes and then stepped out. He walked in the opposite direction of the road that ran in front of the restaurant, getting closer to the beach alongside the river. From there he could see the northern tip of the northernmost of the two islands in the middle of the river, with the Al-Jazeera Recreational Park closest to him. He noted that another car had just driven into the parking lot and proceeded immediately to return to his own vehicle calmly and with no undue hurry. Once there, he started his engine and drove away.

The other car was driven by none other than Joseph. His mission was to see whether any car that might have been parked in the area would leave and seem to be following Mike. He was surprised when he saw a white sedan start its engine and drive toward the exit. He immediately called on his smartphone, being instantly connected to all four *Mossad* agents:

"We may have a customer . . ."

Frank replied:

"I see him. I'm parked about one hundred yards from the exit of your parking lot. He has to keep driving south because of the divider in the middle of the highway. In fact, he will have to drive a bit more than a mile before he can even think of changing direction, unless he drives into one of the side streets, but even there he won't be able to drive northward."

He paused to make sure he had the right directions on his GPS and added:

"Mike, when you get to the roundabout, take the third exit. It's a smaller street, but it's the one that makes it easier for you to return to the restaurant. We'll see what the guy that may be following you does . . . I'll follow the two of you for a while. In the interim, Joseph, keep watch at the restaurant as Josh should be arriving in the next few minutes."

Josh confirmed to his troops that he was indeed less than a mile away. Mike followed Frank's instructions and took the third exit at the roundabout. Both he and Frank were surprised but relieved when they saw the car that had appeared to tail Mike take the second exit. Presumably, it would be driving south, possibly toward the old town, another mile down the road, on the other side of the river. Mike and Frank followed the small road inside Mosul Forest Park, had to make a sharp left a couple of times, and about three miles later found themselves going north on the highway they had taken going south a short while back. They turned north and drove to the next roundabout and returned to the parking lot of the Al Shatee restaurant.

Meanwhile, Josh had arrived at the restaurant. Joseph had followed the same routine as Mike before him, leaving the parking lot to give Josh an opportunity to see if someone was there to check on him. Josh felt relieved as no car seemed to be moving. He parked his car, got out and walked calmly to the restaurant. In the meantime, Mike and Frank were back in the parking lot and would soon be followed by Joseph after he had followed the same circuit as his colleagues through Mosul Forest Park. Five minutes before the time when they were due to meet Josh, aka Abu Musa, another car, with Ibrahim and someone next to him in the backseat drove into the parking lot. It went as far as it could toward the entrance to the restaurant to leave as little walking distance as possible for its two passengers to walk to the front door. The driver opened Ibrahim's door for him and closed it after he had gotten out. The passenger on the other side had to fend for himself. The driver then took the car into the parking lot and found a spot which gave him as much shade as possible. Mike was smiling when he saw the end of the ballet thinking: *the trees and bushes that provide shade for him will also hide me as I get close to the car and place a bug on its rear fender.*

■ ■ ■ ■ ■

Josh had chosen a quiet area with three seats and taken the liberty of ordering *mezze* for three. Ibrahim was all smiles when he approached the table. Ibrahim introduced Rezna by his name but did not spend any time offering any additional details on his role within Ibrahim's organization. Josh noted that Rezna appeared young enough to be Ibrahim's son, but did not take the thought any further. After all, the people he had met when he had last dealt with Ibrahim also included quite a few younger-looking individuals. The way Ibrahim had introduced Rezna led Josh to feel that questions on the role Rezna played within Ibrahim's organization would probably not be welcome. He made a mental note of it and wondered why Ibrahim seemed so protective of his employee.

Ibrahim asked Abu Musa to introduce himself and eventually invited him to speak to what Ibrahim called "his way or earning his living." Josh was quite straightforward as he simply said:

"Rezna, I want to be sure you appreciate that my job is to provide information to parties which feel they couldn't get the same level or detail of knowledge on their own. I'm dedicated to serving what I might call worthy causes and thus wouldn't offer my services to anyone who might seem like he would be endangering peace."

He paused and noted that Ibrahim's eyelids were telling him that he was doing just fine. Turning back toward Rezna, he added:

"I'm currently interested in a rumor which has been circulating in the region . . ."

Rezna asked:

"Rumor?"

"Yes. I have no facts and thus can't corroborate anything. Yet, at this point I have heard that there may an incipient traffic in nuclear waste."

Rezna interrupted all the while briefly turning his eyes to Ibrahim although he almost immediately shifted back to Abu Musa:

"I think I know where that comes from."

Seeing no obvious objection on the part of Ibrahim, he continued:

"It may be something, but it may also be a big nothing. I ran into an acquaintance of mine who introduced me to a man who asked me if I knew anything about nuclear waste. I naturally replied that I didn't and simply asked what he had heard. He quickly shifted the conversation to some other topic and that's the whole lot."

Though a bit disappointed, Josh had to concede that this was exactly what Ibrahim had told him, at least the second time they discussed the issue. He still wanted to try and take the conversation further and asked:

"Rezna, do you feel it would be possible for you to introduce me to the man you met through your acquaintance?"

Josh was surprised when he noted that Rezna was turning to Ibrahim first, before even attempting to reply. He kept thinking: *what in the world does that mean*? His surprise was further reinforced when Ibrahim rather than Rezna provided the answer:

"I'm not sure he would agree to meet you. Don't you think, Rezna?"

Rezna took this as his permission to speak:

"Truth is that I can't really say that I know the man. I do know the fellow who introduced us to each other. I met him first in social circumstances, and, for some reason, have kept in touch. The other man simply seemed quite nice, and we have spoken a couple of times since I met him. I think he is of Arab descent, and he knows I'm Kurdish . . ."

Josh kept asking:

"Could you coach me so that I ask the right questions. He doesn't need to know what I do for a living. I could be a journalist . . ."

Ibrahim smiled and simply said:

"Not sure that would be a lot better my friend."

CHAPTER.17

TEL AVIV, ISRAEL; LONDON, U.K.; FRANCE
AND SOMEWHERE IN THE AUSTRIAN ALPS

Following up on her earlier invitation, Mark called Countess Renate:

"Hello Countess. You said we should talk about the question of these 'orphan sources' in the old Soviet Union. What's up?"

"Ah, dear Mark. Glad to hear your voice. Yes, I remember giving you that message. I must warn you; it's a bit of a long and partially sad story . . .

"I hope it finishes well enough . . ."

∎ ∎ ∎ ∎ ∎

The countess started her story. She talked of a man who had worked for the KGB when the Soviet Union still existed. He was the insider's insider. He knew a lot of people and was liked by many. He never seemed to want to draw anyone into any of his plans, but people did not resent his solitary behavior; he did not lean on anyone and yet was willing to give credit whenever credit was due. Nobody ever managed to get him to break a Soviet secret. He never discussed orders that came from on high; he had a job to do and would obey the orders he was receiving. Yet he was quite personable and one of the first individuals to come to the help of any fellow worker who needed any form of assistance. To many, he seemed like a good man and a first-class employee.

When the KGB was dissolved and the Federal Security Service of the Russian Federation was created as the *de facto* successor to the old KGB, the man was naturally invited to join the new agency. He was happy to accept. He kept rising in the ranks until he was entrusted with the unpleasant job of eliminating dissidents. His faith in the regime remained for a while and, though he did not like what he was doing, he kept his feelings to himself and did what he was asked to do. *After all this was for the benefit of the regime*, he thought.

Eventually, he was asked to eliminate a very prominent dissident, Yuri Zakariov. He did not know much about the man and accepted the mission as was his wont. In the briefing, the man received from his superior, Yuri had been described as a traitor and somewhat of a solitary individual. The man was told that he had no known family, as his parents had already died of natural causes, and nobody was really sure whether Yuri was even interested in women.

After having prepared how he would act, the man followed Yuri during one of his many trips abroad. Yuri initially stopped in London and was due, afterwards, to spend a short week on the French Riviera, near Eze close to the border between France and Monaco. The man, whose KGB code name was Gregory, found a way to slip a polonium-210 pill in the teapot that was being carried to the terrace penthouse of the Dorchester hotel in London, on the last day Yuri was due to be in town. The ultimate in terms of luxury in London, at least according to Dorchester literature, the suite offered lofty ceilings and substantial space, including the terrace from which one could admire the town with Hype Park in the foreground and further south Green Park and Buckingham Palace. To be sure that Yuri had ingested the poison and that the poison did its trick, inducing an acute radiation syndrome, Gregory followed him as he left London and flew to the Nice Cote D'Azur airport, the second busiest airport in France, after Paris and its three different venues.

Countess Renate kept going with the story saying that Gregory had managed to organize a corporate jet charter flight at the last minute, substantially overpaying for it, but money was no object. His bosses did not ask "how much" but rather "did you do it?" He could not get a landing spot in Nice but flew into Cannes Mandelieu, a general aviation airport not more than thirty miles west of Nice. From there, he had booked a helicopter to take him to the Maybourne Riviera complex, on Route de la Turbie just above Rocquebrune Cap-Martin, where he knew Yuri had booked a suite for himself and another for his security detail. She added:

"By the way, I am told that place is something really special. A modern building, planted at the top of a cliff, with floor to ceiling windows in most rooms and with glass balconies. When looking to the sea, there is nothing but water to be seen in the distance; when facing the mountains, you can follow the winding mountain road from the top to the bottom of the cliff."

With a wide smile, she added:

"You shouldn't book a room there if you have any fear of heights . . ."

Back to her story, she explained that Gregory's world suddenly appeared to self-destruct. As he was waiting for the polonium symptoms to appear in Yuri and thus for him to die, he discovered that contrary to what he had been told, a woman and a young girl were with him at the Maybourne Riviera. A couple of enquiries later, he had learned that they were his wife and daughter. That his bosses would have so blatantly lied to him led him to decide to leave the agency then and there. Naturally, as Countess Renate explained, this was much easier said than done. One does not defect from the KGB or its successor agency and live happily ever after to tell the story. Trying to do so is equivalent to committing suicide with the assistance of the Russian secret services. Gregory therefore knew that leaving the agency meant that he would have to die, or at least to appear to die in a credible enough manner that there would be no effort to look for him and thus he would not be traced.

Countess Renate went on to describe the elaborate set up he created to "get killed" on the very road where the hotel was. The road is narrow and has very tight curves, not to mention the many switchbacks. He therefore decided that he would have a car accident. He parked his car in one of the tourist lookouts, a small promontory right by the side of the road, overlooking what was a deep plunge into the sea, nearly five-hundred feet down if not more. He retrieved the electric bicycle which he had folded into the rear seat of his first rental car and cycled down the road until he reached Rocquebrune Cap-Martin where he knew he would find a Sixt rental car agency. Though certainly more expensive than a few others, he knew Sixt specialized in premium German vehicles. He wanted to have a Mercedes G-Class executive SUV, which he chose both because it would be powerful and rugged enough to help him conduct his plan and because Sixt guarantees that one will get that car if it has been reserved.

He booked the car under a different name, which was not difficult as he was always given at least a couple of additional passports to execute his missions. He stopped by a hardware store where he bought a couple of Jerrycans, which he would eventually fill up with gasoline. He also stopped by an electronics store to buy a couple of electric connectors which he would use on the remote-controlled detonators he would need to activate. Finally, he purchased from two different hardware shops the explosives and related paraphernalia he needed to create a small bomb. He took the car back up to the place where he had parked his other rental and waited for dusk to turn to night. That would both provide some cover of darkness for him and make any rescue operation probably slower to be organized.

His first step was to take his first car up and down the road ahead of the parking lot from where he had left it. He was careful to brake quite hard just short of the edge of the cliff a couple of times to be sure that there would be a few tire traces on the road suggesting the driver of the car involved in the accident had tried to stop or at least slow down. Was he going too fast? Had he lost control of the car? Those were questions that he was sure that the police would have to answer later on. It reminded him of the sad story of Princess Grace of Monaco who had died on that road many years earlier. He then positioned the car in a way that was consistent with the tire traces he had made; the hood pointed in the right direction and was already slightly protruding over the side of the mountain. After having liberally doused the car with the gasoline in the two jerrycans, he forced the first car over the edge with the front-end of the Mercedes G-Class applied to its rear bumper; the squarish shape of the Mercedes was exactly what the doctor ordered. He had been careful to align the cars well so that there was no trace of impact on the back of the car that went over the cliff. As soon as that car started to fall at least 500 feet, he triggered the first detonator. It set the inside of the car on fire.

The place he had chosen for the accident would not cause the car to fall all the way down to the water below. If everything worked the way he had designed it, the car's fall should temporarily be interrupted by a small, rocky ledge protruding from the mountain a couple of hundred feet below. Ideally, the falling car would briefly stop for a fraction of a second, bounce and keep falling. At that point he would trigger the second detonator which would blow the car up, throw it into the sea below and, in the process, hopefully set on fire the dry pine trees and bushes on the side of the mountain, a classic but frequent fire hazard in the southeast of France. This would ensure that rescue workers would initially work to get the fire under control, to make sure it did not spread to homes nearby. The story does not tell whether there was or was not a strong wind on that night, but history has proven that a small sparkle in the dry pine trees can trigger a massive fire if the famous Mistral, the strong west to east local wind, is blowing. Anyway, Gregory had figured that rescuers would eventually get to the car, but a couple of hours at least would have elapsed. Additionally, he expected the police to assume that no one could have survived such a fall and would therefore delay a search and retrieve operation until the next morning. Further the explosion would have thrown the body out of the car, though he conceded that there was always a risk that the safety belt would have maintained it on the front seat. Would the police even look for the body of the driver since they would surely not find anything inside whatever was left of the car?

With the 'accident' behind him, Gregory immediately drove the Mercedes G-Class executive SUV to Switzerland. He initially used the A8 which followed the Mediterranean coast to reach Genoa in Italy. There, he veered northward, drove through the Ossola Valley and its major city, Domodossola, the main town at the Swiss Italian border. From there, he went through the Simplon Pass, a high alpine pass leading from Domodossola to Brig in Switzerland. He had no difficulty at the border showing one of his Russian-made passports. From Brig, he took the E62 autoroute west toward Martigny and then Montreux and took the divided highway on the northern bank of Lake Leman and followed it westward until he reached Geneva. There, he had already booked himself into a discreet cosmetic surgery clinic which would ensure that his looks would be sufficiently different that he would not have to risk being recognized, unless one already had other reasons to have serious doubts as to his identity. With no known family, as he had never been married and had lost parents and brothers to the revolution, nobody would miss him, and nobody would be surprised by the change in appearance. With a completely new identity, he could hope that he would be left alone by the Russian secret services.

Mark could only say:

"Wow. I can pick up a few loose ends here and there in the story, but I have to admit that the guy seems to have thought the whole thing through quite well. Anyway, even the few questions that creep into my mind probably reflect the fact that you cut a few corners just to keep the story from ballooning into a novel!"

"Absolutely. I know for instance that he didn't enjoy being an executioner and had much earlier moved some of his money overseas without attracting too much attention. By the way, that wouldn't have been hard for him to do, as secret service personnel in Russia often get bonuses and other payments abroad, quite frankly in so-called tax havens."

She paused for a second and added:

"He also told me that he had started the work to create the papers for a fake identity which he had decided he might one day take. I guess the official lie about the marital status of Yuri was just the drop that got the vase to overflow."

"I assume that Yuri did die, right?"

"Unfortunately, yes. It was widely covered by the western press. If memory serves me right, it was the first time that someone was able to suggest that the Russian secret services used Polonium. But there would be others afterwards, ironically even again in London. However, as Yuri's death didn't occur until weeks after he ingested the polonium, any of the cups or dishes, which might have retained some sign of the contamination in London, had more than once gone through the hotel's dishwashers."

Mark asked:

"Now, how did you meet Gregory, Countess?"

"He was introduced to me by someone he had helped and who coincidentally knew me. Don't ask me how he had met that other gentleman, but Vlad Rheingold, Gregory's new name, told me he had managed to help him get information."

She went on to explain that Vlad never revealed to anyone in Russia, even the co-workers to whom he was close, his real identity. Nobody there ever found out that Vlad and Gregory were one and the same person. He still managed to call on the goodwill which Gregory had accumulated, because he, as Vlad, claimed to be an old acquaintance of Gregory's. He said to me that he concocted a story that he, Vlad, learned of Gregory's accident while staying on the French Riviera. Vlad said Gregory was on the phone with him when the accident occurred. Vlad then said that he had raced to the Maybourne Riviera hotel where Gregory also had booked a room for himself. He told various people that he had been able to go through Gregory's affairs in the hotel after the accident. Vlad would tell Gregory's contacts that he had been a good friend of Gregory's and that he had found the names and telephone numbers of a few of his agency contacts there. He said he always added that he had been at pain to first decipher the code Gregory had used to encrypt all classified information and thus was never sure he was contacting the right person. Though a few people initially had doubts and would eschew helping Vlad, many at Moscow headquarters who had liked Gregory very much, eventually adopted Vlad. Countess Renate concluded:

"At any rate, provided he does not ask things that are too crazy, Vlad believes he can get a lot from the archives of the KGB which were taken over by the FSS."

Mark exclaimed:

"So, you believe that we could get a list of these outposts through Vlad, right?"

"Well, nobody can be sure of anything, Mark. But there is at least one perfectly plausible scenario which one could use to ask for Vlad's help . . ."

"Really?"

"Absolutely. Imagine. A western student might be interested in how Russian authorities communicated with remote provinces. He might have heard that there were a number of them and might be prepared to pay a fee to get to look at either a list or a map of these locations."

"Brilliant Countess. You're assuming that we could surely 'create a student' who would need that information for his or her thesis. So that student would be willing to pay a fee, which I am sure would be requested by Vlad. Knowing how you always operate, Countess, the compensation of The Shadow Experts would be an entirely different matter as per our usual agreements."

"Thanks for your confidence, my friend. So, game?"

CHAPTER.18

MOSUL AND ERBIL, IRAQ

Back in Mosul, Ibrahim and Rezna were about to leave Josh after their pleasant *mezze* lunch. Josh had instructed his three associates to conduct a careful trail of the car in which Ibrahim and his man travelled. They were told that their primary goal was to find out where Rezna lived, as this would eventually allow Josh to learn more about him. Josh had been very clear that he was not interested in finding out where Ibrahim lived, as he knew how to contact him any time he wished, plus he was well aware of the fact that he had more than one place of residence.

The three *Mossad* associates positioned themselves so that one car would be within a short distance from Ibrahim's car, while the other two would travel further back, out of sight. Every ten miles or so, the car that was closest to Ibrahim' car would drop back after having called out to his associates on their four-way internet phone connection. Whoever was supposed to take over would accelerate and take his position a half mile or so behind Ibrahim's car.

The convoy first drove southward, which did not surprise anyone, as the divided street in front of Al Shatee restaurant did not allow any turn to the north. About three miles on, Ibrahim's car veered off to the left taking University Parkway. They were quietly driving through town, passing first under Highway 80. Less than two miles further the car took the first ramp on the right side, effectively joining Highway 2. Josh was immediately interested, though not surprised, when Mike, who was following five hundred yards behind Ibrahim's car, told him about the move:

"Highway 2 is sometimes called the Mosul-Erbil highway, and I know that this is where Ibrahim has some sort of base. After all, it's not that surprising that Rezna should live in the same general area, though I wonder whether Ibrahim will drop him off before getting to the house which he has near the citadel."

He paused and added:

"Joseph, why don't you drive now straight to the Erbil Citadel. After you pass through the main gate, look for the first spot on your left where you can park your car. Then get out of the car and keep a discreet watch over what we know to be one of Ibrahim's houses—I'll send you the coordinates by SMS. I am looking forward to knowing whether Rezna is still with him then and if he is what he does. I would expect him either to have been dropped off beforehand or to have a car or moped in the immediate vicinity of Ibrahim's place so that he can get himself to his home. Hopefully, whoever is right behind Ibrahim's car can then follow Rezna if he is still with Ibrahim. If necessary, jump in the car with your associate and follow him."

Ibrahim's car remained on Highway 2, and drove over the Khost River, which joins the Tigris River only a couple of miles later. Barely another mile further on, the car reached another overpass, which looked at the time to be a major roadwork site. Ostensibly, the plan for the city must have been to extend Highway 2 further south, though it would have to change its name, because Highway 2 then made a 90 degree turn to the left. The bug which Mike had placed on Ibrahim's car made it easier for him to follow from afar. That's how he realized quickly without being right behind him that Ibrahim would in fact stay on Highway 2. In many ways, he thanked his good star, knowing that Ibrahim could not have picked up the fact that someone was following him.

This was the time when Frank chose to pass Mike and be the closest one to Ibrahim. They kept driving between what looked like small villages and a large number of small fields. Frank caught himself pitying the fact that farmers must be having a real tough time at their jobs: the ground was a very light shade of brown, indicating a high sand concentration The few fields which looked cultivated also did not have much greenery, while the most significant element had to be the general lack of trees. Yet about twelve miles on, just before reaching the University of Al-Hamdaniya on the left-hand side of the highway, the landscape changed a bit. The general color palette did not become dramatically different, though two things struck the men. First, what had appeared a continuous construction site rather than farmland on either side of the highway became more clearly dedicated to real agriculture. Second, trees became more prevalent, either as decoration around the homes the men could see from the highway or more frequently as hedges around fields. Further on, as they drove past Hassan Shami, they crossed the Nahr Al Khazir river; this gave them a quick chance to see how people congregated around rivers where they would find it easier to water their crops.

Josh asked on the four-way phone:

"Still no indication that Ibrahim is near to dropping Rezna?"

Joseph replied:

"None. Let me try something, Mike, can you drive closer to me. I'll then pass Ibrahim and as I do, I'll check whether there are still two passengers in the car. I can't see how he might have dropped Rezna off without any one of us picking it up, but it would be stupid for us to keep going if we had missed a drop off . . ."

Mike replied:

"Excellent idea. Let me accelerate ten miles over our current speed. You should be able to turn left at the entrance of Aski Kalat, at the Safran Gas Station, go around three blocks and get back onto the highway just after you pass by the Quran Mosque. By then, you'll be no more than a couple of miles behind me."

Josh noted:

"What that tells me is that you guys are about twenty miles from the Erbil Citadel. I wonder what that means . . . Is Rezna living in Erbil too?"

Mike offered:

"You know, I heard you talk to Frank earlier. Why don't we simply assume that Rezna drove a car or rode a moped to Ibrahim's place in Erbil. The ride from there to Mosul would have given them plenty of time to make sure they were on the same page."

Josh replied:

"I know this makes sense. But I wonder why Ibrahim is staying involved. I can't believe he would get his fingers in that mess. He almost said it himself as he recoiled when I started talking about nuclear waste. So, what does he expect to achieve?"

Mike deadpanned:

"Protecting one of his lieutenants?"

Josh could only say:

"An interesting thought. Yet, if true, it means he knows more than what he has told us. Message to all: let's keep our antennae up!"

■ ■ ■ ■ ■

Meanwhile, Frank had found the place he was looking for. His first waypoint was the statue of Ibn Al Mistawfi, which guards the entrance to the Erbil Citadel. He had taken one of the circular roads, interestingly called the 60 Meters Street, turned left into Halabja Street leaving Aqua Park and Shanadar Park to his right. That's when he found the statue, at the tip of Minara Park. He took Ayubi Street which goes around the citadel and, right after reaching the Shrine of Sultan Musthafar Kawkabri, he made a sharp left and then a sharp right and found the parking lot Josh had mentioned to him. He dropped the car near the Hawler Governorate and, walking back toward Qalat, the last circular road around the citadel, he had no difficulty finding the house which Josh had indicated belonged to Ibrahim, near a leafy square. He sat on one of the several benches provided for tourists and waited for further instructions or Ibrahim's car to arrive, whichever came first.

■ ■ ■ ■ ■

Back on the Mosul-Erbil Highway, Joseph, and Mike, and by telephone Josh, were getting increasingly frustrated. Ibrahim's car was showing no sign that it was going to stop. He arrived close to what the group knew was Ibrahim's house but actually reached it via a different route than Frank. Rather than coming from the southwest of the citadel, they came from the north. As such, Frank could see the car coming right toward him, though it turned right into the street running in front of the square where he was sitting. He saw Ibrahim and Rezna get out of the car and enter the house which he had correctly assumed was Ibrahim's. He called Josh when he saw the main door close after Rezna had entered:

"They're both in the house. Rezna looked quite subordinated as he let Ibrahim go in first and then closed the door behind them."

Josh could only say:

"Let me suggest that a couple of you stay there. I know there is a hotel around the corner, so feel free to book a room and take turns to watch what is happening. I can't believe that in Kurdish culture Ibrahim would allow or even invite a subordinate to spend the night in his house."

He paused and almost hypothetically said:

"I hope they didn't pick any of you up. I'm going to call him tomorrow morning to see if I can meet with Rezna again."

■ ■ ■ ■ ■

Countess Renate called Mark on a video conference line with some good news:

"My contact, Vlad Rheingold, has agreed to help us."

"Excellent news indeed. What do we have to do?"

Countess Renate replied that the issue of the fee would not really be material, adding:

"In fact, The Shadow Experts are prepared to pay it as a part of our service to you. The real issue which Vlad pointed out is the amount of time the process could take."

"Did he give you an estimate?"

Renate told Mark that Vlad did not think that providing an estimate made much sense. She said that he argued that the number of these outposts was probably quite large, and he needed first to find out whether a list of them actually existed. She said he added:

"Normal operating procedures within the old KGB would typically require such a list to be provided by each of the regions. With the exception of of Russia, which was subdivided into several regions itself, all the individual Soviet republics comprised at least one region."

Mark asked:

"Does this mean that no centralized list of outposts exists?"

"Vlad was not sure, though he kept harping back to the same theme. The Soviet Regime tracked virtually everything. Thus, lists must exist, but the question is whether they were compiled into a single overall list or left within regional reporting documents."

"Does this mean that we will need to wait until he can find out whether a single list exists?"

"Don't think so. He said that he would start a few inquiries, based on our original story of a student thesis trying to review how a country with eleven time zones could keep effective communications."

Renate paused and asked:

"By the way, how bad would it be if we could only procure a few of the lists rather than a complete one? I know for a fact that people believe that the KGB was divided into twenty directorates. Yet, Vlad told me that the West only has some idea of what eight of them did . . ."

"Why?"

"That's all they could get from defectors. In fact, he added that he himself wouldn't be able to list the function of all the directorate. Interestingly, he added a wry comment to the effect that the agency was the place which respected the most the concept of 'need-to-know' when it came to revealing any information."

Mark appeared visibly disappointed. Renate immediately noted his demeanor in the tone of his voice and added:

"Don't worry, Mark. I'm sure we will get useful information. After all, you were not planning to attack all of these locations, right?"

"Correct. But still I was hoping that we could initiate a project to go after as many of them as we could. Not to mention the obvious: each of them is a possible source of nuclear waste. Someone is bound to realize this eventually if it hasn't already been done!"

CHAPTER.19

MOSUL AND ERBIL, IRAQ

Back in Mosul, Ibrahim was frankly not surprised when his phone rang. He had been ready to bet that Abu Musa would be calling him. After all, the meeting between Abu Musa and Rezna had gone reasonably well. Yet, Ibrahim could clearly see that very minimal incremental information had been imparted. Abu Musa would surely be trying to learn more.

"Abu Musa, what a pleasure to hear your voice."

"Yours as well, my friend. I suspect you know why I am calling you?"

"I'd be lying if I told you I had no idea, but I would still prefer to hear it from your own mouth . . ."

Josh immediately thought: *Playing it close to the vest. Not a surprise. Very much par for the course.* He replied:

"I would love to have another meeting with Rezna."

"That's exactly what I would have guessed. May I ask what you would like to achieve?"

Josh's mind was running at top speed. On the one hand, he totally understood Ibrahim's *modus operandi*: he was true to himself, trying to get Josh to show his hand before he offered anything. On the other, he could not understand why Ibrahim was remaining so invested in an issue which seemed not to be of primary concern to him: *why is he protecting Rezna? Is he a key close associate? Yet, he seems much too young to be a leader of the Kurdish Resistance?* Remembering that beggars cannot be choosers, Josh had to say:

"I am not sure whether I need much more from him or simply an introduction to his friend's acquaintance, you know, whoever asked the question which piqued your interest and mine."

Ibrahim did not immediately reply. He also felt that they were not going over terribly new territory. They had indeed already talked of some desire on Abu Musa's part to meet Rezna's so-called contact. Yet, he had to concede in his mind that the question had never been as formally asked as Abu Musa just had. He could not duck replying with something tangible. His answer was predictable:

"I am happy to facilitate another meeting, but I doubt very much that Rezna would take the risk of opening up that much. Not sure I would if I were in his shoes."

Josh felt he had to ask:

"Is this because he wouldn't want to or because you wouldn't let him?"

"What do you mean, my friend?"

"Nothing untoward. As the boss, I can easily understand that you want to protect your people. So, I wouldn't be surprised to find out that you don't want Rezna to be found in any sort of compromising situation. After all, for all I know you may already disapprove of him having been involved, however peripherally."

Josh could imagine Ibrahim smiling as his voice changed a bit as he replied:

"Very perceptive as usual, my friend."

Ibrahim stopped right there and seemed to be waiting for a reaction from Abu Musa. Josh was disappointed that Ibrahim did not keep going. However, he had steeled himself for a scenario like the one that was playing out as he offered:

"If you remember, dear Ibrahim, we once met in a situation where I couldn't tell who you were[7]. Could you imagine something similar?"

Ibrahim did not reply immediately. Josh assumed that he was thinking things through and was mildly surprised that he did not seem to have anticipated the comment. Ibrahim quickly proved him wrong as he replied:

"Rezna and I have been discussing something along these lines. I surely do not object to him having gotten ahold of the rumor; he did exactly what I would have done. The problem isn't so much with Rezna's contact meeting you, but with Rezna finding a good reason to introduce you to his friend's contact."

Josh had anticipated that turn of events. He suggested that he could be introduced as someone who has expressed interest in nuclear waste issues. He added:

"How about this? Rezna calls his contact and reminds him if necessary that they had talked about nuclear waste briefly. He adds that he really didn't have much to say then as he truthfully didn't know anything."

"I think I see where you're going Abu Musa, and this might work. Please finish your thought"

"Thanks. Rezna then tells his contact that someone else has asked him quite a similar question. He naturally asks whether the contact would like to meet that someone . . ."

Ibrahim was smiling as he replied:

"That's what I thought you were getting at. I don't want to promise anything, but it might be worth a shot. Personally, trying to put myself in the shoes of Rezna's contact, I would want to meet you. So why would he turn the offer down? The next question would have

---

[7] By the same author, see *Glitter and Smoke*, Barringer Publishing, 2023.

to be whether I would like to meet you in the open or in a setting where you couldn't see me . . ."

Josh acknowledged the point and asked:

"One final thought, Ibrahim. Though I would prefer a face-to-face meeting, even if some disguise is required one way or another, we could have an initial conversation by phone . . ."

"Let me chew over that one. I'll get back to you within the next twenty-four hours."

After he had thanked Ibrahim and hung up, Josh was still wondering what game his friend was playing. What was the story with respect to Rezna? Could he simply be a face in the crowd Ibrahim picked up to disguise the fact that it was he, Ibrahim, who had had the original contact with the fellow interested in nuclear waste?

■ ■ ■ ■ ■

Less than a week later, Josh was again in the company of Rezna and Ibrahim. The "official" motive for the meeting was for Abu Musa to explain to Rezna the scenario which he and Ibrahim had concocted earlier. Josh was still somewhat at a loss understanding why Ibrahim insisted on remaining in the picture and had simply concluded that it had to reflect the fact that Rezna, though younger than one might have expected for such a job, was a key element in the structure headed by Ibrahim. He had taken the thought to a deeper level when he had shared with Mark Levi on the telephone that he suspected that Rezna had been approached by whomever it was not in a random manner but precisely because he was perceived as quite close to Ibrahim. Said differently, in his words:

"The other individual reached out to Rezna because he couldn't get access to Ibrahim by himself or didn't want to come out into the open in front of such a powerful Kurd leader."

Josh had further concluded that he should stop worrying about Ibrahim's real role and thus play the cards he had been dealt. Yet, he had certainly decided that he should be more guarded than ever when dealing with Ibrahim, thinking *he might be a friend, but he is a friend that has secrets. However, after all, it's the same for me: I have secrets for Ibrahim. Nothing dramatic, but secrets can mean surprises. Being on my guard is the best way to avoid unpleasant surprises.*

Rezna, still visibly deferring to Ibrahim, eventually agreed to play a role in the scenario which Josh shared with him. The story said that Abu Musa had been approached by someone who asked him a question which appeared eerily similar to that which the other man, whose name turned out to be Abdullah, had asked Rezna. This time, Rezna decided to contact Abdullah to see whether there would be any interest on his part meeting with Abu Musa, who asked his name to be Ahmed for the occasion. Again, Josh, aka Abu Musa, aka Ahmed could not help but note how Rezna would not agree to any step without first seeking Ibrahim's concurrence.

The meeting between Ahmed and Abdullah was set to take place in Mosul, largely because it was there that Rezna had originally met Abdullah himself. They agreed on a place in the open, right next to the Mosul Cultural Museum, which was almost totally rebuilt after ISIS destroyed it when they took over Mosul in 2014. They finally decided on the Al-Shuhada Park which, together with the Al-Baladia Square, form an oasis of greenery around the Cultural Museum. Also called Martyrs Park, Al-Shuhada offers a wheel-like rotunda in the middle of a large rectangle. The men decided that they could initially meet near the entrance to the park at its southwest corner and proceed toward the center. There they could either walk slowly around the circle or sit on one of the many benches provided.

Ahmed, aka Abu Musa stood out among the people around the entrance as he was taller than virtually everyone, standing a good six foot two inches tall. He had not elected to wear any significant disguise, except for a pair of glasses, whose lenses adapted to the light conditions: they turned darker when he was in the sun and became clearer when he was in the shade or inside a building. He thought that this would be more discreet and in fact seemingly more forthcoming than wearing classical sunglasses; those could be interpreted as an attempt to hide his eyes. The glasses had a couple of undisclosed features which would allow him to record both the conversation and the images of the meeting. Sounds and pictures would both be stored in two memory chips, each inserted in one of the two temples, the arms that hold the glasses in place. He was dressed traditionally, wearing a grey keffiyeh headdress kept in place with an agal, a dark head band. He had a deep brown robe over a lighter brown tunic.

As Rezna introduced Abdullah who had approached from across the street, Josh noted that there was little he could point to that would differentiate him from most of the people around them. His dress was equally traditional while his robe was in light greenish grey. He was definitely shorter than Josh, but the same height as Rezna, one or two inches short of six feet. The three men wore heavy, dark beards and seemed to be in the same general age group, though Josh was probably a few years older. Abdullah started the conversation with the obvious question:

"Rezna tells me that you have an interest in nuclear waste, Ahmed. Is that correct?

"It certainly is, although you must appreciate that my interests are quite wide. I earn my living by being plugged into as many circles as I can and bringing people together when I sense that they may have common interests."

"So, you are not buying or selling nuclear waste, are you?"

"That is correct. I do not trade for my own account. I prefer to rely on commissions which the people I bring together pay me for taking a position in some goods, turning around, and selling them at a profit."

He paused for a second and added:

"You will understand that some of the goods with which I come in contact may or may not be accepted in the broader world. It is much safer for me to bring people together and let them decide to deal or not to deal between themselves. I don't know whether a deal has taken place and thus I do not represent any danger to either party. Their deal is safe and only the two of them know about it."

Abdullah could not miss asking the obvious next question:

"How did you create your network?"

"Oh! Quite simple: the old-fashioned way. I listen to the needs, wants or wishes of the people I meet and work very hard to find ways to help them. You know, Abdullah, people like to have someone who can point them in the right direction and stay out of the way."

Abdullah simply smiled. As he realized that Abdullah was not going to open up without further prompting, Josh asked the next question to keep the conversation going, noting that Rezna appeared somewhat out of his depth:

"Is there a way I could help you, since I hear that you too might have some interest in nuclear waste material?"

Abdullah kept silent for a few more seconds and simply replied:

"I know people who are trying to acquire nuclear waste. I'm told they are conducting research projects which require the use of a small nuclear reactor. They do not have the scale to deal with the big sellers. Plus, they're not only small but are in fact only starting: no track record, and thus low credibility. Ideal candidates for the unofficial market if you see what I mean . . ."

"Ahhh. I do; I do. This could be interesting. I know that certain wastes were stashed away when the Americans and the United Nations came to investigate Iraq. I personally do not know where these are, and in fact I don't know how much there is either."

Josh paused for a short few seconds to gauge Abdullah's reaction and added:

"But I know someone whom I think may know more than myself."

"That would be quite interesting. Is that person in Iraq?"

"For all I know, yes. I met him in Bagdad a few years ago and we have stayed in touch, though we haven't met frequently. He knows how to get to me, and I know how to get to him. I believe he still lives in Bagdad, but I'm not sure. I believe he had a couple of conversations with people I introduced him to but can't tell you anything more. Again, I don't want to know any details. The only thing I know is that someone gave me money for the first introduction and that I gratefully accepted it."

At that point, Abdullah smiled with some visible satisfaction and made a sign to convey his sense that the meeting was over. He asked Ahmed for a phone number where he could reach him and was ready to leave when Ahmed asked:

"Is there any number where I can reach you?"

Josh was surprised and disappointed when Abdullah replied:

"Rezna knows where to reach me through our mutual friend. At this point, I would prefer you to go through him. No offense, but I must remain quite cautious."

"None taken."

CHAPTER.20

The phone on Mark's desk rang. He picked it up and immediately recognized the voice at the other end:

"Countess Renate, good to hear your voice. Can we connect our cameras?"

"Afraid not, Mark. I'm calling on a phone line. It's much simpler as I am on the plane."

"Sorry. I know better than to ask where you are."

He could hear Renate's short giggle and asked:

"So, what's up?"

Renate told Mark that she had heard from Vlad. She was happy to report that the initial information seemed quite interesting. Mark was starting to congratulate and thank her when she interrupted:

"Hold our horses. We don't have anything tangible yet. However, he was able to confirm that regional lists of these outposts exist."

"That's a great first step."

"You bet. He also told me that the story of someone trying to write on the topic of communication within the Soviet Union prior to its implosion struck a bell with the people he had contacted. There were no reasons to suspect anything amiss and, at any rate, concerning as it did developments dating back to the Soviet Union, there didn't seem to be much of a conflict."

She paused and added:

"He said it surely looked like a legitimate history project. Apparently, nobody smelled anything. He volunteered that the only filter someone might impose would be to make sure that no names appear so that nobody with a questionable past might run the risk of being exposed."

With a voice which betrayed the smile on her face, she added:

"He hopes to have something within a week if we agree . . ."

She paused again and asked:

"By the way, Mark, I know why you want the information. But, if we can get it, what do you plan to do with it?"

Mark remained evasive, arguing that he really was not sure until he saw both how many such outposts there were and where they were located. He still added:

"I'd like to make sure that nobody can use them as sources of nuclear waste material. However, what is feasible or not will greatly depend upon circumstances."

He paused a second and added:

"We don't want to start a nuclear war trying to prevent one . . ."

■ ■ ■ ■ ■

Meanwhile, near the Martyrs Park in Mosul, neither Rezna nor Abdullah had noticed three individuals, partially lost in the crowd. Mike, Frank and Joseph had indeed been charged by Josh to take care of three important missions. The first, the obvious one, involved making sure that nothing untoward happened to Josh. Ostensibly, there was not a great deal of fear that something would happen in the kind of meeting which Josh, aka Ahmed, had organized with Rezna and Abdullah, but why take unnecessary risks? More important were the missions which they would have after the meeting had come to a close. They were charged with tailing both Rezna and Abdullah to see where they went from Martyrs Park. Fortunately, the four streets which describe the rectangle within which the Martyrs' Park is located, all offered street parking. It was quite simple for the three men to find discrete parking spots one each near one of the three entrances into the park, all located either due west or south of the park. Though one could leave the park going over the wall around it, it surely would have looked quite suspicious and involve the need to walk on grass that was supposedly off limits. Mike was responsible for following Rezna, while Frank and Joseph would share the task of tailing Abdullah.

Initially, Mike reported that Rezna, who was driving himself seemed to go in the direction of Highway 2, which he knew would eventually take him to Erbil, if he did not stop on the way. Mike had no difficulty following Rezna, as the road on which he was travelling was both straight and with very few important intersections. He followed deceptively simple tactics. He would let Rezna drive somewhat ahead of him, to the point where he might even lose sight of his car, for those parts of Highway 2 where he knew there were no main exits coming up. By contrast, as he was approaching villages such as Hasan Shami, Aski Kalak or even Kani Qirzhala, he would speed up to catch Rezna so that he would be ready to follow him should he exit the highway. In the end, Rezna did not exit the highway and in effect drove straight back to Erbil, to the house which Josh believed was owned or at least used by Ibrahim. Josh kept quiet while Mike was giving his report though he was still wondering why Rezna seemed to want to talk to Ibrahim first after the meeting with Abu Musa and Abdullah. He kept thinking that the situation looked stranger and stranger, but he really did not know what to make of it.

Joseph and Frank proceeded in a different direction. Abdullah, who had a chauffeur, first went due west from the Mosul Museum and Martyrs Park. His car quickly found Highway 1 which goes in a general north-westerly direction. Joseph and Frank took turns being right behind Abdullah's car, though they were always careful to allow for some space between whoever was closest to the car and Abdullah's car itself. Thankfully, there was some traffic on the highway, which made it considerably easier for Frank and Joseph to lose themselves among the rest of the vehicles. They both were thankful for their choices of rental cars which made them very much indistinguishable from many other vehicles on the road. The landscape on either side of the highway was desolate, with grayish brown soil suggesting poor agricultural prospects; yet that had to be where many toiled to provide some of the food needed by the local population. Sixty miles from Mosul, they were surprised when Abdullah's car went across the Iraqi Syrian border, right after he had driven through Rabia, the last Iraqi village before entering Syria. A modest town in northwest Iraq, near the Syrian town of Al-Yarubiyah, Rabia happens to be inhabited by the same Arab tribe, the Shammar, as Al-Yarubiyah; that serves as a reminder of how artificial many of the countries' differences are in a region where tribal traditions dominated until relatively recently. Borders were established, often by powers who had somehow occupied or lorded over territories and yet never spent much time figuring out where borders should or should not be. Rabia's principal economic sector involves illegal smuggling because of its position as a border town.

The men assumed that Abdullah had to show his passport when his car crossed the border, although the passage looked quite routine. The border guards, on both sides, were fully used to people transiting freely between Rabia on the Iraqi side and Al-Yarubiyah in Syria. Numerous people would cross either because they worked on one side and lived on the other, or simply because they felt that shopping on the other side was more attractive. Frank had accelerated as he approached the border to make sure that he would not lose

Abdullah were he to be stopped. The fact that there was one rather than two passports to inspect, helped, and moreover the fact that he was traveling on a Syrian passport was a factor speeding up any inspection on the Syrian side. Joseph, who followed a bit further back, showed his Turkish passport which was barely examined by the border agent. He waited until he was far enough from the border to accelerate to catch up with the other two cars.

From there, Abdullah's driver veered right and took a smaller road which eventually led him to Al-Maabadah, a Syrian village smack in the middle of the very eastern corner of Syria, just south of Turkey and west of Iraq. Interestingly, the majority of the inhabitants of Al-Maabadah are Kurds, with a significant Assyrian minority. In all, the *Mossad* agents figured out that they had driven a full 100 miles. Suddenly, Frank, whose car was closest to Abdullah, could see him veer sharply to the left. He went through a staffed gate and entered an area which looked like a compound, comprising multiple one- or two-story buildings and quite a bit of ground around them. Yet, from where he was, he had to concede that he could not tell how large the whole area was. Frank had to stop at the gate to the compound as it was clearly a restricted area and he would surely not be given permission to come in.

So, Frank made no effort to get in, drove a few hundred yards further on and simply made a U-turn. He drove back toward the gate, but stopped short of it, after having made sure it was both a secure hiding position and a place from which he could observe entry and exit from the compound into which Abdullah drove. Having parked his car in an area which did not look inhabited or too visible, he decided that the one element which he and Joseph could add to their current knowledge would be for Joseph to conduct a reconnaissance drive around the camp, if it was at all possible. He called Joseph who was in fact only a few hundred yards behind him:

"Joseph, I know you can see me on your GPS. I just parked in a spot where I can keep an eye on the gate to the compound, or at least the one gate to the compound I know of. I think I should stay here until we can talk to Josh because we don't know whether Abdullah went into what I'll call the camp until we know better because he lives there or since he needed to talk to someone who does live there."

"Makes all the sense in the world, my friend."

"Thanks. Can you find a way to drive around it and report? I have no idea how large or small it is. I don't even know if there is a road that goes around it, though the GPS seems to show roads of paths which might allow you to drive all the way around. The gate with the uniform personnel makes me think of a military installation, but I can't see anything inside. Beside the wooden fence on both sides of the gate, there are trees at the periphery which obscure any feasible line of sight."

"No problem."

Joseph paused for a second and then casually said:

"You know, looking at the map, there's something interesting, which one of us probably ought to have noticed earlier."

"What?"

"Well, it seems that Highway 1 in Iraq, the road on which we just drove, becomes Highway M4 in Syria."

"So?"

"Highway M4 in Syria takes you directly to Aleppo. That's not earth shattering. But stay with me, after Aleppo, M4 takes you straight to Latakia, you know, the northernmost Syrian port on the Mediterranean Sea, probably not more than 20 miles from the Turkish border."

Frank was still not clear what his friend was trying to communicate. He asked in a slightly stronger tone of voice:

"And what's close to Latakia?"

"The Khmeimim Air Base which is currently operated by Russia as per a treaty that was signed with Syria in August 2015."

"Holy Shit! And by the way, I'm looking at the same map now. Aleppo is a straight shot from where we are to Al Raqqah. And you know what was in Al Raqqah?"

He did not give Joseph the time to reply. Matter-of-factly, he simply said:

"Al Raqqah is where ISIS was supposed to have a base, right?"

"From Charybdis into Scylla! We've got our work cut out."

■ ■ ■ ■ ■

Joseph's remark called back to ancient Greek mythology. Charybdis and Scylla were two sea monsters which were said to be located on the opposite sides of the Strait of Messina. They constituted a whirlpool and a reef both of which were serious dangers for sailors. Avoiding one might only lead the poor sailor to fall into the other. From that legend, a phrase was formed which meant "going from bad to worse": "to fall from Charybdis into Scylla."

■ ■ ■ ■ ■

Back in the shophouse in Mosul where they had eventually all returned, the four men compared notes and discussed next steps. Josh initially suggested that they should for the moment leave aside the issue of Rezna and Ibrahim, arguing that an element was obviously missing, though he added:

"I don't think we should waste our time on it. Let's just wait and see what comes of it. We'll deal with it when something new happens; until then let's focus elsewhere."

They turned then to the issue of the camp where Abdullah seemed either to be residing or at least to have a contact to whom he wanted to report on his meeting with Ahmed, aka Josh. Frank and Joseph immediately agreed that they needed to find out more about the camp, particularly as the proximity to either Al Raqqah or the Khmeimim Air Base pointed to a possible foreign link with two powers who were certainly not on the side of Israel. Frank, who had been the closest to the camp, argued that it looked like somewhat of a well-defended spot, though he added:

"Other than the fact that Joseph did see that the area seemed to be totally fenced in and to offer only one real gate, we don't really know much about it."

Josh immediately agreed though the team could see a smile telling them that Josh might have an idea. He conceded that he had in fact an idea, though he added that there would be a need for careful planning. In fact, he suggested that the first step would be to see whether Mark could organize a drone flyover of the camp, admittedly at a high enough altitude to eliminate most of the danger to the Eitan drone which would be entrusted with the mission. He argued:

"I would like to have an idea of the general layout of the place, inside the fence. We will likely be most effective if we have a sense of what potential dangers await us, and even more importantly where they might be located."

Frank and Joseph were quizzically looking at Josh. He assumed that they were wondering why they should use a fancy military drone like the Eitan when there may be simpler solutions. He explained his choice:

"By the way, we do have access to small discreet drones which we could operate ourselves. You can buy them in several electronic shops near University Park in Mosul. But I would worry that if one of these smaller drones was discovered and presumably shot down, we would find it much harder to do further work: the guard of whoever is in there would likely be up."

He paused and turning to Frank and Joseph, after having apologized for the distance, they had to drive, he asked:

"Could you both do a complete reconnaissance of the immediate surroundings of the camp. I would like to have a good sense of what there is around the camp and a view from the ground as to what we should expect. While you are at it, try to pick a few spots where one or several of us could base ourselves to conduct a careful surveillance of what happens there."

CHAPTER.21

PARIS, FRANCE

Meanwhile, in Paris, Marcel Delagrange had worked with Nathan Stone, *Mossad*'s senior representative in France. He had concurred when Marcel had suggested that they needed a formal contact within the French DGES and GDIS, the two agencies responsible for French security. The DGES, which stands for Directorate-General for External Security, is France's foreign intelligence agency, equivalent to the British MI6 and the American CIA; it was established on 2 April 1982. The GDIS, which stands for General Directorate for Internal Security is the other French internal security agency. It is charged with counterespionage and counterterrorism, focusing also on cybercrime and surveillance of potentially threatening groups, very much like the FBI in the U.S. or the National Crime Agency (NCA) in the U.K.

Marcel had invited Nathan to organize a working lunch so that he could meet Colonel Gabriel Lefevre, the key person at the DGES and Francis Marchand, Lefevre's opposite number at the GDIS. Nathan had decided to remain quite close to the Israeli Embassy in Paris, which is located on Rue Rabelais, a very short street, a stone's throw from the famed Rond Point des Champs Elysees, running from Avenue Matignon to Rue Jean-Mermoz. He chose Pietro, an Italian restaurant, across the street from Kavod, a Kosher restaurant which stood at the corner of Rue Rabelais and Rue Jean Mermoz. Nathan selected Pietro for two main reasons. First, though France is not a strongly antisemitic country, it remains deeply committed to laicity. Thus, specific religious activities are more often than not conducted in private. For an Israeli diplomat to go for a kosher restaurant might have seemed a bit too much, particularly as the three other guests did not seem to be of Jewish descent, at least based on their surnames. Second, Italian food is generally well-liked by most people and offers a variety such that most everyone can find something they like. Both restaurants were patronized with some frequency by Israeli diplomats, as the kitchen and dining facilities at the embassy were reserved for the ambassador, a handful of senior diplomats and a few special occasions almost always involving political guests. Nathan had no difficulty convincing the owner of Pietro to provide a table secluded in a corner of the dining room, away from the windows, facing Rue Jean Mermoz.

Marcel, who was officially playing host, though everyone knew that Nathan was picking up the tab, introduced the various participants. Some usual chit chat ensued as would be typical even in business lunches pretty much around the world. They each ordered a simple aperitif, succumbing to the fashion of the Aperol Spritz, which consists of Aperol, an orange liquor, mixed with *Prosecco*, an Italian white sparkling wine, and some sparkling water. When the time came to pick the food, they immediately agreed to go with the antipasti dish for the whole table, a dish for which Italian restaurants are famous and followed it with various pasta dishes.

The men did not wait until the antipasti were served to dive straight into their topic. Predictably, Marcel, who was the only one knowing all parties, gave a brief rundown of the current issue. He certainly did not disclose anything about himself that the two security officials did not know, explaining why the two French government officials only referred to him as Professor Delagrange. In that, they were following the classical French etiquette which refrains from using first names in most official business meetings and even at times in formal social gatherings. Marcel for his part limited his introduction of Nathan to his role in the embassy, Vice Consul for Military Affairs. He still added that Nathan was a lieutenant colonel in the Israeli army, allowing the French official to refer to him as colonel. Marcel invited Nathan to share all that he could about the situation that brought the four of them together:

"Thanks, Professor Delagrange. Gentlemen, let me first of all thank you for agreeing to this meeting. I know how busy you must be and appreciate your taking this time. Let me add an important cautionary note: what I am about to tell you is top-secret as we speak, and I will therefore ask you to keep it to yourself please."

Nathan noticed that the two French officials nodded their agreement. In fairness, one cannot say that he was surprised. It is common knowledge that officialdom in France is quite prepared to operate in some measure of secrecy; the tendency often found in a few other places, starting with the U.S., to leak information, though present, is considerably rarer—the notion that it is necessary to provide a face-saving solution for everyone is still primordial. He continued:

"Apologies as well for being blunt, but I prefer to give you the bottom line first. You will immediately appreciate both the need for secrecy and our desire to find the underlying cause of the issue as quickly as we can. As you know, Israel is frequently targeted by missiles which usually come from either the southwest or the northeast."

He paused for a second, drank from his glass of sparkling water and added with a smile:

"You must have guessed that I am referring to territories which are controlled by Palestinian resistance fighters, Hamas to the south and Hezbollah to the north."

He was happy to see the two security officials again nod their agreement with an encouraging smile. He congratulated himself for not using the word "terrorists" upfront, in a bid not to risk offending anyone. He continued:

"Well, recently, in the last month to be as specific as I am allowed to be, we found out that one of the missiles which reached us, near Tiberias, on the west bank of the Sea of Galilea, had what we'll call a 'dirty tip.'"

Seeing that Gabriel Lefevre and Francis Marchand were paying more attention when he used the term 'dirty tip' Nathan added:

"Oh! And by the way, by 'dirty tip' I mean that we are sure that the rocket carried a Radiological Dispersal Device, which we euphemistically call a dirty bomb."

"You mean that whatever it was had an RDD, right?"

"Absolutely, Mr. Lefevre. I hope I wasn't pedantic using the full wording for the device, because I was not sure whether the initials were in the same order in French as in English. By the way, should I call you Mr. Ambassador given your illustrious diplomatic career?

"Mr. Lefevre is plenty. Thank you."

Nathan continued his reply to Gabriel Lefevre's question:

"So far, our work which unfortunately had to rely on a relatively small sample of debris, as the device which hit Tiberias was small. We concluded that the radioactive matter primarily comprised caesium-137 and some strontium-90."

Francis Marchand observed:

"This is quite serious. Any victim?"

"Minister . . ."

"Please, just like my friend Lefevre, call me Mr. Marchand. The reference to my having been a cabinet minister once isn't necessary. Let's keep things simple; at times, I dream of being able to be as informal as certain Anglo-Saxon colleagues, but you can't say that in France."

"I see. Thank you. Now to your twin questions. On the victim front, we don't believe that there was anything much to report. One man experienced some minor and brief dysfunction to a pacemaker, but it was quickly addressed and corrected. On the fact that this is a serious development, I couldn't agree more. We've been arguing that this was a nuclear step too far on the part of whoever is responsible. That's why we asked Professor Delagrange's help."

Marcel interrupted the conversation to make the point that he felt the question initially called simply on his experience within the French nuclear industry. He explained that he agreed to help and quickly concluded that there were two elements on which he could offer some help. The first was his ability, in due course, to call upon government specialists, in France or even within the main European countries. The second was to discuss the nature of nuclear waste which could be used to create a dirty bomb. In particular, he described the various sources which he felt were plausible causes, adding that he knew that Colonel Stone's government was dealing with a number of them. He added:

"The one area where the Israeli government isn't able to look without running the risk of creating some diplomatic incident has to do with waste from nuclear reactors. With France a leading user of nuclear energy for its electricity generation, I recommended that we should start here. Yet, we will eventually need to expand our search to Germany, England, Spain and several others, not to mention the U.S. and even Japan."

Mr. Lefevre noted with a smile that Marcel was not including Russia or China in his list. Mr. Marchand took this further adding the elephant in the room, Iran. Nathan interrupted:

"You are absolutely correct gentlemen. We should not and in fact are not excluding anything. However, I have been asked to focus on leaks from nuclear electricity generation. I am sure that other officials in my country's government have been asked to deal with different areas. That is probably due to my being focused on military affairs while others are concerned with foreign policy issues."

Marcel took over the conversation to explain one theory which he wanted to share with Gabriel and Francis. He discussed the possibility that nuclear waste might be stolen during the transfer of used rods, after they have been allowed to cool down. Francis immediately noted that the process was quite seriously controlled. Nathan asked:

"I have been told that it is virtually not practical to assume that rods are stolen when they are extracted from the reactor or even after they have cooled down somewhat. The personal radiation risk is too high, not to mention the extremely high temperatures which are reached, but I am also told that every step of the process is very carefully supervised and monitored."

Francis nodded his agreement, though he added:

"Criminals are usually quite smart. Yet, the environments in which these processes are conducted are almost certainly impenetrable."

Nathan came right back:

"What happens after the rods have cooled down? I'm told that takes five years or so . . ."

"Your information is excellent, Colonel Stone. Once they have cooled down, the rods are transferred into crates which are then sealed and a contractor trucks them away to the site where they will permanently be stored."

"Thanks Mr. Marchand. Are there many contractors?"

Francis replied:

"Not really. Usually, each region has one favored company that deals with all the power plants in that area. There may be a couple here or there, but that would be the exception rather than the rule."

"Sorry to keep pushing, but is there room for mischief there?"

Francis took a few seconds before answering:

"Everything is possible. Yet, for starters, I can't believe that the problem could be with one such transport company so to speak from the top down. The contracts are too high profile, and they are too closely monitored."

"How about individual teams within a company?"

Francis smiled and replied:

"The further down you go in the hierarchy, the greater the risk, obviously. Yet, I know for a fact that the people who work there are screened with a great deal of care. You could assume that my services are asked to review their backgrounds. Additionally, the people who come collect the used rods are known to the inhouse personnel of the powerplant. They are not numerous, a driver and a handler per truck, the man who drives the forklift needed to move the crates . . . They are quite heavy, you know. Most transporters wouldn't have more than a couple of teams dedicated to this activity, to deal with sickness or holidays."

Francis paused and explained:

"Everything is mechanical. The rods are packaged in lead-lined containers—ergo the weight of the containers. They are carried to and lifted onto the truck with forklifts. And then the truck simply drives away. By the way, I should add that there is an inspection as they leave the power plant, to verify that there is the right number of crates."

Nathan was not through with his questions, which in fairness he had discussed earlier with Marcel:

"What happens next?"

Francis replied:

"I assume that you mean between the powerplant and the storage location."

Nathan nodded.

Francis continued:

"The truck simply drives to the storage location, using the normal road network, with a preference for wider roads to minimize the risk to other traffic. The contents of the truck are again itemized and verified when they get to the storage location. That includes checking the wax seal that is placed at the plant, to make sure that the container has not been opened during transit. There would be all sorts of alarm bells if there was anything missing. In fact, come to think of it, the only time I think it happened was due to an error at the origin: there was one too many crates listed on the truck's shipping manifest."

Nathan was not through:

"Could something happen during the trip between the powerplant and the storage area?"

"Quite right, Colonel Stone. Quite right. Yet, once again, it would be difficult, but not impossible. Let me explain. You'd have to start with the wax seal, but there's more . . ."

Francis went on to argue that the truck that carries the waste is, at times but not always, provided with a motorcycle police escort. He justified the original decision to accompany the trucks on the grounds of public safety. Yet, he could not avoid the decisive factor:

"You must remember that nuclear power and everything that goes with it has a long history in France. The first nuclear power plant in France comprised three reactors and was commissioned in 1960. Quite a while ago. Then, with the first oil crisis in 1973, the speed of its development was accelerated. So, I would argue that the transfer of used nuclear fuel has become much more commonplace. As we speak, the protocol is that the decision to accompany a truck or not is randomly made . . ."

Nathan interrupted:

"Are the driver and handler aware ahead of time?"

"Excellent question, Colonel. The right answer is that they should not. They should find out at the very moment they leave the power plant grounds."

Francis had one more comment to make:

"Just for the sake of completeness, let me add one thing: every truck that is used to transport nuclear waste must be equipped with a GPS tracker. It isn't used to track progress on a 'live' basis, but it records everything with a time clock to boot, and its contents are reviewed at the end of the trip."

Nathan could only conclude:

"Makes lot of sense."

CHAPTER.22

TEL AVIV, ISRAEL

Once he had taken the brief phone call with Mark, Josh realized that he needed much more than that to take the next step. He agreed to fly to Tel Aviv, via Istanbul, as dictated by the realities of commercial air travel in the Middle East. A *Mossad* driver was waiting for him at Ben Gurion International Airport in Tel Aviv; he was wearing a uniform and driving a car disguised to look like the services of Nickytravel, a well-known local limousine company. The chauffeur wore a faded blue sport jacket and dark grey pants, with a tie that matched the color of the blazer. Mark had shied away from the Mercedes car offerings, ordering a black Range Rover to ferry Josh to the *Mossad* campus, which was located in the north of Tel Aviv, just about three miles north of Hayarkon Park. The complex was made up of seven individual but inter-connected structures, five of which were arranged as the two sides of a right angle. Each of these five towers looked somewhere between square and hexagonal and had a large internal light well which provided natural light to most rooms without windows to the outside.

Josh went directly to Mark's office, knowing he would always have the time later to book himself in the hotel that had been reserved for him, the West All Suite Hotel, a stone's throw from the Gillot Ma'arav Interchange. Mark was waiting for him:

"How are you, my friend? Sorry that you had to take such a roundabout way of getting here."

"I know the lay of the land, sir. Couldn't be helped. Anyway, glad that we can spend some time together. We may have stumbled on something big, and I know I will need help to deal with it."

At Mark's request, Josh gave him a complete rundown of the group's activity since he had met with Rezna's friend or acquaintance, Abdullah. He told Mark the great job which Frank and Joseph had done following Abdullah on his return trip from the Martyr's Park. Yet, Josh gave every sign that he was impatient to see the result of the Eitan drone flyover which Josh had earlier asked Mark to organize. Mark smiled and said:

"As I told you over the phone, the result of the flyover is precisely why we are getting together here. The images are quite clear and there is no doubt in my mind that we have a base military camp of some sort."

He pulled out a series of still photos from the film taken by the drone to illustrate his next point:

"If you look carefully here, I'm really wondering whether we might not have at least one, may be a couple of missile launchers hidden under the tarps . . . Could be ballistic missile launchers or simply multiple rocket launchers. But nasty stuff nevertheless."

Josh looked quite excited as he said:

"Wow! You're right. Could well be launchers. One thing I don't understand, why is it that the drone couldn't take better pictures?"

Mark simply replied that the meteorological conditions had not been ideal, and they had decided to avoid any activity which might have allowed better results, adding:

"We elected to keep the drone flying quite high. The risk of being discovered seemed unacceptable to us, given the fact that you would be there to take additional steps afterwards.

"Makes all the sense in the world."

■ ■ ■ ■ ■

Mark and Josh spent the rest of the afternoon planning for the actions which Josh and his team could carry out. It became very quickly apparent that the solution they had to choose did not require any incursion by anyone into the camp. This might become necessary at a later stage, but early on they simply had to develop a solid understanding of the layout of the camp and to discover as much as possible about its defensive capabilities. In short, they viewed whatever mission Josh was going to organize as a second step following the high flyover with the Eitan drone. They surely hoped to be able to gather more information, but they wanted to be sure that they would not be discovered and, more importantly, the effort would go unnoticed, at least from the point of view of its main purpose.

They quickly agreed that they needed Marvin's help to be sure that whatever they considered was feasible. Fortunately, Marvin was in his office and available when Mark called. He offered to come to Mark's office, in his words:

"Because there is probably more space for three people to sit in your office than in mine."

Marvin arrived at Mark's office less than five minutes later. He was jovial as usual when he entered, assuming as he did that there would be a few technological challenges for him to address. Josh, who had had the time to consider at least a few alternative scenarios for his next step, started to describe the general direction of his thinking. Having described what had been found about the camp and, more importantly, having confirmed that Abdullah did not seem to have left the camp for three days, he made the point that there was an urgent need to get as good an understanding of what the camp was. Yet, he added that it would be crazy to send people into the camp just based on the data provided by the Eitan flyover:

"Sure, with the pictures you showed me, Mark, we know the general layout, where the barracks are and where there doesn't seem not to be much of anything. We also know or rather believe that they do not have fixed inspection posts along the periphery of the camp. However, we don't know how it is patrolled, if at all."

He paused and Mark added:

"We have seen what looked like a narrow path along the inside of the fence, and there were signs of a few small groups of people on that path when we filmed. We're assuming that this is how they conduct their surveillance. Though we looked as carefully as we could at the fence itself, we were not able to find if any of the posts along the fence were equipped with cameras or infrared detection systems."

Josh offered his initial conclusion:

"Given all we've seen, as I see it, the least dangerous approach is for us to use drones and control them from relatively close by."

Marvin immediately interrupted:

"One issue with that approach, Josh, is that you probably do not want anyone to be able to find out that Israeli agents might have been close by, correct?"

"Absolutely. Thanks, Marvin. I had thought of using drones purchased in Iraq or Syria, just to make sure that they couldn't be traced."

Mark did not have the time to come into the conversation as Marvin replied:

"Makes a lot of sense. Now, the problem with the drones you find in the general retail commerce is that they are rarely terribly good. For one, they tend to be noisy; not crazily noisy, but detectable, nevertheless. More to the point, their cameras are not ideal."

Josh nodded and said:

"To be honest, I kind of assumed that. My plan doesn't rely on one, but on three drones, if only because there are three of us who can control them."

Marvin was about to interrupt when Josh made a sign with his right-hand signifying that he had more to say. He explained that two of the drones would be decoys, although he would still hope that they would be able to detect something. He added:

"Though we did find that the many of the drone controllers on the market in Iraq do not have screens attached to the controllers, we were able to buy smartphones which we could use as screens in order to get what people call an FPV, first person view."

"Excellent my friend. You were telling me that those would be decoys . . ."

"Right, if we see that one or both are identified, we will first fly them away from where the third was. That way, we will ensure that all the local attention is dedicated to the decoys and thus allows the other one to do its job. Yet, if there was any sign of unusual activity in the camp, the decoys would come down further with the goal of being identified and likely shot down, though he added:

"They'd still try a few evasive maneuvers to extend their usefulness, but it was fully my intention that they would eventually be shot down."

Mark asked:

"What about the third?"

Josh smiled broadly, as he got up from the sofa in Mark's office. He walked to the nearby corner when he had temporarily stored his luggage. He grabbed one of the two suitcases he had brought with him. He observed:

"Two suitcases for such a short trip wouldn't make sense if one were not carrying something special. Right gentlemen?"

Mark was smiling as he was starting to understand what his agent had done. He let him keep on with his explanations:

"The drone I have here, which by the way is readily available in Mosul, where I purchased it, is the absolute top of the line. It even has a screen on the controller! I'm sure that Marvin will find it inferior to what we can find in Israel and, more importantly, what he can provide for us, but my hope is that it is a good start on which to build."

Marvin's eyes lit up. He had also understood the plan which Josh had formed. He realized that he would be asked to change whatever could be changed on the drone without being something which might be detected as decidedly Israeli should the drone be identified and shot down. He said:

"Well, let me look at this baby."

He paused and asked Josh:

"Any chance you could find instructions in something other than Arabic?"

Josh pointed to Marvin a set of instructions in English, adding with a broad smile:

"You won't be surprised if I tell you that you don't find instructions in Hebrew in Iraq!"

Marvin went straight to the technical specifications and began to inspect them with a great deal of care. He raised his eyes from the piece of paper and declared:

"This is quite powerful enough for what you want to do. It says the noise level isn't discernable from further away than 30 feet and that is good news, though I want to test it."

He paused to grab his glass of water and concluded:

"The only real weakness is twofold in my eyes. First, the lens does not seem to offer any infrared possibilities. Assuming that you gentlemen are going to conduct the mission at night, that is definitely not ideal. The second is even more problematic: it does not store the pictures which are sent to the controller."

He paused again to see whether Josh and Mark were on board. Mark beat him to the punch line:

"Which means that we have nothing if it is shot down!"

"Exactly, sir. In fact, it does not need to be shot down for you not to have anything! I don't mind that the images are not stored in the drone, very few do, and I don't see any use. But, more importantly, the controller does not store the images it receives; it displays them and then they're gone. They're in the head of the agent who controlled it, but nowhere else."

Mark asked Marvin what could be done in so short a time. Marvin was thinking for a short while and quickly came up with a solution for each challenge:

"First, I can place two lenses where the drone only has one. It will take two movies simultaneously, one with regular light and the other with infrared rays. The images won't be independent, but we'll see the same scenes with two different heat sensitivity. I will need to add another screen on the controller."

Seemingly thinking aloud, Marvin declared:

"Come to think of it, I'd rather place two screens where there currently is only one. Not a big deal. More importantly, I'll add a couple of memory chips to it so that the feeds to each screen are also saved. You'll just need to be sure that you escape with the controller whatever happens."

Marvin paused and asked:

"You don't have the two other drones, do you?"

Josh smiled and replied:

"Drones, no, but I have the two controls. I brought them just in case . . . Brought the two additional smartphones also."

Marvin smiled and excitedly said:

"That's fabulous. I can make the same memory modifications to these two controls as well. I'll use the memory of the smartphones, which should be plenty. You don't expect filming for more than a couple of hours, right?"

"Don't know for sure, but I would hope not. The longer we stay over the camp the greater the odds that we would be discovered."

Josh paused and appeared to be running through an internal checklist:

"Marvin, just a thought . . . The changes which you're making to the two decoy controllers, there wouldn't be any trace of them on the drones themselves . . . Right?"

"I see what you mean, Josh. No. The drones, at least the decoy drones, will look totally bog standard. That does not eliminate the risk that security services in the camp would be bound to wonder why someone was overflying the camp. But they wouldn't find anything different from whatever is found in regular retail drones on any debris if they shot your birds down."

CHAPTER.23

FRANCE

Before they left the Pietro Restaurant, a couple of weeks earlier, the four tablemates agreed on two important action steps. Marcel Delagrange was going to remain vigilant with respect to France but would also contact a few of his closest *confreres* in neighboring European countries to seek their advice. He would surely only mention the developments in Israel in very broad unspecific terms to them but could tell them as well about his concerns. If asked about what stood behind them, he would plead partial ignorance and required secrecy with respect to his sources. Colonel Gabriel Lefevre would for his part tell his most senior officers about the nature of the problem, all the while remaining mum about the Israeli source. He would also reach out to the various heads of national security in the European Union to enlist their help as appropriate. Director Francis Marchand would place his direct reports on heightened alert and contact the most senior members of the police in France; he had said that he could obviously not be specific, though there were enough obvious potential areas of concern that he could point his counterparts in the right direction. Nathan Stone, for his part, would remain ready to offer any additional information that might come up to anyone needing it within the group. He would also be happy to check any lead which did not involve him stepping on any toes. Additionally, and totally unsaid, he would make sure that Mark Levi in Tel Aviv would be fully briefed.

■ ■ ■ ■ ■

A while later, in the middle of the morning, the phone rang on the desk of DGIS Director Francis Marchand:

"Director, we have a report of an unscheduled stop by a nuclear waste transporter."

The caller, Colonel Germain, the chief of staff to the Minister of Defense, wanted to bring a recent incident to Francis's attention. He had been made aware of the event because it had been picked up by the French Gendarmerie, which ultimately reports to the defense ministry.

■ ■ ■ ■ ■

The French Nationale police is divided into two different branches, though a number of exceptions make any generalization fraught with danger. As a rule, policing in large cities, defined as towns with more than 20,000 inhabitants, is the province of a national police force reporting to the Préfet de Police, a senior departmental official from the Interior Ministry. Additionally, there are municipal police forces under the control of the local mayors of smaller cities though a dotted line exists to the Prefet, to ensure efficient coordination. For the rest of the territory, the principal police functions are conducted by the national gendarmerie. It is a branch of the armed forces which therefore reports to the defense minister. Though officially founded in 1791, two years after the onset of the French Revolution, the Gendarmerie is the heir of the *Maréchaussée,* the oldest police force in France dating back to the Middle Ages. Tradition accounts for the fact that members of the gendarmerie often have a more honorable reputation than their colleagues in the national or municipal police, particularly in large cities. It is thus fair to say that all forms of police, members of the military, or of the civil service tend to be viewed negatively by the general population, except when they need them in which cases they surely appreciate their being available. The same tradition suggests that gendarmes, who have operated in more sparsely populated areas than their national police confreres, tended to be more present to the people they protected, as would also be the case for officers of a municipal police in smaller towns. In short, though slight differences exist, the French have the same general rapport with their police protectors as in most other countries, with the notable exception of the British who have always tended to be more supportive.

Both branches have at least one elite group comprising officers who work on motorcycles, referred to as the "Motorized Police." People who have driven on French roads will inevitably one day or another see these officers of gendarmerie who travel in pairs. This reflects the fact that, from a legal standpoint, gendarmes are among the few officials who, in France, are sworn to be telling the truth if two of them agree on a point, unless one could find one credible witness who could prove they were wrong. These *"motards"* as they are called were long called "angels of the road" to convey the notion that they were there to assist drivers, both in the event someone needed help and to ensure that everyone abided by the rules of the road.

■ ■ ■ ■ ■

Colonel Germain was aware of the fact that the two security agencies of France had decided to monitor's the transportation of used nuclear fuel with more care than hitherto. The conversation which Colonel Lefevre, Director Marchand, Professor Delagrange and Nathan Stone had had in the Pietro restaurant a while ago had convinced everyone that the risk of some spent fuel being stolen was real. At the same time, they had all agreed that they had two simple options. The first, which would protect against the risk of waste being stolen but fail to capture any potential guilty party would be to resume earlier practices to have all trucks transporting spent fuel escorted by motorcycle police. The second, which was more definitely aimed at tracking anyone that might be involved in nuclear waste trafficking, required having informal surveillance of these trucks, though the policy change would remain secret; even the management of nuclear plants would not be told of the new policy. The decision was made to follow the second path, though there might also be an increase in the number of transports that were visibly monitored as per current practice with these trucks being selected at random and their drivers informed at the last minute.

The incident report which had percolated up to his office was straightforward, though Colonel Germain immediately noted one weakness in the process that had been approved. The report stated that two members of the motorcycle gendarmerie from St Maximin-La-Sainte-Baume were homebound, riding eastward on autoroute A8 when they noticed less than a half mile ahead of them a white truck which had stopped on the shoulder of the autoroute A8. It had in fact stopped only a few hundred meters short of Exit 34, the exit for St Maximin-La-Sainte-Baume. Yet, before the gendarmes reached it, the truck was getting back on the highway. The gendarmes saw it almost immediately switching its right turn signal on, and taking the exit ramp from the highway. They quickly identified the truck as one of those transporters of nuclear waste and assumed it was coming from the nuclear complex due north of Marseilles.

Though they did not do anything initially, the behavior of the lorry led the two gendarmes to ask themselves questions. Why would it have stopped on the shoulder so close to an exit and then exit? Why not wait until they had left the highway to make whatever stop they needed to make? They knew the truck could not be leaving the divided highway because it was low on fuel; that would make no sense as it passed several gas stations along its route and would find others further on. Similarly, they knew that there were facilities along the autoroute to allow individuals to rest or take care of nature's calls without having to exit the autoroute. The only logical explanation they could agree on speaking to each other on their helmet microphones was that the truck had a malfunction and was going to look for a *bona fide* repair shop.

The report went on to suggest that the two gendarmes decided to follow the truck out of the divided highway and stay with it to see if it needed help. They also agreed not to intervene unless, seeing them in his rear-view mirrors, the truck driver decided to ask for their help. However, soon after going through the toll booth, the truck passed in front of a well-equipped gas station which ostensibly had a repair shop attached to it; yet it did not stop. The gendarmes said in their report that they did not understand why the lorry would keep going if it had a mechanical malfunction. The reason for the stop on the highway's shoulder had to be something else. What was it? The gendarmes radioed to their commanding officer in St Maximin that they were following a truck from a distance and discreetly because of a suspect development which they did not discuss.

Initially, they noted that the truck drove south, in the direction of St Maximin-La-Sainte-Baume, passing close to the famous Basilica of Ste Marie Madeleine, a disciple of Jesus Christ whose remains are interred there. Dating back to the late fourteenth century, the basilica and several of its furnishings are considered extremely important and listed among the major French historical monuments. The truck turned westward on DN7 and, at the McDonald roundabout suddenly veered to the right first and at the next roundabout left, to take D3, a small road. The gendarmes found themselves driving among the multiple vineyards which dominate the landscape in that part of France, famous principally but not solely for its rosé wines.

Their report stated that the truck followed that smaller road for about three miles, passing through Ollieres, a small village, and then when reaching the outskirts of Saint-Hilaire, an even smaller hamlet, turned into a private road leading to a winery in the middle of vineyards located on the left side of the road.

As one took that small, paved path, it was impossible to miss the mansion which suddenly appeared on the right, as if it jumped out from the surrounding trees. It was a typical Provencal castle, a phrase which the French often used to describe a larger than usual mansion rather than edifices like the much more grandiose and better-known castles of the Loire Valley. Probably built in the last two hundred years or so, the three-story structure seemed quite classical, with five windows on each floor, except on the ground floor as the central window made way for what looked like a wide door made of solid oak; a capstone, with carved coat of arms, sat at the center of the stone door frame. The windows were all flanked by light green wooden shutters, which offered a nice contrast to the façade with its ochre color, typical in the area as the Luberon region is believed to have one of the largest ochre deposits in the world. A careful observer might have noticed that the windows of the top floor were not as tall as those on the other two stories; this was in keeping with the tradition that had children and domestic help occupying the highest floor of a house, which thus had lower ceiling heights. The roof had simple gutter-free lines and was covered with antique burnt orange tiles. A triangular pediment topped the middle section of the façade which comprised the front door and the central windows in the two floors above it, giving it a classical look. Cream-colored quoins on either side of that central section which protruded a half foot or so from the rest of the façade lined up with the lowest of the three stone steps leading up to the front door at the bottom and the edges of the pediment at its top. The overall impression conveyed by the house was stately and suggested opulence, but there were no carvings, columns or ostentatious decorations which would have been out of place in this region of France, particularly after the 1789 revolution.

Beyond the mansion, there were numerous outbuildings, all constructed in a much simpler style, though the overall complex did exude charm, with nicely landscaped grounds and fruit trees until one reached the "working part" of the winery complex. The gendarmes assumed that those outbuildings included storage areas where wine barrels containing red wine would be placed to age and the whole winemaking complex, with large cylindrical stainless-steel tanks in which the fermentation of the grape juice was meant to take place. Further away from the entrance to the winery just where the first vineyard could be seen they saw a couple of additional buildings. Seeing tractors and other equipment in front of the leftmost one of them told the gendarmes that it had to be the mechanical area where equipment was stored and maintained. To the right of that building, another, much smaller, almost shed-like structure seemed eventually to disappear into the ground, which was sloping up around the building, probably by twenty or thirty feet. This had to be another cellar, dug into the side of a hill, where the owner would be keeping wine that had already been bottled. The gendarmes noted a station-wagon parked near the entrance to that cellar, but they could not make out its license plate number, and for all they knew it might simply be the winery owner's personal vehicle. Nothing looked terribly odd to men used to seeing wineries of which there were at least ten to twelve within a 10-mile radius of where they were, even though this one was known to them to have the longest history and the most impressive owner's residence.

From where they were, the men could not really see much more than the truck which was parked near the underground cellar entrance. It was standing there with no sign of anything happening under the midday Provençal sun. Though they conceded that something might be happening inside or on the right side of the truck, or even possibly in the cellar whose entrance they could no longer see, they did not feel that there was anything more for them to report. The men noted the name of the winery and its address and reported directly to their superiors on the radio. Their commanding officer, Brigadier Jules Rangade, asked them to stay put while he contacted his local superior, Major Sauvage. Jules quickly came back on the line suggesting that they should avoid being in plain sight, but he did not tell them to hide. He however said that they should keep monitoring the truck unless a more important mission call came from him. They both agreed it all made sense though the truck was still quite a ways from being under suspicion of any specific kind.

They noticed a dirt path that cut its way between a couple of vineyards less than twenty yards to the right; they parked their motorcycles there and took advantage of the shade offered by a couple of large fig trees on either side of entrance to the path. They managed to resist the temptation to grab the easy to access figs on the tree, though they looked ripe and juicy. Jules Rangade told them that Major Sauvage said he would call him back with specific instructions as soon as he had talked to his own boss, Colonel Dupin. Yet, he made it very clear that they should call him immediately if there was a change in the situation. While Jules Rangade was located in St Maximin, Major Sauvage was the head of the brigade to which the men belonged and was in La Valette-du-Var, still not a large town. Colonel Dupin, on the other hand, was the commanding officer for the whole of the Var department and was based in Hyeres, a larger city forty miles away.

It took Jules Rangade nearly an hour to come back on the radio and instruct his men to stay with the truck and report on any subsequent move. They were not to leave the truck without specific authorization. In fact, they did not have to wait long as the truck eventually drove out of the winery and started retracing its steps. One of the two gendarmes signaled the truck to stop on the side of the road. Very politely and smiling he asked whether there was anything they needed. The driver replied that they were fine. Seeing the surprise on the face of the officer, he started laughing and said:

"I see why you're surprised. I'll tell you why we stopped, but please not a word of this to anyone else as it could get us in trouble."

"OK, if you didn't break any law."

"We stopped to buy a couple of cases of wine from this winery. Oh, we don't buy their best, we sure can't afford it. But they have a good rosé that is cheap enough. Plus, we've been doing this a few times since we've started to drive in this area. The owner gives us a discount. You want to see the cases?"

"Without thinking, the older of the two gendarmes said yes."

The man opened his door and pointed to a couple of cardboard cases of six bottles each behind his seat."

The two gendarmes wished him well and let them go on. For a short while, they debated whether they should do anything more. In truth, they felt a bit silly to have followed a truck which seemed to be making a pit stop to buy a few bottles of wine. Yet, remembering the orders they had received, they called Jules Rangade and reported on what had transpired. The officer was not delighted as he shared the feeling of his men; he felt this was probably a major false alarm. However, he was now stuck. He had to have his men prepare a report since he himself had raised the issue with his own divisional superior.

Colonel Germain smiled on the phone as he was reporting the incident to Francis. The simple fact that everyone had been sure to protect their own backsides by calling up for instructions had caused a routine incident to go all the way to him. He added:

"Had it not been for the next development, Director Marchand, you would probably never have heard of it."

He paused and added:

"Still, there is an element which made me think again that this might not be as routine and innocuous as it seemed. In fairness, the gendarmes also noted it. Their report mentioned it in black and white. They were surprised when the driver of the truck asked them not to tell anyone that they had made an unscheduled stop to buy wine. Something didn't make sense. After all, they knew that all these trucks were equipped with GPS trackers. So, how could the driver expect that no one would notice they had made that short extra trip?"

Francis noted that this was an excellent point. Before answering his own rhetorical question, Colonel Germain added:

"But this isn't all. After the winery stop, the gendarmes were going back toward the autoroute as they were returning to St Maximin-La-Sainte-Baume, their home base. They had let the truck go ahead of them and were surprised as they caught up to it and saw it stopped by the side of the road just before it got through a roundabout. One of the exits from the roundabout led to the toll booths at the entrance of the autoroute. The gendarmes slowed to a crawl to see what was going on. They saw the passenger get out, appearing to be messing around for several seconds near the back door of the truck, underneath the spot where the license plate was located."

Francis interrupted:

"Quite interesting. Too early to tell for sure, but this gives me a thought."

Unimpeded, Colonel Germain concluded:

"The truck resumed its trip eastward on the A8 in the direction of Cannes and Nice. The gendarme finally reported that the truck seemed to be behaving normally. By then, they had gone past exit 35 for Brignoles and were beyond the limits of their geographical jurisdiction. They asked whether they were supposed to keep going or pass the baton to another team. Major Sauvage arranged for them to be met by two other gendarmes just before the exit for Draguignan, about thirty miles later on. They were able to exit and take the A8 in the opposite direction to return to St Maximin, while two new motorized gendarmes took over the tail."

Francis asked:

"Anything else?"

"Frankly, no. I think we should start monitoring the trucks which manage nuclear waste a bit more closely, though we should remain discreet. I don't want to let anyone know that something might be amiss. After all, there's got to be someone somewhere who is in the know and we don't want that someone to warn the network, if it exists, that we are on it."

"I can see why you'd do that and totally agree with you? What do you suspect?"

"Honestly, I don't know. The one thing I wonder about is the stops which the truck made both before leaving the highway and as it was about to get back on the same highway."

"So?"

"Well, we know that the men in the truck were aware that they had a GPS tracker. Now assuming they wanted to hide their little escapade, why would they not stop to make sure the tracker didn't know where they were going?"

"Back to the thought I had a few minutes ago. The truckers could disconnect their GPS before they left the autoroute and reconnect the tracker once they get back on it."

"Hey! Interesting idea. Can they do that? I would have thought the tracker could only be modified by whoever placed it on the truck . . ."

Francis replied:

"Don't know for sure and how that would work with the clock that is bound to be part of the system, but I'm certain they're allowed to stop and rest. Let me take this up with a couple of colleagues. Stay on it please. Splendid work."

CHAPTER.24

MOSUL AND AT THE IRAQI SYRIAN BORDER

Back in Iraq, and prior to starting their small expedition toward the camp of Al-Maabadah, Josh, Mike, Frank, and Joseph were carefully consulting the pictures which the Eitan flyover had yielded. Mark had forwarded them via regular email to Josh who had simply printed them. They were at the shophouse since Josh still did not want the three of them to find themselves together at his own apartment. After all, the shophouse had become his *de facto* office and it offered an especially useful setup for him. He laid the pictures down on the tribal rug which was on the floor between the four armchairs. They all kneeled next to the four pictures to get as close a look as they could.

Josh pointed first at the one picture which the drone had taken with the widest-angle lens. It depicted the whole of the camp. The general shape of the camp was somewhat hard to describe. The best the men could do was to agree it looked like two vertical rectangles, with the lower of the two misaligned relative to the first, like it had been rotated thirty degrees to the east. In its longest dimension, the camp measured more than five miles. Mike noted that the camp seemed in part bounded by five villages, one each in the northeast and northwest corners, one where the second rectangle pivoted to the east and the last one at the southwest corner. He also emphasized that a large part of the west side of the camp was near or next to an artificial lake with a dam and a hydroelectric plant at the south end. Laughing a bit he added:

"Note that this is no surprise to Joseph. He couldn't find a way to drive fully around the camp . . . He did see the small dirt road that followed alongside the lake and ran all the way from Girê Pirê to the hydroelectric dam."

He paused and added:

"This could give us a location for operating one of our decoy drones. It would take us about one and a half miles from road 716. We'd have to go slowly on the dirt path, but at least, in contrast to what happened to Joseph, we would know that the path went all the way to the dam."

Returning to the question of entry into the camp, Mike asked:

"I wonder whether there is more than one gate into the camp. So far, I can't see any one other than the one near Sêgirka Çolê, a bit more than a mile and a half from Al-Maabadah. That's where Frank and Joseph saw Abdullah enter the camp. Yet, I can't believe that they wouldn't have provided for a gate near each of the other villages."

Josh could only reply:

"Makes all the sense in the world, Mike. But I don't see anything either. It could simply be because any additional gate is simply a path going through the fence, but without any guard post. Without spoiling the surprise, I can tell you that the other pictures focus on the inside of the camp."

He paused and added:

"Come to think of it, Joseph, when you drove around the camp except for the stretch along the lake, did you see another gate?"

"Truth is, I didn't. Remember the border of the camp does not run next to the roads. It's often a field removed from the closest road or even dirt tracks. At times, the fence was even quite a further distance away from the actual road on which I was traveling."

Joseph suddenly stopped. He remembered something and said to his teammates:

"At Mixeyt, the camp was next to the village. Come to think of it, there had to have been a gate there. Can't imagine how there couldn't have been one. The camp has to employ some of the local people or at least to be ready to interact with them. Not doing any of it would be highly suspicious. Hold it. In fact, I remember that at one point a side road seemed to curve to the right with a house in the middle."

Glancing at the other photos on the rug, Joseph pointed to one:

"Hey, I can see it on this picture. Look, it returns to the main road not more than a couple hundred yards. That's where the gate must be. My fault. I should have driven the side road, just to be sure . . ."

Josh simply replied:

"Don't worry. One thing that means, guys, is that something similar might well be found close to or in each of the five villages we identified. Food for thought."

Turning to the other photos, the men could clearly see a couple of important elements which would be helpful to them. The first one they noted was the near total absence of trees within the compound, except for the occasional tall bush. Frank noted with a smile that the men could not practice any ambushing skill. Joseph deadpanned:

"Where would they use it around here?"

A short laugh later, they discussed the second element which concerned the buildings; they all were along the east side of the camp, between Sêgirka Çolê and Mixeyt. There did not seem to be anything worth mentioning on the west side, closer to the lake. They next turned to photos which had zeroed in further to get as good a sense as they could of where most of the danger was. Josh simply noted:

"I think we should start our exploration from east side of the camp, near Gir Siyareta Çolê."

Mike asked:

"Not that I disagree with you Josh, but what gets you to that conclusion?"

"Couple of things. First, the town is on road 716, which goes in a virtual straight line for more than seven miles, from north of Al-Maabadah to Zexire. Anyone who might come and interrupt our activity from the outside of the camp couldn't sneak up on us: we're bound to see headlights and be ready, whether they come from one end or the other."

Mike interrupted:

"Yes, unless they are setting a trap for us, in which case they could drive without any light."

Josh granted Mike his point and continued:

"Second, the only other place sitting on a main road north of the camp is between Al-Maabadah and Pira Girê-dêra. It would place us more than one mile away from the camp's northern border."

Mike could only reply:

"With my earlier caveat noted, that's good enough for me. Anything else we should be wary of?"

Josh replied that there was not much more that the photos could tell. He noted that there was what looked like a long field in the middle of the camp, suggesting that this might be a practice firing range. Suddenly, Joseph interrupted:

"Guys, my eyes may not be as well trained as yours, but there is something here that I'd love to know more about."

He was pointing to an item about a couple hundred meters south of the closest barracks. There seemed to be a large parking area; the ground looked so dark that it might be asphalt rather than packed up dirt. Taking his point further, Joseph indicated that in the northeast corner of that area, there were a couple of vehicles, maybe trucks, maybe something else. Josh hit his forehead with the flat of his hand and replied:

"Not sure, but do you know what? These could be rocket launchers. Holy mackerel. This could be huge. Well done, Joseph. Well guys, we know at least one area we must investigate very carefully."

■ ■ ■ ■ ■

Now ready for their trip into Syria, the four men packed the three drones into one of their SUVs. There being four of them, they had decided that they ought to take two vehicles to drive to the suspected military camp in Syria. Though on the surface they could have made do with a single vehicle, Josh had preferred to be safe. He had argued that finding themselves stuck in Syria, though they would be there legally and with perfectly valid though fake passports, would be unpleasant if not dangerous, particularly as someone might then notice the drones that they would be carrying with them. Joseph had suggested that they could always leave the drones in Syria after having destroyed them. After all, the most important data, in fact the only important data would be in the memory chips in their controllers. Regardless, the decision was made to avoid using Josh's own vehicle. They should rather use two of the rental cars, on the grounds that losing one of them, if it should happen, would be less problematic than if the one car that was lost was the one registered to Abu Musa, aka Josh Steinmetz, a Mosul resident.

They waited to leave Mosul until the mid-afternoon principally because they wanted to work when night was as pitch black as possible. The fact that outside temperatures would be lower was a welcome additional bonus. They followed the same road which Joseph and Frank had used as they were following Abdullah. The landscape was just as boring in its greyish brown color as other times. The absence of trees except when the highway was running past cultivated farms was noticeable, though in fairness it was no different than what the men could see on the roads in the vicinity of Mosul or Erbil. The border crossing was a mere formality as the men replied that they

were going to visit Al-Maabadah, which had changed its name to
Girkê Legê under the last administration and camp there; they used
that excuse to explain the fact that they needed two cars, the second
containing camping gear prominently laying around the back seat
area.

They had agreed that each of their two teams would be captained
by a seasoned veteran, either Josh or Mike, and include one of the
younger *Katsas*. Mike and Joseph would take one of the cars and be
responsible for the two decoy drones. They would keep patrolling the
northwest side of the camp, initially being careful to keep flying the
drone high enough to avoid being noticed. They would follow the
fence as carefully as they could, starting with the northeast corner
to determine whether there was another gate or maybe more or not.
Josh and Frank would park their car near a tree farm which stood
on the border of the camp less than three hundred yards from the
south end of Gir Siyareta Çolê, on the right-hand side of the road.
They decided to drive into the area in front of the tree farm, as the
plantations began less than one hundred yards from the main road.
They could see that the tree farm was not a part of the camp, as the
fence surely looked like it was west of the farm. They decided to walk
into the tree farm, hoping that they would be hidden from the road,
should anyone pass by. This would still give them plenty of range to
look at the parts of the camp they wanted to delineate as precisely as
possible: the buildings and more than anything else the area where
they thought they might have seen missile or rocket launchers.

Josh would take the best drone and begin to inspect the area
north and west of the field of young trees which though still young
were high enough to provide solid cover for him to hide. Midway into
his work, Josh thought he heard some noise. He motioned to Frank
who had accompanied him with a gun and silencer, just to be on the
safe side, to get back to the car, and to make sure he was ready to
drive away at a moment's notice. Meanwhile Josh continued to film

and as he approached the area that had indeed a tarmac asphalt cover, he mumbled under his breadth:

"My God! These are missile launchers. In fact, for all I know they could launch ballistic missiles. If they're for ballistic missiles, I wonder where they are hiding any rocket launcher they might also have. Could all the projectiles sent into Tiberias have come from here? Are these guys part of Hezbollah? Are they working to set Hezbollah up for reprisals?"

He immediately called the whole team on the ear buds they all wore to let them know of his discovery. He then asked:

"Where are we on the question of gates into the compound?"

Mike replied:

"We've seen at least four."

He stopped and corrected himself:

"Make that five. Just as we surmised. There is one gate near each village, though the main gate is the one Frank and Joseph initially picked up."

Josh deadpanned:

"That means that Abdullah had more than one way to leave the camp when you all first followed him. We still don't know where he is. Things to consider. This one is on my plate. I'll have to take care of it."

He stopped and added:

"I'm walking back to where Frank and the car are. I hear sounds and they are getting closer. Mike or Joseph, can you fly a decoy closer to me and try and attract their attention away. I'd rather not lose this drone, nor would I like them to lay their hands on it."

He started to walk and then ran through the tree farm and was delighted when he saw a car in the distance, parked near the small farmhouse which they believed was uninhabited. Suddenly, Josh realized that the car did not belong to Frank: its headlight pattern was different:

"Damn! If these aren't the headlights of Frank's car, whose are they?"

He called Frank and asked:

"Where are you?"

"Still on the plot of land in front of the tree farm. I had to leave the farm when I saw a car driving onto the dirt track. I wondered whether they were the owners or simply people who were looking for something. I crossed them as they were coming in and I was going out. I smiled at them and then turned right when I got to the highway. There I switched off all the lights and drove back into the farm, you know right behind the shed which is on the left side of the property. I'm sure they didn't see me."

"Where is that car now?"

"Still there. Hey, wait a minute. It's leaving the farm. If they're going to see me, it's now. I'm ready to defend myself but hope it won't get to that."

"Whatever you do, use a silencer and if possible, bullets which won't kill them, just put them to sleep."

"Sure. Wait. They're not coming my way. They're driving straight back to the main road. They're veering north."

"Hold it! I know why they came here. They switched on the sprinkler system. In a minute or two I'll be soaking wet. Forgot that in this part of the world, water is at a premium and people use smart irrigation systems. In fact, the drip lines on the ground explain why the earth is very wet and the trees don't seem more than damp. They must use the few sprinklers to send some water to the leaves."

Josh paused. He asked Frank to come pick him up near the tree plantation itself. In the meantime, he brought the drone to a perfect landing in front of him and was ready to climb into the car with Joseph when he arrived. He called out to Mike and Joseph:

"Where are you two?"

"Still near the dam."

"Where are the drones?"

"North and west of here."

"Wonderful. Return to your car, bring the drones down there. I'm in the car with Joseph and we don't need any decoy anymore. Meet us back between Al-Maabadah and the divided highway. Did you see anything interesting?"

"Quite a bit, we'll discuss it when we're back in Mosul. Bottom line, it is a military camp, we picked up a few signs. Yet, the surprise is that there didn't seem to be any guards looking out. I can't believe anybody saw us."

"Did you fly low?"

"Didn't, as we weren't going to until we heard that you needed us to run interference."

"Well, luckily, I didn't need that. The moment I could identify the missile launchers, I knew what we were seeing and that was all we needed. We'll have plenty of stuff to report to Tel Aviv."

CHAPTER.25

The gendarmes that were now following the truck came from a different unit. Though the French police system is sufficiently flexible, for instance when conducting an active operation, that jurisdictional issues can be overlooked, the current situation was not serious enough to require breaking the rules. Thus, as the truck left the Var department and entered the Alpes Maritime department, the gendarmes from the Var ceded their places to colleagues from the territory in which the truck was traveling. The men had already been briefed and knew that they needed to keep the lorry and its two occupants under surveillance though they were not to interfere with any of the truck's moves: they were required just note them and report. One of the main instructions indeed had been that the men should do whatever they could not to be noticed. In fact, they knew that at some point they were to call for substitutes. These colleagues were following them a couple of miles behind. The first pair would pass the truck and continue straight ahead, while the second took their place behind and at a safe distance from the truck.

The main objective of the current observation effort was for headquarters to know for sure where the truck was going and verify that its cargo was what it was supposed to be. The gendarmes from Nice reported that the truck remained on A8 until it veered off in the direction of Isola, a somewhat isolated village which had been transformed when Isola 2000 was built, a new ski resort remarkably close to the border with Italy. A new nuclear holding site had been created in the valley, when the village was but a shadow of its current self, a few miles short of Isola because of a massive cavern which had been discovered by chance and could be perfectly closed to the outside. The site was considered an interim step before the rods would be sent to Marcoule further west, in fact only a few miles north of Avignon along the Rhone River where they would eventually be recycled into MOX fuel for nuclear reactors designed to use that kind of combustible. The fact that this interim step involves what might appear as unnecessarily long transit distances simply reflects the natural fear from many towns and villages when it comes to storing nuclear waste.

The gendarmes were able to confirm that the truck did go all the way to the nuclear holding site. Once the truck arrived at the gate and had shown the appropriate paperwork, it was invited to proceed all the way to the place where it would deliver the cargo, consisting of half a dozen stainless-steel cases lined with lead. The local handler came toward the back of the truck with a forklift and brought down the cases one by one. The two gendarmes which had been following the truck were given permission to enter the site as well and were invited to witness the unloading operation. An official who was attending the transfer verified that the cases were the right ones, all the way to checking the seal made of red wax which was affixed to the top side of each crate. The seal, which had originally been placed before the cases left the nuclear power plant, was located in a way such that no case could be opened without breaking the seal. That the seal seemed intact confirmed to the attending official that there had not been any tampering with the contents of the cases. That done, the official apposed his signature on the transfer documents, keeping one copy for himself, sending one back with the truck, and using a safe internet transmission to send a copy of the documents to the power plant from where the cases came.

The two gendarmes asked for permission to see the GPS tracker and to analyze what it had recorded. They could only observe that there was an approximate two-and-a-half-hour period during which it recorded nothing, suggesting that the truck had simply stopped. Having called their colleagues in St Maximin-La-Sainte-Baume, whose investigation it still officially was since they had initiated it, to ask if they had any question; they were surprised to hear them ask for somewhat more precise data. Specifically, the members of the Brigade of St Maximin were asking for a detailed map so that he could see whether the point where the recording stopped was the same as where it resumed. The gendarmes noted that there was almost a mile between the two points. They told their colleagues not to mention that observation to anyone at the site, least of all to the driver of the truck and his colleague, though they should clearly include it in their report.

Given the turn of events, the investigation which had transited from St Maximin-La-Sainte-Baume to their ultimate commanding officer in Hyeres, Colonel Dupin, had gained a national dimension. In short, the circumstances were now suspicious enough that further investigation was warranted, and it now involved at least two departments, not counting the fact that Paris and the Defense Ministry wanted to assume overall control. Colonel Dupin instructed the brigade to pass the file onto his departmental office and collaborated with Colonel Severin who was based in Nice and headed up the relevant group for the Alpes Maritimes department. They agreed immediately to create a taskforce comprising two detectives, with the most senior of the two coming from Nice and the other coming from Hyeres, thus allowing both brigades to have representation.

The detectives drove to the winery and asked to see the owner. They were not ready to come out with all that they knew as they had still been instructed not to do anything that might warn the traffickers that something was up. Their visit therefore did not involve any warrant, and its official purpose was solely to ask a couple of questions. They made a story up that, though based on the truth, omitted a few crucial elements. They said that two gendarmes had followed a truck which had driven to the winery the prior early afternoon, a Sunday. They said that their report indicated first that they were surprised that the wine and gift shop of winery would be open on a Sunday and second that the truck drivers had bought some wine. The owner seemed not to understand what the whole affair was about and somewhat flustered simply asked:

"Is there anything illegal there?"

"Surely not" answered the detective from Nice. Yet, he added:

"I would like to have the specifics so that we can close the report which they filed."

"Your gendarmes filed a report for that?"

"The rules are the rules, sir. I'm sorry to inconvenience you but can assure you that it shouldn't take any more than a minute or two."

The owner reluctantly agreed though the gendarmes noted that he seemed uncomfortable. The report in fact stated:

"The owner seems not to welcome a visit, though it is hard to say whether he has something to hide or not. Considering what we know, we have to assume that he has something to hide. We didn't ask any question to avoid giving a hint that there was an ongoing formal investigation."

The detective from Nice followed him into the owner's office, which was on the first floor of the mansion, immediately to the right of the entry hall. The room was tastefully decorated in the style of the residence, though signs of modern technology abounded, with at least two screens on the desk which sat in front of a bookcase which took the whole of the back wall. A door to the left of that bookcase led to another room which served the dual purpose of a wine tasting room and offices for the two staff members dealing with the accounting and administration functions for the winery. The Hyeres-based detective stayed outside and paced around the car in the courtyard of the winery. The owner could see him through the window and asked:

"Would he not prefer to come in?"

He paused and absentmindedly added something he always mentioned to visitors in the hot summertime:

"The air conditioning offers some cool respite to the outside heat."

The senior detective noted that the weather, though quite pleasant, surely did not require respite from undue heat before replying to the original query:

"Thank you, but there is no need to disturb you any more than we unfortunately have already, sir."

What the owner did not know was that the Hyeres detective carried a Geiger Counter on his belt. The detective discreetly walked further and further from the central office, approaching the back of the courtyard, where the two gendarmes had seen both the garage for the equipment and the cellar for bottled wine. He surely disguised his surprise when he heard the characteristic clicking sound indicating that the Geiger Counter had picked up some radioactivity. As the Nice detective returned to the top of the three stairs in front of the entry door with the owner, ready to leave, his Hyeres colleague made a discreet sign. The Nice detective surprised the owner as he asked:

"By the way, back there, what do you keep in that cellar?"

Matter-of-factly, the owner answered:

"Ah! Interesting. I keep older bottled wine separate from the release of the year which is in the building to the left of the equipment garage as we call it. Some of these older wines are for sale, for customers who are prepared to pay more for older vintages. Other bottles I keep for my own collection."

"Would it be possible to look? I've never seen a winery cellar . . ."

"You mean the old cellar or the one that contains the wine currently on sale?"

"The older cellar if that's OK with you . . ."

Though his face clearly told the two detectives that he surely did not relish the request, the owner reluctantly took them to the old wine cellar. The detectives noted that the station-wagon the gendarmes had seen near the cellar door surely was not there this time. One of them asked:

"Do you park your car near here?"

"Why are you asking?"

"Oh. I don't know. Just curiosity I guess."

"Well, the answer is that I do not. It is usually parked in the garage under the main house. You access it from the side away from the road. I maintain a small collection of vintage automobiles which I occasionally drive. The underground garage can hold up to fifteen cars, though we don't have that many now."

They did not think twice about the fact that it had to mean that the station wagon discussed in the report could not be the owner's car; until later. The owner opened the heavy door allowing the men to feel the cooler air that was inside. The detective from Hyeres asked:

"Why such a large temperature difference?"

The owner looked embarrassed as he replied:

"Well, that's why you have cellars. The temperature inside the cellar is always lower. We like to keep it in the mid-teens to be precise. But I should also make a confession."

The detectives suddenly were paying more attention. The owner finished his point with an embarrassed smile:

"In truth we use air-conditioning. It's not illegal and here, given how little elevation we have until you get close to the Montagne Sainte Victoire, we would have to dig quite a long way to get enough of the fresh air we need. So, we help nature a bit . . . Solar tiles on the roof of the equipment garage provides the necessary electricity."

The three men walked toward the back of the cellar and did observe that it was not much longer than one hundred feet, surprisingly short for the kind of cellar which such a substantial winery needed, even though there were three alleys from front to back and thus quite a bit of potential bottle storage. The detectives noted that the racks were all full to the brim. They were ready to leave the cellar when the Hyeres detective told his colleague in a very soft voice:

"Some radioactivity seems to come from the back of the cellar . . ."

■ ■ ■ ■ ■

After Josh had informed Mark that his team had found a base, probably belonging to ISIS, or some subset, or rebirth of that organization and that they had seen two missile launchers there, the word came back quickly that the launchers had to be neutralized. Mark and Josh quickly agreed that Frank and Joseph had done a wonderful job, but that it was time to rotate them out of Iraq. Josh was indeed convinced that the skills he needed were more sophisticated than what the younger agents could offer. In particular, any effort that would be made against the ISIS base required commando skills, and for at least one individual to be familiar with missile launchers and the associated electronics of guidance and firing.

■ ■ ■ ■ ■

Amos Goldberg was the first individual who was selected to be a part of the Iraqi effort. His experience was broad, including commando work in Southern Lebanon in the recent past. However, he had originally pursued advanced engineering studies and while in the army had been posted to units managing rockets and missiles. When Mark told him of the job he would have to take on, his first reaction was to ask:

"Do we know the missile type? Given the range required, I suspect that they are one of three types: Fateh-110, Shahab-2 or Zolfaghar. The Zolfaghar is derived from the Fateh 110 missile. Both are typically fired from a heavy truck. The Zolfaghar is the most modern iteration, named if I remember correctly after Zulfiqar, the sword of Ali ibn Abi Talib, the cousin and son-in-law of the Islamic prophet, Muhammed. They typically have a range of anywhere from 200 to 350 miles, which would be plenty, if they are aimed toward Israel."

"Well, Amos, you know much more than I do on this topic. I bet that Josh will be delighted to have you on the team. You need to get yourself ready to leave within the next forty-eight hours. I suspect that we'll have you transit via Istanbul and fly to Erbil. There is a car waiting for you there, it was driven by Frank Mauser who did a wonderful job during the first half of the mission."

■ ■ ■ ■ ■

Aaron Myer was the other agent whom Mark had selected, to replace Joseph Asher. He had participated in missions within *Shayetet* 13, a unit of the Israeli Navy and one of the primary *Shayetet* units of the Israel Defense Forces. Though *Shayetet* 13 had a special emphasis on navy-type work, Aaron had subsequently moved to the *Shaldag* unit, reputedly the most elite group within the Israeli Defense Forces. Most of its missions are classified. According to the founder of the unit, its name, which means "Kingfisher," is intended to reflect the similarity of its operations to the nature of the bird: a kingfisher dives from its perch toward a prey it has seen in the water from afar and does it with both maximum speed and minimum splash.

When Mark explained to Aaron the nature of the mission, he simply replied:

"ISIS, Hezbollah, they're similar. *Shaldag* was once tasked with a deep into enemy territory mission against Hezbollah. I hope I can help."

Mark replied with similar instructions to those which had been given to Amos, also mentioning the fact that Joseph Asher's car was waiting for him at Erbil's airport.

■ ■ ■ ■ ■

Mike Robert had stayed in Iraq with Josh and was there in the shophouse when Aaron and Amos arrived. The four men greeted one another warmly and then proceeded to sit down together in the back room of the shop. Josh gave a quick update to everyone on where the investigation was and how they got there. He then outlined the plan which he and Mark had put together. Yet, he quickly added:

"The main point is that we don't know what we're going to find. We know that the last couple of times one of us drove close to the base we saw at least one of the missile launcher trucks. We went back at night and using night-vision goggles we were able to conclude that there didn't seem to be anyone guarding the truck."

Aaron asked:

"How far are the trucks from the barracks?"

Josh replied:

"Six to seven hundred feet at most. How noisy are they when they move the missile from its horizontal resting position to its firing state?"

Amos replied:

"Less than you think if they're the type I have seen. It's typically done with an electric motor, which means that other than the odd squeaking of this wheel or that wheel, it should be quiet. Plus, the wheels around which the assembly rotates are visible and accessible from the outside. We ought to bring some extra lubricating oil. Won't eliminate all squeaks but it should help nevertheless."

Amos paused. Aaron took over to ask another question:

"What's the perimeter of the base made of?"

Josh replied that they had not driven all the way around it, but it did not seem to be protected the way typical military bases are. He said they had a few guard posts at the periphery, but they were probably at least a couple miles from one another, if not more. He added:

"You know, these guys are terrorists, not regular army guys. So, they try to disappear among the local population as much as they can; that provides them with useful shields. The only thing that's a bit different is the fact that they have quite a few sheds and garages. I'm guessing that's where they hide their ammunition. In fact, I'm ready to bet that they leave the big trucks out because they don't have space for them in the garages. I'd guess that any rocket launcher is probably hidden away in these sheds."

Amos asked:

"Don't you find it a bit odd that they wouldn't hide things that cost so much money? Plus, what about satellite reconnaissance?"

Josh had to concede that it was not what he would have expected and added:

"Frankly, that's why I'd like us to act quickly. My guess is that these trucks will eventually be hidden under camouflaged tarpaulins or used to launch the missiles. In fact, I should add that the first time I saw images from the camp, in Tel Aviv, the launchers were hidden under tarps."

Amos asked:

"Does that mean that another launch is imminent?"

Josh could only reply:

"Your guess is as good as mine. . ."

CHAPTER.26

TEL AVIV, ISRAEL

Marvin had called Simon earlier on the telephone:

"I received your message. Happy to help, but I still have a crucial question: How much can I tell your team?"

Simon smiled, being in fact quite happy to see how prudent Marvin was with information which he, Simon, knew to be extremely sensitive. Knowing that by "your team" Marvin was referring to David and Mark, he simply replied:

"I wouldn't hold anything back from them. I chose not to tell them anything myself simply because the technological element is too complex. I couldn't be sure that I would do it justice. Plus, I know that I would surely not be able to answer all their questions. So, feel free to go as deep as they need to understand the new weapon."

■ ■ ■ ■ ■

David and Mark arrived at Marvin's office full of excitement. Simon had told them that the conversation would cover a new weapon. which, though still top secret and not 100% operational, had the potential to change their relative power position in the region and the world. As they had met to prepare for the meeting, David and Mark had speculated for a short while on what the new weapon might be. Yet, they quickly agreed that their efforts were futile. They would know soon enough, in fact the next day.

Marvin was all smiles as they walked into his office, though he stopped them immediately:

"Sorry, gentlemen, but I need you to come into the conference room next door. My office isn't set up for the kind of conversation we need to have."

Though taken aback, David and Mark were more than happy to back out of Marvin's office and move to the room next door. It was not much larger than Marvin's office, though it did appear that way if only because everything seemed to be in its place. None of the chaos of papers, blueprints and magazines which covered virtually all horizontal surfaces other than a small portion of the floor and the space for his orchids on the credenza in Marvin's office. The conference table which throned in the middle of the room was made of light-colored wood, quite possibly poplar, with brushed stainless-steel legs whose tops were visible in each of the four corners of the table. The chairs used the same stainless-steel material for their structural elements and were covered in light-brown leather. Sitting in the middle of the rectangular table, Mark and David could see what seemed like a complete video-conference set-up which ostensibly had to be hooked to the two screens, one above the other on the wall opposite the short side of the table.

Marvin invited his guests to sit down on either of the long sides of the table as he took his place at the top, after he had slid the video-conference commands close enough for him to operate them:

"I know that Simon has already mentioned this to you but let me emphasize the fact that this is beyond top-secret."

Both David and Mark nodded and smiled. Marvin returned the smile and added:

"I have used that term before, I'm sure, but this time it really deserves the label. You can count on the fingers of both hands the number of people who know about this in Israel."

Marvin went on to explain the key reason the weapon he was about to discuss was top-secret. He started with an apology for the bit of history which he was going to have to share with them, adding:

"It's indispensable. Without it, you wouldn't be able to understand the whole thing."

As he started his presentation, Marvin recalled that a key element of the new weapon had in fact not been developed by Israel, but by the United Kingdom:

"The UK's Ministry of Defense developed a laser weapon which they called 'DragonFire.' They evaluated it and reported that the tests were successful. What is unique about the weapon is that it brings the cost of anti-missile or anti-drone defense dramatically down. Just to give you an order of magnitude, it may cost a million dollars or more to buy and then fire a traditional anti-missile weapon, and frankly up to $30 million for anti-ballistic missiles. DragonFire would bring that cost down to less than $100 per shot."

David and Mark looked suitably impressed. Marvin smiled and added:

"The only real cost is the cost of the electricity needed to generate the laser beam . . . Obviously, this is after you have sunk the necessary funds to develop and construct the weapon."

Marvin paused and looking his colleagues in the eyes, he took an almost conspiratorial demeanor. David remembered that he had already seen that facial expression and that the news which Marvin had shared then was a true epoch change; it dealt with the use of unmanned vehicles, drones which Israel pioneered. David elected to remain quiet and motioned to Mark that he should do the same, though both immediately had their antennas set to the maximum level of perceptiveness.

"My friends, so far, there is nothing really secret. I should also tell you that we were in fact partially involved with the UK project. So, to start with, let me reiterate that there is no question that DragonFire is truly theirs. You might ask what role did we play and how did we gain the knowledge needed to develop our own weapon. The short answer is that it is quite innocuous. No information we used involved our spying on friends."

He paused allowing David to say:

"I know that's the official line, Marvin, but how much do the British know about what you're about to tell us next?"

Marvin had a broad smile on his face. He conceded that David had exactly understood the key distinction. Marvin explained that Israel, through *Mossad*, had been able to recreate the weapon within its own facilities. He acknowledged that some of the insights they used came from their initial work with the British, adding:

"They knew we were going to engage in our own advanced research and had surely made certain that they wouldn't allow us access to anything they deemed top-secret from their point of view. But let me share another secret: the laser isn't the piece that is crucial; neither is the weapon per se."

He could immediately see that David and Mark had moved a bit forward in their chairs, a sign of their intense interest. Marvin added:

"The point that is absolutely secret is that we have developed a different delivery mechanism."

He conceded that the work which had been done on the laser beam had indeed been common to both, but the different delivery mechanism was what totally changed things. He explained:

"As things stand, DragonFire is primarily a defensive weapon. We will surely eventually buy it and integrate it into our defense systems which, as you know, involve the Iron Dome, together with a couple of other elements, which we call David's Sling and the Arrow 2 and 3 systems. Iron Dome deals with short-range missiles, David's Sling is designed for short- to medium-range missiles, while the Arrow 2 and Arrow 3 systems hit missiles at high altitudes."

Marvin paused and, reiterating an earlier comment, reminded David and Mark that each of these systems rely on complex and thus expensive missiles. He explained that their systems, developed jointly with the U.S. involve identifying threats from afar and firing missiles to destroy them before they could hit their targets in Israel. He noted that there was a fundamental weakness in their effort:

"You can easily imagine an adversary's strategy that would use swarms of attacking missiles or even more likely today relatively cheap drones. We could defend ourselves but could go broke spending upwards of 10 to 100 times as much money on each defensive missile fired as the enemy would have spent on their attacking rockets or drones. Remember these are a dime a dozen to produce."

David could not stop himself and asked:

"We know that DragonFire would deal with that, right?"

"Absolutely correct. It's not available yet, but when it is, we will integrate it into our systems. Now, assuming we are there, what is to stop us from converting the new weapon from a purely defensive use to one which also offers offensive capabilities?"

David and Mark could see Marvin beaming. They chose not to interrupt him as he offered to show a short video, adding that the video was a computer animation of the concept as it was initially approved. The first thing that surprised them was a short passage which depicted a mirror in the sky. They still kept quiet as the video then showed a graphic of a laser beam projected from the earth onto that mirror. The next image showed the laser beam effectively being bounced from the mirror to a target. David waited until the video stopped and immediately asked:

"Why hasn't this been done before? After all, we have seen the conceptual equivalent in several spy movies over the last fifteen to twenty-five years . . ."

Marvin was still beaming and though with all the appropriate deference to David's rank could not help himself as he said:

"My dear David, movies are one thing and reality is another. First, there is the issue of developing the right mirror. Until we found a solution, even a mirror that reflected 95% of a lethal laser beam would still absorb enough heat to burn. The mirror would be next to useless as the beam would be able to reach it only once. That may be why you've seen the bad guys in movies use diamonds to create the surface of their mirrors."

With a chuckle he added:

"One mirror placed in space per shot would make that solution even more expensive than missiles."

Continuing with his explanation, he argued:

"Second, there is the need to control the angulation of the mirror in real time or close to it. Remember, the distances are quite large even when you deal with geosynchronous satellites. It wouldn't take more than an error of a fraction of a degree to miss the target by miles."

"So?"

"I can't go into the details as they are very complex and rely on the very advanced materials we created. But suffice it to say that we have developed two new kinds of materials. One is used as a coating on the front of the surface of the mirror; it prevents most of the energy contained in the laser beam from being absorbed by the mirror. As an aside, remember that heat is the result of the interaction of the energy of the laser beam and whatever surfaces it touches. Thus, minimal heat reaches the surface of the mirror, which heats up only moderately. As whatever is left bounces back, the energy stored in the coating is recaptured and provides an immensely powerful beam."

He paused for a second to drink from the glass of water to his right side and continued:

"Unfortunately, even that modest amount of heat could damage the mirror, maybe not the first time it is used but still over time or if it were called upon multiple times in close succession. That's where the second material comes in handy. It uses the electricity generated by the solar panels of the satellite to cool the temperature of the back of the mirror. Thus, when the laser beam reaches the front of the mirror, any energy which could damage the surface of the mirror is used to warm up the mirror rather than burn it. In short, that second material counters the negative effects of the absorption of the heat in the beam. Together, they preserve the integrity of the mirror and allow it to redirect a beam which is virtually as powerful as the original laser flash. The ambient temperature in space adds the final element in that it maintains the mirror at a low temperature when it is folded back into its protective sheath. Now, gentlemen, please appreciate that I have taken several shortcuts to explain this and thus have certainly said things with which a purist would disagree."

"Wow. And how about the second issue, the aiming mechanism?"

"We were also able to solve the problem with a rather elegant solution."

Mark noted the use of the word "elegant," a Marvin Goldstein trademark when he was about to reveal something new and ingenious. Marvin went on:

"You know how the use of fiber optics has made internet and related communications both faster and more dependable . . ."

"Don't tell me that you can use fiber optics to connect to a satellite?"

"Sure, we can't. But the concept is that light travels faster than anything else, right?"

Mark replied:

"I see that, but how can it be used here?"

"Simple. We convert our instructions from radio waves to light pulses. A receptor on the satellite which hosts the mirror reads these instructions and executes the maneuvers it needs to execute."

Marvin paused as he could see that he had lost his audience. He had allowed some *non sequitur* to creep into his explanation. He explained:

"In plain English, there is a sequence of events that we must ensure is followed properly. The first step involves deploying the mirror, which requires us to send a signal to the satellite."

"Why?"

"Well, Mark, we don't want the mirror always deployed. First, sunlight up there could eventually destroy or at least weaken our mirror protection against excessive heat. But there is also another reason: our satellite is much harder to detect if it looks quite 'normal.' That means like many of those already in orbit: think of a single cylinder with a large solar array to provide it with the electricity it needs to function. Anything with a permanently deployed mirror would generate unwanted attention. We know our enemies have access to anti-satellite weapons. They would use them to destroy our satellite. With our clever solution, our satellite is much harder to detect. The sheath of the mirror is 'parked' alongside the cylinder; when told to deploy, the sheath opens to a 90-degree angle relative to the satellite cylinder. Then the mirror deploys from the sheath."

David noted:

"I noted you just used the present tense to describe the satellite. You said: 'our satellite IS much harder to detect' didn't you?"

"Exceptionally perceptive, David. You're absolutely right. We already have one such satellite in orbit. We will launch more over the coming months."

"So, the new weapon is operational?"

Marvin hesitated for several seconds before replying:

"Well, yes and no."

"What do you mean? It is or it isn't, right?"

"Great question, Mark. We have only evaluated our weapon once in real-life conditions. We placed a target in the desert near Beersheba. I don't need to remind you that it's the capital of the Negev region of Israel and the home of the Ben Gurion University of the Negev and one of the very few centers for the development of our high tech and technology industry."

Mark nodded his understanding. Marvin continued his explanation saying that the test had been satisfactory, though it did not go as smoothly as would be required in the real circumstances of a war. David asked:

"What was the problem?"

"We ran two checks. The first worked like a charm. The target was hit just as desired. However, the second failed."

David asked:

"What happened?"

"Well, the second trial involved placing the target on a robot which moved on the ground at relatively fast speeds, and yet still slower than any incoming missile. We fired the laser twice and missed the target twice."

David followed up with another question, asking what caused the problem and how easy or not would it be to fix it. Marvin replied that the issue had to do with the ability of the sensors to detect the appropriate reflection angle required for the mirror and adjust it quickly enough. He concluded:

"In short, we need to revisit the speed with which communication with the satellite is integrated with our existing systems."

"How hard is this going to be?"

Marvin surprised Mark and David with his reply:

"The issue isn't one of technology or even of cost. We have a fairly good idea of what we would need to do. The real problem is that we do not want people to know we have that capability. So, widening the circle more than it currently exists is a serious issue."

David asked what that meant for the new weapon. He was surprised to see Marvin smile broadly as he simply replied:

"With respect to integrating it along with Iron Dome, David's Sling and others, we're not there and will have to proceed with caution. However, . . ."

Marvin paused for effect and finished his sentence:

"We don't need that integration if we want to use the weapon in an offensive mode . . . I think we'll call it Death Ray; not terribly original, but quite correct, technically!"

CHAPTER.27

PARIS AND SOUTHERN FRANCE; TEL AVIV, ISRAEL

The two detectives had not finished giving their oral report to Colonel Severin, the regional commander in Nice, when he asked them to stop:

"I'm sorry, men, but we need to get Colonel Dupin from Hyeres on the line."

The three men moved to the conference room next to the colonel's office and he dialed Colonel Dupin up on a video conference line:

"Colonel, we may have made an important discovery. I wanted you to hear it at the same time as I did. We may need to call Paris on that one."

Turning to the two detectives, he asked them to give a rapid summary of their report. The face of Colonel Dupin grew increasingly serious as the story progressed and displayed nothing less than total surprise when the men reported that they had found radioactivity signals in the winery, and more importantly, near the back of the underground cellar. Colonel Dupin exclaimed:

"You are quite right, Colonel, we must involve the authorities in Paris. I'm happy to call them as they had initially contacted me, but I'll be sure to give credit where credit is due."

"Thank you. In the meantime, I suggest that we establish round-the-clock surveillance on both the winery and the headquarters of the transporter. At this point, I'd rather wait for orders before bringing anyone else into the picture. Do you agree?"

"Absolutely."

■ ■ ■ ■ ■

The next morning, Francis Marchand organized a meeting in his offices, with Gabriel Lefevre and Marcel Delagrange. As the topic was going to be, in his opinion at least, strictly focused on France, he had elected not to invite Nathan Stone, the Israeli of Vice Consul for Military Affairs. On the other hand, Colonel Germain, the Chief of Staff of the French Minister of Defense, had been invited, while Colonels Dupin and Severin were also connected via video conference. Their roles were to present the report of the detectives and if needed answer any additional questions. They also shared their preliminary instructions with their teams, making sure to mention that they were expecting changes following the meeting.

The group immediately agreed that the report was both worrisome and quite encouraging. It was worrisome to the extent it confirmed that there was at least one center of nuclear waste traffic on the French territory. On the other hand, the encouraging aspect was the fact that its activities had been partially uncovered. Marcel Delagrange was asked to comment on the findings. He immediately suggested that serious caution was warranted to the extent that his could only be informed speculation at best, at least until more information was available. He still argued that there was nonetheless one sequence of events which would fit with the findings as presented:

"To me, the one thing which might make sense would be that the winery served as the locale where the spent fuel pellets are recovered from the used fuel rods."

He paused for a second and concluded:

"As you know, used fuel rods are typically reprocessed or stored. They are stored when the price of uranium is low as the process used to extract the useful materials from the rods, or rather from the pellets inside the rods, is expensive. I will spare you the gory details of reprocessing but suffice it to say that the process requires space: the plants that conduct this sort of activity are not small. You wouldn't hide them in an underground cave, unless it was truly mammoth in size."

Francis Marchand asked:

"Professor Delagrange, what could one do with the spent fuel pellets you are suggesting could be recovered at the winery?"

"Sell them and use the nuclear waste to make dirty bombs, or rather in the official terminology radioactive diffusion devices. In short, you'd place a handful of pellets, even fewer than that, into a conventional bomb and, when it exploded, it would spread nuclear radioactivity within some given perimeter."

Gabriel Lefevre suggested that this would clearly be a major issue. Yet he added:

"Unfortunately, we are in a quandary. We could launch an operation in the winery and maybe recover evidence if we are lucky. Yet, I would suggest that the chances are probably at least as high that the terrorists would simply relocate the operation somewhere else. Sure, we could recover equipment; but it could be easily replaced and set up somewhere else. Plus, I'm ready to bet that if there is anything quite sensitive or hard to replace, it isn't kept onsite."

Professor Delagrange interrupted the flow of the conversation to correct an earlier statement:

"Gentlemen, I may have unintentionally misled you. I said that recovering the spent pellets required space. I was really bypassing a step. You could recover the pellets from the rod in a place such as the cellar you all described. You just need to 'unscrew' the top of the rod, slide the pellets from inside the rod into a container, close the container and you're done. The problem is that the caesium 137 or Strontium 90 must still be recovered: that's when the spent uranium pellets are soaked in water and the two metals eventually recovered. And that's the process that takes space and time."

Colonel Germain thanked Professor Delagrange for the insight and then asked:

"Does anybody know how often these shipments of waste from nuclear power plants are made?"

Everybody seemed to feel that they did not know the answer, although Francis Marchand suggested that the French Alternative Energies and Atomic Energy Commission, or CEA, would be the right place to start asking questions. He added:

"It is a research organization in the areas of energy, defense and security, information technologies and health technologies."

Everybody agreed that such was the obvious next step, though Marcel Delagrange went back to Colonel Germain's question:

"Why were you asking that question, Colonel Germain?"

"Simply because it would determine, in my view, whether we can afford to wait for the next shipment or not."

Seeing that he needed to say more, Colonel Germain expanded his point to argue that in an ideal world he would like to know what happens to the spent fuel after it is broken into pellets at the winery. He added:

"Let's be practical. From what Professor Delagrange said, I have to assume that the laboratory which the winery constructed could be relocated with relative ease; it seems to me that the key elements are the need for discreet space as well as peace and quiet to execute the modest maneuvers that are required."

Colonel Germain noted that Professor Delagrange was nodding his agreement though he said:

"I probably should not say this because I'm sure you all know, but that simple step Colonel German described still involves the need for significant protection. These spent pellets are very highly radioactive."

Colonel Germain continued:

"Thank you, Professor. It is always useful to remember these key elements. Now, any action we take, for instance a search done under a duly issued warrant, would at best only prove what we are assuming. The key people might or might not still be there but, more importantly, we would lose track of the waste at once. So, best case scenario, we arrest one or two individuals. Yet, in the end, I'm fairly sure that the key people would walk away unscathed, and we would be back to square one . . ."

He paused and added:

"Without taking anything away from the great job done by the Gendarmerie Nationale, let's not forget that we uncovered the operation somewhat by chance."

Francis Marchand immediately agreed with the logic. The group therefore decided that the actions taken by Colonels Severin and Dupin were exactly the right ones. Both the winery and the transporter should be placed under tight round-the-clock surveillance. Any indication that a new drop-off had been made should immediately be reported. The point, however, would not be to raid the winery, but rather to learn what happened to the pellets once they had been separated, and presumably picked up to be delivered to the next link in the chain. Marcel Delagrange added:

"I like the idea of keeping a close tab on the transporter as well. This might allow us to discover another place where the pellets are extracted. I would however suggest that we take it one step further."

He stopped to make sure he was on the right track and concluded:

"The CEA which Francis Marchand mentioned must have information on every company that is employed in the transport of nuclear waste in France."

■ ■ ■ ■ ■

Meanwhile, back in Iraq, the four *Mossad* agents were getting ready for their Syrian expedition. First, they had decided that they would try to penetrate the Syrian base through the gate near the tree farm which Josh and Frank had found south of Gir Siyareta Çolê. Their earlier investigations had suggested that the gate was not staffed, although they were prepared to deal with anything short of a small guard brigade. They had made the decision that it was the closest to the place where the two missile launchers were. They had agreed that they would take two drones with them, one to make a quick reconnaissance flight to verify that the launchers were still there and ascertain whether there was any guard nearby. It along with the other would then be used together later to keep an eye on the surroundings. They also had a couple of flexible rope ladders to allow the men who would stay outside to climb over the fence and help their colleagues if the need arose. Mike had suggested that these cautionary steps would be crucial while the men worked on the missile launchers.

The two cars had no difficulty at the Iraqi Syrian border and were able to get to their target location without any trouble. Once parked near the east-end of the tree farm, Mike and Josh stayed outside of the camp, while Amos and Aaron went inside. They were just as surprised as Josh had been the first time when they saw that they could walk through the gate and not be stopped. Aaron, always careful and very attentive to his environment, motioned to Amos to run along the fence toward the north, while he walked carefully with his gun at the ready, silencer already screwed onto the barrel. He approached the window of the small guardhouse and was surprised to see two guards sound asleep. He radioed his findings to the whole team suggesting that this meant that exciting the camp might be a bit more difficult if there was any trouble involving noise or worse yet, some sort of alarm. Josh gave the OK to shoot the guards with tranquilizer needles to make sure that they would be sound asleep for at least another hour.

The two men kept walking in the direction of the tarmac where they knew the launchers were. Josh was keeping them aware of what he could see with his drone around the launchers, while Mike's drone was flying higher and observing the whole area with a wide-angle lens. He would be able to provide quite valuable advance notice if needed. Amos and Aaron could now see the two missile launchers side by side a few hundred feet away. They had earlier completed several simulations on their tablets to make sure that they knew exactly what they needed to do and were able to do it quickly. They each approached the left side of their respective launchers and found the small metallic doors to the guidance module exactly where they expected to find them. They knew that they would need to force whatever lock was there as they surely did not have the keys. It turned out to be quite simple, as the locks seemed at best rudimentary; Amos suggested that this reflected the fact that one never expects a missile launcher to fall under enemy control. They unfolded the keyboard incorporated into the module and found their way into the part of the code where the coordinates of the missiles' targets were recorded. They were able to make the required changes and while doing so were smiling interiorly at the surprise which Iran would have as the missiles barreled toward Tehran, more specifically toward the buildings housing the Supreme Leader and the Iranian Majles, the Islamic Consultative Assembly also called the Iranian Parliament.

While reaching the missile launchers and reprogramming them had proven relatively uneventful, as had been the transition of the missiles from their horizontal resting position to the angle needed for them to be launched toward their targets, all hell broke loose when the engines of the two missiles were fired up. The noise associated with their start, which kept increasing as they rose into the night sky, triggered an immediate response from the terrorists in the camp.

Though the *Mossad* team had hoped not to use the drones in their secondary roles, it quickly became evident that it was the only solution to protect Amos and Aaron.

The two drones which the team had brought along were those that were quite basic. They had been purchased in Mosul and there was nothing in them or on them which could point to any Israeli involvement. Yet, the team had decided to transform them into kamikaze bombs if the need arose. To do that, a sheet of C-4 explosive charge and a mechanical detonator had been affixed to the underside of the drones. The plan, if it came to using it, was that the drones would be flown as high as they could go and then the engines would be suddenly switched off. At that point, gravity would take over and the drones would fall from the sky, gaining speed as they came closer to the ground, triggering the mechanical detonator when they hit the dirt. The limited amount of explosives which the team had been able to attach for elementary maximum take-off weight reasons would not cause massive damage. However, the two explosions were designed to occur in two spots directionally opposite from the way the terrorists would run from their barracks to the missile launchers and more importantly from where the Israeli agents were escaping. That was sure to reduce the intensity of the search for who might have caused the missiles to fire, if not permanently, at least temporarily.

Josh and Mike, sitting on the other side of the fence, could follow the progress of their teammates toward the periphery of the camp thanks to a marker which Amos and Aaron wore on their clothing. They guided them to the closest point they could reach and flung the rope ladders above the fence. They were able to climb over the fence and retrieve the ladders before any terrorist caught sight of them. From there getting back to the cars and driving back to Mosul was just as uneventful as the other leg of the trip, though Amos at one point blurted out:

"By the way, guys, Aaron and I saw that they also had at least a couple of rocket launcher trucks in one of their enclosed sheds. The doors were opened . . ."

■ ■ ■ ■ ■

"David, may I have a minute of your time?"

Mark sounded excited, which was not particularly usual for him, when called David Heller, the head of the Disruption Department of *Mossad* and his boss. David was happy to have a quick cup of coffee with Mark, despite a somewhat heavy schedule that day. He had his assistant, Uschi, prepare a cup of cold coffee, which he knew would be the drink Mark would ask, while he said he would be happy with a cup of hot coffee with some cold milk.

Mark went for his usual spot on the cream sofa in David's office and said:

"Thanks for the iced coffee. Now, I have some important news . . ."

"Yes?"

"Vlad Rheingold, you know, Countess Renate's contact with access to old KGB archives has produced quite a bit of what we asked for. He says that the list of what we call 'orphan sources' isn't complete, and I can believe him, but I think we have a very good start."

"So, let me guess. You want to ask permission to use our secret weapon, Death Ray, on one or several of these targets . . . Right?"

"Can't hide anything from you, Boss."

"Let me talk to Simon. I don't want to go ahead without him having fully vetted the plan and more importantly the use of that weapon. He may even need to have a quick conversation with the Prime Minister, if not the whole War Cabinet."

David paused and as Mark got up from the sofa, he added:

"In the meantime, why don't you select two or three possible targets. I think the motto should be: the more isolated the better . . ."

CHAPTER.27

PARIS AND SOUTHERN FRANCE; MOSUL, IRAQ

Meanwhile, the trap had been set in the south of France. Though the operation had been kept as secret as possible to avoid any leakage, the number of individuals involved in it made maintaining the required secrecy quite difficult. The leaders of the operation kept asking themselves what could go wrong.

The trap, which had been named Operation NW, to mean Operation Nuclear Waste without risking a panic which might ensue if people heard the term nuclear, had several dimensions. Though it had been set up under local control, it had been approved at the highest levels within the French government. The thought that nuclear waste could be stollen and eventually sent into some ring with connections to terrorists was if not the worst nightmare at least quite a bad dream. Fundamentally, the plan was dubbed surveillance as it had been decided not to interfere with any individual or any operation unless one was sure that an arrest could in no way provide any advance warning to the rest of the network. There were two different areas where any new development could be isolated and then acted upon: the winery and the office of the waste transporter. The winery was chosen as it would be the place where action would develop if the network decided to cease activities and clean up the place before leaving. At the same time, it would also be the place where the next "delivery" would take place unless there were more than one such locale in the network. The office of the waste transporter seemed more likely to witness the start of a new action, as the truck which would eventually go to the winery and would first need to leave the transporter's garage and then drive to a nuclear power plant.

Importantly, the need for secrecy required for most operations to be conducted in an "unmarked" mode. Cars or motorcycles could not have any sign indicating they were official gendarmerie vehicles. Individuals could not wear their uniforms; they had to appear to be private citizens. Thus, though gendarmes wore street clothes, which they only infrequently did, they still carried their badges so that they could present them if needed; otherwise, they would seem to be simple citizens going after their routine daily business.

From an equipment standpoint, modern tools made the officers' jobs somewhat easier. In particular, the use of drones allowed them to keep their targets under round-the-clock surveillance without necessarily having all resources on site and ready to act. For instance, though there were always at least two gendarmes in the immediate vicinity of the winery, they did not have to be standing at the corner of the main road and the access driveway. They were in fact "comfortably" installed in a panel van that would periodically move in the neighborhood, never staying more than a couple of hours or so in any given location. That is where day and night drone pictures of all the goings on at the winery could be observed. Also, the personnel in the van would be the ones asking for instructions if a significant development took place. Similar precautions were put in place near the transporter's office and parking lot, though it was assumed that the commercial nature of the enterprise and the careful vetting of its ownership and management made it highly likely that the problem was with a couple of rogue employees rather than with the whole company. However, as Colonel Dupin had said:

"Better safe than sorry!"

It took more than a week before the first indication appeared that something might be about to happen. A truck was seen exiting the parking lot of the transporter and one of the two occupants seemed to fit the description of one of the people who had been briefly stopped near the winery a few weeks earlier. The truck did go directly to the nuclear plant north of Marseilles and from there followed normal procedures as it drove to the nuclear waste storage area: in other words, it was a false alert.

A few days later, another truck left the transporter's parking lot. That time, the two men who were in it both fit the descriptions in the first police report. Though it could, just as it was the prior time, be another false start, the team had its hopes high. They were surprised and their hopes dashed when the truck did not stop to collect the spent rods at the plant north of Marseilles. The truck kept going north on A7 and eventually drove to and stopped at Marcoule, one of the larger nuclear complexes in France. The center is a few miles northwest of Avignon and sits on the left bank of the Rhone River. Once there, it went through what seemed like routine motions, taking a couple of cases made of stainless street and lined with lead. It began to retrace its steps, in a direction quite compatible with a hypothetical goal of journeying to the waste storage area north of Nice.

Things were progressing at the same depressingly slow pace at least for gendarmes used to driving at higher speeds. Yet, they dutifully followed the truck, passing the baton to colleagues each time they went from one department or one brigade's jurisdiction to the next. Suddenly, the gendarmes who had been following it since it entered the Var department, called headquarters in Hyeres. Colonel Dupin was immediately alerted when the gendarmes reported:

"The truck has just stopped on the shoulder of the A8 highway, just before the exit for St Maximin-La-Sainte-Baume . . ."

Colonel Dupin immediately could see that this might be the opportunity they had been waiting for. However, always the consummate professional, he kept his calm and asked what the gendarmes had done. They replied that they both passed the truck seemingly going on their way forward and left the highway at the next exit, because they could not stop without giving away their mission. Colonel Dupin asked:

"What if the truck does not exit and keeps going east?"

"We have planned for this, sir. I'm currently on the ramp getting back onto the highway if they keep going. My colleague will simply need to turn around and speed up to reconnect with me."

"Excellent. Where is your colleague?"

"He has kept going in the direction of the winery. We assumed that if the truck does exit the highway as it should, I could quickly reconnect with it, while my colleague would remain in front of it, riding the motorbike as if he were simply taking a quiet outing among the vineyards."

Colonel Dupin switched his radio channel so that all members of his team could hear the message:

"Everyone on duty converge toward St Maximin-La-Sainte-Baume, but don't interfere with the movements of the truck. Observe and report."

As expected, after having spent less than a minute on the shoulder of the A8, the truck got back on the highway. He never picked up speed as he exited less than a few hundred feet later toward St Maximin. The gendarme who had reported on the radio turned around and raced back toward the truck, though he was careful while in town to respect all the various traffic signs. His colleague, as planned, kept driving toward the winery, having happily seen the truck catching up with him in his rear-view mirrors. He purposefully did not stop as he passed by the winery entrance, maintaining his cover. He did stop a few hundred yards further on when he caught up with two of his colleagues who had been tasked with the local surveillance of the winery. He passed the baton and went straight back to headquarters.

An hour later, the truck left the winery and repeated almost the same routine as on its prior run involving a stop at the winery. Once back on the A8, Operation NW, kicked in again as expected. The truck followed the same routine as on its previous trip all the way to the nuclear waste site. The next major phase in Operation NW was to take place at the winery itself. What would happen? Would someone come to pick up the spent pellets extracted from the used fuel rod? Would the owner of the winery or one of his employees leave with the pellets? And if so, where would that person go with them?

■ ■ ■ ■ ■

The newspaper headlines in Tehran were clear: a couple of missiles had hit the town, causing material damage to buildings and structures. No high-ranking official was hit, though reports did mention a number of victims. The blame was instantly placed on Israel and serious repercussions were promised, as someone noted that both missiles were tipped with dirty bombs. They called the move a step too far, as Israel could thus be described as having made first use of nuclear devices, however weak they were. Israel immediately denied all responsibility arguing that no missile with the potential to hit Tehran was fired, the previous night or, with a bit of arrogant humor, for the prior millennia. It added that it would hold Iran responsible and be prepared to reply in kind if Iran took any action against Israel. Yet, it asked for an emergency meeting of the Security Council of the United Nations to discuss how missiles tipped with nuclear waste could have made it into a regional country, using itself the same terminology which Iran had used against it: a nuclear step too far.

∎ ∎ ∎ ∎ ∎

An hour or so before the truck had arrived at the winery, the gendarmes had noted that a station-wagon had driven into the winery and parked near the entrance to the cellar. They did not pay much attention to it. After all cars came in and left on a regular basis, and in fact they felt they had seen this car at least once earlier. They still noted that two men were getting out of the car. One of them was pulling what looked like a bulky case from the trunk of their vehicle; they thought it could be a case full of bottles, as wine is often transported when it has been bottled but labels and the tax stamp not yet affixed. They could see that his colleague was helping him carry it into the cellar, which seemed perfectly consistent with their assumption that they were looking at a case containing a large number of wine bottles. The cellar door closed behind them.

∎ ∎ ∎ ∎ ∎

After the truck left for the nuclear waste site, the gendarmes were beginning to wonder whether anything would eventually happen. It had been almost eight hours without abnormal movement at the winery, and it was now pitch dark in the middle of the night. The panel van had by now been partly transformed into sleeping chambers as there was no need to have anyone right on the ground; the three officers assigned to the surveillance of the winery would thus take turn; one of them would sleep on the improvised camping bed, one would alternate between parking the truck and driving it for a few miles until it was parked in a different location, while the third was monitoring the electronic equipment, principally consisting of video feeds from the two drones that kept an aerial observation.

The gendarme in charge of electronic monitoring woke his colleague up and called the driver who was also slumbering as the truck was stopped:

"Action at the winery . . ."

The driver immediately started the engine of the panel van and drove in the direction of where the motorcycle of the third gendarme was hidden. The electronics officer added:

"Something odd. The station wagon which we have seen here just before the truck arrived is back; it just entered the driveway of the winery. Why would it come to deliver wine in the middle of the night? Again, it isn't stopping at the main house but is driving directly to the cellar in the back. It's parking there."

The team waited for further information, but none came. A half hour later, the man they thought they had seen going into the cellar left the winery and drove away. The one gendarme who had a motorcycle immediately started to tail him, while he asked for a couple of motorized reinforcements to go to the winery. Jules Rangade agreed though to be safe he called his supervisor, Major Sauvage, to keep him informed.

The gendarme who was tailing the man who had worked in the cellar called thirty minutes later:

"The man has stopped his car and is parked in front of a four-story apartment building. Nothing special to report, other than the fact that it is located within the Sophia Antipolis campus. He left the car and entered the building."

Sophia Antipolis is a large technology park located between Cannes and Nice, on the south coast of France. The campus is quite large, covering close to 10,000 acres. It is known to be Europe's first science and technology hub and to employ people of more than eighty nationalities.

Major Sauvage immediately called Colonel Dupin with the information to ask for instructions. He knew that the current mission orders prohibited any interference with anyone. Yet, he felt that some form of investigation ought to be started to identify the man and make sure he did not disappear into thin air. Colonel Dupin agreed and set up of round the clock surveillance for that man as well. His message was clear:

"I'm not sure what's going on, but the presence of this same car on and off is definitely suspect. What is the man doing when he goes into the cellar? In fact, more simply, why does this man go into the cellar?"

Colonel Dupin seemed to have finished his thought when, suddenly, he said:

"Wait a minute. It's staring us in the face, and we didn't see it."

Major Sauvage was surely surprised, but decided that he should let his commanding officer finish his thought:

"The first time the men reported on the station-wagon, they talked of two men. They were carrying something bulky and presumably heavy into the cellar. We didn't see or noted how many were in the car when it left. Now, the second time the car showed up, we heard that there was one man. He went into the cellar, stayed there for a short while, maybe a half hour, and then left. That's the chap we tailed to Sophia Antipolis. What if there was still one guy in the cellar?

■ ■ ■ ■ ■

Josh Steinmetz's cell phone suddenly rang. The caller ID indicated that his friend Ibrahim wanted to speak to him:

"Ibrahim, hello my friend. What can I do for you?"

"Abu Musa, how can you be so nonchalant. Have you heard what happened last night?"

"Given what I think I know, it looks as if I haven't heard what you have. What happened?"

"Well, my God. You don't know that two missiles tipped with dirty bombs were fired from Syria into Tehran."

"Dirty bombs? Missiles?"

"Yes, that what's being reported. We're told the missiles struck the Majles and the residence of the Supreme Leader . . ."

"That's serious. Any casualty?"

"None from the official standpoint, but there were people killed by debris in the buildings. But did you hear me? The missiles were tipped with dirty bombs . . ."

"Hey! I heard you the first time. That's certainly serious. Is it the first time that dirty bombs have been used in the Middle East?"

"Not sure. I have picked up a rumor telling me that a dirty bomb tipped missile was launched toward Israel a few months ago?"

Ibrahim paused long enough for Josh to reply:

"Hadn't heard that one either. Anything more specific on that one or on the hit on Iran for that matter?"

Ibrahim seemed to hesitate and then simply added the decisive factor:

"We hear that Syria is blaming Kurdish rebels living around the area from which the missiles were fired. You know, the northwest most corner, near the border between Syria and Iraq."

"Is that true?"

"If you're asking whether it is true that Kurds are being blamed, the answer certainly is yes. But we have no idea which Kurdish group might be involved if any subgroup was. Anybody we know told us they had nothing to do with that. They see themselves as scapegoats."

Ibrahim added:

"Syrians don't like Kurds, and this is just one more way to portray them as terrorists."

"I'm with you there, Ibrahim. I don't like the sound of it one bit. But frankly what can we do about it?"

Matter-of-factly, Ibrahim simply replied:

"We should have a coffee together to talk about this. I have a few questions which I'd like to ask you."

"No problem. By the way, do we have any news of Abdullah, you know the acquaintance of your associate Rezna?"

"We can add that to our conversation my friend."

CHAPTER.28

David and Mark had asked for an hour of Simon's time so that a conference call could be set up that included Countess Renate and Marvin Goldstein. The point of the conference call was to report on the first strike using the Death Ray. Mark started the conversation with a quick geographical note:

"As all of you except Countess Renate know . . ."

Simon interrupted:

"I'm sorry, Countess, but I decided that you probably didn't need that information ahead of time."

"Totally understood, Simon. In fact, I thank you for including me in this debrief."

Simon motioned to Mark that he should continue his report. Mark smiled and said:

"The target we had picked was quite close to Zhigalovo, one hundred miles west of the west shore of Lake Baikal and three hundred miles north of the border with Mongolia. The town itself is on the Lena River, but the target was deep in the forest to the southwest of Zhigalovo. I don't need to tell you that 'deserted' is too weak a word to describe that region . . ."

Mark paused, smiling at his own understatement, and continued:

"Bottom line, the ray bounced perfectly from the mirror on the satellite and hit the target right on the nose. I brought before and after pictures to show you the extent of the damage. As you can see, except for some fire damage in a radius of about two miles from the target, we achieved our objective. Nobody will go looking for nuclear waste there."

Simon asked:

"Any local reaction?"

"Very little from what we heard from our sources. However, I don't need to tell you that our sources on the ground there are somewhere between minimal and non-existent. Our man is in Novosibirsk, the capital of Siberia, which is more than five hundred miles away from the target. So, we'll keep monitoring, but at this point things seem to have worked according to plan and the motto which David gave me, 'the more isolated the better' guided us well."

Simon congratulated the team and invited Marvin to add any comment. Marvin, who knew that Simon could be ruthless when he went too deep into rabbit holes simply said:

"I rate this as a success for two reasons. First, the target was destroyed. Second, we haven't picked up any chatter suggesting that anyone understood what happened."

Simon asked:

"Any suggestion?"

Marvin replied that he would have no objection to striking another target, although he added a cautionary note:

"I would take my time before repeating the exercise. We don't want anyone, the Russians more than anyone, to begin to link the various explosions. With only one or maybe two, we can hope they will think of them as random and unfortunate explosions. With more attacks, we'd be only a step away from them looking for the party behind them, and we would obviously be viewed as one of the few states capable of pulling something like that off. We don't want them to try to figure out how whoever did it, did it. I suspect they might still believe in coincidences once or twice, but that should not lead us to behave arrogantly."

Simon inquired:

"And your definition of arrogantly?"

"Repeating the exercise more often than once a month at most. As you know, Simon, a crucial potential use of Death Ray is as an anti-satellite or anti-ballistic missile weapon. I don't want to underestimate the risks associated with the orphan sources of nuclear waste, but they have been dormant for more than thirty years and I find it hard to see them as imminent dangers."

Simon thanked Marvin and Countess Renate for their parts in the success and congratulated David and Mark on the execution. He added:

"Let's follow Marvin's advice. Let's not attack another target for a while and when we do let's make sure the next target is as far away from this one as feasible."

■ ■ ■ ■ ■

The guess which Colonel Dupin had made proved to be quite perceptive. About eighteen hours after he had driven to the residential building, as soon as it was nighttime, the man got back into his car and drove straight back to the winery. He surely did not stop by the main house. He got out of the car and went straight into the cellar and closed the door behind him. About a half hour later, someone exited the cellar, though aerial photographs confirmed that it was not the same person as had entered. It had to be the second person who had gone in the first time. Stepping into the car, he drove back to the apartment on the campus of Sophia Antipolis.

■ ■ ■ ■ ■

When informed of the development, Colonel Dupin called a conference call with Colonel Severin, Colonel Germain, and Professor Delagrange. Colonel Dupin summarized his concerns:

"Something must be going in that cellar for there to be a need for someone there around the clock."

Professor Delagrange immediately interrupted:

"Gentlemen, I must stress that I don't have any more facts than anyone here. Yet, I can offer a simple scenario which would make this a very logical sequence of events . . ."

He paused and hearing no objection, he went on to offer his conclusion:

"This whole thing makes sense if you make a simple assumption: the traffickers steal one or several rods at one point in the process. My guess is that this takes place at the time the transporters make their first stop at the winery. They must act quickly because they have to go through at least three different operations. First, they break the wax seal on the side of the case, second, they extract one or two rods—and remember these rods are heavily radioactive, so that the operator has to wear appropriate clothing—replace it or them with one or two fake rods, and reaffix the seal, which they must have counterfeit."

Colonel Dupin interrupted:

"I believe I follow you, Professor. This must be why you must have people in the cellar before the truck arrives. I don't know whether the special clothing is left in the cellar or not, but this might be what is in the case we saw the men bring in. The switch must be done in the cellar with the case taken into and subsequently removed from the cellar. Let's check the drone pictures to see if we missed that move . . ."

Marcel Delagrange concurred and concluded:

"The last element we need is for someone, either the owner or maybe even one of the chaps in the station wagon to come and pick up the pellets when they have been extracted and encased into something which hides their radioactivity."

Colonel Dupin added:

"This would explain why our detectives found traces of radioactivity near the back of the cellar."

Professor Delagrange concurred, arguing that even if the pellets extracted from the spent fuel rods were collected in the appropriate case, there was plenty of scope for radioactivity to escape and attach to stuff in the cellar. Colonel Dupin then offered a final thought:

"Soon enough, we'll have to raid the cellar. I want to figure out where that makeshift laboratory is. I also want to know what role the owner of the winery plays."

■ ■ ■ ■ ■

Meanwhile, the gendarmes who were keeping an eye on the winery saw a series of developments which they assumed were suspect on at least two counts. A car which they had not seen before drove into the courtyard and went to park right in front of the entrance to what the owner of the winery had called his private cellar. A man stepped out of the car, stuffed something he picked up from the right passenger seat into his pocket and entered the cellar. The gendarmes were surprised that the man would have a key, as they remembered the report which stated that the owner had used a key to enter and exit the cellar when he took the two detectives there. Who was this man that had a key? Within minutes he came out carrying what looked like a heavy suitcase. He placed the suitcase in the trunk, got into the car and drove straight out, without having made a stop near the main house. Why would someone who has a key to a private cellar and who must thus be a known entity to the owner not stop and say hello? A couple of unmarked gendarmes immediately started tailing him. They reported that he was driving eastward on the A8 highway.

Colonel Dupin called his colleague Colonel Severin to organize an orderly handoff if the man who had picked up the suitcase drove into Colonel Severin's territory. Their conversation was interrupted by a message from the gendarme:

"He is exiting A8 and taking D25, toward Ste Maxime."

■ ■ ■ ■ ■

Ste Maxime is one of a handful of upmarket seaside resort towns on the Mediterranean coast which draw tourists during the summer season. It is less than six miles from well-known St Tropez, the glitzy location west of Cannes and Nice.

■ ■ ■ ■ ■

Colonel Severin observed:

"Your man is driving toward the sea. I'd bet that he has a rendezvous with a boat. My guess is that he is more likely to drive toward St Tropez, as they typically park the larger boats either in the harbor which they call the "Honor Harbor" to show exclusivity or just offshore, in which case a small tender craft would be waiting to take him to the large boat a few hundred feet offshore. Please keep me informed. I'll ready a couple of fast boats that could follow whoever gets the package if they come anywhere near Nice. We must know who they are and put a stop to that traffic."

Colonel Dupin agreed wholeheartedly and hung up.

On his end, he contacted the harbor police in the marinas which dot the French Riviera. He agreed with the theory his colleague had suggested but wanted to be ready if the man veered off to the east or the west of the Ste Maxime area. There were indeed more than a dozen harbors that could manage boats all the way up to one hundred feet if not more along the coast, east of Toulon and west of Nice, not counting Monte Carlo or even the few resort towns before or just after the French Italian border. The idea suddenly looked quite good as the man did not follow D25 all the way to the seaside. At the last roundabout, he veered to his left and thus eastward and took Avenue du Preconil. It led him directly to Ste Maxime Harbor. He parked the car in a spot near the jetties and without looking rushed or otherwise preoccupied, picked up the suitcase from the trunk and walked along the middle wharf from which the ferries sailing from Ste Maxime to St Tropez and back typically docked. He walked past the restaurant "L'Amiral" which he could see on the second floor of the building on his left and reaching the end of the pier he suddenly stopped abeam a boat moored in the very last slip, in fact quite close to the harbor exit. She was a colorful speedboat, which many people call cigarette boats. These are among the fastest vessels one can own, reaching speeds up to sixty nautical miles per hour. Except for the various marine police or coast guard boats, very few if any other vessel can reach the same top speed. Further, though they can burn as much as seven hundred pounds of fuel per hour, several of them would have a range extending comfortably more than five hundred miles.

Someone was already at the helm of the boat. He did not waste any time turning on the two massive inboard engines whose total output exceeded 1,000 horsepower. The man helped the captain by throwing inside the boat the two bumpers on each side, which were used at anchor to prevent boats bumping into each other while in adjacent slips. Once ready, the helmsman engaged the forward gear, as the boat had backed into the slip. With all traffic in full view of the local harbor police whose offices were at the tip of the central wharf, the driver followed strictly the rules of the sea, and moved at idle speed into the channel marked with green and red buoys that exited the harbor (on all waters in France when boats are returning from the sea, the red even-numbered markers are on the port side of the channel, while the green odd-numbered marks are on its starboard side, the exact opposite of the norms in the U.S.). The helmsman only kicked the engines to full power when the boat was clear of all restrictions, after navigating further than three hundred yards away from the shore. At that point, it sailed in a southeasterly direction.

There were a number of locations toward which she might be sailing, ranging from Corsica to the south and Italy to the east. Yet, going anywhere further would require the boat to refuel. The gendarme called Colonel Dupin:

"He's in a yellow and red cigarette boat. I'd guess she's a 40-footer or so."

Colonel Dupin replied:

"Excellent, we have a couple of boats that are as fast as his and we should be able to track him. We'll also be using a couple of drones to make sure we know exactly where he is and where he is going."

■ ■ ■ ■ ■

A short while later, at the winery, the gendarmes left saw the owner of the vineyard leave the main house and walk to the cellar. He was in it for less than a couple of minutes and came out with a small pouch which he put in the pocket of the sportscoat he was wearing. Colonel Dupin ordered:

"Verify that nobody else is in the area and if it is indeed clear arrest the individual. The key is that he must not be able to contact anyone."

The two gendarmes ran toward the man. As he saw them coming his way, the owner seemed to be looking for something in his pocket. One of the gendarmes pulled out his service gun and told him to keep his hands up. They showed him their badges and arrested him. They saw that the only thing he had in his pockets was a velvet pouch and that it contained diamonds.

CHAPTER.29

MOSUL, IRAQ; PARIS AND THE FRENCH RIVIERA, FRANCE; TEL AVIV, ISRAEL

Ibrahim was all smiles when Josh, aka Abu Musa joined him at the terrace of their usual haunt, the Al Shatee Café, on the banks of the Tigris River in Mosul:

"Abu Musa, it's nice to see you. How have you been?"

Josh deadpanned that he had been busy, but that did not involve anything much different from the usual. Ibrahim was a bit more insistent when he asked:

"Were you able to meet Abdulah?"

"I would have thought you knew the answer to that question, my friend. Your associate, Rezna, was with me when we all met at the Al-Shuhada Park."

"Touché! I knew of that meeting, but what I heard from Rezna was that little happened. A bit of chit chat, a couple of open-ended offers and that was it. Is that not correct?"

"Just about right. And I should say that has been it! I haven't seen or heard from Abdullah since that day. I am assuming that he has no interest in taking things further. That's a shame for me, but I know that's the way it often goes . . ."

Josh paused and added with a smile:

"You know it well: ten leads and at best one deal!"

Ibrahim returned Josh's smile, though he still seemed somewhat unsatisfied. He explained that he was surprised that conversations did not go any further, as Rezna seemed to think this was a solid lead. Josh replied that Ibrahim ought to have known that things did not go any further as Abdullah had asked that all future conversations were to take place through Rezna. Ibrahim visibly winced as he said:

"I really wonder what happened."

He paused for nearly thirty seconds, visibly thinking, debating in his mind how to prolong the conversation, and added:

"Rezna seemed adamant that there would be a deal if both sides were genuine."

Josh looked surprised and actually made his face appear more surprised than he really was and replied:

"I can assure you that I was straight with Abdullah. I know someone who told me once he had access to the nuclear waste hidden away by Saddam Hussein's supporters. But though I know how to contact that person, I don't have any information as to quantities, prices or even conditions under which he would be willing to deal. Given the sensitivity associated with nuclear waste, what would you do in my place?"

"I can't criticize your position, my friend. The bit I don't understand is why Abdullah wouldn't be interested. Did anything happen after the rendezvous which might have made him hesitate?"

Josh deadpanned:

"Can't see what it could be."

Ibrahim smiled and offered a possible scenario. He suggested that Abdullah might have noticed a car that followed him to where he returned after the meeting and decided that the offer might be a trap. Josh replied that he did not see how that could have happened, as he was alone with Rezna and as each of the three parties went their own ways after the conversation was over. Then he added:

"Hey, wait a minute. Let's assume that Abdullah was indeed spooked by something. Are you sure that Rezna is totally on the level?"

Ibrahim looked almost offended as he replied:

"What do you mean? All my people are straight . . ."

Josh smiled broadly and simply said:

"My dear Ibrahim, don't you remember the bad sheep which hid in your network and whom we uncovered together a few years ago?[8] How can you be so sure?"

Ibrahim had to concede the point and replied:

"I know Rezna particularly well. In fact, he is one of the few people I am grooming to succeed me when I can't do the job."

Josh mischievously asked:

"There wouldn't be a blood relationship by any chance?"

Ibrahim first looked contrite and then smiled broadly as he told Josh:

"You really know our culture well, Abu Musa! Rezna is one of my sons. My oldest son in fact."

■ ■ ■ ■ ■

Colonel Dupin had asked that the owner of the winery be brought to his offices in Hyeres. He wanted to be present when he was interrogated. He was very surprised at how the interrogation went. Mr. Lambert, the owner of the winery, rapidly realized that the jig was up and stunned his interrogator when he said:

"I might as well tell you the whole truth now. But first, please go to the winery and ask my wife to follow you. Bring her here."

---

[8] By the same author, see *Glitter and Smoke*, Barringer Publishing, 2023.

The sergeant who was doing the questioning immediately called Colonel Dupin. Claude Lambert explained that he was but a victim in the scheme. He said that the whole thing started when his son, Philippe, was somehow arrested in Syria. Colonel Dupin interrupted Claude and asked him to explain what he meant.

Claude explained that a year ago or so, maybe a bit more, he had heard that certain people from the Middle East were interested in purchasing a winery in the area, adding:

"The area was truly broadly defined. I heard that they were looking as far east as Bandol and west as Arles."

Seeing that the detail did not seem to interest Colonel Dupin, Claude continued and said that his property had been visited, though he said that he was not really interested in selling, confiding:

"However, you know, every man has a price . . ."

Colonel Dupin's half smile encouraged him to keep going. He confirmed that he said he was not selling. His son, who had been present when the visit occurred, told him he met one of the visitors a short while afterwards, in Cannes, in a club. Claude concluded:

"To make a long story short, Philippe told me that he was going to go on a pilgrimage, a solo pilgrimage, in the steps of St Paul. Our family is quite devoutly catholic, and I wasn't surprised of Philippe's interest in St Paul. He hadn't been gone for a week when I received a call from someone who said he was a friend of Philippe. Apparently, he had been arrested because a woman there, in Syria, accused him of rape. I asked what I could do, and they simply said they would call back. Bottom line, I'll spare you the details, but I finally realized that he had been kidnapped and was being used by his captors to extort me."

"Blackmail?"

"Yes, Colonel. Our only son, my intended successor at the winery. The kidnappers were trying to get me either to do what they wanted or to sell them the winery. I decided to do what they asked, hoping that I would at some point find a way out."

Claude sighed and became visibly emotional, at which point he was given a couple of minutes to regain his composure. He asked whether his wife had arrived and was told that she was still on the road, safe in the company of gendarmes. In truth, she was being held in an office nearby, but Colonel Dupin wanted to have a chance to cross-examine her and did not want to have to explain that to Claude at the time.

Claude continued his story saying that nuclear waste traffickers contacted him and told him that their son would probably receive the death penalty if Claude did not cooperate. They asked for access to his cellar, adding:

"They must have seen the cellar when they visited the winery and decided that it would allow them to do what they wanted to do without being seen. The one thing I quickly found out is that the first time I was allowed back into it, it had been substantially cut back in size. You see, the gallery is around 180 feet long and when I saw it, it had been about cut in half. The back end was missing! They had installed some sort of false back wall, electrically powered. So, they could conduct their business in the back of the cellar without anyone knowing anything. In fact, I know that a couple of detectives came and visited the cellar with me; they didn't seem to find anything strange."

Colonel Dupin was not about to tell Claude about the traces of radioactivity . . . Claude went on detailing what the traffickers were doing, though he claimed that he knew next to nothing. He even added:

"I know nothing about nuclear stuff, so I really can't even imagine what they could be doing and why they needed my winery."

"How did you find out about the nuclear stuff as you call it?"

"They told me not to interfere with their work, warning me that there was radioactivity there . . ."

"O.K. That's another story, Mr. Lambert. Now, tell me, why didn't you come to us?"

"And cause the execution of Philippe?"

Colonel Dupin nodded and replied with a sad voice:

"That's exactly what kidnappers of all types expect victims will do. Keep things to themselves, don't call the police and effectively sink deeper. And yet, we have ways of operating. By the way, why tell us now?"

"I know it's over. You've caught me. Whether I tell the truth or not, I'm not sure I'll see my son ever again. That's why I wanted you to get my wife. At least she is safe. And I bet they don't know about our daughter and her family; they've never talked of her. Thank God for her having taken the name of her husband."

He broke down in heavy sobs again. Either the man was a first-class actor, or he was telling the truth. Colonel Dupin asked further:

"By the way, let's put your daughter and her family under close surveillance until we feel she doesn't need it. OK?"

Claude nodded his agreement. Colonel Dupin was not finished with his questions:

"Why did they need to pay you? In diamonds? After all, wouldn't you be prepared to do it for nothing?"

"Nothing? The life of my son, Colonel!"

"Grant you that. I misspoke. So why the diamonds?"

"They're not for me. I deposit them in an account in Monaco. I don't know who gets them. Maybe an intermediary; maybe the big guy. Who knows?"

"I'm sure we'll be able to find out . . . With your help, of course. Now, tell me, how long has this been going on?"

"Less than a year, Colonel. They kidnapped Philippe seven months ago, almost to the day. In fact, the time your detectives visited me was only after the second transshipment as the traffickers called it. Actually, another tidbit comes back to my mind: your men asked about the temperature in the cellar. I told them a half-truth."

"Never a good idea . . ."

Claude looked repentant as he interrupted:

"I know, but anyway, I told them that we had air-conditioning to help maintain the cellar at the appropriate temperature."

"Well?"

"That's where the lie is. I never installed an air-conditioning unit because we never needed one. The temperature in the cellar when it was the full couple of hundred feet long was quite acceptable. The traffickers installed it. I'm ready to bet that it was meant to eliminate the radioactive air from the back end of the cellar . . ."

"I know this is a rabbit hole, but let me ask you anyway: where does the air from the cellar come out?"

"In a small clump of trees, at the end of one of our vineyards. In fact, I heard that someone in the village saw a rabbit that looked quite sick."

"Useful tip. Radiation sickness probably. We'll investigate. Anyway, back to our main topic; did you receive the same quantity of diamonds each time?"

"Hard to tell, sir. I'm no diamond expert. I sure counted the stones, and the number was about the same both times, around 100 stones; they all looked similar in that they were all brilliant cut, but they varied in size, from what I'd describe as small to a bit larger."

"Let me ask this differently?"

"Did the bank where you deposited the diamonds give you the same amount of money for them each time?"

Claude seemed surprised by the question. He replied:

"I'm not sure I understand your question. I never received any money from the bank. Just a receipt that stated the number of stones I had deposited."

"And you had no access to that account?"

"None. I was told that Philippe would die if I tried to get anything out of it."

"Did you keep the receipts?"

"Sure did. They are in my safe at the winery. You're welcome to them any time you want."

Colonel Dupin then surprised Claude:

"Well, thank you, Mr. Lambert. I'm going to ask you to stay in this office while I have a short talk with your wife . . ."

With an air of both surprise and relief, Claude asked:

"She's here?"

"Yes, safe and sound, next door. But I will not let you speak to her until I have had a chance to ask her a few questions before. I'm sure you'll understand.

■ ■ ■ ■ ■

Colonel Dupin had asked his assistant to organize a conference call with Colonels Severin and Germain as soon as possible. He had in fact told his assistant:

"Tell them this is top priority. Interrupt me the moment you have them on the phone."

Less than fifteen minutes later, Colonel Dupin was called out of the room where he was checking Claude Lambert's answers with his wife, Christine. He apologized for the disruption and went straight back to his office.

He picked up the videoconference which had been organized on the computer that stood on his desk and stated:

"Gentlemen. We have a break in our case, but we may also have just run into some serious complications. Let me explain . . ."

He went on to recapitulate the key points of the conversation he had had with Claude Lambert and added:

"So far, everything he said seems to fit with what his wife told me. That doesn't mean that they're not accomplices and thus have previously rehearsed that line of defense. Yet, my instincts and my experience lead me to think they likely to are telling the truth."

Colonel Germain asked:

"Are you saying that we should abort the current chase of the man with the nuclear waste?"

"I'm tempted to say yes, though there may be a better solution. Can we engineer a double cross?"

Colonel Severin laughed:

"Excellent idea, but at least one of our boats has our name written all over it . . ."

"Can we not broadcast a message to all and sundry talking of a coast guard fast boat having been stolen?"

"How about their being in uniform?"

"How easy is it to get fake uniforms?"

"OK, I see your point. But can we act in good conscience for as long as we don't know where Philippe Lambert is held captive?

Colonel Germain concluded:

"Leave this one with me. I need to confer with the Minister and a couple of other people here in Paris. I should be back to you within the next twenty-four hours at most."

CHAPTER.30

The first individual Colonel Germain called was Professor Delagrange who quickly insisted that Nathan Hole, the Israeli Vice Consul for Military Affairs should also be on the conference call. The three men quickly came together on an electronic video conference and Colonel Germain provided a quick summary of the current situation. Nathan was the first to reply:

"Though I don't know much about the topic myself, I know we have teams in Israel which specialize in hostage situations. I'm sure you know we've had our share of people kidnapped and held for ransom. Let me take this up with one of my contacts there and I will come back with a possible solution . . .

The next morning, Nathan was back on the conference call, but he was not alone. He introduced Malkiel Lindberg, aka Mark Levi, a man whom he said was a specialist in people security, which he described to mean specialized in providing for the security to individuals who asked for special protection. Ostensibly, this was nothing but a trivial lie, given Mark's position as deputy to David Heller, Head of the

Disruption Group of *Mossad*. Yet, there was some truth to it, *Mossad* did get involved in hostage situations . . .

The conference call was briefly interrupted by a call to Colonel Germain. It came from Colonel Dupin, who was informing him that the cigarette boat, on which the man with the nuclear waste package had been, was now clear of both French territorial waters and the contiguous zones. Combined, these two zones represent thirty-six nautical miles. Colonel Dupin added:

"The handoff can occur at any time from here on out. The speedboat has sailed between Italy to the east and Corsica to the west, going almost due south."

Colonel Germain kept Colonel Dupin on the line as he brought the latest information to the attention of the four people on the video conference call. Malkiel, aka Mark was the first to react as he asked:

"We are assuming that the package is to be transferred to a yacht, correct?"

Colonel Dupin confirmed that this was the current assumption, yet asking:

"Do you see many other alternatives?"

Mark agreed that the very fact that the man had chosen to travel by the slowest possible means, a boat however speedy it might be, suggested that there was to be a rendezvous at sea. Yet cautioned the group:

"This wouldn't be the first time that a transfer at sea is done via a helicopter . . . So going with the assumption that you are looking for a yacht makes sense, but it isn't the only option. From what you're saying, the boat will never be terribly far away from land on either side."

He paused for a second and asked a different question:

"Do we know for a fact that the hostage isn't on the yacht, if they are going to use a yacht?"

One could have heard a pin drop. Everybody looked surprised that they did not have the answer, while simultaneously they appreciated how relevant and even crucial the question was. In the absence of a reply, Mark simply said:

"Gentlemen, I could be quite wrong, but my advice to you is to allow the transfer of the package, if it is to take place, to eventuate. If the transfer occurs via a helicopter, we must also allow it to take place and must find a way to track the helicopter if we are to know what the eventual destination of the nuclear waste is. If it occurs onto a yacht, I think we also must not intervene directly: too much risk if the hostage is on the boat. Once the transfer has taken place, then there are two important next steps."

Mark paused to verify that everyone was on board, and, hearing no objection, continued:

"The first step involves the man in the cigarette boat. We can't do anything until we hear that the hostage is safe. So, the second step, intercepting the yacht if that is what we have must happen before you can take care of organizing a special reception committee for the man on the cigarette boat. Let's keep monitoring the movements of the yacht."

He paused again and asked:

"Would you need Eitan drones to monitor from the air, or are you set on that?"

Colonel Dupin replied that he did not feel he needed additional drones, though he thanked Mark for the offer and suggested he might change his mind at a later date. Mark simply replied that there were no problems, though the drones would take several hours before they reached the western part of the Mediterranean Sea. He added:

"Now, with respect to intercepting the yacht with a possible hostage onboard, do you have what you need?"

Colonel Dupin suggested that they might speak again offline to compare notes and discuss that very point. Mark agreed and added:

"I am confident that I have the equipment we would need to take care of the yacht, even if the hostage is on board."

■ ■ ■ ■ ■

Meanwhile, back in Mosul, Josh was continuing his conversation with Ibrahim:

"How does that change anything my friend?"

"Well, Abu Musa, I think the time has come. I must make a confession."

In line with the traditional customs in the Middle East, Josh took an understanding demeanor and by his posture encouraged Ibrahim to talk without inferring any sort of criticism. Ibrahim surprised Josh by telling him that he had originally known quite a bit more than he let on. Josh interrupted, politely asking about what. Ibrahim replied that when he approached him with the rumor about some sort of nuclear waste traffic, he knew that it was more than a rumor and had second thoughts himself.

"Ibrahim, I totally respect what you are saying and am touched by the trust you have in me, but I am now totally lost. Can you go back to the beginning and help me?

"Sure."

Ibrahim told Josh that he had heard about the traffic from a Kurd friend who had heard that someone was looking for the nuclear waste which had been hidden when Saddam lost power. He had then asked his son, Rezna, to help him investigate, as the source of the rumor had told him that the people who had contacted him were from his son's generation. He added:

"I was assuming that he would find out more easily, as he tends to associate with people of his generation while I move in circles that are a bit older."

"Makes sense. So?"

Ibrahim continued with his story, telling Josh that Rezna quickly found out first that the rumor was true: people were looking for that waste. But more importantly, he met someone who had a great deal of influence in Arabic circles. Josh interrupted:

"That wouldn't be Abdullah, by any chance?"

"Precisely my friend. So, Rezna continued to meet with him when the opportunity seemed to be available and pretty soon was asked if he knew anything which he might be willing to share."

Ibrahim continued saying that Abdullah told him that they were going to fire a test rocket with a very modest amount of nuclear waste. Rezna asked why and what the target was. Abdullah explained that they were taking apart the tip of the missiles which Iran was supplying to them and inserting radioactive material in it to transform them into a dirty bomb. Ibrahim further suggested that the terrorists, as he called them for the first time, felt they needed to fire one of these missiles to make sure that the modifications they made to the tip did not change the missiles performance characteristics.

Josh asked:

"Is that why they fired in the direction of Israel?"

"Yes. That is something else I knew but didn't tell you."

"How did they manage to coordinate their test with an actual series of bombardments by Hezbollah in terms of both timing and the target area?"

Ibrahim conceded that he certainly did not know any of these details but explained that he had learned from Rezna that Abdullah maintained some contact with the Palestinian resistance. He added:

"I jumped to the conclusion that these contacts were less than genuine. Abdullah simply wanted to find out what they would be doing and would use their next operation against Israel as a cover to launch his test. Now, by the way, I wouldn't be surprised if we found out that Abdullah's crowd also fired rockets in addition to the dirty-tip missile."

"What makes you say that?"

Ibrahim simply replied:

"Rezna told me that something which Abdullah said made him conclude that they had Iranian rocket launcher trucks as well."

Josh took advantage of a pause by Ibrahim to ask whether Abdullah was in fact more than a member of the group, wondering whether he might have in fact been the leader. Ibrahim replied that his experience with these people told him that they rarely have a single leader. He added:

"Most of the time, you have two or three key individuals. I am convinced that Abdullah is one of them with respect to this group. Yet, I don't know that he is the leader."

Josh changed the topic and asked his friend:

"Why would you get involved into this stuff? What did you have to gain or to protect?"

"You just said it, Abu Musa. I had nothing to gain per se, but I surely had a lot to protect. One of the things which Rezna had hidden from Abdullah was both our blood relationship and thus the fact that he had a personal allegiance to the Kurdish movement. Abdullah one day told him that they wanted to destabilize the area by chasing Kurds out of eastern Syria. You may or may not remember, but Hezbollah was known to have performed serious ethnic cleansing in Syria, primarily among Sunni Arabs, but it also included Kurds."

Josh interrupted:

"Now you make sense."

He paused and with a sincerity which Ibrahim could not doubt he asked:

"What in the world did you expect me to be able to do that you couldn't do yourself?"

It was Ibrahim's turn to smile. He simply reminded Josh, aka Abu Musa, that he had seemed quite able to find ways to bring certain forces to bear that helped the Kurdish cause. He added:

"If you look at what has happened since I told you about the rumor, you can't deny that you achieved quite a lot. I think I now understand how you managed that . . ."

Josh stood more erect in his chair expecting the worst, but Ibrahim had something else in mind. He had apparently bought Josh's story that he was selling information to influential people and therefore was under the impression that Abu Musa had brought foreign agents to help him deal with the threat. In fact, Ibrahim added:

"I know you won't tell me, but I really wonder who has helped you. I can't imagine that you would yourself been able to get into the camp in Syria, but you must have been able to get some help. Was it CIA? MI6? Who else? Can't imagine *Mossad* would deal with an Arab, but who knows?"

Josh simply smiled and replied:

"You're right. I won't tell you. But now let me ask you: why did you want to have this chat with me?"

■ ■ ■ ■ ■

Mark Levi had immediately called David Heller, his boss and mentor, to give him a full report and ask for his approval of the next steps he was considering. David was all smiles when David told him the story, though he added:

"The one thing we still don't know is who fired the dirty bomb that hit Tiberias . . ."

Mark conceded the point, though he said that great progress had been made on several issues. He pointed first to the fact that he now had a list of where many of the so-called "orphan sources" of radioactive material are located arguing:

"As you know, I have a plan to deal with them, but we'll have to proceed with care and method to ensure that we don't reveal either our being behind anything that happens to certain of them and of the weapon we will be using."

He paused and almost immediately resumed his story:

"More to the point, we have uncovered a network of nuclear waste traffickers in France. We should be able to neutralize the network, although we need to do something beforehand to ensure that we protect the French hostage. By the way, any news on the Iranian threat to reply to the missiles fired from Syria?"

David interjected:

"Not really. But they have stopped threatening. I wouldn't be surprised that they have also been able to analyze debris and note that the missiles that fired at them were of Iranian origin . . ."

"That couldn't hurt. Right on, sir."

"So, what is your next move?"

"If you agree, I want to stage first a surveillance of the delivery of the nuclear waste by the cigarette boat to the yacht and later on to organize an interception of the yacht. Yet, I can't do that without talking to Marvin Goldstein to find out whether we have any tool that would increase whatever protection we must provide to the hostage, if he is on board. And if he isn't, we must find out where he is and rescue him."

CHAPTER.31

MOSUL, IRAQ; TEL AVIV, ISRAEL

Marvin was cheerful as usual when he heard that Mark needed to ask him a few questions. His love of technology was well known, and Mark was among those who tended to have the oddest and most challenging requests.

"Mark, what can I do for you? Note that I made space for you to sit on the sofa."

Marvin's office was a well known mess though he would argue that he knew where everything was and had never yet been caught not finding what he was looking for. He had placed whatever was on the right side of the sofa on top the pile he had been building on the left side. There was also just enough space on the so-called coffee table so that Marvin's assistant was able to place a jug of fresh water and two glasses. Mark went straight into the conversation:

"Marvin, I find myself in an unusual position with an unusual task. I want to find out from you what is the best equipment I should plan to use."

Marvin seemed to be jubilating and asked:

"What kind of task are you talking about?"

"Let me give you the headline and we can go into details when it is necessary. I believe that I need to commandeer a luxury yacht at sea, in international waters."

"Nothing terribly challenging here if I can say so myself . . ."

"Agreed, my friend. What makes this a challenging and dangerous operation is that there may be a hostage on board?"

Hold a second here. Is there or isn't there?"

"That's the question."

"How will you find out?"

"Well, that's the other part of the question. Let me take you through the key details."

Mark explained that a young man in his early thirties had been kidnapped and was being used as a hostage. He went on:

"He has been used as a hostage to force his father to allow nuclear waste traffickers to use the family winery. We assume that they use the place to take nuclear pellets from spent fuel rods and package them in a way that allows the pellets to be safely transportable."

"Very ingenious. Wonder why they're going through such a complex process, but this is unimportant."

"Agreed. So, French police working with one of Countess Renate's experts seem to have managed to locate one such package. I'll spare you the gory details, but long story short, a man took the waste package from the winery, drove it to a marina, where he boarded a superfast boat and met a yacht outside of French and Italian territorial waters,"

"So far, so good. But I don't see where the young man comes into play."

"That's where we are totally in the dark. We have no idea where he is. One thought that came to me was that there are two alternatives that seem more probable than the others. The first is that the young man is kept somewhere in Syria, which is where we believe he was kidnapped. The risk to him in that case is that if we were to try to stop the yacht, the man, or men onboard would use him to be allowed to keep sailing."

"What do you mean?"

"Simple: you let us go or our people will kill the hostage . . ."

"I see. I see,"

"In that case, we have no real option but to let the boat go and start looking for the young man and try to rescue him the old-fashioned way."

Mark paused to drink water and turned to the second alternative:

"While that might work, I placed myself in the shoes of the terrorist and decided that there was a better solution. What if we simply placed more value on killing the terrorist and recovering the package, somehow hoping that we would be able afterwards to seek to find the hostage? That led me to the idea that they might have taken the young man along. The moment we make a move to intercept the yacht, they get the hostage from his cabin and bring him to the stern platform. They threaten to kill him if we make any move?"

"To some extent, the life of the hostage still hangs by a thread, right?"

"Right. But with the hostage right there before our eyes, the terrorists would have to think we will find it harder to forget about him . . ."

Marvin nodded and asked:

"Different topic, Mark, if I may. How are you going to intercept the yacht?"

"I would hope to be able to use our two disguised supply boats . . ."

▮▮◼▮▮

The two disguised supply boats to which Mark was referring were heavily modified and still as partially secret as could be. They were able to reach speeds considerably higher than outwardly similar boats because they could transform into hydrofoils with a couple of simple maneuvers. The foils, which at rest were folded into the hull at the bow of the boat, could be extended; at speed, the boat riding on these foils would rise higher on the water, creating less friction with the water and thus more speed. To accommodate the fact that the boat could rise higher on the water, the angle and length of the two propeller shafts could also be altered so they would still operate at full power and with full effect at top speed. That alone made them quite different from any supply boat and would allow them to outrun virtually any boat, particularly as their twin engines were double the power which boats of that size would normally have. Unfortunately, with the need for more power came the requirement that fuel capacity be substantially increased as well: they weighed more, but that would not be visible to someone from the outside, as the extra space for fuel was taken from the cargo-carrying capacity below deck.

A couple of important modifications had also been made but would likely not be of much value in this operation. First, the vessels were equipped with an air lock which allowed the boat to pick up or deliver loads underwater. Also, the lower level of the front deck, under the bridge tower, hid a full gamut of electronic surveillance equipment. It offered space for a couple of operators to work while allowing them to move from that space to the modest living quarters on the bridge without stepping out in the open. Finally, the vessels could easily change identity. They each had three names on rotating supports on each side of the bow of the ship. Simply rotating the support would allow the ship to change its name. At the same time, each of the names corresponded to a country of registration. Currently, they were using Malta, Panama, and Gibraltar, but any other country flag could be substituted if needed. Thus, the flagpole at the very aft of the ship would display the flag corresponding to the registered name through a clever mechanism inspired by the multi-color ballpoint pens of the past: each flag would roll around its own axis and the whole retract into a sheave. The captain could therefore "dial up" the flag he wanted. The ultimate disguise, however, dealt with the color of the hull's middle section. The top of the hull would always be white, while the bottom, the part most often immersed into the water, would always be black. The middle section, however, comprised small-section vertical rotating equilateral triangles which could display one of three colors: red, dark green, and white.

∎∎∎∎∎

"May I ask why you feel you need them both?"

"That's what I hope to be able to organize with you. My thinking is that only one vessel would serve to intercept the yacht, but the other one would be somewhat further behind and might be able to deploy one or two additional weapons."

"Here we go. What do you have in mind?"

"Well, one of the weapons would have to be some form of observation drone, which would be remotely piloted by officers on board the boat. I'll grant you that this wouldn't necessarily require a second boat, as the drone could be maneuvered from the same boat that did the interception. However, I am thinking of doing a lot of observation, hopefully without the yacht noticing it."

"So?"

"I was thinking of having the intercepting boat coming from the bow of the yacht and thus was looking to have another boat further back."

"Belt and suspenders?"

"Yes. Anyway, the second subject is even more important, do we have what I might call 'sniper drones'?"

∎∎∎∎∎

Back in Mosul, Josh had asked the question with a smile on his face. Ibrahim replied with just as broad a smile:

"First, my dear friend, I wanted to come clean. I don't like the fact that I may have put you in some danger for a purpose of which you were not aware."

"Thank you, but you know that I have an interest in the cause. After all, as I said to you earlier, I work for 'worthy causes' as I call them. Nuclear proliferation does not fit under that header. Anyway, is there a second purpose?"

"Yes, and it is related to the first. I believe that Rezna has been exposed to risks by being closer to Abdullah than he was ever supposed to be. So, I am really wondering whether there's a way to dismantle the camp in Syria."

Josh looked genuinely surprised as he said:

"Well, you surely did play that one close to the vest. Early on, I was under the impression that it was not even a sure thing you would help me. And yet now you tell me that you were almost setting me up?"

"I know and this is what bothers me. I should have asked for your help since it looked like that, again, we were on the same side. Anyway, I don't know who helped you, but with the same people's help and using our own Kurdish fighting resources, if necessary, I would like to make sure that the camp can't do anybody any harm anymore."

"Ah. This is quite interesting. What do you have in mind?"

"Without knowing whether Abdullah is the top guy or just one of the top guys, I think he has to be eliminated. Whatever overall role he plays, I am convinced that he is the mastermind behind the nuclear tipped missiles. We can't have this in the Middle East. It is a step too far. One of these days, Israel will retaliate, and this will be terrible for the Kurdish men and women who only looked to till the land and keep their traditional culture alive."

"I'll see what I can do, but I must tell you that this quite different from what I do on a day-to-day basis. Let me approach those who did the heavy lifting and tell them of your request. I'll hide your identity but will have to mention the Kurdish dimension. Is that OK?"

"I'll be indebted to you again, my friend."

CHAPTER.32

MEDITERRANEAN SEA, MALLORCA, SPAIN, HYERES, FRANCE; MOSUL, IRAQ; TEL AVIV, ISRAEL

Early in the day, Colonel Dupin, Colonel Severin, Colonel Germain, Professor Delagrange, and Nathan Stone had been on a second conference call with Malkiel Lindberg, aka Mark Levi. Mark opened the conversation with a discussion of his plan. He said that given the route taking by the cigarette boat, the rendezvous could be either at sea or in one of the numerous small marinas which dot the coastlines both in Sardinia and Campania in Italy. He added:

"In plain English, that means that the speedboat will need to refuel before returning to the French Riviera. Until we can determine whether the rendezvous is at sea on in a marina, we must remain flexible. The main advantage of a hand off in a local marina is that the package could then be shipped to its ultimate destination via air; it wouldn't be hard for a terrorist to have a private jet waiting for him at the airport. Our best response would be to shoot the jet down if we can't force it to land. But we must be able to determine whether the hostage is with the terrorist or not; personally, I would assume that he would be: what better insurance against our shooting the jet down?"

"He paused and discussed the other alternative:

"Now, the downside of the onshore scenario as I might call it is that jets involve controls and potential inspections. So, a handoff at sea is still quite plausible. Whoever is to pick up the package will be on a larger vessel. I'm assuming a private yacht because I can't believe a commercial cargo boat would take that risk. However, I'm on soft grounds on this one. If a yacht, she could be anywhere as we speak and be going anywhere afterwards. Intercepting her will be difficult."

Mark concluded:

"I've organized for two boats from the Israeli Navy to sail toward the western Mediterranean. I'm told they have top secret capabilities, but I'm not sure what they are; the message simply was: "no boat can go any faster than they." Fortunately, they were already near Malta on a training mission, with a tanker and a couple of other boats with them. They were able to fill up to the brim and immediately sailed further westward. They won't be able to reach the area before the rendezvous but should get there soon enough afterwards to be useful. We've airlifted a couple of important pieces of equipment to them during the night."

Colonel Dupin asked:

"What do you expect will happen?"

"I assume you mean after the rendezvous."

Seeing Colonel Dupin nod on the video screen, Mark continued:

"If the rendezvous is onshore, I think we know, and we've already discussed it. If at sea. I really don't know what the yacht will do. One option would be for the package and the passenger or passengers to be picked up by helicopter once the rendezvous has taken place. Whether we're talking of a yacht or a cargo vessel, there should be space either to land a helicopter or have the helicopter hover above the boat while the package and human transfers take place. If that's the case, we will need some help from the authorities of the countries around the Mediterranean where the helicopter might try to land . . . We know that the copter couldn't fly from there to the Middle East."

Colonel Germain interrupted:

"That's possible, but I must concede we're talking of a tall order."

"I understand this, Colonel. Now, I personally assume that this won't be the preferred option. Given what's in the package, I am pretty convinced that the individual wouldn't want the package to transit through unfriendly territory."

"What do you mean by unfriendly?"

"Excellent question, Colonel Severin, I mean any country which does not at least unofficially support Islamic terrorism. I can only think of Libya as a potential candidate in the immediate neighborhood. That should give us the time to act before the yacht gets there."

■ ■ ■ ■ ■

The two French police cruisers had been following the cigarette boat from afar. They were far enough away that they were convinced that the cigarette boat could not suspect anything, though the captain of the cigarette boat had to be able to see the two cruisers on his radar. The occasional flyover by something which looked like a drone might have seemed odd, but many people travelling on yachts have been reported to use drones for fun, and at times to look for activities which might give photographs some financial value. Nobody was terribly surprised when they saw the boat sailing virtually due east initially and veering south as soon as it had cleared the limits of French territorial waters and their contiguous zone. Though the speedboat would have reached international waters faster had it sailed due south, it would also have found itself in the middle of a vast expanse of water, with very limited opportunities to reach the coast if the need arose. The route it had chosen would keep it far enough from the coasts of Italy, Corsica, Sardinia or even Sicily further south, and yet be able to find refuge in one of marinas along the way if needed. This also helped it deal with issues of fuel consumption. The helmsman knew indeed that his boat's fuel consumption skyrocketed when he was using full speed. Yet, full speed was what was needed if he wanted to elude any possible follower. Colonel Dupin, who was monitoring the situation from afar, commented:

"Keep a close watch on where the speedboat goes. Use the drones as they are faster than our boats. By the way, also send a small tanker so that our boats can refuel. We don't want them to run dry . . . One thing I really want everyone to be on the lookout for: make sure that the boat does not veer west into the straits between Bonifacio in Corsica and Santa Teresa Gallura in Sardinia. We'd have a tough time getting the right resources in place."

The two police cruisers dutifully launched aerial drones both to track the speedboat and to keep as good a photographic record of the handoff of the nuclear waste package which they believed could happen at any time then. They had been well aware that the odds of a handoff before the boat reached international waters was unlikely. After all, the traffickers had to know that once in international waters, no arrest could be made without more than what they thought was a suspicion. The pilot of the cigarette boat, for his part, was trying to reach these waters as quickly as he could, feeling as he did that nothing could be held against him if he was arrested after the handoff. He knew very well that there was absolutely no incriminating item on board once the package was no longer there. Additionally, he and the man who had collected the package at the winery had placed it on the back seat of the boat to maintain as much air movement around it. That should minimize the risk that any form of radioactivity would be detected.

The first of the two cruisers radioed to her sister ship and officers onshore:

"The speedboat has passed the point where it would have enough fuel to return to harbor in France. She will need to refuel somewhere. The two options must be Sardinia to the west and mainland Italy to the east."

Colonel Dupin's reply was very short:

"OK. I'll advise our *confreres* in Italy."

About thirty minutes later, the radio officer on the cruiser spoke again:

"I see a yacht due south of us, probably twenty nautical miles away judging by the range finder on my binoculars."

Colonel Dupin answered:

"Could be our target."

"The yacht has a helicopter on the stern side of its upper deck."

"Ah! Interesting. We'll warn the Air Force, both ours and Italy's. I'll also inform our Israeli safety consultant."

The next radio message confirmed Colonel Dupin's suspicions:

"The speedboat is slowing down. The yacht is a large one, mostly white though it has a large grey band just under the gunwale. Must be over two hundred feet!"

The onshore radio operator replied:

"Location?"

"Tyrrhenian Sea, 40.2 degrees North and 11.5 degrees East. Virtually midway between Naples to the east and Cala Gonone in Sardinia to the west. Assuming a 50-knot speed, the cigarette boat is a couple of hours from Sardinia and less than three from Naples."

Colonel Dupin came on the radio:

"Malkiel Lindberg's assumptions are proving pretty close to the mark. Message to Cruiser one: Reposition your drone so that it captures everything that happens during the transfer. Maintain 10,000 feet altitude and navigate to the west of the yacht. Hopefully, you haven't been located by the yacht's crew."

"Understood."

Colonel Dupin continued:

"Cruiser number two, maintain distance with speedboat, but bring your own drone closer as well. Maintain 11,000 feet altitude and navigate to the east of the yacht. Cruiser number one is flying its drone 1,000 feet below yours. Stay with the yacht if the two boats move away from each other. Don't appear threatening and stay far enough away that the yacht does not suspect anything."

■ ■ ■ ■ ■

A couple of hours later, the French Gendarmerie Nationale and the country's Coastal Police were treated to a front seat observation of the speedboat briefly docking alongside the stern of the yacht, which was flying a Panama flag. A man wearing a white thobe, a long and loose-fitting tunic-like garment often made of cotton and linen emerged from the inside of the yacht. He seemed to be wearing white pants under his thobe, with plain brown sandals and no socks. He did not have a head dress, showing off a thick, dark head of hair. With his full beard, only his nose and a small part of his forehead were the only skin that was readily visible. His sunglasses covered his eyes and made it difficult to make out much of his facial features. He stood at the rear gunwale, just above the swimming platform. The driver of the speedboat approached the yacht from the port side and tethered the boat to the yacht. His passenger climbed onto the swimming platform and handed the package he had brought on board to the man with the white thobe, who seemed to be handing a small package to him in return. Within seconds, the helmsman had untethered the speedboat from the yacht and put its engines in reverse to back away. As soon as he was far enough away to be able to swivel the boat in a westerly direction, he gunned the engines to full throttle and raced away. Colonel Dupin announced:

"He's going to refuel in Sardinia. Let me call the Italian Coast Guard."

"Thanks. By the way, we are still tracking her with our drones, as our boats can't compete with her speed."

"Understood. Call back if you have any news."

■ ■ ■ ■ ■

An hour later, Cruiser one came back on the radio with some news:

"The speedboat looks like it is going to Marina di Arbatax, to the north of Tortoli.

Colonel Dupin replied:

"This is consistent with her need to refuel. I'm going to get permission for you to go into the marina. Over."

Cruiser one quickly called back:

"Change of plans. The speedboat has entered the marina, but I see a helicopter now approaching the jetty. Could the passenger be seeking to disembark?"

Colonel Dupin replied:

"Hold it for a minute. I'm looking at the detailed map of the Tortoli area. Damnit! The Tortoli-Arbatax airport is less than a couple of miles aways as the crow flies. Cruiser one, keep up the surveillance and let me know if anything changes. I need to organize for the man not to be able to board his flight."

CHAPTER.33

MEDITERRANEAN BASIN; TEL AVIV, ISRAEL

Nathan Stone had routinely forwarded to Mark in Tel Aviv the
videos of the handoff between the passenger on the cigarette boat and
the man in the white thobe on the yacht. He had just returned to the
office from his lunch break when the phone with the secure line on
his desk rang:

"Nathan, we have a virtually positive identification of the man in
the white thobe: it's none other than Abdullah, the fellow which Josh
Steinmetz and his team followed to the military camp in Syria . . ."

"Oh, my God!"

"You can say that again. I won't say we have finally closed the
circle quite yet, but things have become a lot clearer. We must stop
him. The fact that he took care of the errand himself raises in my
mind the probability that the hostage is with him. Such a man needs
protection . . ."

Nathan listened carefully as Mark detailed the plan which he
wanted now to execute and was tasked with informing the French
and Italian authorities that the man on the yacht was a high security
risk, sought by Israel. Nathan was to let them know that the man was

under suspicion of being involved in a bombing which included the use of a dirty bomb.

■ ■ ■ ■ ■

Unfortunately, the speedboat's passenger was able to board his flight at Tottori despite Colonel Dupin's best efforts. A medium range Citation VII twin jet was ready for him. He boarded it quickly and the jet immediately took off to the southeast. Colonel Dupin's call to the Italian Air Force had however triggered an instantaneous response. A couple of Eurofighters Typhoon took off from Decimomannu Air Base, ten miles to the north of Cagliari, the capital of Sardinia, and forty miles from Tottori. The airport is named after Colonel Giovani Farina who died in combat in the skies of Sardinia in 1942. They quickly caught up with the Citation and intercepted it. They firmly instructed the pilots not to disclose to the passenger the reason the plane was returning to the Decimomannu military airport. Once on the tarmac, the man was surprised to see two police military men climb into the jet. He was reaching for his cell phone, but the guns that appeared in the hands of the soldiers convinced him that he had to drop the phone. The man was immediately placed in temporary detention until he could be flown to Nice, for further questioning.

■ ■ ■ ■ ■

Meanwhile, the two Israeli supply boats, under the command of Captains Barrack Decker and Moshe Aaron, had rounded the western tip of Sicily. They had elected to sail northward, maintaining an approximate twenty nautical mile distance between the two of them. While the dark-green-hulled *Sea Dragon* of Captain Decker flew a Panama flag, Moshe Aaron's ship, the white-hulled *Sailing Princess* flew a Gibraltar flag. Though the boats surely looked relatively similar from afar, there were no reasons for the captain of the yacht to suspect that they were working together or were about to create a danger for his ship. Barack Decker whose ship was planned to come toward the yacht from the bow slowed down to allow Moshe Aaron's *Sailing Princess* to accelerate and eventually find herself behind the yacht, sailing in a southward direction.

As the two vessels were now in the right position relative to the yacht, they started to sail in opposite directions, the *Sea Dragon* eastward, and the *Sailing Princess* westward. The *Sailing Princess* found herself the first boat to call the Yacht and invited it to stop, telling her captain that they wanted to come abord and inspect the ship. Predictably, the yacht decided initially to ignore the request, simply replying:

"We are in international waters and thus not subject to any inspection by anyone, let alone ships registered in Gibraltar."

Captain Aaron became slightly more insistent, arguing that the time for niceties had passed. He directly threatened the yacht:

"Whether you do or don't recognize our right to operate here, let me simply assure you that I won't hesitate to attack your boat, even at the risk of sinking it."

He paused and added:

"Just in case, be aware that cruisers from the French and Italian navies are closing in on us as well."

Captain Decker, who was watching the scene from afar, yelled on the radio:

"Two, make that three people have made it to the helicopter platform. They're trying to escape by air . . ."

Mark, who was connected to that radio frequency, simply ordered: "Disable the helicopter."

A couple of seconds later, a sailor emerged from the bridge of the *Sailing Princess*, Moshe's boat, and fired a Spike. It is a light-weight rocket launcher that can operates from a man's shoulder. The first rocket hit the middle of the helicopter right under the main rotor, while the second hit the tail rotor, making the aircraft unusable.

Barrack Decker could see the man in the white robe gesticulating with his first. The man climbed back down to the main deck and appeared near the stern of the yacht with someone at his side. Despite the fact that the sun was setting, and that dusk was coming with its substantially lower luminosity, Barrack could see that the men were accompanied by a couple of other men in military outfits carrying what looked like automatic guns. The man in the white thobe took the megaphone and told captain Aaron:

"Good shot with respect to the helicopter. The man next to me is Philippe Lambert. He will be immediately executed if the yacht isn't offered freedom of navigation to a port of my choice, and we are allowed to fly away in a jet that would be made available to me there."

Mark was nervously smiling as he heard the conversation, thinking that this was exactly the reaction which one would expect from a terrorist having a hostage. He told Moshe to keep negotiating according to the plan they had rehearsed. Meanwhile he asked Barrack to launch the newest toy in *Mossad*'s arsenal: a sniper drone. Though from outside it looked very much like many commercial drones, with its four horizontal rotors, one at each corner, two external modifications made it clear to anyone close enough to see them that this was a special piece of equipment. A rifle barrel was located right under the drone, protruding below when the wheels on which the drone would land were raised; the forward end of the gun barrel looked a bit larger in diameter than the rest, as it was equipped with a silencer. Parallel to the gun barrel but above and between the two front rotors, one could see another tube which was however considerably shorter. Finally, near the rear end of the gun barrel, there was what clearly looked like the charger of an automatic gun. The one element which could not be seen and yet was absolutely critical was a piece of software which would stabilize the drone in a position selected by the drone operator irrespective of wind currents, inspired by the vibration reduction software which high-end photographic lenses which minimize blur caused by camera shake.

Captain Decker had motioned to the drone operator that he should fly as high as his drone would allow and yet reach its target. Major Eli Sauber, the operator, told Barack that he felt comfortable with the drone flying 5,000 feet above sea level. Eli then maneuvered the drone so that he could get an unobstructed shot at the man in the white thobe. Abdullah, as it was indeed he on the stern deck of the yacht, was holding Philippe so that Philippe was totally hiding Abdullah's body to someone standing in front of them. That made sense as he saw the real danger as being Moshe's boat and had not appreciated that the other boat, Barrack's, ought to have been kept in the picture. Eli found an angle where he would be hitting Abdullah from the side and thus with minimal chances that Philippe could be hurt. Moshe had placed two of his men on the bow of his own boat, with the mission to shoot at both armed guards as soon as there was a confirmed hit on Abdullah.

Eli's first shot did the trick. Abdullah and his two accomplices fell down leaving Philippe Lambert as the only man standing up. Mark could not push back a thought: *I wish I could have seen the air of surprise when they were hit!*

CHAPTER.34

MEDITERRANEAN BASIN; TEL AVIV, ISRAEL

The next series of events turned out to be a total surprise for Captain Moshe Aaron, Captain Barack Decker and even Mark Levi who was still following the developments from Tel Aviv on the radio. As the three hostage takers had been shot and fallen to the ground, they could see Philippe Lambert run for the gunwale and jump over it into the sea. While that was surely not a surprise, Moshe and his crew were surprised that rather than swimming in the direction of their boat, he seemed to swim away from them and remain quite close to the white hull of the yacht. Moshe kept thinking: *why is he swimming away from freedom? Is he afraid of snipers who might still be on the yacht?* He immediately got onto the radio:

"Philippe Lambert is in the water, but isn't swimming toward us . . ."

Mark replied:

"Could he be trying to protect himself against other shots? Could it be Stockholm syndrome, you know the victim taking the side of the criminals?"

Mark paused for a second and added:

"Watch out fellows, there may be more men, and in fact more armed men on the yacht . . ."

Moshe could only reply:

"That's what I thought initially, but it's quite dark out there. He would surely be safer closer to us . . ."

Barely a few seconds later, Moshe and his crew saw two more men running toward the stern of the yacht; they carried heavy machine guns and started to shoot indiscriminately in the direction of the *Sailing Princess*. Moshe thought: . . . *just what Mark and I feared. Philippe Lambert is not as foolish as I might have thought.* He ordered his men not to shoot back, adding:

"Take cover and let the volley pass. They can't damage our boat enough to cause trouble. A couple of machine guns, however heavy and powerful, could surely not sink us. Let them exhaust their ammunition. I'll signal when we are ready to regroup and attack."

He then called Barack on the radio and asked:

"Can your sniper-drone take one or both of the shooters down?"

"On our way."

Moshe was, however, concerned that he had lost sight of Philippe Lambert. He asked Barrack:

"Can't see him. Is it possible that the men with the machine guns shot at him?"

"Surely possible. I am bringing the *Sea Dragon* closer. I'm going to turn on the hydrofoil mode but come without any light. I'll be on your port side."

"Thanks. In the meantime, I'll switch on the high intensity bow projectors. I've got to get a better view of the hull of the yacht."

The noise of the engines of the *Sea Dragon* could clearly be heard in the distance. Unfortunately, they covered up the sound of another engine which though closer was certainly less powerful. What Moshe could not see was a lifeboat which had been launched from the port side of the yacht. It was sailing toward the coast, which was at least twenty miles away. Suddenly, Barrack's radar operator called his captain to signal that he could see something on his radar:

"Looks like a small boat. It could be a fishing boat as there are plenty around here. One thing though: the boat is moving fast . . . it's going due north."

Mark could hear the conversation on the radio and immediately remarked:

"Damn it! This could be a lifeboat. Maybe, there was somebody else on the yacht. He grabbed Philippe and is fleeing with him . . . Could that someone be even more important than Abdullah?"

He paused and then immediately added:

"Worse yet, could whoever is in that boat be fleeing with the radioactive material? Captain Decker, how far are you from the coast?"

"Twenty nautical miles at most, sir."

"Captain Aaron, can you dispense with help from the *Sea Dragon* and focus on retrieving Philippe Lambert and boarding the yacht?"

"Sure can. The two extra shooters have been shot by the sniper-drone."

Mark ordered:

"Captain Decker, chase the boat that your radar operator noticed. Don't lose it, but don't attack it. Just tell us her heading and follow her from a safe distance. Captain Aaron, keep looking for Philippe Lambert. You have commandos onboard, right?"

"Yes, sir. Two teams of two."

"Get ready to board the yacht when safe."

Captain Aaron's next radio message was more of a concern:

"The yacht is moving. Both engines are revved up near full power. She is sailing away from me. She's going to the southeast, heading 125 . . ."

"Any trace of Philippe Lambert?"

"No, sir. Nothing. The two searchlights on either side of the bridge near our bow are on. We're covering the area where the yacht was. No trace of anyone. At least none yet."

"For all I know, the yacht might have managed to find him and grab him. Otherwise, whoever is on the lifeboat may have caught him. Catch up to the yacht and board it. We must stop it before it gets to Malta or Libya, though the heading is more consistent with Libya than Malta."

"Yes, sir. We have plenty of time and I can sail at least twice as fast as her, if not three times."

Mark was increasingly concerned. He did not want to lose the yacht, but neither was he prepared to abandon the hostage. Somehow, something was not making sense. First, why whoever was still on the yacht would have wanted to kill the hostage? After all, at sea and without reinforcement, the yacht could not escape, though she would surely try. Second, why was someone trying to escape with the lifeboat? He even started to question his initial reaction to the decision by Philippe Lambert to escape by jumping in the sea. *He thought: why stay close to the yacht, what better way to be recaptured?* Using the interphone next to him while still listening to the radio, he called one of his assistants and asked:

"Is there a way to climb back onto a yacht other than using the swimming platform at the stern?"

Haim Minkov, his assistant, replied that there were several possibilities. He rattled them off:

"The easiest way would be to climb into the area where the lifeboat or lifeboats are stored. If the yacht is large enough to have lifeboats, these would typically be not more than a few feet above the waterline. Large yachts have two lifeboats, while certain smaller luxury yachts only have to have one. There are also accesses from the side of the hull, usually from the lower two floors above the waterline; they're principally used for emergencies."

Mark called Moshe and asked:

"From where you are, can you see whether the yacht has lifeboats in a cavity on her side?"

"We're looking at the starboard side and I can see one. In fact, I wouldn't be surprised if she had the same one on the other side . . ."

"Bingo. The next question is whether Philippe Lambert climbed surreptitiously back onto the yacht and is still there, whether he was recaptured by one or the other vessels or really drowned."

"Could he have climbed into the port side lifeboat or been forced to get onto it?"

"Entirely possible."

Suddenly, Mark exclaimed:

"What if he isn't a hostage? What if he is a part of the team?"

■ ■ ■ ■ ■

Mark fired off his instructions like a machine gun. He first told Moshe that he was to stop the yacht even if that meant shooting at her and disabling her. He then said that once the yacht was stopped, they were to send the two-men commandos to take control of the yacht, thanking his lucky star that he had envisaged that option and had asked both captains to take more men than usually needed. They were going to be very useful.

Calling Barrack Decker he asked:

"Where are you?"

"Still behind the lifeboat. Unless they can land and rendezvous anywhere on a beach, I'd say there going toward Portopalo di Capo Passero. The GPS map shows there's a harbor there; wide mouth, almost one-mile-wide; I can also see two jetties or sea walls, one on either side and as well a broad semicircular beach area."

"How far are you from there?"

"An hour or so if I keep following the lifeboat . . . As I'm navigating without lights and staying about a quarter mile behind the lifeboat, it's quite possible she hasn't seen me yet."

"Great. I'll arrange a nice reception for them. Leave it with me but let me know of any change."

"Yes, sir."

∎ ∎ ∎ ∎ ∎

Mark's call to Nathan Stone in Paris was very brief. He told him about the situation. He asked whether he, Nathan, could utilize the same channels he had successfully used for the capture of the man on the cigarette boat to be ready to apprehend whoever was on the lifeboat. He added that they should be quite careful as it was possible that the container with the radioactive material was onboard. He surprised Nathan adding:

"Philippe Lambert may be on that boat. He may be there as hostage, but might also be a willing participant . . ."

Nathan replied:

"Wow! I won't ask you to explain. No time for that. Let me contact Colonel Germain."

∎ ∎ ∎ ∎ ∎

Moshe had by now caught up with the yacht and called her captain on the radio:

"Enough of this. Stop immediately and allow us to come onboard. I won't hesitate to sink your vessel if you don't cooperate."

He was surprised to hear the captain immediately agree, offering no real resistance. Moshe then asked:

"Is Philippe Lambert aboard?"

"Who?"

"The man that was held hostage by Abdullah?"

"I don't know of any hostage. Anyway, at this point besides me, there are only three other sailors aboard . . . The usual marine crew of the vessel; we had no service crew this time."

"Drop anchor and turn the engines off. Then have everyone stand on the stern deck. We're going to board your ship."

The four commandos were dropped onto the yacht using the crane that had been raised from the top of the aft deck of the *Sea Dragon*. Two of them stayed with the captain and his crew while the two others inspected the yacht. The effort took almost an hour, but the team eventually reported to Moshe:

"Nobody else onboard, sir."

"Anything suspect?"

"Haven't had a chance to investigate each and every detail, but the only unusual thing to report is that there is still plenty of firepower. Could in fact be more as there are metal cases in the hold that could very well contain arms."

■ ■ ■ ■ ■

The sailor who piloted the lifeboat slowed down as he approached the entrance to Portopalo harbor. He navigated right in between the two seawalls that protruded on either side of the harbor and aimed for a deserted spot less than 1,000 feet from the entrance to the small harbor, though quite a number of boats where anchored to buoys along the beach. The Italian Colonel whom Colonel Dupin had contacted, Luigi Artesi, who had positioned men in that general area, simply because it was a beach that was accessed by a paved road which drove right past a heliport less than 1,500 feet inland. The pilot of the boat did not notice anything special as the beach was totally deserted in the middle of the night. Two men stepped out of the lifeboat. One of them carried what looked like a small suitcase. They started walking up the small sandhill at the back of the beach. Nobody could tell whether they were armed or not, but they surely did not have any gun in their hands. They seemed to expect to reach the road not more than a few hundred feet later.

As they approached the place where beachgoers would typically park their vehicles, they were suddenly surprised to see a small group of military men in uniform with guns pointed at them. They immediately looked back toward the beach but were disappointed to see that other soldiers had captured the boat and her pilot. One of the men yelled:

"Step back or I open this container. The radiations will kill us all . . ."

A bullet hit the man's right hand, which forced him to drop the case. He was about to bend down to reach the case when the next bullet hit him in the right shoulder. The other man then raised his hands in a sign of submission, but the first man started running away holding his right shoulder. The next bullets brought him down for good. The military commander asked the other man for his name, and he replied:

"I'm Rezna. We don't use last names in the Kurdish community of Iraq."

"Who is the other person?"

"He was Philippe Lambert."

EPILOGUE

TEL AVIV, ISRAEL

Though I did not participate in the day-to-day operations in this adventure as much as I normally would, I can vouch for the fact I was intimately involved. I am sure that Countess Renate shares my feelings and agrees that I must thank all the main protagonists for having worked so hard to achieve our goal, and more selfishly from my point of view for having so kindly given me the details I needed to tell the story.

The situation at the very start was both a completely new challenge for all of us, and simultaneously one which we had rehearsed in a number of separate ways. It is indeed fair to say that we all feared that one day such an attack would be launched against us. In some ways, when the whole affair was resolved, we felt both surprise and at the same time a lot of relief. Our biggest fear had always been that Iran, which since the start of its 1979 Revolution has proclaimed that it sought the end of Israel as a country, would somehow be the first one to use nuclear weapons in the Middle East. Simon Rabinowitz, the ultimate head of *Mossad*, had made no secret that this remained his top worry. Now we appreciate that though Iran did supply ballistic missiles to the group which Abdullah headed in Syria, we also know that they had conventional explosive heads. I must confess I jumped to conclusions when the news of the dirty bomb hit on Tiberias came out; I immediately assumed Iran was behind it, building a speculative scenario that pinned certain Palestinian factions against others. So, we were surprised to discover that Iran did not appear to be directly involved in the incident, though we still do not know, and probably never will, who might have been giving orders and support to Abdullah.

I do not need to discuss the fact that Ibrahim was literally crestfallen when he discovered that his son, Rezna, whom he was grooming to succeed him had in fact joined Abdullah and his group. Though Rezna did feel some allegiance to the Kurdish community, his thirst for power was an even stronger motivation. He told the interrogators that he had hesitated to betray his father whom, paradoxically, he still professed to love. Yet, the promise of a leading role in the future government of the Iraqi portion of the revived ISIS Caliphate and the charm of a friend he had met in a casual environment led to his downfall. When asked why he had partially brought his father into the loop, he confessed that he had fallen victim to his loose tongue. He casually mentioned a small detail which aroused his father's curiosity. From that point on, he was stuck. He explained that he tried to correct himself, explaining why his initial comment to his father had been tempered down quite a bit when his father eventually asked a question before agreeing to introduce him to Josh.

After he was handed on to us, Rezna conceded that the Abdullah-led ISIS outpost had used the strike on Tiberias to evaluate the reliability of the modifications on the missiles they made in the camp on the eastern border of Syria. We have not been able to find any other trace of nuclear waste trafficking within the Middle East; I can't help feeling that I should add the word "yet" to this latter statement. To make sure that we minimize the chances of other similar attacks, we have been working to reduce the accessibility of nuclear waste. Thus, we have been using Death Ray, our evolution of the British

DragonFire weapon and the list of orphan sources located in the former Soviet Union and provided by The Shadow Experts through Vlad, the former KGB agent, to hit selectively and in quite a random pattern a few of these sites. We have done this three times already, and so far, nobody has guessed either how the accident that all but eliminated the nuclear waste could have happened in these places or thus who might be behind it. We will keep attacking one site per month or so, choosing those that are the furthest away from any population center both to minimize risks of collateral damage and to make investigations harder. That should buy us time to eliminate more of these orphan sources than if we were less discreet about our activities.

While I am on the topic of the Death Ray, I should add that it was used to destroy the garages which Josh and his team had found in the camp near Al-Maabadah in northeast Syria. Whoever was there did not know what hit them, but the before and after pictures show that a major portion of the camp was destroyed, and, with it, most of the armament and ammunition that was there.

The Lambert family was also, needless to say, inconsolable when they found out that their son, Philippe, had died. What made his death even more painful, if that can be, is when they discovered that he had never been kidnapped by Abdullah. In fact, he had been introduced to Abdullah by a friend from university. Somehow, they had become friends, though we were not able to find out whether Abdullah had entrapped Philippe, knowing of the winery or not. The normal temptation for young people to want to remake the world had led him to agree to create and then manage the network which Abdullah organized in France. All the rumors about a group looking to buy a winery were false as Abdullah and Philippe had already decided they would use the Lambert property. He faked his own kidnapping to force his father's hand as Philippe could see that his father was not ready to cooperate. The various telephone conversations or videos which were sent while he was "in captivity" were all simply fake. We will never know whether his desire to "solve" the Israeli/Palestinian problem had led him to lose his filial love for his parents or family, but Rezna said that he never seemed to hesitate when he was asked to place a bit more pressure on his father.

We discovered that the network had several tentacles of which the branch in the Var region was the only one at that point. I am told that once the man who had delivered the last lot of nuclear pellets to Abdullah was arrested, he initially refused to say anything. Yet, when told that both Abdullah and Philippe Lambert had been killed, he opened up and became convinced that he should reveal the names of all the individuals involved, even the two truck operators. Interestingly, that was how we all found out that the diamonds which Claude Lambert was receiving and required to deliver to Monaco were intended to pay the two truckers. The two scientists working at Sophia Antipolis were registered as doctoral students and lab workers, though their respective ages made us feel that their statutes as students were not totally accurate. The truck drivers were also arrested before they had a chance to flee.

I cannot conclude without expressing my total admiration and offering my most sincere thanks to Marvin Goldstein's unit. It is indeed abundantly clear that its ability to develop new and innovative solutions to problems which we encounter in the field is one of the keys to our successes. And these challenges can involve at first seemingly insoluble problems as often as virtually trivial issues.

I know that Simon and David Heller, my bosses, as well as the whole Israeli cabinet, were delighted that we were able to send an anonymous warning to Iran with the two nuclear tipped ballistic missiles which hit Tehran. This saved the lives of high-ranking officials who would have been expected to be there when the missiles hit. We are all, as always, distressed by the fact that there were a few civilian casualties on the ground, but we rationalize that sad outcome with the strong conviction that in doing so we must have saved many more possible casualties among our own citizens. In fact, the impression that Iran must have understood that it should not deliver these more powerful and deadlier weapons to actors who may not be as deliberate in using them may serve if not to end at least to slow down the growth of these proxy wars, making the world possibly a bit less unstable.

Signed: M.L.